Christmas 1960

To Mom
from Connie and Bill

By Gladys Hasty Carroll

Novels

AS THE EARTH TURNS

A FEW FOOLISH ONES

NEIGHBOR TO THE SKY

WHILE THE ANGELS SING

WEST OF THE HILL

CHRISTMAS WITHOUT JOHNNY

ONE WHITE STAR

SING OUT THE GLORY

COME WITH ME HOME

Collected Short Stories

HEAD OF THE LINE

Nonfiction

DUNNYBROOK

COME WITH ME
HOME

Gladys Hasty Carroll

Come With Me Home

Little, Brown and Company
BOSTON   TORONTO

Published simultaneously in Canada
by Little, Brown & Company (Canada) Limited

PRINTED IN THE UNITED STATES OF AMERICA

TO
MY HUSBAND

Come with me home.
The stars rise, the moon bends her arc,
Each glow-worm winks her spark,
Let us get home before the night grows dark;
For clouds may gather
Though this is summer weather,
Put out the lights and drench us through;
Then if we lost our way what should we do?
    — CHRISTINA G. ROSSETTI: "Goblin Market"

COME WITH ME
HOME

~~~~~ *1*

WHO knows Miss Rosamond Lacey?

She lives in the big house at the end of Lacey's Lane, which to many would seem the end of Nowhere. All beyond is wilderness. No one goes by except hunters, and fishermen who know of the narrow trail through an alder thicket to Lacey's Pond where a leaky rowboat, chained to a rock, bobs among the lily pads.

I am a fisherman.

People think Ichabod Lacey built the house in 1776. They think this because the trim on the left of the front door has seven grooves while that on the right has six. There may be some other reason for this curious circumstance. Ichabod may have been seventy-six years old when his house was built. A workman may have been poor at counting or grown tired of carving. Nobody knows. Nobody is old enough to remember.

It is on record that Ichabod had sons and one of them was Daniel who had another Daniel. The second Daniel had four girls and Jonathan. Jonathan married Louisa Hutchins from a neighboring town and had a daughter Rosamond. All lived in the big house.

Now there is only Rosamond. But she is not alone.

I write of her because of the reason she is not alone. For this reason she is too rare, if not unique, in the world today. She knows beyond all doubt and in great detail where she has been, and foresees with crystal clarity where she is going. I wonder that a four-lane highway does not lead to her door and airfields surround her. I wish they did; yet, even as the wish swells, I murmur, "God forbid." For could even Miss Rosamond and the big house survive the onslaught? Perhaps the kernels of truth she holds can be shared with only one, or a few, in a season, and need the protection of the stubborn shell which is two miles of unimproved road from a village with one store and three churches near the mountainous border between two rural states. Perhaps it was intended that Miss Rosamond should live in obscurity.

She would say so.

She would say, with Pope, "Whatever is, is right." (Though she would mean, "Right for the moment: right as a springboard.")

In case it was so intended, I am not, I think, revealing her whereabouts to anyone who does not already know it, only spreading the word that she does exist.

Her house has seventeen rooms besides the three in the ell which is the new part the second Daniel built.

The day I was there the second Daniel sat in his cushioned, banister-back armchair beside the parlor fireplace, hands crossed on a gold-headed cane, bearded chin resting on his hands, and narrow, rheumy eyes regarding me quizzically. His wife, Mercy, was praying in the small library across the hall; when the door is closed, she is praying. In the one of two large front chambers which she shares nightly with Jonathan, their daughter-in-law, Louisa, was dressing the canopied four-poster. Before drawing up the lower sheet she smoothed the featherbed with a broomstick. The starched pillow shams smelled of spice. In one of the rabbit warren of rear chambers Daniel's daughter Ruth was studying church creeds because before night she had to write one; she had called a meeting of neighbors who wanted a new church. At the end of the spacious upper hall, another daughter, Rachel, modeled a gown of plum-colored silk her dressmaker had just finished. It had a looped overskirt of black velvet and the bodice and sleeves dripped black lace. She whirled in a dance step before a long mirror with a gold-leaf frame, and the crisp silk whistled, the velvet hummed. In the great attic, a third daughter, Caroline, knelt before a sea chest, sorting letters and account books and newspapers, dating and tying them into packets with string. The youngest daughter, Pauline, was out on the hill with her sheep. I saw her through small, thick panes of colored glass. She sat on a cobalt-blue ledge and green lambs nuzzled the ruby notebook where she was inscribing, in a spidery hand, pastoral songs which the clouds and the hickory trees and the nibbling sheep sang to her.

Old Daniel and I were the only men in sight. Caroline's husband, Lute, was in the old mill inventing the gasoline engine. Jock was down by the river painting a picture, wishing for a studio with a north wall all of glass.

Ten Jersey cattle grazed at pasture, and four black horses in the stable tossed their heads in scorn at whatever the meaning might be of the sounds Lute was making in the mill.

You might or might not be conscious of the presence of these people and creatures in and about the quiet Lacey house. But Miss Rosamond is. And I was.

I found her in the ell part, for her big kitchen is there, her small sitting room with windows full of geraniums, and a smaller bedroom. She was busy, for there is always much to do. In 1959 she still cooks over a wood fire as she always has, draws her water from a copper pump at the end of the sink, kneels to scrub the bare, hard-pine floor, and lights the rooms with oil lamps. A shelf filled with lamps runs the whole length of one kitchen wall, and every chimney shines. At no time of year is there any heat in the house except from the cookstove, a chunk stove in the sitting room, and the fireplaces. In winter a boy fills the woodboxes every night, but only Miss Rosamond feeds the fires.

It was summer when I was there. God willing, I shall be there again next summer.

Miss Rosamond often says "God willing," implying "If it is part of His plan" — not that He is unpredictable, capricious, One who can be coaxed or flattered into throwing up overnight a bridge which a human being would profit by building.

I found her because, being a fisherman, I was told during a summer holiday of the trail from the end of Nowhere through the alder thicket to the boat among the lily pads; because I do not fish only for fish; and because on the corner of a weatherbeaten, shingled building she had fastened a sign which said ANTIQUES. *I have been arrested by hundreds of signs which bore that promising word, but never by another so intriguing as hers. The black letters stood out against such a rosy rising sun as was often used to decorate the high backs of early sleighs. The pointed, golden rays of the sun were also those of an old sleighback. But among and beyond the golden rays were varicolored balls representing the planets of our solar system: violet Venus, red and green Mars, orange Mercury, dark Jupiter stabbed with fire, turquoise Neptune, blue Saturn, gray Uranus, and little silver Pluto. The course of each was indicated by a line in its own color so slender yet following with such precision the half-circle of the sun that it seemed it could not have been drawn freehand; still, I was sure it had been. I sat in my car and stared at it.* ANTIQUES, *like a flag across space. A chart of the heavens at the end of Nowhere.*

I left the car, and walked across the yard.

Miss Rosamond was busy, but she saw me.

She said through the open window, "The pond is about a half a mile farther on. You'll have to walk in, but there's a boat —"

I said, "I've been told about the walk and the boat, but not about the antiques."

She laughed and came to the door.

"You're the first one to see the sign except ones who live around here. I only put it up a week ago, to see what would happen. I have a few things I'd sell. Not much."

I wonder what you imagine she looked like, standing in her kitchen door, speaking of selling. A sturdy peasant? A shy countrywoman? A shrewd bargainer?

Miss Rosamond is extraordinarily tall, and reedlike. Her grandmother used to say she was slim as a slipperstick. She wore, that day, a clear lemon-yellow blouse with rolled-up sleeves, a blue denim skirt, and leather sandals. Her face, framed in short, curly white hair, is round as a child's, pink as a child's. Her blue eyes first disarm, then caress or singe you in accordance with what you have said and done deserves. She is a graduate of Wellesley, Class of 1920, and her motions are queenly. She speaks as a queen, even when using the language of commoners. Her voice is like a glockenspiel in play, sometimes reverberating as from a church steeple, sometimes rippling as softly as water running among stones; and it often fades away into the ether so gradually that you still hear the ringing after it has stopped.

She went with me to the shingled building which had been first Daniel's carriage house, then Ruth's meetinghouse (for two years until a Free Will Baptist church was built a mile away), then Jock's studio. Three walls were still covered with his paintings. On the north side she had set bookcases without backs and filled them with art glass. Light from the big window Jock had inherited from the interim church streamed through.

"The glass was Aunt Rachel's," Miss Rosamond said. "She collected it for years. Then she lost interest in it. I never cared for it. Do you?"

I shook my head, but said that many people did, that competition for it among collectors was now very keen, and that it brought high prices.

"For instance, that pitcher. I think it is plated amberina. If so, it is almost priceless."

"No," she agreed, as if she had not heard my words but noticed only my gesture and warmly approved of it. "The people who made those pieces were very clever, and perhaps fancy glass blowing was their greatest gift. But it serves no purpose except to be ornamental, and it is too elaborate, too obvious for my taste. It would be more beautiful, I think, if it were simpler. And more meaningful if it had a practical use. Come in the house and see our glass bowl. We always have fruit in it. Purple grapes are best. It is plain, on a heavy standard, and slightly misshapen, but the glass has a life of its own. I'd never part with that. It was in the house when my grandmother came here as a bride. She thought it was Waterford, but it may have been made at Salem in the first American glassworks."

I followed her into the house. She took me into every room, and introduced me to all the Laceys. She showed me their portraits, too. Her father, Jock, had painted them all except his own. Then she invited me to lunch, and we ate at the kitchen table — peas and potatoes brought from the garden that morning, simmered with rich milk into a creamy stew and served in deep, tricolored ironstone plates; hot cheese biscuits, a tossed salad, thin glasses of sherry, and small, luscious golden pears from the Ichabod Lacey bowl. I did not have to write down the menu to remember it. Afterward we walked by the river with Jock and sat on the hill with Pauline and her flock, talking.

I went no farther that day. I have not yet seen the leaky boat among the lily pads. But I have begun what I hope will be a long friendship with Rosamond Lacey. She is many years older than I am and speaks with the tongues of generations which preceded her own, yet her vigor, her incisiveness, her enthusiasm, her unblinking courage in the face of current events, and her simple but in these days revolutionary faith which suggests that of a precocious child combine to make me feel painfully old.

I told her so, and she said, "I'm glad it is painful. I hope *it becomes a scourge. For one of your age to feel old is worse than nonsense. It can be fatal. And not only for you. No one is old until he wants to be. It is the beginning of the death-wish. If it comes to many who are young, and stays with them, it augurs the end of civilization."*

I am going back next summer to study with Miss Rosamond. If I lived near her, I would study with her every day. She knows secrets I want to uncover, many of them written in symbols unfamiliar to me, spoken in terms I only half under-stand. I am not sure her language can be translated. I must learn to think in it before I try.

But I shall try. Because she is on a highroad between the past and the future. If I cannot travel it with her, it may at least show me the direction and I can find a trail of my own through this worse-than-an-alder-thicket in which I am now helplessly entangled, along with everyone I know except Miss Rosamond.

—J. P. S.

*   *   *

In his small, crowded office at the head of the stairs in the old bank building, where a few minutes before he had brought down his fist upon the brass stamp of the notary public to make official the sworn statement that an essay by Judith Crawford was written entirely by her and that her age was eleven years, Judge William H. Morrison carefully returned the newspaper to its original folds, laid it on his desk and stroked it slowly as if it were a deed or a will ready for record-ing at the county seat.

Judith's mother, a little blond woman in plaid slacks and a black fur jacket, bounced impatiently on the edge of her chair.

"She doesn't really live in this town, does she? I told Wayne it was impossible — *too* much of a coincidence — that some-body here should be written up in his home-town paper in Minnesota. His mother sends him a bundle of them every now and then. Lots of times he doesn't even look at them. He's been away from there so long he says there's hardly ever any mention of anyone he knows. But last night he saw that column, and it caught his eye because he likes to fish and the men at the plant have been telling him that this spring they'll take him out on Lacey's Pond somewhere up in the woods. He said it *could* be that this woman lives there. He said if anybody would know, you would, because you're a native; and since I was coming anyway about Judith's essay he insisted that I show you the newspaper. Of course I was curious, too. But it seems so unlikely —"

Judge Morrison had not looked at her until she paused. He was a big man, and he had sat there in his oversized chair behind his huge, ink-stained desk, stroking the folded newspaper with the palm of one big hand and staring at a blue Delft cow which he used as a paperweight in his letter basket, and which was the only ornament, the only spot of color, in his oak-paneled office.

When the room was still he cleared his throat in legal-sounding fashion and said, "No."

He slid back in his chair, rested his elbows on its arms, and brought the tips of his fingers together. The attitude was familiar to his clients. Dottie Crawford had seen it before, when the papers had been passed in October on the house she and her husband had bought because there was none in town which they could rent until they built their own home; and on occasions when she had consulted him about school problems. He was the chairman of the local school committee.

"No," he said again. "Not at all unlikely. There are a surprising number of coincidences in life. Haven't you noticed that the unexpected happens about as often as the expected?" He went on slowly, in deep, measured tones, as if he were taking an oath in the courtroom or leading the responsive reading in church. "Those who know — Miss Lacey — might say that nothing about this matter — is so unexpected as that — she should be engaged in any kind of business — and put up a sign on her property. But the truth in this case is that it is typical — of Miss Lacey — to do the unexpected — and thus it might well be expected — of her."

Mrs. Crawford had begun to fidget, he noticed. Late years women were no better than schoolchildren at sitting quietly and putting their minds on what was being said. He was not sure they had minds. But they were bundles of energy.

He rose heavily to his feet.

"If you have no further use for this newspaper, Mrs. Crawford, perhaps you will leave it with me. I may drive out to see Miss Lacey. It is conceivable that she has not attended to the — legal aspects of her business, being unfamiliar with business. And it might interest her to see that she is in the news, so to speak."

"Well, all right," Dottie answered, hopping up. "But bring it back after she's read it and I'll pick it up some day. I'd like to show it to the PTA Board. Maybe some of us will go antiquing and get acquainted with her. If she's such a wonderful person as all this, maybe we should have her speak at one of our meetings."

"I've never — heard of her doing any — public speaking," said the Judge.

"Oh, well, there always has to be a first time. Ten years ago I never had either. But I do it now on the slightest provocation."

Judge Morrison had no doubt of that.

She was halfway down the stairs when she heard his voice again. She turned to look back. He was standing in his doorway, filling it, blotting out the pale light behind him.

"The road," he said. "The road out that way — is hilly and narrow. I would advise you — not to drive over it before May. At this time of year it is icy. And when the frost is out of the ground — during the spring rains — there are places where wheels sink to the hubs."

"Oh," replied Dottie with a shrug, "my little German can go anywhere." She added impudently, "If you can go, Judge Morrison, I can go."

"Ah," said the Judge calmly, "but I know the road. You have lived here only a few months, Mrs. Crawford. Until yesterday you had never heard of Lacey's Pond. I was fishing it before you were born."

He stepped back into his office, closed the door, and bolted it.

A few minutes later his telephone rang.

He had just reached, in his rereading, the paragraph which began with the question, "I wonder what you imagine she looked like, standing in her kitchen door . . ."

He let the telephone ring several times before his hand groped for it.

"Hello?"

"Long distance is calling Judge William H. Morrison."

"Speaking."

"Hold on a minute, please . . . Here's your party."

"I have Judge Morrison for you, Senator."

These remarks were all in feminine voices faintly reminiscent of Mrs. Crawford's, and the Judge had kept on reading until he heard the title "Senator." Even then he did not give the conversation his full attention; it was not unusual for him to receive a call from the State House during the legislative session and he was now reading, "Her blue eyes first disarm, then caress or singe you, in accordance with what you have said or done deserves. She is a graduate of Wellesley —"

"Hul-LO, Bill. How's everything back home?"

The Judge's massive face brightened. He pulled the telephone toward him, and bent close to it. This call was not from the State House, but from Washington. This voice, which he would have recognized on a rainy night in the jungle, was that of the young Governor the state had lately sent down to the United States Senate; and he was the only person who ever called the Judge Bill, though they had not met more than three times.

"Why — glad to hear from you, Senator! Everything here is

going along as usual, as far as I know, but you left quite an empty space when you went away."

"Well, it's been something of a wrench for me, I can tell you. But I hope to get back to see you all in the summer. Have to find out what you want me to do down here! Listen, Bill — I just left a meeting of about twenty of the boys. As it was breaking up, something was said about fishing, and a few of us told some tall ones — letting off a little steam, you know — and then Bob Frye from Minnesota asked if any of us ever heard of Lacey's Pond. He said he'd heard that it was quite a place for trout fishing, but couldn't remember where it was, or even what state it was in — thought maybe some of us had been there. None of us had, but on the way back here to the office it kept running through my mind — *Lacey's Pond* — and it connected with you. Did you or didn't you tell me years ago, when I was campaigning the first time, that if I could ever stop in North Pelham long enough, you'd take me fishing on Lacey's Pond?"

The Judge glanced down at the Minnesota newspaper open on his desk, cleared his throat, and told the truth, not only because it was constitutionally impossible for him to lie but also because he considered the Senator capable of finding out sooner or later anything about his state which he wanted to know.

"You have a phenomenal memory, Senator," he said slowly. "I did indeed. Lacey's Pond is near the southeast corner of North Pelham." He added, "But it is small. And secluded. It hardly merits an out-of-state reputation. And should many fishermen from a distance find it, I couldn't promise them the excellent fishing I promised you some four years or so ago."

The Senator laughed.

"Check, Bill. I get it. I'll try to keep this information confidential, except to Bob Frye. Him I must amaze. And some day he and I'll drop into your office to take you up on that invitation, if it still holds."

"Certainly. Certainly it holds. But the boat may not. The only one on the pond was leaky three years ago."

"We'll patch it. Or we'll bring our own boat. Great talking to you, Bill. Frost going out of the ground yet?"

"Not yet."

"Leaves are coming out down here. Be sure to stop in if you're in the District. Either at the office or at home. We sent you our address on the Christmas card, didn't we? Wife and children would be as delighted to see you as I would. So long, Bill."

"Good-by, Senator."

The Judge sat for a while with his hand on the receiver, as if he might be about to raise it and put in a call. But there was no one to call. Later he edged slowly back in his chair and brought the tips of his fingers together in vain. It did not provide the customary reassurance. He was a lonely outpost. Two scattered volleys had been fired. He did not know whether this was a skirmish or the beginning of a battle, even of a war. He waited for what would happen next. Nothing did.

After half an hour the office was nearly dark. He did not turn on the lights, but stood up, folded the newspaper carefully, tucked it into the pocket of his thick black overcoat, put on his overshoes, a gray scarf, the coat, gray suede gloves, and a black felt hat, in that order, went out and locked the door behind him. A gold-headed cane waited for him at the foot of the stairs. It had once belonged to Lawyer Forbes of Hilton, Forbes, and Morrison. This in hand, he made his way down the icy street to the only brick house in town. The brick house had been built about a century before by Lawyer Hilton. Lawyer Forbes had added bay windows, shutters, and two verandas, all painted yellow. The light was on over the front door. Inside, the only light was in the dining room where the table was set for one, and in the kitchen where Mrs. Eustace was preparing dinner. The Judge climbed his steps as Sandy Weymouth drove through the village on his way home from the University.

Sandy was always later if his car was in running order and he had the money for gasoline. When he had to hitchhike, he tried to be in the village by half-past four, the time shipyard workers were coming through. Unless Joe Barron or Paul Lee or one of the Pulaski boys picked him up, it was a long, dark walk to the end of Lacey's Lane, added to the half-mile over and back and another half-mile beyond in weather when he could not take the short cut through the woods.

At the old watering trough, now filled by the North Pelham Garden Club with small fir trees in red wooden buckets (next summer it would hold pink petunias and hanging vines), Sandy turned left off the main street and left again a few hundred feet farther on at the Soldiers' Monument. Here street lights fell behind. As lighted windows became more and more scattered, the power line ended. From here on the occasional farmhouse was oil-lit, and as likely to be a quarter-mile off the road as beside it, a ruddy eye blinking softly as the moving branches of trees now obscured and now revealed it.

Sandy knew well all the women who had filled and lighted the lamps; all the men who were sitting down to supper at this hour and those who, having lately reached home from shipyard, plant, or shop, had carried lanterns to the barn to do their chores; all the children who had come home from grade or high school on the bus two hours ago. If he had opened any door, nothing he would have seen would have surprised him. He knew who was saying grace and where men were swearing at dogs and children, who was ill and who was getting better, where a baby was being rocked to the tune of a ribald logging song, even who was talking and who was listening or not listening.

"I feel as close to them," thought Sandy, "whenever I think of them, as if I were with them. I always have."

But as he turned up Lacey's Lane, shifting into low gear and hunching forward over the wheel to see what was left of the tracks he had made the night before, skidding a bit and hearing bushes whip the side of the car, he realized guiltily that he did not think of his neighbors as often as he used to. Sometimes days went by when he did not think of them at all, when he did not even see their lights as he drove by at night, saw only the woods which seemed to reach out to him, to enfold him, to give him the peace he had been waiting for in which to think through the bewildering, enchanting, disturbing, or infuriating events of his crowded hours on the campus.

The chief events in Sandy's life now were mostly new ideas. But not altogether.

Creeping across the narrow bridge, he saw the moon rising behind the ruins of the old sawmill. Climbing the steep little hill, his engine sputtered. When he forced it, turning into the yard, it backfired twice, like gunshots.

Rosamond Lacey opened the kitchen door, stepped out onto the porch, and held up both hands.

"Have pity!" she called. "What would you with me, sir, after all? I am but an old woman, and poor. In my purse there is naught but a few coppers, in my cupboard naught but a cold johnnycake, in my stove naught but a few embers, in my woodbox naught but a stick or two of firewood. If it is these you have come for, take them and go. But first, prithee, bring me a few more sticks from yonder shed that I may hotten the kettle in which congeals a cupful or so of boiled beans left from yesterday."

"*Boiled* beans," grinned Sandy. "You mean stewed beans. And you're going to split and butter the johnnycake and heat it in the oven. Hie thee hence in out of the cold, lady, and set another place. I'm not expected home before ten o'clock."

He disappeared into the woodshed with his flashlight. A minute later, not hearing the door close, he called, "Are you still out there? You don't even have a shawl on!"

She called back, "Leave me be, Sandy Weymouth. I am looking to the moon."

The last night her father had come to the supper table, he had let his plate cool, sitting with his head turned toward the window, toward the still, bare, black branches of the big maple trees he had set out as saplings and the unearthly blue light on the snow. She had doubted that he was seeing it, and asked, "What are you thinking, Father?" He had answered, smiling but not turning his head, "I'm not thinking, child. I'm looking to the moon."

When Sandy came into the kitchen with the first basket of wood, he peered into the box behind the stove and said, "No fooling — you *are* low!"

"I've been spending wood today," she told him, "like a drunken sailor. The spirit moved me to sweep and dust the chambers, so I built a fire in Grandmother's room. It took three armfuls just to start the frost out of the hearth brick."

"Couldn't the dust wait until spring? Or at least until tomorrow? And I'd have taken the wood up for you."

"The dust could, maybe," said Rosamond. "I couldn't. I told you the spirit moved me."

He filled three boxes while the beans were heating, the johnnycake was toasting, and Rosamond was bringing pickles from the cellar. Then he hung his jacket on a hook in the back entry, washed at the sink, and sat down opposite her. With a slender silver ladle she dipped steaming brown beans and thick, rich broth from a huge, dark-blue tureen to fill his plate. Sandy bent over it and breathed deep.

"Um," he said. "Best smell in the world."

"Well, I don't know," said Rosamond. "Hot roast stuffed turkey smells good, too. And steak broiling over the coals. And lobster baking in seaweed at the beach. But right now stewed beans is the best because it's what we have. Grandsir always said half the nourishment in food came out in the smell. Nobody told me until I was in college that one should pretend it doesn't have any smell."

"Nobody's told me yet."

"Maybe because you don't live on campus. Or maybe the rules of etiquette have changed. There were never any such rules in France. The French openly sniff what is served them in the finest Paris restaurants. They know that the fragrance

is as much a part of food as the bouquet is of the wine . . .
No other people know the full meaning of *joie de vivre* like
the French. They have an extraordinary talent for it. They
suck it out of every experience as they do the juice of oysters
and snails from their shells. Perhaps they have too great a
talent for it, as they seem to have too little for accepting the
sober responsibilities of life and for profiting by what is
bitter."

"Do you think any people has the talent you say they don't
have?"

"Certainly. The Anglo-Saxons. That's our special forte. The
Puritans who came to this country demonstrated it at its
zenith. It doesn't wipe out the capacity for joy, either, as many
people think. It does temper and channel it. Anglo-Saxons
enjoy much which the French do not enjoy and therefore tend
to ignore . . . We aren't the only ones. I believe the Africans
are like us in that. Maybe the Russians and the Chinese are;
but they have yet to prove it in this age."

"How do you know how the French eat snails?"

"Aunt Rachel and Uncle Jim lived in Paris for several years.
He was in the diplomatic service."

"I thought they had a hotel in Florida."

"That was later."

"He was the one who went to the Klondike?"

"Yes. That was before. Soon after they were married. Aunt
Rachel stayed here while he was gone. Her first child was born
here, the other two in Paris."

"None of you visited them over there?"

"No. We all had too much to do here. Besides, we didn't
need to. Aunt Rachel wrote frequent, voluminous, and very
penetrating letters."

"Now everyone figures he has to go to see for himself."

"We could read," said Rosamond.

She speared a long, crisp pickle and held it across the table
to Sandy.

"What's the excitement at the University today?"

"Mostly over bids to the fraternities and sororities. They're supposed to be out the first of next week. The fellows in my house are at each other's throats about whether they'll take a freshman named Mo Coen. The Jewish members want to take in at least one Jewish fellow a year, and in this freshman class there are only three and the other two are as good as pledged to other houses. Some of the fellows think we have enough Jewish members, and some of them say they don't like Mo, and the rest are boiling mad at the idea of anybody being kept out by race prejudice."

"What side are you on?"

"Neither."

"Why?"

"I don't know Mo."

"Excellent reason. As far as it goes. I'd like to line your 'fellows' up and tell them all a thing or two. Mo shouldn't be taken into any college organization because he is a Jew any more than he should be left out because he is a Jew. It's prejudice either way — unfair and undemocratic. It isn't his inheritance that should count, but the way he has used it, what kind of person he is. What would you say are the characteristics common to most of the members of your fraternity?"

"Well, most of us are serious students — all of us, I guess. All preparing for public service of one kind or another — pre-med, pre-law, the ministry, government work, and so on. Of course I'm not in the house much, but they're a very decent crowd. No serious drinking, no girl trouble. Everybody's 'gung-ho' about the House Mother. They don't do much she doesn't approve of. They're a very talky bunch. Some nights I've stayed over we've talked until four o'clock in the morning."

"Then make a point tomorrow of looking up Mo Coen. Find out if he's headed for public service. Find out whether he drinks much and what his attitude is toward girls. Find out whether he'd cause your House Mother trouble, and if he's likely to join in long talk or be a good listener . . . Then when you vote for or against him, tell the fellows what you were voting for or against, and what you weren't."

"You could do that, Rosamond. I don't know whether I can or not."

"Nonsense. Of course you can. That's the *least* you can do. If I knew your fraternity brothers as well as I do you, and they were more like you than they sound, I'd say you should take Mo in no matter how serious a student he is, or how service-minded, or how race-conscious — even if he is irresponsible and has bad habits. Because apparently the boys in your house have many good attitudes to share with someone who lacks them. But I gather they still have some self-organizing and growing up to do before they're ready to tackle living with anyone less well equipped than they are . . .

"You know, Sandy, you've been almost too fortunate so far. In your lifetime, there's never been any racial or religious prejudice here, either way. You really don't know what it is. But you're going to see plenty of it. It seems to be instinctive to dislike and distrust those who are markedly different from ourselves, until we get to know them. Cats and dogs don't like each other until they know each other — and they have no wish to get acquainted. Civilization among human beings has now reached the stage where many know that prejudice against is unreasonable and wrong — so they've bent over backward so far they're practically falling on their heads. Prejudice against and prejudice for are sweeping the world like tidal waves from opposite directions, and people with sense have to stand like rocks while the waters eddy around them.

"There are good and bad, wise and foolish, intelligent and stupid in every race and every nation. That's a truism to us here because for more years than you are old we Scotch Protestants have had French Catholic, Polish Jew, and Negro neighbors. We know most of them are fine people, but we are afraid that Rita Thibedeau, unbeknownst to her parents, is a bad girl, cut out by the same pattern as Suse George whose ancestors were among the first settlers in town; and we know Roger Lee is breaking his folks' heart. We didn't tell you when you were in high school not to run around with Rita because the Thibedeaus are French Catholic, or Suse because she lives in a dirty house, or Roger because he is colored. We told you to steer clear of them because they're not fit company for any young person. The rest of the Thibedeaus and the rest of the Lees we all know to be fine people; and even the Georges deserve a good deal better than Suse . . .

"But most people in this country, Sandy, have never lived *close* enough to people of other races and other religions to see them as human beings, each with his own character — or lack of it. So they think, 'If he's like me, I can at least put up with him. If he's different from me, I can't stand him.' Or else 'So many narrow, benighted people can't stand him that, even though I don't know a thing about him, I think he's wonderful and I won't believe a word anybody says against him.' So what is a truism to us would actually be a brand-new idea to a good many people, and I hope you'll start spreading it tomorrow morning."

Sandy watched her whipping cream in a cracked pink lustre bowl and piling it on a square of gingerbread.

Taking the plate she offered him, he shook his head a little and groaned.

"The things you're always calling on me to do for the world! I *wish* you'd go out and do some of it yourself. It would be a lot more likely to get done."

"I sent you," said Rosamond comfortably. "I'm an old woman. All I can do is cook. The only reason you want me to go out in the world is so that you won't have to bring up my wood every night. You don't have to. I've told you time and again I can do it myself."

"The pay is good," said Sandy. "And I like what you cook."

"More coffee?"

"Please."

Before she poured it, she took off a stovelid and stuffed the firebox with misshapen apple tree branches from the trimming Sandy had done in the orchard in the fall. The flames shot up and she drew her head back from the heat and light which made her face glow. As she replaced the cover, they subsided to a merry chatter, like the voices of women bent over a quilting frame beyond a closed door.

The two in the kitchen did not speak again until the gingerbread was finished and Sandy lit his pipe. It was a meerschaum, one of a dozen or more fine pipes which had belonged to Rosamond's father and which she had given to Sandy on the understanding that he would smoke them in preference to cigarettes.

Scooping the tobacco out of Jock's pigskin pouch, tamping it into place, striking a kitchen match with his thumbnail, leaning back in his chair, Sandy felt suddenly old enough to be his father's brother, on a level in maturity with his instructors at the University.

Rosamond, watching him, thought how young his face looked behind her father's pipe; scarcely old enough to go to high school.

"Good tobacco," she said. "What kind?"

"Holiday . . . I think it, or the pipe, or both, will get me a date for Saturday night."

"You do, do you? What kind of girl makes a date with a lighted pipe?"

"The best, naturally."

"I doubt it. That she's dating smoke, I mean."

"Well . . . Of course, it's not definite that she's dating me *or* my smoke. But she did say, 'Hey, that smells good,' in the cafeteria line today. Which gave me the courage I needed to barge in and sit with her and her crowd at lunch. She's in my one-thirty class, so we walked over together — me smoking like a chimney — and in the hall, just before we went into the classroom, I asked her if she was going to be free Saturday night."

Rosamond knew how he had done it. With the same feeling

that he had once set out to follow other boys across a beam in the top of a barn, or off the ledge head first into the pond. Probably mumbling, and looking at the wall.

"What did she say?"

No, he had not been looking at the wall.

"Well, for a minute she didn't say anything. She tossed her head — her hair is dark and soft — and tipped it on one side, twinkling up at me through her eyelashes. She's got the darnedest eyelashes. I guess she was waiting for me to say something else, but I didn't know of anything else to say. Finally she asked, 'Free for what?' "

"Fair enough."

"Sure. Only I hadn't had time to think up 'for what.' So I said, 'For whatever's going on. That you would like to do. That I could take you to.' She said, 'That's better. When some fellows ask if you're free they mean free to ride around in a car until they're ready to bring you home.' I said, 'I don't have that much gas.' "

Rosamond laughed aloud.

Sandy stared at her.

"I wish you'd tell me what's funny. Sheila laughed, too."

"Maybe she laughed because she thought you meant it to be funny. Or because she knew you didn't, and was pleased. Depends on Sheila and how intuitive she is. I laughed because it was so unexpected — or would be to anyone who didn't know you and your father."

"What's my father got to do with this?"

"Nothing. Only that there's so much of him in you. It's a great satisfaction to me that I know so many families all the way back for two or three hundred years. But don't let me interrupt. What did Sheila say then?"

"Well, she said she might have to go home this weekend; she wasn't sure yet. She asked me if I liked to dance and I said I wasn't very good at it. She asked me if I belonged to a fraternity, and would there be a party at the house, maybe, Saturday night. I said I hadn't heard of any, but I'd find out.

Then the last bell rang, and she said, quick, 'Okay. You ask around, and I'll ask around, what other kids are doing. See you Friday after this class. By then I'll know whether I'm going home.' "

"So I suppose you'll stock up on tobacco for Friday," said Rosamond.

She began picking up the dishes. Sandy pulled the teakettle to a front cover of the stove and stood moving his hands slowly over the spout, waiting for the steam.

"I was a fool not to ask her before," he said. "Nothing to it."

"You've been wanting to quite a while?"

"Since the first time I saw her. She didn't come until last fall. Transferred from New Jersey; some girls' college, somebody said. She must have plenty of dates. Two or three of the fellows at the house have taken her out. I'm lucky she isn't going steady by now."

"Mr. Right hasn't come along."

Sandy looked across the stove at her. She was stacking china, putting a handful of silver into the dishpan. The lamp between them cast a rosy light on her cheek and put a gleam in her hair. Her shadow on the wall was long and slight.

He said, "I guess sometimes he doesn't."

"Usually, though," said Rosamond cheerfully. "Nearly always, I think."

The steam had pushed his hands away. The teakettle had begun to sing. She came to get it. As she passed him, she gave him a light tap on the shoulder.

"And you're Mr. Right for somebody, that's sure."

A minute later he said, "I hope it's for Sheila."

From beside the sink Rosamond answered, "You don't know yet. Wait and see. Takes more than eyelashes."

An hour or two later Jay Schuyler sat before a typewriter in St. Paul, ashtray overflowing beside him, facing a sheet of paper from which a few introductory lines stared back at him, introducing nothing. Dottie Crawford, wearing fireman-red cotton flannel pajamas, was curled in the corner of a sofa-bed, talking on the telephone to a superintendent of schools in a nearby city who was politely but firmly refusing her invitation to address the North Pelham PTA. Judge Morrison, filling a big, leather-covered chair in his long living room, unthinkingly stroked his cocker spaniel's back with his left hand while his right held a Minnesota newspaper at arm's length and close to the light which came from beneath a fringed, green silk shade. The silk was old and beginning to split. United States Senators and their wives were at dinner; work had kept them from their dining rooms until nearly nine o'clock. On the University campus five of Sandy Weymouth's fraternity brothers were visiting Mo Coen in his dormitory room. At one of the sorority houses Sheila Kent was trying to call her home town and finding the line busy. But in the southeast corner of North Pelham the only light was in the gable end of the Weymouth house where Sandy sat on the side of his bed looking at a piece of paper torn weeks ago from the University *Hijinks*. It had a picture of the Winter Carnival Committee, and Sheila was a member of it. All the other windows in the neighborhood were as dark as those at Laceys'. Rosamond was asleep.

~~~~ *2*

THE NEXT day a blinding blizzard wrapped every house in North Pelham and surrounding towns in its own cocoon. Telephone and power lines snapped. Not a wheel could turn on country roads. Beyond the outermost tall, peeled pole, no stranger could have told where the roads ran. Sandy came to Laceys' in midafternoon, on snowshoes, to fill and heap the woodboxes, and left at once to get home before dark.

The storm ended in the night, having dropped eleven inches of snow. At dawn a strong wind came up like an invisible giant with an invisible rake to drag those eleven inches into ragged white windrows four and six and eight feet deep. Rosamond knew Sandy was shoveling out his car, his yard, and watching anxiously for the town plow, for tomorrow was Friday, the day he was to get Sheila's answer after class. She had smiled when she saw high blue and blinking red lights creep past the end of the lane close to midnight, just as she rose from her prayers before the open bedroom window. Every night since she could speak she had knelt in the dark to pray before an open window, with her elbows on the sill, her chin in her cupped hands, and her eyes wide open to the moonlit sky or the stars or the dark clouds which hung like a veil between the brilliance of the Face of God and the vulnerable vision of worshipers as yet unready for full revelation.

Sinking into the featherbed, tucking comforters about her shoulders, reaching with one toe for the hot soapstone in its flannel bag, she was still smiling.

"So remarkable," she murmured. "When I was a child, and there were men in every rural section to gather in groups of five or six and talk and laugh as they threw out shovelfuls of snow until their section of the road was clear and they came together with the next group to stand leaning on their shovels, steaming in the cold, talking and laughing all together and looking proudly up and down the long stretch of open high-way . . . when it was not necessary to find a hard, black base, for sleds and sleighs needed ice and snow beneath them . . . when none of us suspected that a great machine with high blue and blinking red lights would ever come along our road hurling the snow ahead of it (how terrified we would have been then, if it had suddenly appeared!) . . . even then You had it ready and waiting in the brains of men — to be here on this stroke of midnight, so that Sandy will be on the University campus tomorrow to get his answer from Sheila! . . . Is it so important whether Sandy and Sheila have a date on Saturday night? . . . Surely not that alone. But something about it, having it or not having it, may be important — a part of something big . . . Something You know all about, and we know nothing about . . . nor need to, yet; or we would . . ."

The big plow could not come up to Laceys'. The trough between the banks of the lane and the railings of the bridge by the mill were too narrow. But a small plow came Friday afternoon and turned into Rosamond's yard. She called the two men to the kitchen for coffee and warm molasses doughnuts, though she had never seen them before. They seemed surprised by the invitation and came sheepishly, each trying to walk behind the other. They pulled off their caps and stuffed them into jacket pockets with their gloves, but would not come farther into the room than they had to to close the door behind them.

"You got a nice clean floor here, ma'am," said one. "We won't drip all over it."

"I wish you would," said Rosamond. "A floor needs to be dripped on once in a while." She filled the mugs and offered sugar and cream on a tray. "Were you out plowing last night?"

"All night long. Ain't slept sence night before last. Started at five o'clock yesterday morning. But this is the end of it. We got to you last, some way."

"Known we'd get doughnuts like this," said the other, munching, "got here sooner."

"I wasn't in any hurry," Rosamond said. "Whether I can get out or not, I stay here. Mostly."

"Don't blame you, neither. Nice snug harbor."

"It's been called that before. My aunt once painted a sign and put it on the gate — Snug Harbor. But my grandfather made her take it off. He said it was the Lacey place, always had been and always would be, and no use calling ships because tidewater didn't run up this far."

The men laughed. Each took another doughnut as they left. Pausing on the step to put on their caps and gloves, they held the doughnuts in their teeth.

Sandy came later in the track they had made, tire chains clanking. He sprang out of the car, slammed the door, waved and grinned, galloped into the shed, and a few minutes later came up the stairs whistling.

As he set down his basket beside the woodbox, Rosamond said, "Obviously Sheila turned you down. She is very sorry but she has to go home as her great-grandmother has chickenpox. She is very sorry but she plans to spend the weekend in the infirmary as she has multiple laryngitis. She is very sorry but —"

"She is very sorry," Sandy chimed in, "but she isn't as quick-witted as you so she couldn't think of an excuse, so she is very sorry but she and a sorority sister and some fall guy are going to teach me to play bolivia tomorrow night. Bolivia is a game which everybody in the world but you and me knows how to play. She is very sorry but after she has taught me to play this game or given up trying, we are all going to a place called Philippa's on the road to Sybridge for pizza. And I am very sorry, but I must bring you enough wood to last until Sunday as I expect to spend all tomorrow afternoon tying my tie. Also don't tell me what you are having for supper because no matter what it is, as soon as I have brought you enough wood to last until Sunday, I have to bomb along home and do two nights' studying in one."

"I also am very sorry," retorted Rosamond, "but, much as I shall miss you, it will be worth it if you can find out what to do with a tie. The last time I saw you with one on it was traveling toward your left ear. Also I am getting very short of groceries and am grateful not to have to share them with you. Here are two lists; one for your father's vegetables and one for the store. And money to cover. Until you fill these orders — Monday will do — this restaurant is closed."

But as he placed the last stick from the last basket of wood she relented and handed him a paper bag.

"Molasses doughnuts," she said. "With coffee they may help keep you awake to study. And just one reminder, Sandy. Whatever happens tomorrow night — it's your responsibility to see you use it in a way that, whether by much or little, will truly enrich your life. Waste nothing."

"Especially doughnuts."

"More especially experience."

Sandy leaned forward suddenly and kissed her cheek, closed the door, and was gone.

The next afternoon Judge Morrison's Buick was in the Lacey yard when Dottie Crawford drove her Volkswagen in.

"Oh, for heaven's sake!" Dottie exclaimed. "I hoped I'd get here first. Well, anyway, this will show the old duck I *could* get here. Neither he nor the road could prevent me!"

"Why should he want to prevent you?" asked Eileen Struthers uneasily.

"Can't imagine," Dottie answered cheerfully, "but he did his darnedest. All to no avail."

She opened the door and sprang out.

"Shouldn't we wait until he leaves? Maybe their business is confidential. You didn't tell me he tried to persuade you not to come. Maybe she's shy, and doesn't appreciate having strangers barge in."

Eileen's soft mouth, which always irritated Dottie, had grown softer, almost trembled, and her soft blue eyes, equally irritating, swam in anxiety.

"I'd never have brought her," thought Dottie, "if anybody else would have come with me. But I did think two —"

"Then she shouldn't have put out an antiques sign and got in the newspapers. And maybe he isn't here on business at all. For all we know they're romancin', and without another soul within a mile, in which case it's our plain *duty* — so come on!"

She opened Eileen's door.

"I don't see any antiques sign," Eileen demurred, peering. Eileen had remarkable powers of concentration.

"Well, *anyway*, we're here, and chances are they've seen us, so chin up. We're big girls now. Come *on*, Eileen!"

Dottie strode up the narrow walk between drifts which had melted a little at noon and were now locked under an icy glaze. She was wearing gray flannel slacks today, and red stadium boots, and a red wool jersey under the black fur jacket. Her close-cropped head was bare, and her breath went before her like billowing cheesecloth. Eileen in her dark suit, dark topper, small green hat, and decent black overshoes followed timidly, not appearing to breathe at all.

Rosamond Lacey opened the door to them. Dottie thought she would have recognized her anywhere, even at a convention in Chicago.

"Hello there," said Dottie. "We're interested in antiques,

and heard you had some to sell — I mean, that you have a shop — but maybe we came to the wrong place — we don't see a sign out —"

Eileen had never before known Dottie to be at a loss for words. She glanced in alarm from one face to the other and made small noises in her throat, stroking the fingers of her gloves.

"You must have heard it from fishermen," said Rosamond. "I did have a sign last summer but set it inside before the ground froze, not expecting custom in cold weather."

"Oh . . . Well, could we see the things?"

"I'm sorry. They're in the studio, and there's no path." Her voice was crisp, but she looked sympathetically at Eileen. "It's too bad, since you've driven over these roads. Would you like to come in and get warm?"

"Oh, thank you, no. We won't trouble you," Eileen said quickly. "We shouldn't have come without telephoning." But Rosamond pointed out, "You couldn't have done that. I have no telephone," and Dottie, having partially regained her poise, cried, "Frankly, I'd love to." It seemed to Eileen that all had been said before she had finished speaking, and that she was carried on a warm wave with the other two into the room where Judge Morrison sat at the kitchen table with a cup of coffee before him and a half-eaten slice of applesauce cake.

He stood up to introduce Mrs. Crawford and Mrs. Struthers to Miss Lacey, adding uncomfortably that he should be going. But Rosamond said, "No, indeed, Judge Morrison, you haven't finished your coffee. Sit down, ladies, and I'll pour some for you. Take off your coats or you won't feel them when you go out again."

She took Eileen's coat, and the Judge made a gesture toward draping Dottie's over the back of her chair. The coffee was poured from a pewter pot. Dottie longed to turn it upside down and see if it was marked. Boardman? Gleason? Dunham? The coffee came in pink lustre cups, Eileen noticed, and the little cake plates, she was quite sure, were soft paste.

"Your china, Miss Lacey," she almost whispered. "It's too beautiful to use."

Rosamond smiled and shook her head, sitting down.

"We have never felt so," she said, "and though we have fewer perfect pieces, for that, as the years go by, we find beauty in the chips and hairlines. Should anything — or anyone — grow old *unused?*"

Dottie wished she knew whether Judge Morrison had yet shown the newspaper story to Miss Lacey. Not knowing, she picked up the first cue she heard, in case there should not be another.

"How absolutely true!" she cried. "I use every antique I own. Luckily they're mostly iron, wood, tin, crockery, and so forth. Because I have four children and Judith, the oldest, is only eleven, and you *can't* expect children to be *careful* with things. After all, their home is their home and you can't fuss at them every minute they're in it. And I love what you said about people being useful. That's exactly the way I feel. There's so *much* needed in this world I can't understand why more people don't try to provide it instead of hanging back, trigging the wheels of progress."

"What do you feel the world needs?" asked Rosamond.

"Oh," thought the Judge, "now the evidence will come out."

Dottie slid forward to the edge of her chair, whipping up enthusiasm for her topic as she did before rising to make a speech.

"Oh, in general, naturally, more tolerance of different races and religions, more understanding of those who are in trouble, more eagerness to help others. But those are distant goals. It will take so long to achieve universal brotherhood, won't it? In the meantime, we can fill the needs we see right around us. North Pelham should consolidate with the other towns of the union to build a central high school with a gymnasium, an auditorium, and so on. But too many are prejudiced against that, or say we can't afford it." She cast an impudent grin at the Judge. "So we have to keep *fighting* for it, educating parents to the importance of it, get the children behind the project, and of course make every effort to raise money for playground equipment and study aids and to get the adults out for inspirational meetings and to organize all the children for recreational activities. Last year women who really couldn't do anything else painted the walls of the subprimary room and all the little chairs. This year we're doing first grade. Children love bright colors. There's need for everybody somewhere. If only, as you say, they all realized how important it is to be useful! Miss Lacey, I'm going to ask a favor of you. Would you speak at one of our PTA meetings? You could use your own question as the topic. *Should anyone — or anything — grow old unused?* That's *so* intriguing. You could refer to antiques for illustration, because quite a few people in town pick up antiques at auction, especially glass and china, and most of the pieces are cracked or chipped. *Would* you do that? It would be *such* a help, and we'd appreciate it *so* much."

"I'm much too far away," said Rosamond instantly.

The Judge was surprised that she made such a feeble excuse.

"Oh, I'd come for you," said Dottie, as the Judge had known she would. "And bring you home. Any alternate Tuesday beginning March 14. We have our speaker for the next meeting —"

"I didn't mean too far away in miles," said Rosamond. She had not moved, and did not move now, except that the pupils of her eyes, as she faced the Judge, turned toward Dottie. A round spot of color darkened in each cheek and her voice rang out resoundingly. "I meant too far away in philosophy. And in time. If I were to accept your invitation, Mrs. Crawford, you would regret that you extended it. Because I always say what I think, and I think that if your distant goals are ever realized on this earth it will have become a sponge full of human insects dying for lack of enough strength anywhere to keep them alive. I think we need less wishy-washy tolerance and more respect for convictions wherever they exist, whether in ourselves or in other people; more concentration on solving our own problems and more practical encouragement to others to solve theirs in their own way; more determination to help ourselves and less frittering away of time and energy on group projects and group activities. I've known a time when most people stood on their own two feet. I hope to know it again. There is grandeur in that for everyone who does it, and it can be gained in no other way. There will be no universal brotherhood except where full manhood and womanhood has been achieved. Things have to be used by people to be useful. People are not useful for anything or to anybody unless they are first useful to themselves.

"As for your immediate goals, Mrs. Crawford, I consider them also dangerous. Because you have lived where there are consolidated schools with gymnasiums and auditoriums, you are trying to teach North Pelham that it must have what you consider to be advantages, whether it wants them or not, whether it can afford them or not. How do you dare? How can you be sure you are right and they are wrong? Don't you think God is as likely to speak through them as through you? What do you consider an inspirational meeting — one by which people are 'inspired' to do what you want them to do? The only inspiration to be trusted comes directly from God, or indirectly through an atmosphere or a book or a person with the gift of persuading an individual to seek God in his own mind and heart and so to come to his own independent conclusion.

"I have never had a child, but I am sure children can and should learn to value and to preserve family possessions. They can learn this only from their parents. Having learned this, they are likely to respect the property of others.

"I taught seventeen years in one district school — this district — and I know that for a good education children actually need only protection from inclement weather with a teacher who cultivates and rewards their natural curiosity and their God-given drive for personal achievement and mastery of their environment. Children working hard to acquire information they want do not notice the color of the chairs they sit in. There is the brilliance of a constellation in the column of figures they have added correctly, all the shades of the rainbow in new words, all the glory of earth, sea and sky in the maps and charts they draw.

"And not all children do love bright colors, Mrs. Crawford. If you gave them paper and access to all the paintpots of Arabia, some would choose grays and browns, others black and white, and theirs might be, though not the gayest pictures, the most meaningful and the most promising. Just as not all children need or can profit by organized recreation; some must find their own, and perhaps find it alone.

"God made us each one an individual; that individuality is our one priceless treasure, to be preserved and enhanced at all cost as our passport to eternity . . . Or so I have believed all my life, more convinced of it every year."

Her eyes turned toward the Judge, and she smiled.

"May I have your cup?"

He passed it to her and she filled it.

"Mrs. Crawford?"

Dottie shook her head, tight-lipped. "We must be going."

They all stood up.

Eileen was startled to hear her own voice. "I wish you would come to our church some Sunday, Miss Lacey."

"Your church?"

"The Methodist Church. My husband is the pastor."

"Laceys were once Quakers," said Rosamond thoughtfully. "Some of them were disfranchised for that, and proud of it. Later we were Congregationalists. Then my Aunt Ruth and some of her friends drew up a very simple creed and became members of what they called the Church of the New Disciples. They built over Grandfather's carriage house and met there. Aunt Rachel thought that whole idea was silly. She liked ceremony in her religion and became an Episcopalian. When I was a child my parents and I went to the little country church a mile or so up the road. It has fallen to ruins now.

"There were no locks on its doors. We could go there at any time, alone or with others, to worship, and it existed solely for that purpose. Our minister was a carpenter, and earned his living by his trade. We called him the Elder, and I could see the halo behind his head as plainly when he stood on the roof of a barn as when he stood in the pulpit. He spoke to us on Sunday afternoons because it was his joy to bear witness to the greatness of God and the grandeur of His creation. The offering on the collection plate was to buy the materials with which the men of the neighborhood, including the Elder, kept the building in repair. He held baptism in June and September in the river which flowed behind the church. He came to pray with us in times of trouble and of rejoicing, and held weddings and funerals in our parlors, because he loved us.

"Wherever he went, God was with him. When the Elder died, we had no one to take his place. . . .

"Perhaps such a church would no longer meet the needs of others (though I believe it would), but it met mine. I could not substitute for it an organization so concerned with money-making to maintain itself and its social program, to enlarge its vestry and decorate its walls and buy a new pipe organ, that it takes people from their homes and fills their time and minds and hands with group activity mistakenly assumed to be religious and which dulls them, distracts them, prevents them from spiritual contemplation — the only avenue by which the human spirit reaches God's . . . And I gather from my reading, dear Mrs. Struthers, that this is what too many Protestant churches are, and are doing. If that is true of yours, and if your husband is a deeply spiritual man, capable of sharing his great gift with others, ask him if he feels he is doing that where he is, if he is conscious of growing in grace himself, if he has the serenity, the joy, the sense of fulfillment which comes to a man from living as in his heart he knows God wants him to live. If his answer is no, tell him an old woman you met up country has a notion the call he heard was to a different kind of service than this which he is struggling to render."

Her fingers gripped Eileen's shoulders for an instant as she helped her on with the dark topper.

"I'd like to see you in blue," she said. "Like your eyes."

Dottie was already opening the outside door.

"Thanks for the coffee and cake," she said over her shoulder. Then, over her shoulder to Eileen, hoping the door had not yet closed, "But *not* for the sermons. Did you ever hear anything so ridiculous, or anyone so brassy? Why, she's against *everything*. Lucky for her she *doesn't* get out in the world. It would soon have her in a can with the cover on."

"What a dreadful thought," Eileen said with a shiver. She paused and looked back. Through the kitchen window she could see Rosamond lighting a lamp. As she took her seat in the Volkswagen, she said, "I think she's wonderful. Like something out of an old book. Or out of a book which has not yet been written."

"You and Jason P. Schuyler!" snorted Dottie, shifting into reverse. "How blind can you be? The woman's a crackpot."

Neither of them spoke again all the way back to town.

Judge Morrison raised his eggshell cup in both big hands and across its rim studied Rosamond.

"There go two potential customers never to return," he said. "On the basis of this performance I could not feel justified in investing any of my clients' funds in your business. However, I do appreciate the blow you have struck for education as you and I have known it."

"It was a good blow, wasn't it?" said Rosamond, eating her cake with relish. "Even though it never tells. I do admire your patience and stubbornness, William, in putting up all these years with people like this Crawford woman, keeping the schools going in spite of their running interference which I am afraid is constantly on the increase."

"That it is, indeed," sighed the Judge. "And they honestly

think they are being helpful. Some of them are, of course — or could be if they were not hurried, pushed around, intimidated by those who talk loudest, fastest, and most raucously. It's hard to find anyone who can stand up to groups run by women like Mrs. Crawford. Teachers and superintendents who can and will eventually tire of the battle and either try to find another situation where they can work in peace or change their vocations. Only weaklings let themselves be swallowed up. Sometimes I wonder how much longer we can find anyone to stand as a candidate for the school board."

"Mrs. Crawford would, I suppose?"

"I doubt it. Though far from as smart as she thinks she is, she is probably too smart for that. She has not made herself liked, to put it mildly. She would have small chance of being elected. If she were she would be the prime target for the pot shots she has taught so many how to take. The ones who most enjoy shooting least like to be shot at."

"I'm sure you don't enjoy either, William. Unless time has changed you more than I think."

"No. I don't shoot. A long time ago I decided that all I wanted to do, that I could do, was to begin building a wall around North Pelham, walling in what we had when you and I were growing up that seemed to me of permanent value, walling out passing fads, destructive trends, pernicious influences, buying on margin, bankruptcy. That work has been my life, through my law practice, my court, my church, the school system, and local and state politics. My hands have been too full of other tools for me to carry a gun. And I must have acquired a coat of mail, for it is many, many years since a shot fired at me made any impression whatever. I don't even hear the shooting except from a distance. I only notice what is happening to the wall. I get a little piece built, a bomb goes through it, and I have to decide whether to fill in the hole next or leave the hole until I have added more bricks at the end. After forty years, Rosamond, I am not at all sure the wall is as long or as high or as firm or as effective as it was at the end of my first year. But that is not my fault. I have worked hard and enjoyed the work. I shall keep on building as long as I live."

"I would expect you to feel that way. You have lived as you know you were meant to live. The results of doing that need not concern you. They are out of your hands and depend upon many elements in human nature, much for which you are not responsible, much which may happen after your building is done. Your effort has brought you peace of mind, William, I can see that, as simply living has brought it to me. Perhaps I should feel guilty because it has come to me so easily, indeed that I have always had it without effort of any kind."

"No. Not guilty. Grateful."

"I am. Grateful both for the inheritance God gave me and for the environment in which He placed me. Grateful that I had my family for so long, and that I still don't feel I have lost them. Grateful that I am sixty years old, not so much as a year younger or a year older. Grateful for my friends, old and young."

"You have no wish for the course of your life to change?"

"No, William."

"But what if it did?"

"I don't know. That would depend upon how it changed. Why?"

"Because it may. I don't know that it will, of course. But it may."

He brought his overcoat from the cold entry, spread it open over a chair beside the stove, took the newspaper from the pocket and handed it to her, touching the Jason Schuyler column with a big forefinger.

As she read, he drained the coffeepot to fill his cup for the third time. He noticed that she read without glasses. As she read, he sat watching the expressions which flitted across her face, and remembered a spyglass his mother had kept in the parlor and put within his reach, as a child, only when she had callers and considered it proper that he should be present but quiet.

When she finished, Rosamond asked, "Where did you get this?"

"Oddly enough, Mrs. Crawford brought it to me. It had been sent to her husband. She had heard of Lacey's Pond. It is in connection with this, of course, that she and Mrs. Struthers came here today. I knew she would be coming soon, and I had hoped to warn you —"

But Rosamond was not listening.

She glanced at the name of the newspaper and then folded it, passed it across the table to the Judge.

"I don't think he told me he was from Minnesota, but I remember he had a Midwestern accent. That has always fascinated me, since I first heard it in college. I kept wishing he would say more, but he was a very quiet young man. I liked him, but to me there was something unreal about him. Almost as if he were sleepwalking . . . I wonder if he really will come back."

"I suspect he will. And others may come too. Because of what he has written."

"Oh, I can't imagine that. Why should they? He writes well, but it sounds as if he made it up. It's all so ordinary — a country road, a country house, a country woman, an ANTIQUES sign — but he makes it fantastic. Who in this great, rich, wonderful, challenging world needs the ordinary or the fantastic?"

"An incredible number, I would suspect, lack, need, and search for an appreciation of the one and a glimpse of the other. And you, my dear, are both."

"Nonsense. Besides, I've never heard of that town where the paper is published. It must be a small one. And it's so far from — the End of Nowhere."

"Every American town is the home town of many people, most of whom are no longer living there. You remember the saying about building a better mousetrap."

"I've built no mousetrap."

"Perhaps you have," said the Judge, heavily. "Perhaps you have, without effort, as you say you have built your life."

Suddenly Rosamond stood up and laughed.

"Well, don't be so portentous about it. If I have I didn't mean to. And surely it's no crime, Your Honor. If it happens, it should be good for business. I'll put up my sign again the minute the frost is out of the ground. Now I hate to hurry you, William, but your coat is well warmed and you should get out of the lane before it grows any darker. Mrs. Eustace will be worrying about you. It's clouding up, so there'll be no moon tonight."

"Mrs. Eustace," said the Judge wryly, picking up his coat.

"Oh, now! She's the best cook in town. Her angel cakes have been famous as long as I can remember."

"I prefer applesauce cake. Yours."

"Then I'm glad I made one this morning. I'd give you what's left, but she wouldn't like that. I wouldn't, if I were she."

"I could smuggle it in and up to my room."

"What a thing for a Judge to do!"

But she quickly wrapped a large square of the cake in waxed paper, put it in a stationery box, and handed it to him.

"I'll flourish this as I pass the kitchen door," he said solemnly, "and say I must get some letters written immediately after dinner."

"Your trade," said Rosamond, "has taught you tricks. You used not to be so devious. My mother always praised your absolute honesty."

"I did not know then that a man's worst friend is a girl's mother."

"Oh, my mother and father were truly your friends, William. And so am I."

"Of course I know that, Rosamond. And I am yours. Though we meet so seldom."

He had reached the outside door. His hand was on the

latch. But he did not lift it. Instead, he stood for a minute with his head bent, thinking, and then turned to her.

"I liked what you said to Mrs. Struthers of your church here, as it used to be. Now, you said, it is going to ruin. Is it beyond repair?"

"The windows are out. One of the last things my father did was to board them over. The roof leaks and the ceiling plaster is off. The platform in front and the steps leading up to it have rotted and are unsafe."

"If that is all, are there men in the neighborhood who would restore it, if they had the materials?"

"I think so. They don't like to look at ruins. There are too many faiths here now, among the relatively few families (some have no religious interest) for any worship service to be supported. But I think the church would be used for special services — weddings and funerals."

"And you would go there to worship in your own way, as you used to? As if it were a wayside chapel?"

"Yes. I. And others."

"Then I would like to provide the materials. Anonymously. As an offering on the collection plate. If you can arrange it."

"I will arrange it, William. Come spring. Bless you."

They shook hands. As she stood in the doorway he saw the glint of tears in her eyes. He hurried down the narrow path to his car. The sky was clouding over, but there was a dull glow behind the pasture pines, and in the east, though unseen, the moon was rising.

~~~~~ *3*

ONE Sunday in early March, Rosamond cleared the gate-
leg table in the sitting room, raised one leaf, and covered it
with a white linen cloth. It did not seem necessary to move
it out from the wall as it was a large table and she and Sandy
could sit at the ends, with Sheila between them. The day
before had been unseasonably warm, so she had washed and
starched the muslin curtains and hung them on the line.
While they were drying she had scrubbed the white woodwork
and waxed the pine floor and furniture. In the evening she
had pressed and rehung the curtains. The room still smelled
sweetly of naphtha soap, wax, outdoor air, and a hot iron.

She set the table with her mother's Haviland china, hum-
ming as she worked, taking quick steps between the sitting
room and the kitchen where she was fricasseeing a chicken,
baking potatoes, steaming squash, and mixing buttermilk biscuits. Over a green-sprigged, cream-colored thin wool dress
edged in old hairpin lace at the neck and wrists, she wore a
big, crisp white apron with a bib held up by two small gold
pins.

It was a day like yesterday, with water running in silver
streams from the roof, sunshine flooding both rooms, and the

geraniums in the sitting-room windows bursting with pink and white and red blooms and the kitchen begonias as lush and extravagant-looking as orchids.

"I do think we're going to do Sandy proud, don't you?" Rosamond said, speaking to her parents, grandparents, and all her aunts. "What Sheila may be used to, I'm sure I don't know. I doubt if Sandy does. Anyway, I haven't asked him. He must have thought we're all right, just as we are, or he wouldn't be bringing her here for dinner before he takes her home to meet his family. And I've done my best by us. We're much cleaner than we were day before yesterday. In fact, we're sparkling clean. And the food smells good. And we have flowers. See how your star of Bethlehem is blooming, Aunt Pauline, here on the wall bracket. *Do* you remember the time you found I had hung popcorn-and-cranberry chains and gilded walnuts all over it, pretending it was a Christmas tree? I shouldn't have been more than four or five, to do such a thing, but I may have been older. You all spoiled me so, I was dreadfully late starting to grow up. Not that I mind. There's been time enough for that . . . though actually sometimes I'm not sure I'm grown up yet. Whatever would people say if they knew I often skip through these rooms? Ridiculous . . . I *must* remember that I shall seem very old to Sheila. By her standards, I am an old lady, and I must try to act like one . . . Oh, here comes Sandy's car now. Quick — where did I put my dignity?"

She went to open the door, hastily unpinning her apron, and was astonished to see not one but three strangers in the yard with Sandy; all three in gray flannel trousers and plaid jackets with hoods hanging like small capes across their shoulders. The jacket zippers were open, revealing rows of pearl buttons on white shirts, and lean young necks. The three bare heads were close-cropped. The three strangers were talking and laughing together, not looking toward the house. Sandy in his brown gabardine suit, green tie, and unbuttoned tan topcoat, with his hair neatly parted on the side, was looking at Rosamond; and everything about him seemed separate and uncertain.

She went across the porch toward him.

"Hello, Sandy! It's like spring today, isn't it? I heard the ice breaking up in the brook last night. If this keeps on there'll be a freshet —"

One of the strangers turned then and said, "You call him Sandy? We call him Wey." It was a girl's voice.

"Sometimes Mr. Wey," said a boy's voice. He was not looking at Rosamond, but at the girl who had spoken, and now she was looking at him, amused.

"His name is Charles," said Rosamond, with the feeling that she was shouting down a rain barrel. "But we have always called him Sandy because his father is Charles. He has brought you to the back door, but it is the one he always uses. Come in."

The three strode up the walk and the wet soles of their shoes left marks on the dry porch floor as they passed Rosamond.

Sandy, stooping beside her to take off his rubbers, said low, "Don't think you have to feed them, Rosamond. I didn't invite the other two, of course. Just Sheila. When I went to get her, she said a sorority sister wanted to come and bring her steady. Kippy was right there, so I didn't know what to say. I did tell Joe when we picked him up at Deke House that only two of us had been asked to dinner and he said he wasn't hungry, had just had breakfast."

He straightened up, but not very straight, and looked at her helplessly.

"I'll feed them," said Rosamond, trying not to sound grim.

As they went into the kitchen, a girl's voice which Rosamond had not heard before said, "My mother'd like to know how your mother gets house plants to bloom like that, Wey. Hers all run to leaves, and then the leaves dry up and fall off. Cripes, hers are a washout."

"She isn't my mother," said Sandy. "I told you we were stopping at a neighbor's first."

"Oh, that's right. I guess you did."

"She is Miss Lacey. Miss Rosamond Lacey. This is Sheila Kent, and Christine Donaldson —

"Kippy!"

"Kippy. And Joe Kowalski."

"Joe the Deke," said Joe, hands in pockets and weight on his heels.

"Joe the Cutest," said Kippy, thrusting her arm inside his and rubbing her forehead against the point of his shoulder. "The cutest and sweetest boy in Deke or any other house. Look at him. Isn't he cute?"

They all looked at Joe, and he liked it.

Rosamond thought, "He is preening himself." She wondered if he or Kippy would know the meaning of that word.

She said, "Well, take off your coats. You can wash at the sink, if you like. Dinner will soon be ready. Sandy, if you will open the desk in the sitting room, the girls can set the glass and china over there while you and Joe move the table out from the wall."

Sandy was the only one who washed. The others dropped their jackets on the kitchen couch, and went in to where the table was set.

At the sink Sandy said, "You needn't have gone to so much trouble. We could have eaten here in the kitchen. You needn't have used your best things."

"I wanted to do you proud," Rosamond told him. She added gently, "Sheila is a *very* pretty girl."

"I thought you'd say so. I hope you'll have a chance to get acquainted with her, but it's not easy in a crowd. I wish —"

He followed the others.

Sheila was pretty, especially when she smiled, but she seemed to smile only at Joe. It was a smile which went on and off like an electric light. When it was on, her dimples flashed, her eyelashes flickered provocatively, and her dark hair shone.

When it was off, her full mouth drooped at the corners, her eyelids lowered, and she had a sullen, sulky, sultry look which Rosamond supposed might also be provocative to a man. It was as if Sheila were saying with a shrug that she could take it or leave it.

Kippy, on the other hand, was saying that she was determined to have it, and nothing could stop her, whatever it was, and whether she really wanted it or not. Kippy was short and stocky, with hair bleached to the color of broomstraw, pale blue eyes, a poor complexion, and large teeth she tried to cover with her hand when they escaped her lips. But Kippy bounced, she was irrepressible, she was indefatigable, she was invulnerable.

When the pan of biscuits was in the oven, Rosamond put extra china, glass, and silver on a tray and went into the sitting room. The table had been moved to the center of the room, but the plates and goblets were still on the open desk. Sandy stood uneasily by the stove with his pipe. The other three sat on the floor smoking cigarettes. They had taken saucers from under the plant pots to use as ashtrays. Kippy and Joe sat back to back, like book ends with no books between. Sheila was curled up with her cheek against the wall, facing Joe and smiling at him now and then as he told in a booming voice what had happened when a fraternity brother came in "on cloud nine" at five o'clock that morning.

Rosamond set down her tray and adjusted the white cloth to cover the second leaf. She reset the table, stepping carefully around Kippy's outstretched feet. She went to the kitchen for a pitcher of water and filled the glasses. She took warm plates from the shelf of the stove and heaped them with brown fricassee on crusty biscuits, potatoes split and crowned with butter, cinnamon-sprinkled squash, and scarlet cranberry sauce.

She drew out the Hitchcock chairs with the russet apples and gilt leaves splashed across the backs and the thirteen gilt stars in a row on the front of the seats and said quietly, "I think everything is ready now. Would you like milk or coffee to drink?"

Both girls said, "Coffee, thanks," and Joe said, "I'm a milk-man myself," for which Sheila smiled at him and Kippy laughed rather hysterically, giving him a shove which toppled him over on his side.

Rosamond went to get the milk and coffee, growing more incredulous with every step. When she came back they had picked themselves off the floor and were in the Hitchcocks. Joe was tilted on the two back legs of his, and still smoking. He had brought the plant-pot saucer to the table with him.

They ate, Rosamond thought, like stevedores. If they were not hungry, what they would have consumed had they been hungry hardly bore thinking on. They ate almost uncon-sciously, as if the forks and cups or goblets they raised were empty, like properties of a dinner scene in an amateur play; and there was no hesitation between lines. Joe did most of the talking, with Kippy filling in. An extraordinary number of uninteresting experiences had made up Joe Kowalski's life so far, and each one he recalled reminded him of another. The time his car got stuck in the snow and so he went parking with a girl he couldn't stand the sight of; the time the doctor didn't think he had broken his arm, but he knew he had, and broken it proved to be; the time his mother got a vicious headache waiting up for him to come in from a prom, and that was how she learned he was too old to wait up for . . . The time an examination called for him to write all he knew about the Peloponnesian War, he wrote "I know nothing about the Peloponnesian War," and he took the failing mark all the way up to the school board before he gave in and accepted this injustice, because it was true and accurate that he knew nothing about the Peloponnesian War.

Sheila listened, sometimes with her chin in her hand, by turns darting a swift smile at Joe and letting her heavy-lidded eyes caress his features in slowly sweeping, mesmeric fashion.

When Rosamond took away the dinner plates and brought in a deep bowl of brown Betty, still bubbling from the oven, and a Bennington jug of heavy cream, Sandy spoke for the first time at the table.

He said, "I told you she'd have brown Betty, Sheila. She calls it her winter company dessert."

Sheila glanced around at him as if surprised he was there.

"Did you?" she asked vaguely. "I've heard of brown Betty somewhere. But I don't think I ever ate any."

"Nobody else around here can make it taste like hers," said Sandy. He added with a note of desperation, "Maybe she learned how at Wellesley."

Sheila raised her eyebrows. "Did you go to Wellesley, Miss — Lacey?"

"Yes," said Rosamond, serving pudding.

"Did you *really?*" cried Kippy. "Isn't it — wasn't it — an awfully stuffy school?"

"When I went there we didn't think so," said Rosamond. "I doubt if the girls who go there now think so." She could not resist adding, "And we call it a college."

For the first time a hush fell. Rosamond could hear the kitchen clock tick. Then everyone bent to the pudding.

"Laceys have lived in this house ever since it was built," said Sandy, suddenly. "Nearly two hundred years. Maybe more."

"Is it *that* old?" asked Sheila. She looked about and flashed at Rosamond a smile intended to be reassuring. "Nobody would know it. You must have taken wonderful care of it."

"I've tried," said Rosamond modestly. "During the first hundred years I was sometimes a little careless, but during the second hundred I've grown quite conscientious."

Kippy laughed nervously. Sheila looked affronted.

"Of course I meant all the — Laceys," she said.

"Yes, dear," said Rosamond. "I assume you must have."

"Where are we now?" Joe asked Kippy. "They've lost me."

"Poor darling," said Kippy. "He's lost. Isn't he cute?"

"I suppose we're all more or less lost," said Rosamond. "Whether we know it or not. Whether we care to admit it or not. Some of us all the time, or most of the time. Some of us just now and then." She was looking past Kippy and Joe, at Sheila. "It's a bad feeling, isn't it?"

"Do *you* feel that way, too?" Sheila asked slowly. "I didn't suppose — older people ever felt that way."

Suddenly it was as if they two were the only ones in the room.

"Oh, they do," Rosamond answered. "Usually for different reasons than young people. All of us are led by the hand when we take our first steps. We follow someone else's path for years. Then something tells us we should have a path of our own, that there is one waiting for us somewhere. So we pull away, but not far, pick a few flowers and are satisfied, and come back. But each time we go out alone we go farther, until by and by we don't want to come back, couldn't come back if we wanted to. But we still don't see the path we are looking for.

"That's the first time we're lost. Either we see no path at all, or we see many paths and go a little way first on one and then on another and then on another. That's confusing. It's frightening too. It's like someone who doesn't know how to swim exhausting himself trying to keep afloat. But anyone *can* swim if he will, if he doesn't panic, if he lets his mind and his muscles work with him instead of against him. And there *is* a path through the meadows and the thickets, for every one of us, and we all find it in time if we look for it earnestly and intelligently, don't keep on darting this way and that, trying to go everywhere at once . . . Once we have found it, we get lost only in the thickets, when we come to a barrier and wander off in search of a way around it. Usually there isn't any way around it. Usually you have to climb over or chop your way through."

"Can't you get lost in meadows, too?" asked Sheila. "I mean,

I know lots of older people who aren't getting anywhere, not accomplishing anything, just doing what they have to to make a living and the rest of the time hacking around, going to cocktail parties, making out with other people's wives or husbands, or just eating and sleeping and puttering in the yard. They seem happy enough, I guess. They don't really *care*. If you tell them you've got a problem, they say, 'Oh, it's just a phase. Forget about it.' If you ask them who they're going to vote for, they say, 'Oh, politicians are all alike. None of them can be trusted.' If you say then how can a democracy stay strong, they say, 'Who knows?' Then they fill up the glasses and tell some jokes or eat a big meal and go to sleep and snore."

"I think people like that have been in the thicket and met a barrier — or at least got near enough to see it — and backed up. Or, using the other figure, they have learned how to swim but have chosen to forget, and only remember how to float because it's so easy."

"But that isn't living, is it?"

"Of course not. In the middle of the most exciting, the most challenging, the most promising period of human history, they have chosen to withdraw, to close their eyes, to die, and bury themselves. Because for all that is happening they take no responsibility, in all that is going to happen they will have no share."

"What's going to happen?" asked Joe.

"That depends on you."

"Who, me?" He put his hands, palms out, before his face as if to ward off a blow.

"On you and Sandy and Sheila and Kippy and all the fellows in your fraternities and all the girls in your sororities and all the fellows and girls you don't take into your fraternities and sororities, and all the young people who go to secretarial and trade schools, and all the young people who go to work, when they finish high school, in factories and mines and stores and garages and on farms and bridge and road construction. And just because there are so many of you, don't think any one of you can leave it to the rest. It's going to take every one of you."

"*What* is?" persisted Joe.

"Getting things done. Big things. Making men and women of yourselves. Men and women worthy of and equal to your opportunities. Then the biggest things you can think of. Maybe bigger. Proving democracy can work, by making it work. Giving the lie to those who say politicians can't be trusted. Producing. Distributing. Inventing. Discovering. Making successes of yourselves. Showing what freedom means, and what can be done with freedom. Giving every man, woman, and child in the world reason to want it. Using every ounce of everything God built into you. Knowing your world, and more than your world. As lately as a few years ago people thought pioneering days were over. They have barely begun."

"Why is it all on *our* shoulders," demanded Kippy, "after the generation before ours got everything in such a mess?"

"To each generation its own burdens, its own opportunities, and its own rewards," said Rosamond. "You weren't expected to fight Rome, be Christian martyrs, find and settle North America, fire the shot heard round the world, free the slaves, stand with England when her back was to the wall, nor even to save South Korea from the Communists. But now it *is* your turn, and you *are* expected to demonstrate that God's creation of mankind was good and is worth saving, that the human spirit is more noble than base, that human ambition and courage and industry and vision are equal to whatever they may be called upon to do in any generation, and that the individuals, whether from your generation or the next, whom you send into outer space, perhaps to settle other planets or to meet other races there, will take with them a breadth of knowledge and understanding, a wealth of ability and confidence and simple decency, a joy in life and in high purpose, a faith in themselves and in their mission to which you, their fellow men, can contribute mightily . . . I have loved my life, exactly as I have lived it, but I have just now realized that if I could I would give it all away to be less than twenty years old today. Like all of you."

She stood up, and began clearing the table.

"We'll help you," said Sheila.

"No." Rosamond smiled at her. "I might go on talking, and I've said enough. It's after three, and Sandy's mother will be looking for you."

They were all in the kitchen now, and Rosamond was passing out jackets.

"I haven't done this since I taught school," she said, "and sent the children out to recess."

"Would you come over to our sorority house for dinner some night?" asked Sheila. "And talk to the girls? If Sandy could bring you?"

"No," said Rosamond again. "I rarely leave home. But if you would like to come here with Sandy again, I'd be glad to have you. And after you and I are better acquainted, you may bring some of the other girls, perhaps . . . You see, Sheila, it has been years since I have known any young people except those who live in this neighborhood. Here we have long been a little world unto ourselves. Our young people go into the outer world and come back, but they don't become part of that outer world usually. You can see that in Sandy, I'm sure. So you and Kippy and Joe were quite a surprise to me. Today has been an experience which I shall be assimilating for days to come."

"It has been an experience for us, too. I hope we didn't shock you."

"Yes, you did. But I have learned from you. By and by, you must come back so that I can learn more. I have lived a long time but I still have an insatiable curiosity, along with my many fixed ideas and strong opinions."

"What is your most fixed idea, your strongest opinion?"

"That men should be men, and women should be women," said Rosamond promptly, "and that there is work for all, and everyone should decide as quickly as he can on a job he wants to do, and *do it*. Do it with joy. Do it with a sense of dedication. Do it with faith in God and humanity."

Now they were at the door, and Kippy and Joe were climbing into the back seat of Sandy's car.

Sandy stood on the step beside Sheila, looking down at her, his eyes glowing.

Sheila was not ready to go.

She said slowly, "I can't quite believe this. I never met anybody like you."

"Nobody is really like anybody else. We're all individuals. It's silly to pretend we're not. Silly and wasteful and ungrateful."

"The dinner was delicious. You saw how we ate."

"I did. There's hardly enough left to pick up for one woman's supper."

"You can always stew some beans," grinned Sandy. "After I take these kids back to campus, I may stop by to find out if you did."

"I was afraid of that."

They had reached the car when Sheila ran back and said low, a little breathlessly, "Next time I come, Miss Lacey, I'll wear a skirt."

From the porch Rosamond reached down to lift a strand of Sheila's hair.

"And let this grow a little?"

Sheila flushed, laughed, nodded, and ran to the car. Sandy had already started the motor.

Rosamond stood in the sunshine and watched them go. She waited, looking through the filagree of maple branches and twigs at the blue of the sky, until a rumble dying away told her that the car had crossed the mill bridge. But it was not yet spring, and a wind was rising as the sun dropped lower, so she picked up Pansy, her big yellow cat, and went in to do the dishes. The fire was down, and as she fed it, the flaring heat felt good. She filled a blue willow soup plate with broken biscuits and chicken gravy and put it on a newspaper under the hearth of the stove. Pansy, purring, stopped purring to eat, stopped eating to purr, and ate again.

"You're like the people Sheila knows," said Rosamond, indulgently. "But not for the same reasons. You're a cat."

She sang to herself as she washed and dried the dishes. When she had hung up the dishpan, Pansy was asleep in the rocking chair and did not wake as she was gently picked up, did not even uncurl. Rosamond sat down on the warm cushion, stroking the cat in her lap, rested her head against the quilted pad, and thought about Sheila and Sandy, even a little about Kippy and Joe.

When Sandy came in with a basket of wood at half-past six, he found them both asleep. The closing of the latch waked them. Pansy jumped to the floor, stretched, purred, and rubbed against his ankles.

"You back this soon?" asked Rosamond without moving, only opening her eyes.

"It's not exactly soon. As you may note, it's getting dark." He put down the basket of wood and lit a lamp. "What, no supper ready?"

"Not yet." She yawned. "We just had dinner, didn't we? But you didn't eat much. Hungry?"

"No. And believe it or not, that's the truth."

"Then I'll just make some fresh coffee and we'll finish the brown Betty."

A little later, across the table, he said, "Well, don't keep me on tenterhooks. What's the word?"

"The word on what?"

"Sheila, of course. What do you think of her?"

"How can I say? I don't know her well. I don't know how many Sheilas there are."

"There's only one Sheila. The one you talked to just before we left. The one who said some pretty significant things. The one who listened to you."

"Then — forgive me if this hurts you, Sandy — who was that

who ignored you to concentrate on Joe, who ignored me while I set the table and served the dinner and brought the coffee and dessert, who appeared to feel that everything is lost and nothing gained by the passage of time in the life of a person or of a house?"

"I thought that was obvious. That was Kippy's sorority sister. It's the way she always acts when she's with any of them. It isn't Sheila. What worried me, when I found Kippy and Joe were coming, was that you might not get a glimpse of Sheila herself. But you did. In spite of them, for a little while she was with you the way I see her, the way she is when she's alone with me. Didn't you like her then?"

"Yes. I liked her very much. And I agree with you that that is the real Sheila. But — I have to say this — doesn't she spend much more time as a sorority sister than she spends with you? And what effect do you suppose all that time spent in not being Sheila is having on Sheila herself? How long can anyone pretend to be what she isn't without becoming what she isn't, unless she is absolutely sure of what she *is?* And very few young people are sure. You feel you know the real Sheila. I think I have seen the real Sheila. But does Sheila know and value the real Sheila? Until she does, there is always the chance that she never will."

"Isn't that true of all of us?"

"Yes, but it's safer not to pretend, particularly if one can do it as successfully as she does. It's safer not to fall into the habit of following any group pattern. To find one's self, one has to search, and the search is within. I wish Sheila would look there, long and hard, and act on what she finds."

"She does, sometimes. She will more and more. But it takes some degree of maturity to acquire maturity, doesn't it? I mean, until the time comes that you have the self-confidence to stand alone, there's a need to lean; so after you feel too independent to lean on adults, you lean on your contemporaries; at least, most people do. And for quite a while none of them have the strength to stand up to the leaning, so there they are, all bent in the same direction like tall grass in the wind. And all the time they're leaning postpones the day when any of them can stand alone. At least, that's how I've figured it out."

"You figure very well, Sandy. Maybe that's because you've never belonged to a group. You've stood enough apart so that you could observe and understand."

"I've had a lot of advantages which other students consider disadvantages. I've never been subjected to the pressures many of them have. . . . But Sheila is going to fight her way out, I'm sure of it. I can help her. And so can you."

"I hope you're right."

"What was it you said to each other last? When she came back to the porch?"

"Why didn't you ask her?"

"I did. She wouldn't tell me."

"Well, I'm not going to satisfy your curiosity. It was — woman talk."

~~~~ *4*

MARCH melted away and April blew in. Toward the end
of the month the spring rains were over, the gale winds had
softened to breezes, the sun came near enough to feel, and
Sandy returned the sleighback with its wheeling planets and
its single word to the corner of the shingled weathered building which had been a carriage house, a church, a studio, and
was now an antiques shop. The next morning — that was a
Sunday — Rosamond went mayflowering.

Bareheaded, in a wool skirt and old leather jacket with yellow canvas gloves sticking out of the pockets, and carrying low
rubber boots, she went out of her yard, Pansy following, and
along the hard-packed clay of the lane. Pansy's scampering,
padded feet made no sound, but Rosamond heard her own
steps in the stillness, and gradually she heard other sounds, so
many that there was no stillness anywhere. It was as if her own
steps had started others, her own movement set others in motion. Somewhere ahead of her a boy was taking cattle to pasture, as until twenty years ago some boy of one family generation after another had taken his father's cattle over the lane to
pasture every morning and brought them home every night
from May through until after the second mowing of the fields
in September.

She heard her mother saying, "Your grandmother told me

that when Enoch Walton was a boy and started to take the cows to pasture, she had the only garden anywhere around. Other people had lilac bushes and syringas, and maybe a rosebush by the doorstep, but she had a garden fenced in with pickets, with a privet hedge inside, and beds with walks between, the good soil of the beds kept in and grass kept out by wide boards set edgewise deep in the ground with just the edges showing. She had set out bulbs there, and plants which had come from Boston, and seedlings she had tended in boxes in the house. The first time Enoch came by, the first tulip had just bloomed. Enoch had never seen a tulip before. He must have thought about that tulip all the way over the lane and back, because when he passed the picket fence the second time he suddenly jumped over it, having taken a running start, and pulled up the tulip, bulb and all. Of course he had landed on other plants, and as he could not get a running start back he broke off privet branches climbing the fence.

"He was almost out of sight toward the mill bridge when your grandfather called him back and asked him what he had in his hand. Enoch said truthfully that he didn't know. Your grandfather said, 'Not likely you would, Enoch. I wouldn't have myself a year ago. But it's no wild weed, as you and I might think. It's some dad-ratted thing Mercy calls a tulip. She sent up to Boston for it, and *they* had to send all the way to Holland. Mark my words, Mercy sets great store by her tulips and everything else she's tending inside that fence. Didn't, she wouldn't have had me put up the fence to keep out the cows and hens and whatever might eat them off or pull them up or break them down, not, of course, having any notion all the trouble she's had getting them this high. Now, I don't know what it's done to that tulip to be out of the ground. Maybe it'll grow if it's set out again, and maybe 'twon't. But Mercy says you can have it to set out and see what happens. You dig up a nice little bed for it, and water it, and keep the weeds away from it, and if it lives it'll bloom next spring. It'll be a mite of work, but worth it if anybody likes garden flowers. They don't mean much to me, but they do to Mercy, and they must to you if you wanted one so bad.'

"Nine-year-old Enoch put his free hand in his pocket, the way your grandfather had his hands in his pockets — your grandmother was watching them from the parlor window — and said, ' 'Taint me, neither. It's Sophrony. She's crazy for ary thing with a bloom to it. She's been abed with a swelled-up throat for two weeks. Mayflowers is all gone by, and laylocks is hardly budded. I aimed to take her suthin.'

"Your grandfather nodded. 'That's thoughtful of you. Enoch. I hope she's getting better. Let's see, Sophrony's what now — fifteen, sixteen? Well, since Mercy's given you the tulip, I don't see as you need to say anything to Sophrony about how you jumped over the fence to get it and broke the privet getting out. It might worry her; being that old, she knows, of course, what garden fences are for, and that people are supposed to go in through the gate. After this, if you want to go in, you come to the door and ask Mercy. Anything she can spare she'll let you have and tell you what to do with it, and by and by maybe you'll have a flower garden of your own for Sophrony. That would just suit Mercy. She'd like to see a flower garden at every house she rides by.'

"Your grandmother said Enoch didn't have green fingers, or lacked time and patience ever to have much of a garden, but he never jumped the fence again. If she was out there when he went by, he would come in, and sometimes he brought Sophrony, and your grandmother would cut flowers for them to take home. Later on when their little brother John was old enough to drive the cows he would look over the picket fence and say, if your grandmother was there, 'I never jump into gardens. Enoch said you might break things off that way, and then they'd never bloom again. What's them blue things?' Your grandmother would tell him, 'Larkspur,' or 'Bachelor's-buttons,' and cut some for him to take home. When I was taking care of her garden, Enoch's boys, one after another as they grew old enough, came by day after day, morning and night, and each in his turn told me, 'Pa says not to jump over the fence. He says if I want to go in, you'll let me in by the gate. I won't come in; might break suthin. I like flowers that smell good,' and I'd give him some sprays of flowering almond, or a bunch of spice pinks. They were good boys. All the Walton boys were good boys."

Rosamond heard the sharp hoofs of cows striking the outcrop of ledge on Steep Hill, the crack of small bushes as a heifer plunged toward a muddy ditch, a young Walton's shout of "Hup! Hup out o' ther'!" and the thick soles of his boots racing to bring the adventurer back into line; heard it as clearly as if the lane had not been unmarked by any hoofs but deers' for many a year. She heard, too, the creaking wheels and the lumbering rumble of a dumpcart in the meadow on the far side of the hill. Though the Wentworth meadow had long ago grown up to alders, and the 'Lijah Wentworth house had crumbled into its cellar, she could hear 'Lijah's gentle voice speaking to his horse — " 'hoa; 'hoa now" — and then to Nimbly, the boy boarded with the Wentworths by the State ('Lijah and Em called him Nimbly because he was so quick on his feet), "Stand back a mite, dear. I'll fork it down and you kinda spread it round . . . That's right. That's good. Time we git the barn cleaned out and let it lay here a fortnit, and then plow it under, we'll have us a good crop of fodder comin' to keep our cutters contented and the rich milk a-streamin' out while the north wind sets on the ridgepole next winter. We can set, then, easy as you please, beside the stove with bowls of that milk on our knees, a-spoonin' popcorn out of it. Maybe if we git on the right side of Em, she'll make us some cornballs, too. Em, she makes the best cornballs ever I et, when she takes a notion. Jest in case, you 'n' I'd better plant us two, three rows of good poppin' corn."

And from high on the side of Mount Franklin, beyond the frog pond and the Black Swamp, rang out Paddy Michaud's solitary ax which rose and fell in even strokes, slowly but surely bringing down the hardwood trees to let in the sun on the pines, splitting logs too crooked to be sawed into boards, and piling up the cordwood which would be hauled out by horsesled next winter to keep the fires which powered the sawmills and the railroad engines. Paddy had come down from the north, down from Canada a hundred years ago with nothing but the clothes he wore and the ax he carried under his arm. A year later he had his own cabin at the foot of Mount Franklin. Two years later he had a horse and rode it home to Canada, bringing back another horse with Anna-Marie, his bride, riding on it. Each year for a long time after that a new Michaud baby rolled and kicked in the sweet fern beside the cabin, while his father's ax rang out high up on the mountain. His father's name was Jacques, but people called him Paddy because of the song he sang as he worked, day in, day out, and which sounded to them like "Paddy me for norsaw, paddy me for norsaw, compare ici, compare ici, paddy me for norsaw." Paddy's grandchildren had gone to the district school with Rosamond. Now one of them had a portable sawmill, another a grocery store in the village, one was a director of the local bank; among his great-grandchildren several were priests and nuns, and at least one was a lawyer with a Boston firm. But when his grandchildren had walked home from school with Rosamond, they sometimes stopped in the lane and said, "Hark! That's mon grandpère up there choppin'." Rosamond, listening with them, had heard both his ax and his song, and heard it now. "Paddy me for norsaw, paddy me for norsaw, compare ici, compare ici, paddy me for norsaw."

At the foot of Steep Hill she sat on a boulder and changed her shoes for the rubber boots, leaving the shoes under a juniper bush. At the edge of the frog pond she turned left, following the road the horsesleds had made, skirting the pond, but wading through a marsh where the muddy water reached above her ankles.

Pansy pursued her, in one leap, as far as the first hummock of grass. There she said, "Meow," in distaste and warning, and leaped back to the clay bed of the lane.

Rosamond laughed.

"You're right," she said. "This is no place for a lady without boots. Go home, Pansy. Go home and wait for me. I'll bring you some mayflowers. I know where they grow pinkest. Up by the Frenchman's Shanty."

She went on through the marsh and started up the long slope which led to the foot of Mount Franklin, walking the trail horses' feet had made in the rich, dark compost of rotted leaves and pine needles. On either side of the path ran velvet ribbons of gray-green moss. Here there was a quiet so deep that even Paddy's ax could not penetrate it. Nothing spoke here which had not been born here; only the wind out of caves near the top of the mountain stirring the tips of the trees, spreading the clean smell of pine, balsam, black spruce, and budding leaves on the hardwood branches; the brook laughing as it raced over stones and roots from the spring on the mountainside to murmur among the marsh hummocks and then whisper its way among the alders; the birds whistling signals as they searched for the nests in which they had come out of their shells last year, or built new nests in the home trees to hold the eggs they were to lay and keep covered for the hatching of their own young, who would next fall go south with the flock and wing their way again in the spring to whistle signals as they searched for old nests or built new ones.

"For water and wind and rooted things, and for creatures guided solely by instinct," thought Rosamond, "life is a steady progression from birth to death and birth again, all in one groove. But for us who have minds the future is forever unpredictable, because none of us knows where his thinking will lead him or how the thinking of other men will affect their lives and his. We think a wheel, and the wheel is good; but where will it roll to? We think a fire, and a fire is good; but how hot will it be, how far will it spread? We think an engine, and an engine is good; but how many times will its power multiply, and then can we control it or will it control us? We think a fine, free way of life, fight for it, establish it, but what we establish has all the evil as well as all the good which is in those who establish it, those who maintain it, and those who use it; freedom has as enemies those who do not respect the freedom of others, and those who do not know or serve the sources of their own freedom, who assume freedom is license, not knowing that it is compounded as much of responsibility as of privilege; what are we able and willing to do with and for the freedom our thinking created?"

She went on, crossing the old bridle path which once had been the only route between the southern and the northern settlements in the county, and touched as she passed it the granite ledge which had been a resting place for her great-grandmother each summer as she rode north, going cousining, with her newest baby before her in the saddle.

Just beyond, a clump of white birches ringed around by poplars marked the spot where the Frenchman's Shanty — the Michaud cabin — had stood. She did not know why it was always birches and poplars which sprang up where once walls and a roof had kept the sun from touching the earth. This was one of many questions she had meant to ask her father, but postponed too long. Perhaps Charles, Sandy's father, knew the answer. She must remember to have Sandy ask him.

A little way south of the clump of birches she reached down suddenly, separated thick green leaves, and picked her first spray of mayflowers, careful to break off the branch clean, not to disturb the roots. She touched it to her lips and it felt cold and glassy smooth, like wax, but smelled of everything in the woods — moss, evergreen, bursting leafbuds, sun and shade, rich soil, running water, wet stones — and still more of itself, a delicate fragrance that was like a soft radiance, a scent that was almost visual. She held it off, and studied it, seeing it as a cluster of pink stars grown small enough, cool enough, come close enough to lie in a woman's palm.

Then she looked up to where the tallest pines left an opening to the sky.

"God," she said, "the boards and the shingles have come for

the repair of the meetinghouse, and William has written a check to pay for them. The men will start the work this afternoon. You know they have only Saturdays and Sundays at home nowadays. The rest of the week they work away, in schools and factories and in the Navy Yard. They plow and work on their cars and trucks and tractors on Saturdays. They would not do these things on Sunday afternoon but they think it is right to work at Your House on Sunday afternoon, and so do I. It will be a fine thing to have a church again . . .

"But here is a church, too, God. Here is Your House, too. Here where nobody is but You and me. Here where the Michaud babies used to roll in the sweet fern while Paddy chopped cordwood on the mountain. Here where under thick green leaves are hundreds of stars still smelling of heaven. Here — in the palm of my hand . . . Here where I have come everything is good. Here there is no evil, except whatever may be in my own mind and heart.

"Where did the evil in man come from, God? You did not put evil in me, did You? I did not put it there, did I? But it must be there because I am a human being like other human beings, and any evil I have ever seen has been in us; there is none anywhere else in Your whole creation . . . But in us it seems — it does seem — that there is more than there has ever been before. So much that everyone is troubled about it — deeply troubled — everyone, even the most evil. Because we all hate evil in all its manifestations. So why can't we rid ourselves of it? . . . Or *is* it evil, God? Do you have another word for it? If You do, I wish You would tell it to me, because the word itself is bitter to my tongue when I frame it . . . Is what we call evil (since we find it only in thinking creatures) wrong thinking, mistaken thinking, confused thinking, and the result of that wrong, mistaken, confused thinking? . . . I believe it is! I believe You are telling me it is! . . .

"You know the human race is very young. We are beginning to feel old, in the way adolescents feel old — that desperate feeling that everything earlier generations have done has been wrong and much which should have been done has been left undone, so we must do it all and do it right, and *quickly;* we are still full of questions but there are no answer books, so somehow quickly, quickly, we must find the answers, the right answers, in our own heads; we must act and act fast, to save ourselves and to save humanity, for we stand at the edge of the precipice, at the brink of the falls. But you see us as older people see adolescents — tall children in the long, painful process of beginning to grow up, clinging to one another because they lack the confidence and courage to stand alone, afraid to speak for fear others may not agree with them, struggling to get loose from what is familiar, struggling to avoid the rapids of the unfamiliar, trying to escape from the past, trying to understand and explain and conform to the present, trying to prepare for the mysterious future, convinced that they must do all this *now,* today, for tomorrow will be too late . . .

"You did not give us minds with which to create evil, did you? You gave us minds to *use,* minds with which to seek and find and know You in ways that the birds and the trees and the brooks and the mayflowers never can.

"But You are patient — more patient with us than we are with ourselves or with You. You know it takes a long time for a person or a race to grow up; a long time to learn to spell properly even the short words, to say nothing of the long ones; a long time to understand even the simplest book, to say nothing of those which contain the most wisdom; a long time to apply skillfully one hand tool, to say nothing of operating an infinitely complicated mechanism. When a boy gets on a bicycle for the first time, we are not surprised that he falls, and falls again, or even runs into another bicycle. When a girl first picks up a needle, we do not expect her to make a tailored suit; she pricks herself, she stains the cloth, the stitches are uneven, the material is bunched, she may throw the work aside and say she will never sew again. But we are not surprised. We wait for tomorrow, knowing the boy will try the bicycle again tomorrow, the girl will take up the needle again tomorrow, and sooner or later he will be driving a car, she perhaps making her own clothes and her mother's too unless she finds other, better uses for her time. So You, too, knowing how young we are, what our capacities are, how much more time there is than we think (they are always saying, 'There is less time than you think,' but there is more, isn't there, God? There is all the time You planned for us to have — and that is time enough, more than we can imagine), You wait calmly while Your human race does all the wrong (not *evil* — it is not evil to misspell or misread a word, or to make a mistake in multiplication, or to fall off a bicycle, or to take uneven stitches), all the wrong thinking it seems to have to do in every area, in every period, in the face of every new problem, every new situation in the trial-and-error process of learning how to use the minds You gave us. You can wait calmly because You know that many times already in human history the human mind has achieved and created magnificently and will again, and that when such achievement, such creation is the rule and not the exception the mind You gave us will again be one with Yours.

"Looking at ourselves, as we are, how can we think such glory as that can be ours quickly or soon? It will take ages. It will require mighty effort and perseverance. It will test our patience, as well as Yours. It will demand stern self-discipline . . . We must understand that. We must accept that. But if we never give up — and You will not let us give up — we shall have served Your purpose and earned the privilege, by becoming the friends You would like to have there, of sitting at Your table.

"Thank you, God, for helping me to think this through. Help me to do more thinking, more than I ever have, for the more I think the more clearly and logically and decisively I can think. I realize here — now, with this mayflower in my hand — quite suddenly, that all my life I have done many things, said many things, without knowing why I did and said them, without even wondering why. I have kept house as my mother kept house. Most of my ideas were my father's ideas. Many of my judgments have been the judgments of my teachers. Even my faith is my grandparents' faith. I have spent most of my life in close association, close communion, with people I loved and trusted who were of earlier generations than my own. If I have not made serious mistakes, it is to their credit more than to mine. And I have even depended upon what I called my woman's intuition. What would have happened if my 'intuition' had been wrong? What would have happened to me if I had grown up in an entirely different environment, in a house that was not well kept, with a father whose ideas were unsound, with grandparents who had no faith, with teachers whose judgment was poor? Would I have *known* that? Not unless I had learned to think for myself. I must *think* . . .

"The world I live in, the world I have always lived in, is the past. How much of it is a part of the present? How much has come into the world that my parents and aunts and uncles and grandparents knew nothing of, and what is it? I don't know. I must find out. Because they are gone, but I am still here. I am living now. They had their time and contributed to it. This is my time, and I must contribute to it. I must add my mite to civilization before my time, too, is over. To do that, I must first see it for myself, see it working, and then I must think about it . . ."

Looking down at the mayflower in her hand, Rosamond saw between her parted fingers the silvery saffron of running evergreen and among it a fleck of waxy pink. She stooped to pick a second blossom, and a third, moving on slowly, a few steps at a time, and finding more where a minute ago none had seemed to be. In half an hour she had as many as she could hold by their stems and sat on a mossy stone to make them into a tidy bunch, stripping off many of the leaves, and tying the flowers together with a strand of evergreen.

She rested her elbows on her knees, letting the nosegay

dangle lightly from her looped hands, and watched the poplars quivering among the birches like ballet dancers on point ready to run out from behind the slim pillars which gave them balance while they waited for the signal which had not yet come; listened to the brook running brightly, bravely from the spring on the mountainside and down the steep slope, not knowing what it would find at the end, or whether there would be an end, but running anyway because it was a brook and a brook must run; listened to the wind stirring the tops of the pines, always the same wind, it seemed — but was it? — coming out of the mountain caves and going back into the mountain caves, deathless, eternal, though a pine tall enough long enough was either cut down or blown down to make room for younger pines for the wind to play with and make to sing; breathed in the fragrance of the flowers and the leaves and the needles and the stones and the moss and the wet earth and the noonday sun of May streaming down on them all and on her. Nothing but beauty could she see; nothing but music hear; nothing but sweetness smell. It was as near to heaven as she could imagine. It was perfect peace. As far as she knew she was not expected anywhere. She might have stayed there a long time, until the sun set and dusk came down.

But she said, "God, I think I shall buy a car."

And she stood up and began walking swiftly past the birches and the poplars, across the bridle path, and down the long slope toward the marsh.

She did not know that in southern Minnesota it was a very hot day, that the heat had come suddenly as it always came there at the end of the long cold winter, putting into sunsuits children who had played in snowsuits a week or two ago, and that Jason Schuyler was driving too fast along a broad, straight, flat highway toward Duluth and the north shore of Lake Superior.

He said to the girl beside him, "The North Shore isn't Maine, but it's more like Maine than any other place. And it's nearer."

"You must have seen a very colorful girl on some Maine beach last summer."

He glanced around at her. She had slid down in the seat until her head rested on the back. Her knees, bare below madras bermudas, pressed against the instrument board. Her silk shirt clung to the soft curves of her breast, and the big gold earrings he had given her shone between her short, blond curls. Her coffee-colored eyes were half-closed.

He said, "No. Yankee girls are not colorful compared with Scandinavians. Especially brown-eyed Scandinavians. Of which you are probably the only example extant."

"My mother was French."

"Nice combination. Odd, but nice."

"Frankly, I've always thought so. But then what is this with Maine? I imagine it as one log jam after another. With bears leaping about, wielding peaveys . . . Besides, it's almost at the bottom in percentage of the number of its young people who go to college."

She was a student of education at the University.

"Maybe that's because there are so many other things to do in New England besides go to college. So many other ways to learn. Other things to learn than are taught in colleges — at least lately."

"Such as?"

"I can't say yet. Tell you more after I've been there again . . . Maybe I'll take you some day to see for yourself."

"And then again maybe not, darling."

"And then again maybe not. Darling."

Clouds of smoke from a prairie fire rolled across the highway, and he drove faster to get clear of it, his eyes stinging.

Rosamond did not know that in Washington Congressman Robert Frye from Minnesota and a friend of his who was virtually certain of the gubernatorial nomination in Indiana were just coming out of church and had encountered a Senator on the steps. The three stood together as in a football huddle during a backyard game, with an arm of the Senator about each of the others.

"How about coming home with me for that fishing trip, if this session ever ends? What would suit you? Salmon? The herring run?"

"Whatever they stock that lake with. What do you call it? Embroidery Pool?"

"Lacey's Pond. That idea stuck with you, didn't it? Good enough. Stop in at my office some day soon and we'll set the date. Then I'll give the Judge a ring and he'll tell the trout to wait around."

Rosamond did not know that as near as the village Eileen Struthers was saying to her husband in the parsonage kitchen, "I'm sure there must be a way, dear. There *must* be. Let's go out this afternoon and talk with Miss Lacey."

She did not know that even nearer, at the end of the lane, a Chrysler Imperial had stopped, and its driver was saying, "We're taking a chance if we try to go over that road. Do you think a car ever has?"

His wife responded impatiently, "Of *course*. That Mrs. Sturtevant drove her German over it away back in the winter. She told me about it at the county meeting. You know I've been dying to get there ever since. She said the woman is a regular battleax, but I don't care about *that*. It's in out-of-the-way places like this you find real treasures. And bargains, Ray!"

The thought of bargains persuaded him, as she had been sure it would, and he pressed the pedal, easing the sleek nose, the spread wings of the Chrysler Imperial between the steep banks of Lacey's Lane.

Rosamond, having changed back to her heavy-soled shoes, and carrying her rubber boots in her hand, was swinging toward home, unaware that the world was coming to learn from her just as she had decided to go out to learn from it.

~~~~ 5

WHAT an unusual sign! It's an old sleighback, isn't it?"
Rosamond turned from unlocking the studio door, and nodded.

Her first customer of the year wore the air of the city. The sheer wool beige suit, the mink fur-piece with little tails dangling like a fringe, the filmy blue hat, the handsome alligator bag and matching pumps with pointed toes and pencil-thin heels had all come either from New York or from a Boston branch of a New York shop. The face below the hat was small and sharp with quick, shrewd eyes; the eyebrows were too heavy, too dark for the skin color and texture, and so were the wings of hair too dark above the pierced ears with the cameo earrings. The hand holding the gloves had glossy brown nails, and the gloves were of blond doeskin, soft as butter. This was a woman who often fooled others, always to her own advantage, but never fooled herself.

"I've seen a sleigh with original decorations. The sun rising or setting, or whatever it's doing. But what are all those swinging balls?"

"My own addition," Rosamond answered.

"You painted them in?"

"Yes."

"Fascinating! What for?"

"They are the planets. Our sun's planets. The man who painted my grandfather's sleigh didn't know about them. He thought they were stars, like all the other stars he saw in his quiet sky at night, and he thought all stars went to bed when the sun came up. We have learned otherwise. So I added the planets."

"Oh? But what has astronomy to do with an antiques shop?"

"It's not only astronomy. It's the present and the future."

The customer made a wry face and an exaggerated shudder.

"But why here? I go to antiques shops and collect antiques to forget the dreadful present. To say nothing of the ghastly future."

"And are you successful?"

"Only briefly, I must admit."

"Then," said Rosamond quickly, with her first smile, "I think you earn such brief surcease." She threw open the door. "Come in. Here is yesterday. Here, that is, are some of the problems solved yesterday, some of the dreams realized yesterday. Yesterday's smiles caught in glass and painted on china; yesterday's tears turned to silver and gold. Everything here is finished and at rest. Nothing can be added to it, nor anything taken away."

While she was speaking, they had gone inside, and she moved about, raising shades and opening windows. The late April sunlight streamed in across the shelves. It was like lighting the candles on a Christmas tree.

The customer stood still, staring, and drew in her breath.

"Oh," she said, "you — you have —" She paused and then in quite a different tone said, "You have some very pretty things, don't you?"

Rosamond laughed.

"You were about to say I have beautiful things. But you're an experienced collector. You thought that if you said that I'd raise my prices. So you changed it to 'some very pretty things.' Now that's no way to get your surcease. Beauty is in the eye of the beholder. If you like these things, say so. Liking them isn't buying them. As for my prices, they are reasonable, and the more you buy, the lower the prices. I want to sell in quantity, if possible. I hope to sell everything I have here within a month."

"*Everything?* Within a *month?*"

"That's right. If I haven't, I shall have an auction as soon as the Harbor season opens."

"You're — going out of business?"

"Oh, no. I've only just gone into it. But I want to get all new stock. Antiques, of course. But a different kind of stock entirely."

"Really." The customer had stopped listening. Her shrewd eyes had narrowed, grown shrewder. She was moving forward softly.

Like a cat, Rosamond thought, toward a leaf moving so little that to any eye or ear but a cat's it would seem motionless.

"There is a good deal to see," said Rosamond. "Take your time. I have some paper work to do." She sat down at the table which had served as a pulpit of her Aunt Ruth's church and was now brilliantly spattered with her father's paint, and opened a drawer. "Notice there are six sections of shelves. I will sell the contents of any section — your choice — for a thousand dollars."

"A — *thousand* dollars? Really, Miss Lacey, you don't actually think you have a thousand dollars' worth in just one of these sections?"

"More than that, as I am sure you know," replied Rosamond calmly, secure in the information gleaned from Jason Schuyler that one of those shelves held an almost priceless pitcher. "And you would have your choice, as I said. But you would have to decide rather quickly. I am only beginning to learn values, and the price is likely to go up at any time."

Her back was toward her customer and she did not turn her

head, but began to write words and figures in a small ledger. It was one in which her Aunt Pauline had inscribed pastoral poems, and Rosamond was using a clean page toward the end.

A half hour or so later a tall, thin man in a gray flannel suit, a red bow tie, and a hound's tooth checked cap came to the door. He held a cigar between his thumb and forefinger.

"How much longer?" he asked his wife.

She said, "Oh — I'll be right along. You haven't finished reading the *Times?*"

"I certainly have. It's past one o'clock and we must be an hour from any place where we can get dinner."

"We didn't finish breakfast until nine."

"That's four hours ago. We'd better get going."

"Well, I suppose . . . How much is this bowl, Miss Lacey?"

Rosamond looked up from writing "Priceless pitcher $35. Priceless pitcher $135. Priceless pitcher $1350. What price priceless? Priceless pitcher —" and said, "Fifty dollars."

"Fifty dollars for a plain Pomona fingerbowl? You couldn't get that much even if it had cornflowers."

"Personally," smiled Rosamond, who had never heard of Pomona before, "I prefer Pomona without cornflowers. My tastes are simple. Anyhow, as I told you, my prices are lower on large quantities. I believe it is called wholesale."

"She wants to sell the contents of a complete section of these shelves at a time," the woman told her husband.

"Either that or at auction," said Rosamond, "as soon as the season opens at the Harbor."

The woman seemed to be trying to tell her husband something with her eyes. He trod heavily, reluctantly, toward the shelves and stood staring at them.

"If you were to buy a section," said Rosamond, "not that you are, of course, which would it be?"

The woman shrugged.

"Oh, I like several pieces in this section," she said, nodding toward the one she stood beside. "But certainly not at the price you quoted. Believe me, you'd be doing well if you got half that. At an auction or any other way. But I *would* give you half."

The section she indicated was not the one which contained the priceless pitcher. There was something — perhaps several things — here which she preferred to a plated amberina pitcher. And she was, clearly, a canny and experienced collector of glass.

"I'm sure you would," said Rosamond, "but I couldn't consider it. A thousand dollars is a very reasonable price for what is on those shelves and I couldn't take a dollar less even from a dealer."

"Good lord," roared the husband, goaded. "She wants a thousand dollars for that stuff and you're offering her five hundred? You must both be crazy. Come on. We're getting out of here. Right now."

As she was being propelled into the yard, the woman shot Rosamond a furious glance.

"You have no idea how to run a business," she shrieked. "No idea at all."

A minute afterward, when he had slammed the car door and was going around to his side to get in, and Rosamond was passing with her mayflowers toward the house, the woman said in a different tone, low and conspiratorial, "I may telephone you."

"I have no telephone," smiled Rosamond.

She heard the woman's gasp of frustration drowned out by the roar of the powerful engine, and, standing on the doorstep, watched the car disappear around the curve and down the hill toward the mill bridge.

"It's at least four times the size I want," she thought.

She meant the Chrysler Imperial.

"So I suppose it cost four times what mine will. And her clothes. Even his cigar smelled expensive. So there's no question but that they can pay a thousand. If they want to. It depends on the real value of that glass. They want their money's worth and more. If they come back, it is worth $1500, at least, or she will have persuaded him that it is. And she knows. I'm sure she knows."

Pansy uncurled in the corner of the porch and stretched.

"Why, good day to you, milady," said Rosamond. "Do honor me by stepping across my threshold, and taking a thimbleful of cream."

They went in together and when Rosamond had raked up the coals and baited them with chips and edgings, Pansy lapped under the stove while the kettle came to a boil on top and Rosamond arranged her flowers in Franklin mugs, a redware beaker, and a brown toby jug marked Bennington.

As she sat eating her lunch, the flowers surrounded her saucer of seckel pears, her bowl of strong tea, and the slices of homemade bread she had toasted by holding them with a long-handled fork over the coals.

The wind had quickened and was rattling the windows a little. The sun, beginning its downward swing, came through the northwest windows like a great, invisible brush and struck elongated blocks of light on the cellar door. The clock on the shelf ticked softly, steadily, as if time existed only to be measured.

"Why do I think of moving out of my orbit?" asked Rosamond. "I am so at peace in this room, in this house, and anywhere within easy walking distance. I know it all so well — the meaning of every sound, the position of every object, the routine of every day and night. I have no obligation to leave it. I could stay here, along with you and a neighbor dropping in now and then, until my life is done. Why don't I? Why do I take any risk?"

She was speaking to any and all who had ever sat around this table, and she heard them answer her as she had heard God answer her in the woods.

"Because you do have an obligation, Rosamond. An obligation, at least to yourself, to learn what we could not teach you because we knew only our own times; to find out what has gone on in the world while you have been living in ours; to see what your fellow men are doing, what motivates them, and where they are heading; to judge whether or to what extent you are their kind, or they yours. It has never been your way to lie back against a cushion. You never have until very lately. You are a thinker and a doer."

"But isn't this like — going to the goblin market?" Rosamond asked. "And am I Lizzie or Laura?"

She did not know why the Christina Rossetti poem came to her mind now. She had not thought of it for years, yet when she had jumped up and run into the library still thick with the cold, dead air of winter, her hand went straight to the green and gold binding of the volume she wanted. She brought it back and sat with it in the warm kitchen.

> ". . . Look, Lizzie, look, Lizzie,
> Down the glen tramp little men . . ."
> "No," said Lizzie, "no, no, no;
> Their offers should not charm us,
> Their evil gifts would harm us."
> She thrust a dimpled finger
> In each ear, shut eyes and ran:
> Curious Laura chose to linger
> Wondering at each merchant man.
> One had a cat's face,
> One whisked a tail . . .
> One like a wombat prowled obtuse and furry,
> One like a ratel tumbled hurry-scurry . . .
>
> Till Laura, dwindling,
> Seemed knocking at Death's door:
> Then Lizzie weighed no more
> Better and worse,
> But put a silver penny in her purse,
> Kissed Laura, crossed the heath with clumps of furze
> At twilight, halted by the brook;

And for the first time in her life
Began to listen and look . . .

One may lead a horse to water,
Twenty cannot make him drink.
Though the goblins cuffed and caught her,
Coaxed and fought her,
Bullied and besought her,
Scratched her, pinched her black as ink,
Kicked and knocked her,
Mauled and mocked her . . .

In a smart, ache, tingle,
Lizzie went her way . . .

That night long Lizzie watched by her,
Counted her pulse's flagging stir . . .
But when the first birds chirped about their eaves
And early reapers plodded to the place
Of golden sheaves . . .
Laura awoke as from a dream,
Laughed in the innocent old way . . .

"For there is no friend like a sister,
In calm or stormy weather,
To cheer one on the tedious way,
To fetch one if one goes astray,
To lift one if one totters down,
To strengthen whilst one stands."

"Am I Lizzie or Laura?" Rosamond asked again.
"I think you know. If you are not sure, that is the first thing
to find out."
"If I am Laura, I have no sister to save me."
"No. No sister. Only us."
"If I am Lizzie, who is Laura?"
"That you will learn. Perhaps you have met her already,

perhaps not. There may be many Lauras. If you are Lizzie, anyone will be Laura whom you see wake as from a bad dream and hear laugh in the innocent old way."

Rosamond's eyes fell again to the fine print on a page bordered by a red line.

". . . O Laura, come: . . .
Come with me home.
The stars rise, the moon bends her arc,
Each glow-worm winks her spark,
Let us get home before the night grows dark . . ."

Every goblin laughed
When they spied her peeping:
Came towards her hobbling,
Flying, running, leaping . . .
Grunting and snarling,
One called her proud,
Cross-grained, uncivil . . .
Lashing their tails
They trod and hustled her,
Elbowed and jostled her,
Clawed with their nails,
Barking, mewing, hissing, mocking,
Tore her gown and soiled her stocking . . .

"What are these horrid creatures?" Rosamond wondered. "They must be human mistakes, all the wrong motions, all the steps in the wrong directions, all the inaccurate additions, subtractions, multiplications, divisions, all the x's made to stand for what y stands for so that it is as if $4x$ (cups of sugar) were often mixed with y (an egg) instead of four eggs with a cup of sugar. And to these mistakes the poet has given wombats' bodies, rats' tails, bats' wings, sharp nails, and snarling voices —"

She blinked at the sound of a knock on the entry door at the end of the stove. She had been too absorbed to hear a car drive into the yard, or steps on the porch, or the outside door opening. If the outside door had been closed. Perhaps she had left it open.

She said, "Come in," and was surprised to see a woman whose face was only faintly familiar followed by a man she had never seen before.

"How do you do, Miss Lacey. Please forgive us for coming so far in before being invited. The outside door was open, and you didn't hear us knock. I don't suppose you remember me. I called one day in the winter with — Mrs. Crawford. I am Eileen Struthers."

"Of course I remember," Rosamond said. "Let me take your coat. And this is your husband?"

"This is John. Yes."

"Give me your hat, Mr. Struthers. Come into the next room. Do sit down. How nice of you to drive out! But it's a beautiful day for a ride, isn't it? I've been mayflowering. That's why you found me at the lunch table so late. Besides that, I was lost in some reading —"

They were sitting together on the small sofa, opposite Rosamond in the wicker rocking chair. Eileen, in a blue rayon dress with white dots and a round white collar, hair brushed straight back and pinned, and hands clasped tightly in her lap, was like a child with an old face. John was as restless as Eileen was still. He unbuttoned his coat and buttoned it again, his feet were in constant motion inside his shoes, he moistened his lips, his cheek twitched, and his eyes snapped from one object to another in the room pausing nowhere.

"I'm sorry we interrupted your quiet afternoon," Eileen said.

"This is a welcome interruption. My reading, though absorbing, was not exactly pleasant."

"But what we have come about is not exactly pleasant, either. We are in trouble, Miss Lacey. And you are the only one I could think of to turn to."

"Then I am glad you came. Though I am rather surprised that you thought of me."

"I've thought of you many times since the day I was here. You suggested a number of questions for me to ask my husband. I never dared to ask them. But lately he has been answering them without being asked. Because he *is* a deeply spiritual man, Miss Lacey."

Rosamond bent a little toward him. There was only interest in her face, but a lively interest.

"So what is your trouble, Mr. Struthers?"

He said uneasily that it might be he was tired. He was not feeling well, had headaches which came on suddenly and were almost intolerable, but the doctor could find no cause. He said he had felt somewhat the same at this time last year, while they were in their first parish in western Massachusetts and he was commuting there for weekends from his theological studies. But after getting his degree, having a month's vacation with relatives in Canada, and being called to North Pelham, he had felt much better. It distressed him to be feeling this way again so soon for it interfered with his work and made Eileen anxious. The doctor told him the only cure was rest, but he could not rest, knowing how much waited, needing to be done.

Rosamond nodded slowly, thoughtfully.

"You work beyond your strength and still the work is never finished nor even at a point where you can lay it down until tomorrow with peace of mind. A few weeks of that kind of struggle is enough to wear out any man or woman . . . Is it possible that you are attempting too much, John?"

"He is," Eileen said firmly. "That's it, Miss Lacey. He is."

The eyes of both were fixed on Rosamond. She looked only at John, as if Eileen had not spoken.

"If you are, why are you? Do you believe God expects more of you than He gives you strength for? Would that be the way of a loving father? Would that even be — humane?"

John sighed, the intake of air in short gusts like sobs, and the outgoing breath long, spent, the sound of complete exhaustion.

"God expects a pastor to meet the needs of his flock. And He expects a husband to meet the needs of his wife. That is not too much to expect . . . But I am doing neither. The harder I try, it seems, the farther short of both I fall."

Now Eileen was staring at him in amazement. She unlocked her hands and reached for one of his.

"John, what are you saying? I have never complained. I have nothing to complain of. *Nothing . . .*"

He gave no sign that he heard Eileen, or felt her touch, or knew that there was anyone but himself in this room with Rosamond. It was as if a curtained circle had been lighted for these two leaving the rest of the world mute in the dusk beyond. Even within the circle, the sounds seemed not those of voices but of John's thoughts speaking. Rosamond's words — and Eileen's — were the reverberations of John's thoughts.

"My wife has never complained," he said. "She never will. I know that. Sometimes I wish she would. If she thought of herself, she might save herself. But she thinks only of me, of what more she can do to help me serve the needs of our parish. So both of us are giving all we have, day after day and night after night . . ."

"And still it is not enough?"

"Not nearly enough . . ."

"Not enough for what, John? What are the parish needs you are trying to serve?"

"Inspirational services," he said slowly, "to bring the people closer to God in worship and to go with them through the routine of their daily lives. Personal spiritual guidance during periods of grief, anxiety, emotional confusion, wavering of religious faith. The example of a pastor and his family finding life good, as God's children, enjoying what He has given us to enjoy, wrestling bravely, confidently, with whatever is wrong in the world, scattering encouragement, comfort, hope simply by walking down the street or lighting the windows of the parsonage . . . But I can't do that. I thought I could, but I can't. Because . . ."

"Why can't you do that, John?"

"Because . . . *so much else* is needed!"

"What? . . . What else?"

He sighed again, more painfully than before, and began again, more slowly than before.

He spoke of the children of working mothers who roamed the streets asking for coins with which to operate jukeboxes in preference to going into empty houses; of adolescents lacking supervised social activities; of the despairing, too-early-married young; of the lonely ill, the aged neglected and deserted in nursing homes, the men and women who came to him in desperation because they could no longer communicate with their wives or husbands; of financial crises in families, political crises in town affairs, the insoluble problems which led to resentment, bitterness, hate; of projects to raise money for a better organ, a more musical bell, new pew cushions, new kitchen equipment with which to earn more money for organ, bell, and cushions; of the rivalry among church congregations to enlarge; of fundamentalist members seeking to avoid all contact with the world, and progressive members urging a close relationship with it, contribution to all its good works, participation in politics, education, public health, recreation; of pacifists seeing patriotism as un-Christian and dangerous, patriots suspecting any reference to the desirability of peace as an effort to promote peace at any price and thus as inspired by the enemy . . .

At a restaurant beside a superhighway thirty miles away, Elise (née Alice) Burrage was asking, "Dessert, Ray? Or just coffee?"

"In case the coffee is as bad as the steak, we'd better have dessert."

"Coffee will do for me. My croquettes were all right."

"Can't understand your ordering croquettes in a place like this. No knowing what went into them."

"I don't dwell on thoughts like that. They tasted all right."

When he had ordered, she lit a cigarette and smiled at him.

"I was afraid the steak wouldn't be good, but I'm sorry it wasn't. Both for your sake and because I do want you in a good mood."

"Why? What are you going to hit me with now?"

"Something that can't wait, unfortunately."

"If it's anything that will slow us down getting home, it will have to. I'm expecting a telephone call around seven o'clock. Important."

"So is this important, Ray. To me. And so, to that extent, to you. I know you have a very big week coming up, and both of us will have to be at our best. I'm prepared to outdo myself. I really am. I really want to. But I can't unless I have a clear mind. And I can't have a clear mind until — I have in my cabinet several things I saw at that Miss Lacey's . . . If we shouldn't be home at seven sharp, surely your call —"

"You mean you want to go back there today and buy some of that stuff at her prices? You said yourself it wasn't worth half what she asked."

"Ray, for heaven's sake! Of course I said so. But it is. Not the bowl alone. But the section —"

"Elise! She said *a thousand dollars* for a section, said she wouldn't take less; and I believe her."

"So do I."

"Then — if you're trying to tell me you've reached the point in this craze where you expect me to write a thousand dollar check for a bunch of old glass, you must be sick, sick, sick."

"I'm not sick even one time. I know what I'm doing. This is no ordinary bunch of old glass. It's a fabulous collection. I've never seen anything like it outside the Parke-Bernet Galleries."

"Well, I'm not the Parke-Bernet Galleries."

"You paid much more for my mink coat."

"When Mitchell's wife turned out in a mink cape, you had to have a coat. That was business."

"You pay much more for a new car every year. Beside the trade-in."

"That's business, too."

"Well, so is this. If you won't buy that glass for me, I'll use my own money. It's not only something I want. It's an investment I'm going to make. Ten years from now it may take me on a round-the-world cruise."

He pushed away his half-eaten pie and chuckled, a half-exasperated, half-amused sound. She had so little money; something less than $3000 left her by an aunt five years before, all she had ever had except what he gave her since she came to work in his office twenty years ago; and she was always threatening to spend it. But for him it would have been gone by now. Poor Elise, talking about investments. She knew no more about business than a child.

"I'm afraid you mean that."

"I do."

"What on earth do you think is so fabulous about the stuff?"

"In that one section with the Pomona bowl there are a dozen — a complete dozen — morning-glory wines, and even one is an advanced collector's item. They retail, when they can be found, for about a hundred dollars apiece. There is a holly amber jelly compote worth four hundred dollars. To say nothing of a Burmese perfume bottle, glorious color, which in a Charles Street shop would have a price tag of a hundred and twenty-five, an Agata creamer I don't know the value of except that it must be out of this world, along with odds and ends of coralene, Mary Gregory, cut velvet, and signed Tiffany which must bring the total value up to twenty-five hundred at least; probably three thousand."

"Whew! You've never talked in figures like that before. I thought when I paid a hundred dollars for a pair of vases with dingle-dangles around them —"

"Not dingle-dangles. Prisms. Not vases. Lustres. We got them at a show on the Cape, and they were worth what you paid but no more. At a thousand dollars that section of Miss Lacey's is an absolute steal." She bent forward and held her lighter to his cigar, her blue eyes below the blue hat crinkling at the corners. "So — are you going to steal it for me, or do I have to steal it for myself?"

In her wicker rocking chair, beside a window full of pink geraniums, Rosamond was saying, "It does sound impossible, John. Impossible for any one man — or man and wife — to meet so many demands, to fill such a breadth of needs."

"I was afraid he couldn't get through his sermon this morning," Eileen said. "He was so tired. He had to speak at a PTA board meeting last night. Then he worked on his sermon until after two o'clock. Looking up at him in the pulpit, I was scared. His face was grayish and sometimes he swayed. I thought he might faint."

"It was this . . . *that* headache," John said. He brushed a hand across his eyes, winked rapidly, and suddenly smiled for the first time. "It's gone now. You worry unduly, my dear. I told you it would pass. We've taken up too much of Miss Lacey's time. I hardly remember now what I've said. I hope nothing I shouldn't have. If I did, you won't repeat it, will you, Miss Lacey? And please forgive me my protesting, as in my prayers tonight I shall ask God to do. As His servant, I should and do welcome every task He assigns me."

"I have nothing to forgive," Rosamond told him, "and I am sure God will tell you the same. I hope and believe He will tell you that you have not so much protested as begun to use the judgment He gave you; that what you have protested against are not His assignments but the burdens heaped upon you by your fellow human beings which are preventing you from doing well what in your heart you know He called you to the ministry to do, and what He brought you and Eileen together for . . . On your way home, John, while your head no longer aches, I wish you would consider whether what you said to Eileen a little while ago may not be what God is saying to you. You said she never complains, and sometimes you wish she would, because if she thought of herself she might save herself. As Eileen's health, peace of mind, happiness are important to you, and yours to her, so that of you both is important to God Who loves you both even more than you love each other. Or thus I was brought up to believe, and do believe."

John was looking at her in a puzzled way, but Eileen's eyes were shining. They stood up to go, and Rosamond rose with them, but said, "Won't you have some tea and a piece of cake with me? I have a problem too, and perhaps you can help me with it."

"Fair enough, isn't it, John?" Eileen cried. "Now we couldn't refuse even if we wanted to. Which we don't."

"As long as we're back in time for the young people's service —"

"I'll see we are, John. Trust me? And don't think of time again? . . . Oh, Miss Lacey, I do love your kitchen. My grandmother had a wood stove. May I slice the cake?"

As the women moved between cupboard, stove, and table, Eileen exclaiming, Rosamond explaining, John Struthers walked slowly along the wall, pausing to touch an iron latch, feel the curve of the thumb rest, watch the thin, uneven bar rise from its socket and drop back into it, to rub the heel of his hand up and down a corner post as smooth as an adze, time, and wax could make it, to study the pine boards of the floor white from much scrubbing and worn into hollows around the knots.

As they sat at the table over steaming cups, Rosamond asked, "If you had not gone into the ministry, John, how do you think you would have earned a living and supported a family?"

"As a contractor, almost certainly. I earned the expenses of my education by working for one on Saturdays and during vacations."

"You enjoyed that?"

"Oh, very much. He built houses, mostly. I never got beyond being a helper. But first I helped on the rough work, then I learned to help with the inside finish. When I left him I was just beginning to do a little cabinetwork. I'd like to build some cupboards for Eileen around her sink, if I had time. The parsonage kitchen has only one cupboard and it is inconveniently located."

"The last minister I knew well — and that was a long time ago — was a carpenter. That was his trade and his livelihood. All he did for us — his parish — was to live his life among us, as a good neighbor, and to speak to us in the church on Sunday afternoons. But it was enough. It was a great contribution. With his example to go by, his people did the rest — took care of themselves and one another."

"Those were less complicated times."

"Only because we did not think of them as complicated. Nothing is complicated except by having many parts. Each of the parts is simple. Whenever we cannot deal with all the parts combined, we should separate them and deal with one part at a time. Like a mechanic with an engine. If it isn't running properly, he doesn't try to push the whole stubborn mass, or to lift it up and shake it . . . And now I've brought the conversation around to my problem."

"Good. I was just about to. What is your problem, Miss Lacey?"

"I've decided to buy a car and learn to drive it. I haven't driven at all for forty years and never very much. I know nothing whatever about modern cars, and what I'd like is a Model T Ford. I do know they haven't been produced for a long time, but can they still be bought second — or should I say tenth — hand?"

John laughed aloud. Eileen looked at him in astonishment. He so rarely laughed lately that she loved to hear him — but was he laughing at Miss Lacey?

"I'm laughing out of pure pleasure," he said quickly. "This

is such a neat, tidy problem compared with what I expected! Though I don't know what I expected — surely not that you would have any problem I'm accustomed to having brought to me." He pushed back his empty cup, and his eyes actually twinkled. "Now let's see. A Model T. Yes, I think one could still be bought, but it might take a long time to find it. When you did, it would be a collector's item and I guess you know what that means because I understand you sell antiques."

"I try to," said Rosamond. "I try. Do you mean that a Model T Ford would cost as much as a priceless pitcher? Or more?"

"What does a priceless pitcher cost?" asked Eileen.

"I wish I knew, dear. If you and John don't know more about cars than I know about priceless pitchers, you aren't going to be able to help me at all. All I know is that I have a pitcher which has been called priceless, and I certainly would like to trade it for a Model T Ford, or even half a Model T Ford."

"Why do you want a Model T Ford? As advertising for your business?"

"Good gracious, no. I want one because I would have some idea how to drive it, and because I supposed it would be cheap."

"I don't think it would be cheap. An antique car ready for the road is quite a property. If it isn't ready for the road, it may take a good deal of time and money to get it there. And when you had it on the road, you might find it difficult as well as expensive to keep it there. Parts aren't easy to get, you know, nor mechanics who know how to put them on or in," he grinned suddenly, "even though they are simple!"

"See?" said Rosamond quickly. "It isn't only complexity that stumps us. Simplicity does it just as readily nowadays. We're so used to attempting too much that everything seems difficult . . . Well, all right. No Model T. So what is the cheapest and best car for me to buy?"

John put his elbows on the table, his hands together, and rubbed his chin on his thumbs.

"I'll tell you," he said. "Any car in good condition would cost at least twelve hundred dollars. For that, you should have a pretty wide choice in secondhand cars. But you always take a chance on a secondhand car, and most of them use a lot of gas and oil and need replacements every little while. I think if I were you I'd get one of the new compact cars. They handle more like early cars, the initial cost is low, and they're very inexpensive to run."

"How much do they cost?"

"The cheapest I've heard of is about twelve hundred. That's very cheap for a new car. Being small, of course not only the operating cost but the registration and insurance is low too."

"About how much is that for the first year?"

"Maybe a hundred."

"Thirteen hundred, then. Besides driving lessons so that I'll be sure to get a license. I do have to pass a test to get a license, don't I?"

"Oh, yes. But with a few lessons I'm sure you'll pass it, Miss Lacey."

"I'll pass it," said Rosamond. "With flying colors. In a cloud of dust. And all that."

"I just can't imagine anyone refusing you," said Eileen. "Either he couldn't bear to, or else he wouldn't dare. Anyway, I'm sure you'll drive like an angel. Johnny, it's lucky she gave you such a big piece of cake and that whole pitcher of milk. Because we can't go home before Young People's. If we dash now, straight to the church, we'll just make it. Miss Lacey, how can we thank you? I don't know when I've had such a good time!"

"Come again," said Rosamond, waving them off. "That's all. Come again."

The sun had set. From the dusk above a red line along the western horizon Vega had slipped out, a queenly actress between the curtains of the cosmic stage. Rosamond, before she closed the door, stood straight for a minute, in the growing chill, to honor this royal entrance.

She thought, "I have known them all, all my life. I know them so well, from a distance. Soon now — perhaps even in my time — men will be meeting them face to face, go into their homes. What kind of men? Will they enter by invitation or invasion? Shall we be welcomed or hurled back? . . . God, don't let this mission be undertaken until mankind is worthy."

She lit a lamp and was placing it on the table when she heard a quick knock and saw that the yard was flooded with light. What now?

"Come in," she called turning down the wick slightly because the flame threatened to smoke the chimney.

She had a sudden feeling that it might be anyone. Anyone at all. Even the First Lady of Vega. But she had no sense of surprise, of apprehension, of awe, only of fulfillment, of serene readiness for contact with whomever, whatever, might be abroad in this remarkable universe of which she was a part.

It was only Elise Burrage, hatless, flushed, a little out of breath, and looking quite girlish, almost mischievous.

"Hullo. Here I am again. If *only* you had a telephone you'd have saved me *so* much trouble! After I achieved the miracle of getting my husband to come back, we lost our way. If he misses an important call that's supposed to come in around seven o'clock, I may be Reno-bound. And let me give you some advice: *Never* mention price before a sulky husband (or wife) if you can possibly help it, if you want to sell! But in spite of your best efforts, so to speak, you've sold that section of glass. I'll be back for it some day this coming week — say Wednesday. Don't pack it, please. I like to do my own packing. You'll take this check for half? I'll bring another for the rest when I come."

Rosamond looked at the slip of paper.

"I would take the check, Mrs. Burrage. But it isn't for half."

"What do you mean?"

"I warned you my price might go up. It is now thirteen hundred and fifty."

"You're joking!"

"No. I did warn you, you know."

"But that's ridiculous! Raising your price at —" she glanced at her watch "— at the rate of nearly a hundred dollars an hour! *Where* do you get such *ideas* of values? Did you buy that glass?"

"Oh, no. It was my aunt's. Aunt Rachel collected it when it was new, most of it. And she had everyone giving her glass for Christmas and birthdays and anniversaries and each time she had a child. She described what she had as a passion for glass."

"Oh-h . . ."

There was a loud blast on the horn and Elise jumped.

"Well, I don't *dare* stay to argue with you. This is simply preposterous, but I too have a passion for glass. My husband is risking a coronary by agreeing to pay a thousand, but I will pay you the three hundred and fifty extra out of my own funds when I come on Wednesday. I can trust you, I hope, not to raise the ante again, and not to remove anything from the section? Because I remember exactly what is there."

"I'm sure you do, Mrs. Burrage. And you can be sure that you will have everything you saw in that section when I have your checks totaling thirteen hundred and fifty. In the meantime, I'll have my lawyer investigate this check, since we are strangers."

"You will find it well supported, Miss Lacey."

"I assume so. But this is business. For me it is big business. The first I have ever done in my life, but I don't intend that it shall be the last. I have learned a great deal from you, Mrs. Burrage, and I am grateful. I shall look forward to seeing you again Wednesday, and hope you will come often. Perhaps we shall become friends."

"Hm," said Elise, looking back warily over her shoulder. "I don't know about *that*. But we may enjoy fencing, more or less. You must have enjoyed this first match. You won it."

"For my purposes, I won it," said Rosamond calmly. "But for your purposes you won it. You know that perfectly well. You're no creature of impulse like my Aunt Rachel. Your passion for glass is not so overpowering that you would pay me thirteen hundred and fifty dollars for this unless it were worth much more. So, congratulations! And see you Wednesday!"

As the Burrages went down the hill, Elise said, "Ray, that is the most extraordinary woman I ever met in my life. I can't *wait* to get back here on Wednesday!"

Her husband, faced with the problem of meeting another car, and barely avoiding a ditch, said only, "She seems to be building quite a business. I wish she'd hurry up and build a better road."

"Heavens," murmured Elise, "now who can *that* be?" If it were any other week than this week, she thought, she wouldn't wait until Wednesday. She would be back tomorrow. Surely it couldn't be a customer coming in over this road after dark?

If it had not been too dark for her to see Sandy's lean, young face, the round neck of his T shirt above the open zipper of his windbreaker, or even to guess the age of his car, she would have been reassured.

He was the next to thrust his head into Rosamond's kitchen, and he had not knocked.

"Need any wood?"

"No. I've used very little today. Did you come by the church?"

"Come by it!" He stretched out his arm and flexed his muscle. "I've been working there all afternoon. So's Dad, and Andy, and Paul Lee, and Ben Farraday, and Timmy Walton, and the Pulaski boys. Even Joe Thibedeau brought over his jack to use with Dad's so we could get a rotten timber out and replace it with one we got from the George barn that fell down under the weight of snow last winter. The roofing was delivered yesterday, and we've started putting it on. Soon as that's tight we'll be ready to put new windows in, and then lay a floor. I've got an idea for next weekend. I'll see if I can't get some guys from the frat over to put in an afternoon's work. Good exercise for 'em."

"Fine," said Rosamond. "I'll fix supper for any of them who come to work."

"That should bring 'em," grinned Sandy.

"By the way, are you hungry now?"

"Yes, but the Pulaskis have asked me down there to supper, and I'm saving up for Maria's spareribs and sauerkraut, with banana fritters for dessert. That is, I'm sure of the spareribs and kraut, and hoping for the fritters. It's at least a year since I had either."

"Fine," said Rosamond again. "So there'll be no supper here tonight. I feel lazy, and shall go to bed early."

"What have you done today? Besides go mayflowering?"

He bent and sniffed.

"People have been here. A minister and his wife from downtown —"

"Why? Had they heard we're repairing the church?"

"I don't think so. They didn't mention it. And I had business callers."

"Business?"

"I am in the antiques business. Or didn't you know?"

"Oh, that. They didn't buy anything, I suppose? A plate or anything?"

"They didn't buy a plate. But the main thing I've done is to come to a decision. I think it will surprise you, sir. I have decided to buy a car."

He dropped into a chair.

"A *car!* *You?*"

"A car. Me. A compact model. You must take me where I can see some for sale. I think I'd like a red one. Or else yellow. I want to be sure the drivers of other cars see me coming."

"You expect to drive it?"

"Certainly I shall drive it. After I learn how. And don't be afraid I'm going to ask you to teach me. I shall require," she tossed her head, "a professional instructor who will come here and ride with me along the lane until I am ready for thoroughfares."

"Rosamond, are you serious?"

"Never more so."

"Well, who am I to say this? But . . . what has come over you? Can you *afford* all these things? The materials for restoring the church, *plus* a new car, and professional driving lessons? And why do you want to, all of a sudden?"

"My dear boy, how curious you are about an old woman's whims! But I don't mind. The answer to your two middle questions is yes, I can afford it. As to what has come over me — I've heard the voices of the goblins. As to why I want to, all of a sudden — well, I've been to the goblin market once and I want to go again. And again. And again."

He repeated, "Goblin market," and looked so honestly alarmed that she laughed.

"Oh, don't worry, Sandy. I'm perfectly sane. The references to goblins are from an old poem you probably never read. It has fascinated and puzzled me since I was a girl, and at last I've found a way to apply it to my own life. I'll answer you in plain English. Take comfort from my assurance that I am not paying for the materials for the church; an anonymous benefactor is. And I can afford the car because it will be, among other things, an investment. I shall buy the cheapest new one available. I'm told it will cost under twelve hundred dollars. And this very day I sold thirteen hundred and fifty dollars' worth of antiques."

He sat staring at her.

"You mean you actually had stuff worth that much out in your father's studio — and nothing to fasten the door but a spring lock that anybody could take the screws out of in five minutes?"

She nodded, widening her eyes.

"Of course I didn't know I had. But I found out. Better not tell anybody. And I haven't sold quite everything, either. There are quite a few pieces of Aunt Rachel's still there. So maybe you'd better think of some safer way to lock it. I feel almost guilty having this unexpected legacy from Aunt Rachel, just because she stored her barrels of glass here, but I *am* her nearest living relative . . . And of course whatever I get for the rest I shall use for buying new stock. To find it, I'll need the car . . . Besides, I want to go out and see the world."

"Well!" said Sandy. "That, you know, I've long thought you ought to do, but I wouldn't have bet a thin dime that you ever would!"

~~~~~ *6*

LIFE for Rosamond became an intricate kaleidoscope, sometimes dark, sometimes brilliant, sometimes soft-colored, but never cloudy, and never twice the same combination. And she never knew, each morning when she picked it up, at which end she would find herself — whether among the shifting patterns, or at the eyepiece looking down a long, narrow but gradually widening tunnel:

*   *   *

It is May. The lilac bushes in full bloom, out early this year, and the apple blossoms are still as wet with dew as if it had rained last night, though the sun is climbing. Rosamond stands by the studio door and is all but dizzy from the fragrance. She is examining in the strong light a small yellow mug she bought yesterday, and she thinks, "It is as if the mug had been filled with good wine and I, unaccustomed to wine, had just drained it. May is almost too beautiful to bear. This is the time to reach deep and turn the furrows, bring earth and sky together in a powerful embrace; time to let the cattle out of the barn and into the greening pastures; time for release, for freedom, for even the voiceless to cry out with joy." She sees forklike lines on the base of the yellow mug but knows that they are of no consequence for they do not go through to the inside; they are not cracks but true age lines. She runs the tip of her finger around the lustre rim of the mug, touches the black transfer of a little girl with looped apron pushing a wheelbarrow filled with grapes and melons, and the black script on the other side, beyond the applied handle: A PRESENT FOR CATHERINE. "It is strange," she thinks, "in a universe where one senses so much more beauty than the human eye can see or the human mind grasp, now and then we seem to hold it all in the hand — or in the heart. For a breathless instant."

A bell rings in the house. She is not annoyed by this interruption of her thoughts as she had rather expected to be when the telephone was installed. She finds it exciting to be called. It changes the pattern. She lopes across the yard like a long-legged colt not yet broken to harness.

"Hello? Rosamond Lacey speaking."

"Oh — Miss Lacey, this is Eileen. Could you possibly come down? John made up his mind last night. He really couldn't do anything else for he's no nearer being able to preach tomorrow than he has been the past two Sundays. So he had me ask Mr. Porter to call a meeting of the deacons this morning, and he has dressed and gone over to give them his resignation. I don't know how he'll get through it. He was as white as a sheet and walked as if he didn't have much control of his legs. I don't know what is going to happen to us. We'll manage somehow, of course. But if you could just be with me when he comes back — or here to wait if I have to go to get him —"

"I'll be with you in ten minutes, Eileen. Go make the bed and freshen the room. If I'm not there when you've done that, do your dishes or start fixing something for his lunch. I'm on my way."

She has a car and a license now and can go wherever she is needed.

She gives her hair a quick brush, puts an amethyst ring on her finger, turns a key in the house door, swiftly crosses the yard to turn a key in the studio door, breaks off a few sprays of lilac, lopes over to the shed, and slides into the little yellow car which sits beside the stairs.

"Oh, for mercy's sake!" she says. Pansy is asleep on the seat beside her. "Wake up, Pansy. Go catch a mouse. But *not* a bird. Remember now — no birds!"

She turns on the ignition, lifts the choke, puts in the clutch, pulls the gear into reverse, feeling wonderfully efficient, and backs out into the sunshine, wheeling to the left.

"They said it would turn on a dime," she exults. "It does. That thin dime Sandy wouldn't have bet." The top of the car is rolled down and fastened with strap and buckle. She looks up at the pale, soft, new maple leaves uncurling above her head, and smiles, and waves toward the house as she starts down the Lane. "Back soon!"

The hill. The old mill. The mill bridge. Another hill. No more scrunch of gravel or jar of ledge. The main road is newly hard-surfaced, glossy black under the morning sun. Her little wheels spin over it. As leaves unfold, miles unroll. The air is clean, vibrant, smells of lilac, apple-buds, new grass, pine trees, river water. Her face tingles. She begins to sing. The hills smile down. White, peeled poles, lately set, march beside her like footmen in seven-league boots. The wires hum. The outline of a young moon swings in the blue sky like a fairy hammock.

"Everything is so alive," she thinks. "So intensely alive. Everywhere. It doesn't all know it. But I know it."

She enters the parsonage by the kitchen door, carrying lilacs. John has already come back from the church. He is slumped at the table with his head in his hands, a steaming cup of broth unnoticed before him. Eileen stands beside him, her hand on his shoulder, and tears are dropping on her hand.

"Well, *now!*" says Rosamond cheerily. "What's the trouble?

Wouldn't they accept your resignation, John?" She drops the lilacs in a heap on the table.

He raises his head, looks at her, and nods once slowly. There are dark shadows under his eyes, dark hollows in his cheeks. Eileen has a haunted expression. She has lost much weight in the last month. A faded pink cotton dress hangs baggily on her once chubby little figure.

"They were — very kind," John says. "They will go to services at the Baptist church until the end of June — before beginning to hear candidates — and continue to pay me a salary during that time, in case I — should be able to — take up the work again.. But I don't think they think — I told them I didn't think — I believe they — I believe they are — *relieved* —"

He hid his face again, and sobbed.

"Well, and so should you be," Rosamond said. "You two poor, tired children! Eileen, go put a few things into a bag. Just what you need for overnight. We can run down tomorrow for anything you forget. You're coming home with me to stay until you both feel better." . . .

*   *   *

Rosamond has wakened very early. She seems to wake a little earlier each morning and to be unable, unwilling, to go back to sleep, too eager to begin looking for what the new day holds. She has come out to the kitchen in her nightgown and lit the fire laid last night. The kettle has boiled and she has bathed and stepped into clothing which still smells of yesterday's sunshine blown into and all through it by the wind which whipped it on the line. She is standing by the open window drinking coffee and eating a toasted half of a biscuit spread with jam when the Judge's car comes up the hill and William gets out ponderously, followed by three other men who are much more agile. It is still only five o'clock.

She goes to the door with the new sense of emancipation to which she hopes she will never become so accustomed that she is not aware of it. It is a feeling usually encountered only in dreams where one enters what appears to be a strange building and discovers not only that its rooms are familiar but that it is happily inhabited by loved ones until now unseen for many years; or where dolls come alive and seize their little mops and pans and begin to clean their little house and bake in their little oven; or where trees stride down to converse with the river as it passes, pick up the children who are dancing on its surface and toss them to topmost branches where they squeal with laughter, then spread their wings and fly back to dance again on the water. Even as a feeling of incredulity begins to rise at the sight of such unusual activity, it subsides deliciously with the thought, "It isn't unusual. It only seems so because I haven't seen it before. It has been going on all the time where I wasn't. And at last I am here."

"Well, William," she says, "good morning. How nice to see you."

"Good morning, Rosamond. Knew you were up because we saw the smoke from the chimney. You recognize the Senator, of course. And these are his friends, Congressman Bob Frye of Minnesota and Governor-elect Sid Lamie of Indiana."

Rosamond says, "Good morning, gentlemen," and shakes a hand of each, adding, "You've come to breakfast, I hope?"

They stand there with twinkling grins like four schoolboys playing truant. The Senator runs his tongue over his lips and bends his head close to the Judge's ear.

"Did the lady say what I thought she said, Bill?"

"They flew up from Washington last night," the Judge explains. "Reached my house after midnight. Wonder I hadn't gone to bed. As it was, all I could give them for supper was what little was left from my dinner. Mrs. Eustace comes in at eight to fix breakfast, but they wanted to get out to the pond early. So the best I could do before we left was to mix up some frozen orange juice. I thought we could fish a couple of hours and go back for breakfast, but —"

"It's downright imposition," says the Congressman, "but if the trout are biting, we're not going to want to leave in a couple of hours. And when we saw woodsmoke coming out of your chimney —"

"You asked Bill if she said what you thought she said, Fred," says the Governor-elect. "She said what you *said* she'd say, and you know it." He shook a finger at the Judge. "And *you* didn't deny it."

"It's my fault, Miss Lacey," says the Senator, ducking. "I try to be modest, but there's one thing I can't help bragging about, to save my life, political or otherwise. That's our state's hospitality."

"Then don't apologize," says Rosamond. "It's part of what we sent you down there for. To brag about us. And if the American people have legislators who neither slumber nor sleep, the least we can do is feed them to keep their strength up. William, take these boys for a quick trip around the Lacey estate and be back in ten minutes. I can get a better meal together quicker if I don't have to do it over four pairs of feet."

Fifteen minutes later they are deep in crisp home-cured bacon, eggs with yolks trembling under gold-brown jackets, wild blueberry preserve ("High bush, of course — huckleberries," says the Senator, and Rosamond nods), and crusty buttermilk biscuits heaped with pale country butter.

There are footsteps overhead and the Congressman's laden fork is stayed in midair. Rosamond does not understand the startled expression on his face.

The Judge says quickly, "Someone is visiting you, Rosamond?"

Rosamond says, "John and Eileen Struthers. He has been ill, and resigned from his pastorate in town. Perhaps you'd heard. Their families live in Canada."

"I knew he'd resigned. I didn't know where they'd gone. His people have been coming to our services lately. They say they will begin hearing candidates soon, but we're trying to persuade them to unite with us into a federated church. Neither congregation is large enough to support a full program."

"That sounds like an excellent idea. I think John's illness was entirely the result of trying to do the impossible. They've been here only ten days, and he's very much better."

"No wonder, on meals like this," says the Governor-elect.

"Pretty fine of you to take them in," says the Senator. "Was he your pastor?"

"No. I have no pastor. We are lately being given a church, but it has no pastor. Perhaps you would like to show them our church, William, before you go back to town. A crew of boys from the University will be working there this afternoon . . . And the gain is all mine in having the Struthers here. John is a good carpenter, and is showing the boys how to lay the church floor and put in windows. This leaves the men of the neighborhood free for their spring planting. And Eileen does a great deal to help me. She and I will give you lunch if you come back from the pond about twelve o'clock. If you haven't come by then, we'll pack a lunch and John will bring it over to you."

"I see what you mean, Fred," says the Governor-elect. "If this is a sample, your state's hospitality is unbounded."

"Fred is a lucky man," says the Congressman. "He gets not only votes but the best food in the country. That statement is off the record, of course."

"I'm quite sure I don't get Miss Lacey's vote," says the Senator. "If I'm not mistaken, she's a Republican."

"Rock-ribbed," says Rosamond. "So is the Judge. But we can respect a good Democrat when we see one."

"Question is," grins the Senator, putting his hand on the shoulder of the Governor-elect, "do you know a good Republican when you see one?"

"Is he a Republican?" asks Rosamond. "Have another doughnut, Your Excellency. I thought you had a special quality."

They are all standing now, thanking her, moving toward the door.

"I wish you luck," says Rosamond. "Too bad you couldn't have come when the ice was just going out."

"We thought this session would never end," says the Congressman. He is the last to leave and from the porch says, "I hope to see you again when I come back. I notice you have an antiques sign. Perhaps I can find a gift to take home to my wife."

"I'll be glad to show you what I have."

They climb into the Judge's car, the Senator on the front seat beside William, and Rosamond knows that William is proud — proud of his passengers, of his car, of the breakfast she has provided, and of her.

She waves, watching them go, hears the birds singing in the dooryard maples, and feels the promise of June in the air. It is not yet six o'clock. She goes back into the kitchen and Eileen is there, getting hot water for John's shaving.

"Who in the world have you been feeding at this hour?" Eileen asks, with a gesture toward the littered table.

"Half the United States government," says Rosamond, picking up dishes. "They may be back for lunch, or John may have to take it to them at the pond. They've gone fishing."

John has to take it to them. Rosamond and Eileen fill a thermos jug with split pea soup, thermos bottles with coffee, pack a dozen man-size sandwiches, boiled eggs, glass jars of caper greens, and a warm apple pie. At noon John drives away with it all in Rosamond's little car, looking absurdly tall, and is gone over an hour for he has stayed to eat with them, at their insistence, and comes back with nose and cheeks reddened from the wind and the reflection of the sun on the water. He says they are all sun-burned and that none of them has yet caught a fish except the Senator, and that they say they will not come in until each has at least one trout. There is not a crumb left in the basket, nor a drop in any of the containers.

"It is a long time," says John, "since I have seen four men having such a good time. I always thought the Judge a very serious, even a pompous man, but he is like a boy over there today. They're all laughing about how he weighs down the boat. I wonder whether it is politics or getting away from politics which makes them so happy."

"Both, I suspect," says Rosamond. "They like their work, and they like a holiday."

A long line of cars is rumbling into the yard. A tangle of boys and girls emerge. The girls come toward the porch carrying cartons, chattering and laughing. The boys and John crowd into two of the cars and ride away, leaving under the maples a '42 station wagon with a weather-beaten wooden body, a '48 Buick sedan with three broken windows, and a rusty black hearse with the words IF YOU WANT TO GO WHERE I'M GOING GET ABOARD painted on it.

"Does anyone imagine I operate a used car lot?" asks Rosamond. "Hello, girls. Who are you, except Sheila and Kippy?"

"We're Sigma Phi," says one. "And they're Alpha Sig."

"And what's in all these cartons?"

"Supper for the boys," says Sheila. Her hair is so long now she wears it in a pony tail, held smooth behind her small, pink ears with shiny metal pins. "And for us. And for you and John and Eileen. And anybody else who comes bombing in."

"That's good," says Eileen. "Because you never can tell who's going to come bombing in here next."

She looks excited, and almost as young as Sheila. She is wearing pedal-pushers and a brief blue sweater over a white blouse. She is peeking into a carton.

"We *know* that," says Sheila. "They said last time you fed them all. And that isn't fair."

"Camembert," cries Eileen ecstatically. "I *love* Camembert! So does John!"

"It's going to be a cookout," says Kippy. "My Pete stopped at his house and got his mother's outdoor grill and a bag of charcoal. Isn't he an angel?"

So Pete is hers now; and to whom does Joe belong? And is Pete the angel, or is it his mother?

"Simply loads of hamburgers all made up," says a girl with a face as freckled as a swamp lily and as enchanting. *"With* onion. Buns to put them on. A case of coke and a crate of apples. Boxes and boxes of sesame seed crackers to go with the cheese, of course. Doesn't it sound divine? And over at Commons they'll be eating — ugh! — baked beans!"

"Stay out of my kitchen to avoid extreme torture," says Rosamond. "In my oven two pots of baked beans are bubbling and the smell of them is spreading through the house."

"Oh, *your* baked beans are something else again," says Sheila. "Commons baked beans are skinned peanuts boiled hard for seven days and served with goose grease."

"With all this protein, we should have a green salad," says a red-headed sprite who looks like a ballet dancer but is obviously a major in home economics. "But that stuff in packages is never fresh and all we saw today was even older than usual. I doubt if it had one vitamin left in it."

"I'll show you where there's plenty of green salad with vitamins practically oozing out of it," says Rosamond. "As soon as I've put my brown bread on to steam."

Eileen scurries to find baskets and sharp knives. Rosamond puts on rubber boots and, carrying her shoes, leads the way to the deep woods where the fiddleheads hide, the dock, and the wild mustard, leaving a few scouts in each location, and finally to the brook where the capers are a dark green mass starred with yellow flowers.

"You can take turns wearing the boots," she says, taking them off and putting on her shoes. "Pull mostly those that haven't bloomed yet; just a few that have, for they are tougher, but they do add flavor."

She and Eileen go back toward the house and, as they go, Rosamond's hand swings out for Eileen's and finds it warm and soft like that of the little girl who used to wait to walk home from school with her teacher.

"Let's sing," says Eileen.

"Start something."

"No, you."

> "Vacation time is coming,
>   The bright time of the year,
> With happy hearts and voices,
>   We hail its advent here —"

It is the same song Miss Lacey and Dolly Walton used to sing, walking home from school together on a late May afternoon. Eileen does not know either the words or the melody, but by the second time through she has picked them up.

When they have pushed the steamer back on the stove and added boiling water to the baking beans, they bring from the studio the old sawbuck table Rosamond bought of Ben Farraday yesterday and which he delivered to her in his truck after supper last night. They scrub the top with soapsuds and stiff brushes, and as they work they hear the busy hammers at the church, the voices of girls in the woods and fields, the cawing of crows, the drone of a plane too high to be seen, and the staccato whistle of a Buddliner.

"Fiddleheads and crows have been here since before the memory of man," thinks Rosamond. "They followed on the heels of the receding glacier. Our kind brought hammers with us and have used them ever since, which is a long time. Droning planes and Buddliners are Johnny-come-latelies and already all but obsolete. What will Sandy and Sheila see come to pass before they are my age? Wonderful things or terrible things? Both, no doubt, for that is human experience and always has been. The one essential to living well is to be interested in life. Passionately interested in every minute of it."

"Tell me what you're thinking," says Eileen.

Rosamond tells her and Eileen straightens to listen, pushing back a lock of hair with the back of a hand which holds a brush. Listening, she nods. Her eyes are wide like an earnest child's.

They open the cartons and spread out the packages of food, set out the paper cups, weight down the stack of paper plates with a stone. Pansy comes to investigate, lifting her yellow feet high. Eileen catches her up and cuddles her. Pansy looks indulgent, like an adolescent being petted by an infatuated aunt.

Suddenly the girls are coming from all directions, displaying their full baskets, their cold, earth-and-chlorophyll-stained hands. They have to be shown how to give their greens a first cleaning at the pump in the yard, and then go in to the sink for more careful washing, for cutting and breaking and tossing in garlic-rubbed bowls with oil and vinegar and seasoning.

Now the boys are coming, whistling, yodeling, horns blowing. John is one of the boys. He and Sandy get soap from the shelf under the sink and they all wash at the trough in the yard. They are splashing and shouting and boasting of what they have done today, and are such a crowd that it is a few minutes before Rosamond realizes that the fishermen have come with the carpenters, are scrubbing with the same soap, splashing and praising the carpenters and boasting of the fifteen trout they have caught.

"Fry pans, quick," says Rosamond to Eileen. "Three. Clear the top of the stove of all but the big coffeepot."

She goes to the door and calls, "William? If you gentlemen want your fish fried, clean them and bring them in. If you'll share them with us, we'll share with you our Saturday night baked beans and brown bread, also our Sigma Phi and Alpha Sig hamburgers and so forth and so forth and so forth. John, will you get us a piece of salt pork from the cellar and slice it? Sheila, the corn meal is in the cupboard above your head —"

The stove is covered with browning trout, Eileen is taking luscious lumps of pork from the beanpots in the oven, hamburgers are sizzling in the yard, the girls are carrying out the great bowls of salad when a car stops in the lane because there is no space for it in the driveway.

Rosamond takes a quick look and calls like a clarion, "Come and get it, everybody! Help yourselves! I have a customer!"

She runs like a quarterback past all interference and reaches the car. She grasps the side of the open window and half hangs there, breathless and laughing.

"What on *earth* is going on here?" demands Elise Burrage. "The county fair?"

She and Rosamond are well acquainted now. It is no secret between them that Elise secured an extraordinary bargain when she bought the contents of a section of the shelves in the studio, that her checks provided Rosamond not only with a car in which to go about renewing her stock but with the opportunity to make contact with other dealers and with reference books, and that — since Rosamond is a rapid learner — neither Elise nor anyone else will ever get such a bargain from Rosamond again. Elise comes every weekend and sometimes in midweek, buying a piece at a time and marveling mournfully that the first day she came she did not observe that the amberina pitcher was plated. Its price now is $1200 and Elise has little doubt that Rosamond will one day be paid that for it, but not by the Burrages.

"There *is* a limit," Ray has said, and Elise knows this is true.

"Oh, no. Just a few friends having a cookout. Won't you join us?"

"This is fantastic . . . That tall man isn't — your Senator, is he?"

"Yes. They've been fishing over at the pond, four of them. Caught fifteen trout and I've just fried them."

"Well! That's who Ray said it was. I told him nonsense, he was having illusions. He said if it wasn't your Senator it was Abraham Lincoln. That really scared me. But I guess —"

"Will you come have something to eat?"

"Of course not. We'll go along, and maybe come back tomorrow."

"Elise, we can *not* come back tomorrow," says Ray. It is

plain that he wants to stay. "You know we're leaving early to drive to Albany."

Elise says, "I'm embarrassed. Two more added to such a crowd as this —"

"What is two more," says Rosamond, "but more fun? Drive your car in front of the studio, Mr. Burrage. Just leave room enough for us to walk past when we're ready to go over."

Until some of them overhear the introductions, none of the University students have known who the fishermen are, and they are too young and too hungry for it to matter much to them now. There is no formality at a cookout, even if heads of state, including royalty, are present. Everyone is eating ravenously wherever he finds himself; some standing, some on the well curb, some in cars, some on the porch floor and railing, some (four boys with crew cuts and two girls with smudged faces) at the kitchen table. The Judge is carefully splitting his trout to share it with Elise. Two girls in black leotards and Scotch kilts are serving Mr. Burrage more salad. The minister is sitting tailor-fashion beside Sandy on the roof of a car, and both are munching hamburgers. The Governor-elect has gone into the house for another plate of beans and Eileen has gone along to help him. The Senator is spreading the last of the charcoal in the three-legged iron pan and replacing the grate. Between bites the girls lead cheers and the boys sing; everyone is talking and the laughter is loud.

Sheila says to the Senator, "This is a change from Washington, isn't it?"

Her face, sharply tilted toward him, is fresh-colored and bright. Rosamond remembers an old simile, *bright as the sun on the sea.*

The Senator answers easily, as he always speaks, "Yes. And no. It's what Washington is all about. If we ever forget this, down there, that's when trouble starts."

Today's sun is growing small now and hangs like a red moon over the pasture pines.

- *III* -

The Congressman comes to Rosamond and says, "When you're ready, will you show me your antiques?"

She is ready now, and as they go toward the studio, the Burrages follow them, and so do William, the Governor-elect, and the Senator.

Rosamond takes matches from a tin box and lights the oil lamps, a railroad lantern, and several candles in glass and brass and pewter sticks.

The Congressman says, "It looks like a studio. It doesn't look like a shop. It is charming."

Elise says, "The first time I saw it she had only glass. Now she has added more primitive things. In wood and metal and pottery. The kind of things men like better than glass, I think. Ray, see the copper washbasin."

Rosamond notices that the Senator has not come in, and goes to the door to look for him. He is standing before her sign, studying it, and gives her a slow smile.

"Interesting," he says. "The universe on an old sleighback. Shows how far we've gone in this short time. I can remember when sleighs were still used, up north. And I'll soon see our machines bringing back reports from these neighbors of ours. Some of those young people over there may go on expeditions to some of them, may even make a settlement on one of them."

"But before they can," says Rosamond, "a great deal has to be done, and it will cost a great deal of money. Also genius."

"The genius we have," he says. "But Republicans don't like to spend money."

"They will spend it when they're convinced it is a good investment," says Rosamond. "Democrats are all too willing to spend it on what is comparatively trivial. They must learn to put first things first and space exploration is the next first. America does have the genius. We must put it all to work and give it what it needs to work with. America has the money. We must use it to become strong. Stronger and wiser than we have ever been."

"I agree with you there."

"And on the extent of the sacrifices we can and must make to do it?"

"I think so."

"Then be making up a list and tell us what they are. That's all we need, and we'll get about it. *Never underestimate the American people.* That's the one thing I've been wanting to say to you all day. It's a message I want to send by you and Mr. Frye to your colleagues. Tell them all that a true statesman never underestimates his people, but that politicians too often do. The times call for statesmanship . . . Now, if you like, laugh at an old country woman for sending messages to the United States Senate and House. I don't mind."

"I'm not laughing, Miss Lacey. We need to know your views. You're a citizen and one of those I have the privilege of speaking for — even though you are a Republican."

They go into the studio together and Rosamond does a lively business. The Governor-elect buys a set of Georgian silver serving pieces in a blue-silk-lined leather case, just as Aunt Rachel brought it home from London. The Judge takes a miniature shaded lamp, ridiculously tiny in his big hand. ("Delft, isn't it?" he asks, and Rosamond nods.) The Senator chooses hand-wrought andirons with rings in the heads, and Rosamond tells him they were probably made by Sandy's great-great-grandfather in his blacksmith shop in the hollow between Tearshirt and Tanner Sam's hills.

"In those days," says Rosamond, "everybody knew how to do at least one thing well. Better than anyone else around. That's what made them all so independent. That's how we became an independent nation. Not by leaning on one another, but by learning to stand straight."

Because the other men are buying, Mr. Burrage takes the copper washbasin. The Senator admires it and Mr. Burrage offers to give it to him. The Senator shakes his head and laughs.

"No Oriental rugs," he says. "No copper basins."

"No fur coats," says the Governor-elect. "And no deep-freezes."

Elise brings over a pink rose bowl gleaming with large gold flakes.

"This is one way to get trade," she says low, and rather nastily.

"We stop at nothing, you and I," says Rosamond in the same low tone. And louder, above the crackle of the newspapers she uses for wrapping, "That's vasa murrhina. A month ago I wouldn't have known. The credit is yours, so you may have the bowl at dealer's price. That's twenty per cent off. One good turn deserves another, even if the first wasn't intentional."

The Congressman comes up with a candlebox. It is of thick pine boards, dovetailed, has a sliding cover, and wears its original blue stain of milk and indigo.

"The price may seem high, but it's a good piece," says Rosamond. "It comes from the neighborhood. I bought it yesterday. I'm quite sure it is seventeenth century. You will find one like it pictured in Nutting's *Furniture Treasury*."

"I would be glad to pay twice this for a piece half as good," he says. "Miss Lacey, I've been looking forward to today for months, and it has been one of the most enjoyable of my life. Thanks to you."

"To me! To the Senator, I should think. And to the Judge."

"To them, too. But primarily to you. Because it is very unlikely I should ever have been invited to come here if I had not asked for the invitation. And I should not have known what to ask for if I had not heard about you from a young columnist in my state who called here last summer. A young man named Jason Schuyler. You gave him a most memorable afternoon and he wrote about you for his paper. Did you know that?"

"Oddly enough, I did. Someone in the village received the paper and brought it to William who showed it to me. It was exceedingly complimentary. I couldn't quite understand it.

I hope you didn't come here expecting to find what he described."

"Perhaps not exactly 'expecting.' I'd say I came to verify his conclusions, and I feel I have. The more important ones. But he presented you as in a way a recluse, and I have never met anyone who seemed to me less so."

Rosamond laughs.

"There are Rosamond Laceys young Jason wots not of," she says. "My mother used to tell me I had too many bees in my bonnet, too many strings to my bow." She adds, more soberly, "But I *was* more of a recluse last summer than I am now. My life has changed quite remarkably in the last year." She frowns suddenly, and then laughs again. "Come to think of it, it is probably largely as a result of that column your young friend wrote. So you may thank him for me, when you go home. Tell him I am enjoying my new life enormously."

"I am sure he would be glad to know that. But he is not my friend. That is, I have never met him. I do read his paper, along with all Minnesota papers, from time to time . . . Miss Lacey, a question has been in my mind all day. Does North Pelham have a little hotel, an inn?"

"Oh, no. Nothing of the sort."

"Any home which is open to summer guests?"

"No, I don't think so. Not so far as I know."

"I'm sorry to hear that. I have to go abroad this summer, with several members of the House. My wife has been thinking of taking our two daughters on a tour of New England. The girls have never been farther east than New York. It will be a leisurely trip and I wish they could spend a couple of weeks in this beautiful section."

"Our coast is famous for its beauty. North Pelham is not noted for such attractions. There are five hotels at the Harbor."

"How far from here is the Harbor?"

"About twenty miles."

"I suppose that would do. They could drive over. My wife

would be delighted to see your antiques. I — want them to meet you, Miss Lacey. I particularly want my older daughter to meet you."

Rosamond says she would be happy to meet Mr. Frye's family.

They notice that while they have been absorbed in this conversation the other men and Elise have left the studio with their purchases. The Congressman puts his candlebox under his arm and pays for it. Rosamond picks up her cashbox and a lantern, blows out the candles, turns out the lamps, and locks the door behind them. The Burrage car is no longer in front of the studio. It is quite dark now, and Rosamond swings the lantern in half circles but sees only cars in the yard. There is nothing to show that there has been a cookout. The sawbuck table has been carried to the porch by people who do not know that it belongs in the studio. There is not a person in sight.

"They must all be in the house," says Rosamond, holding the lantern high while the Congressman puts his candlebox in the back seat of William's car. She wonders if the andirons and the silver have been stowed away together in the trunk, and if William has tucked the little Delft lamp into the glove compartment. "What odd secrets would be revealed," she thinks, "if people knew and told why they buy what they buy!" She says, "Let's go see what they're doing."

"I should like that. But it has been strangely pleasant being out here. As if we were apart from the world."

"I know. And we all need a little of it. But too much, as of a drug, is dangerous, isn't it? If all the world's a stage and all the men and women on it merely players, nevertheless we all have our appointed roles. Our lines are being written and we must deliver them. Without a cast, the stage would be terrifying in its emptiness of all but the wordless elements. If a few of us stay offstage long, the other actors run away with the play. And this is the only play in which we shall ever have a part as human beings."

A roar of laughter comes from the house.

"That must be our cue," says the Congressman.

"Quick. We're on," says Rosamond, and runs up the path and across the porch, he close behind her.

Are they lady and lawmaker, or anonymous children of eight or ten? The same hearts quicken under the same ribs as did at that age. The only difference is that they quicken sooner.

In the entry, with her hand on the latch of the kitchen door, Rosamond turns and says, "I said we're on. But of course we are always on, even when we imagine we are off. Wherever we are, whatever we do or don't do, thinking or not thinking, it all counts one way or the other. People say, 'I'm not going to take the responsibility,' without suspecting that the decision not to take responsibility is a heavy responsibility to take."

She does not wait for a reply, but opens the door. The kitchen is filled with girls but very neat. They have done the dishes. Eileen is lighting lamps.

She says, "Oh, here you are. Sheila was just coming out to ask if we may take the girls through the house. They want to see it."

Rosamond says of course they may. The Congressman says he also would like to see it. As they pick their way in single file among the boys lying on the sitting-room floor, the Senator and the Governor-elect come out of a corner and say they would like to go too.

Even without them, the sitting room is much too crowded, and Rosamond suggests that those not taking the tour move into the parlor. They are all there when the others come back, and a fire is crackling on the hearth to banish the winter chill, peg lamps are lighted in the mantel candlesticks, candles are burning in all eight sconces on the wall.

Rosamond sees the Congressman glance at the empty banister-back armchair beside the fire.

"Do sit there," she tells him, motioning. "Everyone else has avoided it, I suppose because William told them it is about three hundred years old. It is sturdier than anything just out of a furniture store."

But the Congressman takes another.

He says, "I've heard that is where your grandfather always sits."

"Not nowadays," smiles Rosamond, "when there are people here who have not been introduced to him. If he were to meet everyone who is here tonight and listen to the conversation, I suppose he would think he was dreaming."

She directs the Governor-elect to Daniel Lacey's chair. The Senator is already on the floor with John and the students; he sits with his knees drawn up and his chin resting on them. The Judge shares the sofa with Eileen and Rosamond.

The talk has been and continues to be constant. One topic after another has led to the next.

"Mac says, 'Imagine what the world will be like when we have total disarmament. Never any more fear of war. All the money that has gone into weapons available for social welfare of all kinds — education, public housing, medical and other scientific research—' "

"Then what about the population explosion? Everybody so well cared for they live practically forever, whether fit or unfit, and multiplying like rabbits? They say that by and by women ninety years old will be having babies."

"You don't mean we have to have wars to kill people off?"

"If I did, I wouldn't be the first with that idea. No, but it's appalling, what's in the cards. There *has* to be more than standing room for each person."

"Maybe before we're too overcrowded, some of us will be settling other planets."

"Many parts of the world are already dangerously over-crowded. China, for instance. We've got no time to lose. And we're already behind in the race for space."

"Hey, do you remember back in high school, when kids who talked about space travel were stared down as weird-os? Anybody who thinks we can get along without arms is a weird-o; that's sure."

"Why? Can't we learn to talk out our differences, to get along, to be kind, to share? If nobody has weapons, won't we *have* to do that?"

"Some of us could and would. But it wouldn't always be wise. And it wouldn't work."

"Not now, maybe. But —"

"Nor in the foreseeable future. It scares me when people seem to take it for granted it would be a fine thing. If local, state, national, and international laws couldn't be enforced, do you think everybody would keep them? Take away nuclear weapons and you fall back on stockpiles of small bombs, shells, bullets, and bayonets, both for offense and defense. Take them away and you use pocketknives, rocks and clubs. If they could be taken away, it would be fist, tooth and claw. By then numbers would be all that counted."

"I suppose there would be an international army for defense. Like a police force."

"How large an army would that have to be, to insure every boundary? And is *it* going to be armed — use its modern weapons against masses of humanity pressing forward to find food and shelter wherever it still exists?"

"Look, the more fortunate have to care about the unfortunate, try to solve their problems —"

"Sure, and we've been trying to do that for years. Hasn't it created as many problems as it's solved, if not more? Who wants his solved problem handed to him on a platter? They take it because they don't know what else to do. But what they want is to get up there on their own. And how much have we done or can we do for, say, China? It's worse than useless, being generous and gentle to brutes and criminals. They don't understand it, they don't appreciate it, they certainly don't admire it; they only take advantage of it."

"What about the Golden Rule, Mr. Struthers?"

"It tells us to do unto others as we would that they should do unto us."

"Fine, but how do we know what that is unless we are in their places?"

"Like tonight. See how many really wanted baked beans instead of hamburgers or even fresh-caught trout."

"Well, even for ourselves, as individuals, most of the time we're not sure what we want. We think we want what other people have if it looks good, but when we get it we may not like it. A man with ulcers may long for pizza. But does he really want it? I may think I want a jet plane, but if I can't fly it, what good is it to me?"

"Can anybody think of just one thing that every human being, deep down, really wants from other human beings?"

"Understanding."

"I don't. Not from more than a few, and I don't like for *them* to assume too much of it. I'm me, and there's nobody like me. I pride myself on that."

"Sympathy."

"Oh, no, thank you. I see us all drowning in seven seas of sympathy. It's too much like pity. I know it's often well intentioned but I hate it. I fight it."

"If you needed it more, you wouldn't."

"The more I needed it the more I'd hate it. When I'm in trouble I can't get myself out of I want help or nothing."

"Help, then. I think you're all being difficult."

"People *are* difficult, let's face it."

"A little help in a bad time, yes. The right kind, if anybody can figure out what it is. But I can't see the human race lying on its back bleating, generation after generation, 'Deep down, more than anything, I want help from everybody.' "

"If it won't make anybody upchuck to hear the word, I'll suggest — love."

"What's that, Kippy?"

"I didn't think you knew."

"No, but what *is* love that everybody could give to everybody else, or want from everybody else? Not sexual love, I take it. Not a child's love for his mother. Not parental love. What other kind is there?"

"The love of a friend."

"Oh, but that's based on personality and personal association. Nobody could expect or would even want that from everybody."

"Besides, everybody can't love everybody, by any definition. Only God can love us all. Human beings aren't God. Let's not kid ourselves."

"Faith, then."

"You don't get that from other human beings."

"Well, sometimes, in a way, I guess you do. But —"

"How about justice?"

"Wow! Who knows what that is?"

"Anyway, does a thief want it? Do the Soviets want justice meted out to them for what they did to Hungary, for instance? Does Castro? Does anybody want justice if it would bring hardship to him?"

"Wait a minute. Let's think about that. I wonder if they don't. They may not realize it, consciously. Until they get it, they may not know what it is. But, deep down as somebody said, isn't that what we're all looking for? Maybe a criminal act is always a desperate attempt either to straighten out what seems absolutely unfair or to get some attention and be straightened out. Maybe there is something even in the Russian leaders and Castro which suffers, aching to be stopped, to be prevented from this headlong, brutal, lying course. But nobody stops them, and they hate the sad, gentle bystanders for not stopping them."

"I know when I was a kid the only thing I hated more than being pushed around for what I hadn't done was being allowed to get away with things. Not so much when I thought I'd been devilishly clever and nobody knew what I'd done —

but when it was plain as the nose on my face and the family or the teacher just overlooked it. I despised them for that. Then something drove me to do worse and worse until they *couldn't* overlook it."

"You must have been a darling little boy."

"Seriously, maybe we've got something here. Say that basically everybody wants justice, and so that's what the Golden Rule means. One great thing about treating people justly is that it's no favor, so nobody has to feel grateful for it. Justice is his right."

"Well, I say again, who knows what it is?"

"People used to. They often spoke of 'common justice,' implying that everyone knew what it was."

"But did they? If they did, a lot of them didn't deal in it, by my book."

"That's a different thing altogether. You may know what the truth is, and still lie; or what honesty is, and still steal. But if you don't know what the truth is you can't tell it even if you want to; and if you don't know what justice is you certainly can't exercise it. If justice is what everybody wants, everybody better make up their minds what it is."

"There would be as many different ideas of that as there are pressure groups."

"Then one would be right, maybe, and the rest wrong. If they were all on one subject."

"Oh, old Mr. Right and Mr. Wrong. Also old Mr. Truth. Mac tells us *every day* (well, every other day) they're absolutes and therefore *don't* exist. Everything is relative."

"Once I was all screwed up by that concept. No more. Whether it's *relatively* true or not, it's beside the point. At least, in this discussion. Our business as human beings is to work at getting as far away from wrong as we can, and as close to right, truth, justice, and so on as we can."

"So what can we base a decision on, if we're trying to be completely just?"

"On what is fair. It certainly isn't fair for some people and some nations to be 'haves' and other ones 'have-nots.'"

"Isn't it? This country and most people in this country were 'have-nots' first, and effort, ambition, and ingenuity (wherever it existed) eventually made them 'haves.' Was that bad? The people who have the easiest lives aren't the happiest. The happiest are those who are digging in, climbing, on the way to getting what they want, getting it for themselves."

"What about people who don't have drive, ingenuity? Is it fair for them to suffer for what they can't help?"

"Well, should they be rewarded for what they lack? If they knew what the rewards are for having them, they might develop them. Would it be fair to carry a child everywhere so he never had a chance to learn to walk and run and swim and climb?"

"Come. So I am asking. What is justice?"

"Justice is relative."

"All right. Relative to what? Injustice. All *right*. But if we're *trying* to hit the target — even if it is a mirage — what does it look like?"

For the first time, a brief silence falls. Sandy puts a log on the fire.

"It's justice when you get the grade you earned. Whether it's an A or a C or an F. Of course opinions may differ as to what you earned. But if the instructor is just and the student differs it's not an opinion the student has. It's a wish."

"It's justice when if you speed or go through a red light you get stopped and given a ticket. And you know it, curse your luck as you may."

"Even though other people do it and don't get caught?"

"Sure. You got justice; they didn't. And sooner or later they will. Or you'll live a heck of a lot longer than they do."

"It's justice when you get and hold a job because you're capable and honest; not because you are or aren't a member of a particular race or nationality or organization."

"What if somebody else *needs* the job more than you do?"

"What about the employer's need, the public need? If the job is worth doing, *it* needs the workman who is most capable. What would happen to an airline if it hired pilots and mechanics and dispatchers according to how much they needed money?"

"Not all jobs are that sensitive. It sounds awfully cold-blooded to me."

"I wouldn't say justice is either warm or cold. It's just just."

"Didn't Shakespeare say justice should be tempered with mercy?"

"Yes. How about old Shakespeare?"

"Maybe in a world where everybody was absolutely just (I'm ducking, Mac!) a little mercy would be needed now and then to fall like the gentle rain from heaven —"

"That was sleep. We don't have to wait, now, for it to fall from heaven. We can get it out of a bottle."

"If you don't shake the wrong bottle and get no-doze!"

"If we're right on this thing, looks as if the free world's worked itself into a state where we're overloaded with mercy and we'd better at least temper it with some justice. But fast."

"So who'll suggest where to begin?"

Joe gets to his feet, rubbing his eyes.

"Let's sleep on it. The gentle rain's been falling on me for an hour and I'm soaked. No Sominex for me tonight."

Swamp Lily says, "*I* think the way to begin is by thanking Miss Lacey for taking us in after the cookout, and especially for letting us troop through the whole house. It's better than any museum, Miss Lacey, because when you're in it you feel as if it's then and you're part of it — all relaxed and safe and peaceful — until these guys start talking about nuclear weapons!"

"We always feel safe in history," says Rosamond. "Because we know the human race survived whatever it was involved in then. If it hadn't, we wouldn't be here. But now is our time, and our responsibility . . . Thank you, boys, for your work at the church this afternoon. Thank you, girls, for the supper you brought and cooked and served. Thank you all for the latest in a series of good discussions. John, may we have a blessing?"

"*May the Lord watch between thee and me while we are absent, one from another. Amen.*"

The students unwind, pick themselves up, shake themselves or stretch like so many puppies and kittens who have played until they dropped, had a fine dream, and now are ready to start out again by whatever door is opened; or like subprimary children who have been for an hour in the land of Oz or on Crusoe's island or in Kipling's jungle, and now the teacher says, "Time to go home. Don't forget your boots. Be sure to look in both directions before you cross the street." They glance about half-dazed and take steps without direction. Some of them say good-by to Rosamond, Eileen, and the men; some shake hands with them; but most tumble out of the room, out of the house as if this were a fire drill in the night, and all were going out together, all coming back in a few minutes. There is a full moon and the yard is almost as light as day. The cars look like gilded chariots and the oldest of them begin to mutter, tremble, cough, roar, and, carrying their cargo of what is dearer than life to parents who may be wakeful in their beds, they move off down the lane, past the abandoned mill, and along the highway toward the future.

"Remarkable," says the Senator. "This goes to disprove what some of the newspaper columnists and intellectuals are saying — that people aren't expressing their views and young people aren't thinking any more. Ours obviously are."

"But it's new to them," says Rosamond. "They needed encouragement to do it. That's largely to John's credit."

"I noticed you spoke of a series," says the Congressman.

"It began the first Saturday night after they worked at the

church with John. This is the third. Last week a number of older men of the neighborhood who had been working with them came in. I wish you could have heard that one, Senator. On the kind of people who ought to be elected to political office. Particularly to high political office in these critical times. They want people with strong convictions and deep devotion to the cause of freedom. They don't want leaders who believe in peace at any price."

"Do I hold political office?" asks the Senator. "I had almost forgotten —"

"Those students certainly did. Did you notice how they treated whatever you said exactly as if one of them had said it? And the same with the rest of you. It's always like that. They get so absorbed in ideas that they seem totally unconscious of where or whom they come from."

"Perhaps this is the only place," says John, "where they can talk with adults as equals. I imagine it is and that that is why they talk so eagerly. They are free and they are challenged, and don't know that it is maturity which challenges them. They want desperately to be mature, to think maturely, yet have no respect for authoritarianism, and most adults speak authoritatively to young people, probably in self-defense. This builds a brick wall just where no wall should be and where no one really wants it."

"I'd like to see get-togethers like this in my state," says the Governor-elect.

"I'd like to see them in every small town and city ward in the country," says the Congressman. "But I'm afraid there's only one of Miss Lacey and one of Mr. Struthers. I feel I've learned a great deal myself tonight. I only wish my wife and daughters could have been here. Especially Margaret."

"There are many places where John and Eileen and I could make no contacts at all, even if we were there," says Rosamond. "But there must be people who could. It is very easy if you have an open sesame. Sandy — who has done my chores since he was eight years old — was ours."

"And the influence of the church — the experience of working with one's hands, all together, on a place of worship," says John, "has played its part."

"So we all owe a great deal," says Eileen in her soft voice, "to the anonymous person who is providing the materials for the work at the church."

Trying not to look at William, Eileen looks at John, and seeing again, but as if for the first time, the brown strength in John's features, the confidence in his eyes and slow smile, the health in the way he stands there, feet apart and hands in pockets, she is suddenly overcome, rises on tiptoe like a child to kiss William's cheek, dissolves in happy tears, and runs upstairs.

"I think, Bill," the Senator says, "the secret is out." They all laugh, and the Senator puts an arm around William's shoulders. "But it's safe with us. And now, mine good host, will you drive us to the airport?"

"Airport!" says William. He looks at his watch.

"There's time," says the Senator. "I have it all figured. There's a flight out in just an hour. We'll be at my mother's by midnight. I want Bob and Sid to see a little of the northern part of the state in the morning. That has its points, too, you know. And they have reservations for a flight out of Boston at five P.M. tomorrow."

They stand on the porch shaking hands with John and Rosamond. The Senator breaks off a bit of woodbine and puts it in his buttonhole. Rosamond tells the Congressman she will be looking forward to meeting his family. Pansy comes purring. Rosamond picks her up. The last car fills. It purrs like Pansy, and, purring, dissolves into the night. The moon has set. It is very dark. The first whippoorwill of the summer speaks liltingly.

"Whippoorwill?" . . .

*   *   *

There is the day that John takes downtown the check he has received from the treasurer of the church from which he has resigned as pastor. He and Eileen resolved, before it came, to donate it toward a new communion service for his former church. Rosamond suspects that they have very little, if any, money, but at present they have no need of any. They know they are welcome to stay with her and that they are more than earning their board by what they do for her and by John's work at the church. She has offered to pay them, and they have refused this, too. They say they are amply paid by John's almost miraculous recovery and by their happiness in being with Rosamond. But they do not intend to continue as they are indefinitely. The church is now repaired and being painted. As soon as that is done, John will go to work for a contractor building houses at the Harbor. In his free time, with his own earnings, he will make a shop for Rosamond in the big red barn, and rebuild the studio into a home for himself and Eileen. Eileen has whispered to Rosamond with shining eyes that perhaps they are going to have a child. John will hold services at the restored church, beginning the first Sunday afternoon in July. They feel strong and proud, and Rosamond is proud of them. She thinks it most suitable that her Aunt Ruth's interim church, after serving for a while as a temple of art, should become a parsonage. Business, since it began to thrive, has been out of place there. The antiques Rosamond is now stocking can be more attractively displayed in the barn. And for the first time in her life she will have near neighbors.

She is in the yard spraying her grandmother's seven sister, hundred-leaf, and Scotch rosebushes. They haven't budded yet but will any day now. She thinks of how pretty Eileen looked riding down the lane beside John in their old station wagon, wearing a blue cotton shirtwaist dress she had made from a wrapper of Aunt Rachel's and little white ballerina slippers Sheila had given her because they were too small for Sheila. It is the first time John has gone into town since he came to Rosamond's. Rosamond and Eileen have brought up the few Struthers possessions from the parsonage, and Eileen has spent two days there cleaning it. But John has waited until the day of the first board meeting, when he could go as a whole man, a free man, and make his parting gift. She thinks of how tall he sat behind the wheel, Eileen happy beside him. Thinking again of Eileen's feet in the ballerina slippers, she thinks of Sheila, and of how Sandy has not spoken of her lately. Indeed, Rosamond has hardly seen Sandy alone since the Struthers came. She tries to remember whether he and Sheila were much together the night of the cookout.

It is startling to see Sandy's car coming up the lane, as if he had heard the questions in her mind and were coming to answer them. But it is unlike Sandy to come in mid-afternoon.

It is not Sandy in his car. It is his parents, Charles and Vera Weymouth, who do not have a car of their own.

The car stops in the driveway and Rosamond goes toward it.

"Well, this is a surprise," she says. Her voice does not sound like her own. She clears her throat. "Hello, Vera. Hello, Charles. It's a long time since you two have been over." She knows very well that they never have.

Charles, looking oh, so much like Sandy, glances at her, lets a smile like Sandy's begin, then nods, and looks with concentration at the barn.

Rosamond is on Vera's side of the car. Charles is wearing a hat, but she can see, below it, that his thick, once sandy hair is white.

"Well, we don't go much of anywheres," says Vera. "Or anyway, I don't get to. Where they come with tanks for the milk, way they do now, we don't even have to keep a truck. So we don't. Don't do anything we don't have to, seems like. Go down after groceries once a week, night the stores are open, if Sandy has the car to home, and that's about it. Rest of the time it's stodge, stodge, stodge. Sometimes, I tell 'em, I feel like walkin' right out and lettin' the work do itself or stay undone. Trouble is, I've got too heavy to walk far. Trapped in my own flesh, you might say."

"Oh, no, Vera," Rosamond says, forcing herself. "If anything's trapped you, it's habit. I was just the same for years —"

"Fat?"

"No, but a stay-at-home. After I stopped teaching, I stayed close to take care of my mother and father, and after they went I stayed here from habit. Oh, I still walked, but mostly in the woods and fields. I thought I could get along without people. But now I know what I was missing, since I got a car."

"Yes, Sandy said you had a car, but I don't see you driving it up our road —"

"I know I haven't yet. I guess I was waiting for you to come over first. Well, we keep talking here. Let's go in the house and have some coffee."

"No, no. We can't stop. Charlie's got to get back to milk. To tell the truth, I've felt kind of slighted you didn't come up since you got a car and been drivin' around to other places buyin' up stuff. Didn't you think we had anything good enough for your trade?"

"Vee," Charles says, low, "don't talk like that."

Vera laughs.

"Charlie's always afraid somebody's going to take me wrong. I like my little joke. Life'd be as dull as dishwater, I tell him, if everybody was as serious as he is all the time."

Charles? Serious all the time? Charles Weymouth was born a clown. The classic clown who inspires a laughter close to tears; tears warm with tenderness and with only a grain of the salt of sorrow which comes of sensing how much is not which might be. Rosamond remembers that quality in Charles now more clearly than any other. In the little boy across the aisle in the district school, ruefully twisting the long, damp, straw-colored hair around his ears into curls and making girlish faces, pulling at the ends of the big plaid bow under his chin until it came undone and carefully spreading the soft silk over the collar of the coarse black serge jacket which had already rubbed a layer of skin off his neck; and later, at the Academy, in the tall boy with arms so long that his hands hung below his knees, who when he had been sent to the principal's office for setting his section of the study hall to laughing, returned apelike, slightly stooped and arms dangling loosely, and set the whole study hall to laughing. It was as if he said to onlookers, "I don't know what they're trying to do to me, but whatever it is they can't do it; see? I'm one jump ahead of them all the time. That may not be far, but a miss is as good as a mile."

"Just the same, I've been kind of wishin' you'd come after I heard you'd been buyin' of Farradays and ones like that," says Vee. "Long as you didn't, I been after Charlie lately to bring me over here."

"I've only been to buy where people have sent word they had something they wanted to sell," says Rosamond. "Do you have something you want to sell?"

"Come to that, I don't have anything it would break my heart to get rid of if it's worth anything. Trouble is, I don't know the worth of any of it and I don't want to get gypped."

"I know just how that is," says Rosamond. "I was exactly the same way myself until lately. But I've been studying into it, and I think I know values now. If you want to sell anything I think I can sell, I'll give you a fair price for it."

"I stuck some stuff in the back seat there, if you want to look it over."

"I'll be glad to."

Rosamond opens the door, but Charles is getting out of the car. He comes around and takes out three cartons, puts them on the grass before Rosamond and opens the covers. He says nothing. He looks so miserable that she thinks perhaps there are Weymouth family pieces here which he does not want to part with.

"Do you *both* want to sell everything that's in these boxes?"

"It's all hers," Charles says, low.

"Stuff they got out of my folks' house in Tuftwood Center when it was burnin' down," says Vera. "They stayed with me after that, you know, long as they lived. This and a lot of other stuff was brought over in flour barrels and put in the shed.

Never opened afterwards until I dug into 'em yesterday. Far as I could see this was about the best of it."

Rosamond and Charles stand with the cartons between them, looking down at the chipped rims of plates, the cracked handles of cups which stare bleakly back at them from a litter of scorched rags and shredded newspaper.

With an effort Rosamond reaches down and takes out a teapot. It has no spout.

Rosamond thinks, "I cannot bear this."

With both hands around the teapot as if it were a bowl, concealing its poor, jagged stump, she says, "Charles, I've been using the studio as a shop but I'd like to move the business into the barn. While you're here, would you be good enough to look at the underpinning and see if it is sound?"

His face brightens a little.

He says, "Glad to," and goes.

Rosamond does not let her eyes follow him. She says briskly, "Now, let's see," kneels, and quickly unpacks the cartons. Vera watches curiously with one big, bare arm hanging from the open window and swinging slowly back and forth like a giant clock hand.

"Now!" says Rosamond again. "This is almost all china, Vera, and every piece of it more or less damaged. Of what isn't china, the enamel teakettle and the silver-plated pitcher are not old enough for an antique shop. There is a secondhand place in Mumford where you might sell them. The pewter tablespoons are good, and one of them is marked. I could pay a dollar apiece for the five that are unmarked, and five dollars for the marked one. I can't sell damaged china unless it is very, very old. Most of this isn't. But this strawberry sugar bowl is and even though one handle is gone and the knob from the cover, I could have it repaired and I would pay ten dollars for it. Also this little plate, which has two cracks, is an ABC plate with children playing a game — rugby, I think. There are collectors for them, even for damaged ones, and I'd pay — well, five dollars for that."

"Makes twenty-five all together, don't it?" says Vera.

"Yes, but if you don't want to sell for that, don't. You grew up with them. You must have memories associated with them. They may be worth more to you than to anyone else."

Vera laughs scornfully.

"Not worth twenty-five dollars to me, I can tell you that. Tell you the truth, I was hopin' to get ten for the whole lot. Shows how much I know about old stuff. Why, for twenty-five I can get enough linoleum to cover the kitchen floor, and Sandy can help Charlie lay it before he goes to work at the Harbor."

"So you do want to sell it to me."

"I'd be a fool not to."

"You won't think you've been gypped? I can give you the name of some other dealers you could check with first. They might give you more. I don't think they would, but they might."

"No, no. I don't have any idea you'd gyp anybody, Rosamond. Some way we've never got very well acquainted since I come over here to live, but everybody's always spoke well of you."

"I'm glad to hear that."

"And you've been awful good to our boy, I know. He thinks the world and all of you. Sometimes makes me a little mite jealous."

"Don't be, Vera. I'm only the first teacher he ever had. You're his mother." She had put the enamelware and broken crockery back into the cartons, and now stood up, the strawberry sugar bowl in one hand and the spoons on the ABC plate in the other. "Sure you won't come in with me while I get your money?"

"No, no. I'm gettin' so it's awful hard for me to get into and out of a car. Besides, Charlie's startin' this way. I don't doubt he's anxious to get to milkin'. Sometimes I tell him I don't believe he ever thinks of anything but cows."

Charles? Charles Weymouth who had read half the books in

the Lacey library before he stopped coming to Laceys' altogether; who learned a whole section of *The Christmas Carol*
to recite at a Sunday School concert when he was eight years
old; who was valedictorian of his Academy class and then
took a two-year correspondence course in draftsmanship, getting in the high nineties on every paper he sent in? Rosamond
hurries into the house and does not come back until Charles
has loaded the cartons and is again behind the steering wheel
of Sandy's car.

She tucks folded bills into Vera's hand and says, "How is the
underpinning, Charles?"

"Sound," he says. "Nothing to worry about there. Your folks
always took good care of what they had . . . I mean, they never
let any leaks develop. If wood is kept dry it lasts just about
forever."

"I've heard them say that. But thanks for checking it. You've
been working at the church, too, haven't you? I like knowing
it's being taken care of. I hope we'll have some services through
the summer anyway. If we do, you folks will come, won't you?"

"I don't see how I can," Vera says, "unless I find enough
more old culch to sell to you for money to buy me a hat. All
this is going into linoleum. I need a linoleum on my kitchen
floor more than I need a hat to my head."

"You can have a hat if you want it," Charles says, staring
straight ahead. "And you could have had a linoleum before
this if you'd said so."

"Anybody ought to know it was needed without being told,"
Vera says to Rosamond. "Old one's worn right through in
front of the stove. Course I keep a rug there, but time and
again the rug's been out at the door while I was moppin', and
there was the holes right there swearin' a blue streak when he
come through on his way to the sink. Like enough with mud
on his boots, too . . . Well, anyway, I'm going to have a new
one now. I'm real tickled to sell this stuff, Rosamond, and first
chance you get, come over. Maybe I can scare up some more."

The car is moving. Vera holds her unfolded bills in the breeze the car's movement is making and they look, waving there against the landscape, almost shocking, as a towel would if unfurled from a flagpole, or a paring knife if stuck in a candlestick, or a mail-order catalogue if placed among fine bindings on a bookshelf, or an ill-smelling weed if set out in a Wedgewood pot.

Rosamond remembers sitting by a poplar tree with a little girl, watching the trembling of the delicate leaves, thinking of the explanation she had been given in her own childhood for this trembling — that the cross Jesus had to carry was of poplar wood, and ever since poplar leaves have trembled with the agony of recall. She remembers the little girl saying innocently with wide starry eyes, "Just think, Miss Lacey, if every leaf was a silver dollar" — and her own quick, horrified reply, "Oh, that would be *dreadful!*"

She stands in her yard now, alone, looking where Sandy's car is no longer to be seen, and says, "Oh, poor Charles!", adding in fairness, "And poor Vera!" For money is a good thing in its place, and a new kitchen linoleum is a good thing; and she knows it is true that all her married life Vera has had little she wanted for herself, not because Charles was not willing to give her more but because he did not have it to give.

Rosamond sighs deeply and still there is a tightness in her chest. She picks up her spraying can and takes it to the shed. On the way back she pauses in the shed door, feeling unequal to climbing the shallow slope to the house. She looks across the field and sees how the bushes are coming in along the fences because for so long there has been no one with a scythe to clip the grass the tractor-drawn blade cannot reach. She sees the old apple trees, scattered where once they stood in orderly rows, most of them now with only one branch in leaf, the other branches like black skeleton arms against the blue sky or already blown off and rotting on the ground.

"We are all old together," she thinks. "Old. And such a little while ago we were young in a world that seemed clean and full of promise."

She shivers, and forces herself to walk slowly toward the house.

"I must start the supper," she thinks. "I'll make caramel custards. John likes them very much."

She keeps looking out of the kitchen windows each time she passes, watching for John and Eileen. John and Eileen are young and happy and in love. It will be fine to see John and Eileen coming in.

But when she returns from the cellar with a jar of pink Wolf River applesauce they have already come. John stands close to the stove, looking down at it in a puzzled way, as if he hears the fire crackle at a great distance but cannot feel its heat. Eileen is sitting on the couch, very small in the crumpled blue dress and childish white ballerinas, her shoulders folded in and her hands locked together between her knees, one foot resting on top of the other. Her hair has been pushed back behind her ears, and her face is blotched from crying.

Rosamond says nothing. She closes the cellar door and leans against it, waiting.

Their eyes turn toward her in heavy wonder. They expect her to say something. They have been counting on her as she has been counting on them. They wish she would ask a question but she cannot. They are in trouble and it will come out, but she cannot ask for it tonight. She can only wait, with her back hard against the cellar door.

"We — have had a strange afternoon," says John at last.

"Oh, Miss Lacey," cries Eileen, "it's been horrible. I can't believe it yet."

It is very close now, whatever it is. Rosamond hears herself ask stiffly, "An accident?" The old station wagon may have been demolished. That would be a shock to them. John will need transportation to his work. But somehow that could be arranged. If someone has been injured — a child perhaps — it is a serious matter. It would be serious for anyone, but especially for Eileen and John. If they have injured anyone, it will be a long time before they sleep again, whether it was their fault or not.

"By no means," says John. "All that has happened was carefully premeditated."

Rosamond is conscious of relief. One cloud has been lifted. She comes to a chair and sits down. The tall pink jar lies in her lap.

She can say, "What happened? You went to the board meeting?"

"We went to the door of the board room. It was closed. I knocked, but there was no answer. There were loud voices inside. They were talking about — us. A voice we know well — that of a man we have respected — was shouting that there was no question in his mind but that this was a put-up job — that there was nothing the matter with my health, that I had been secretly *paid* to resign suddenly, either by — by you because you were in a hurry to fill the pulpit of the church you're fixing up, or by the Judge because he thought a sudden move like that might force this church to unite with his, a move he had been quietly advocating for a long time because he needed financial help to keep his open."

"I wanted us to leave right then," Eileen sobs, "I didn't want to hear another word. I wanted to run to the other end of the world — into a wilderness where nobody was!"

"But we couldn't leave because we had already heard these words. What we had started had to be finished. Another voice shouted agreement with the first, adding, 'So I don't see why you sent him that check. He doesn't need our charity and we can ill afford it.' The treasurer said, 'I sent it because we had promised it to him.' I knocked and someone told us to come in. We went in. There were all those familiar faces around the table, and the chair empty where I used to sit. I apologized for interrupting their meeting, and said Eileen and I had brought back the check they had sent us, wishing to donate it toward a new communion service. Then there was quiet and some of them looked angry, the others sad. One of the women who looked sad said that was generous of us, that we had more than earned this extra payment, and did I mean that I still wished my resignation to be accepted? I said I did, that I was not ready for full-time ministry now and might never be again. No one else said anything. Then I said I felt I must tell them that we had overheard a little of their conversation before we came in, that if they did not feel the check which had been sent to us was ours to donate they should use the money in whatever way they thought best, but that they must believe we had left them because of my illness and that no one had paid us or in any way sought to persuade us to do so."

"It had been awful before," Eileen says, "but then it became worse. Because they began arguing fiercely among themselves about John and about the church. One asked why we dashed straight up here and one said probably because we were invited, and somebody said yes, for what purpose, and why didn't we turn to our own people for help if we needed it, and one said probably because none of them had paid enough attention to us to realize we were in trouble, and another said they had all they could do to worry about the church and keep it running, and somebody said that was because there were too few of them and their church needed to federate with the Judge's at least as much as it needed them, and two women began to cry — they're sisters — and said they had sat in the same pew as long as they could remember and that was nearly seventy years, so they would go on sitting there the rest of their lives even if there was no one else in the whole auditorium and the roof was falling in —"

"Then," John says, "I said these were matters only they could decide, and we must not intrude. And Eileen and I went out and closed the door. If I — if I had felt I could provide the leadership they need, I would have offered it — even if I could last no more than six months —"

"I knew you would," Eileen cries, "and I held my breath for fear you would decide you must try. And you *would* have lasted no more than six months, and that sacrifice would have been a total loss. Because what you have to give — so *much*, John — they're not ready for yet. It's something we don't have that they need now. I don't know what . . . We went to the car. I felt wooden. It was like a nightmare when you know you have to run but you can't because your feet are shod with lead. And when we got there —"

"Eileen, I don't see how any good can come from telling her —"

"But she has to know, John. It must be our being here that's doing this to her. We have to talk about what it is best to do. We can't go away without telling her why!"

Rosamond says, "Of course not. If you are thinking of going away, you must tell me why." Her voice sounds to her like the voice of a stranger.

"Well . . . When he got to the car, Mrs. Crawford was standing beside it. She was waiting for us, smiling, and I didn't know a smile could be so mean. She said, 'Well, Eileen and John!' (She never called my husband by his first name before.) 'What a change of bosses for you! I hear you're working for Cupid now, and isn't he the little devil, though! What we want to know is will Rosie come down to live with the Judge or will the Judge go up to live with Rosie? We hope it's the latter because one of them is more than enough of a load for us to carry. Both would be *too much*. Are you going to tie the knot, John? Do you still have your credentials? *Somebody* must be going to pretty soon. They can't keep on carrying on this way much longer. Your wings aren't covering them, you know. They don't even cover you any more. They're moth-eaten. Are you getting rich out of this, or what?' . . . You wouldn't think we'd have listened this long, would you? But I told you we were shod with lead. Only at last I gave one of those plunges you do in a nightmare, and I said, 'One more word and I'll slap your face here on the street. I didn't know before that a human being could have such a dirty mind.' We got into the car and rode off and left her there. But she was still smiling . . . I never knew I could feel like that — speak like that. John and I never said a word all the way home. I thought it was — wonderful he could drive . . . Miss Lacey, what's happening to us all?"

Rosamond says, "Now let's think about that. Quietly. Exactly what *is* happening on this little patch of earth where we put out our feelers?"

She sets the jar of applesauce on the table, picks up Pansy and sits stroking her. The very act of stroking seems to clear her mind.

She says unexpectedly, "There was an old word for this. For stroking a cat. My grandfather used to call it 'poring.' He would say, 'There, get down, cat. I've pored you long enough,' or 'Some people like to be flattered the way a cat likes to be pored.' "

After a minute she says, "There'd be no hope for the world if nothing happened in it. Things are happening all the time. Different things in different places. Some things make the places where they happen better overnight; but they may not stay that way when different things happen. Some things that happen seem to make a place worse, but maybe that's only temporary; sometimes a place has to get worse before it gets better . . . I'm just thinking aloud, Eileen . . . I think what is happening in North Pelham is that a few people are trying very hard to keep it just the way it always has been, because that seems to them the best way, and another few people — newcomers — are fighting hard, sometimes viciously, to make it completely over into something it has never been. The majority of people stand in the middle, looking first in one direction and then in the other, wanting some change but not too much, but wanting above all else not to get caught in the cross fire. Which is where you two and I are, to some extent. That is, when we go into town, where the battle rages . . .

"I think this happens to anybody, these days, who opposes any pressure group or even openly refuses to go along with it. It didn't happen to you before because you were giving your lives to helping everyone who came to you, to sympathizing with everyone who seemed to be trying to do good, and to doing whatever your church people asked of you. It hasn't happened to me before because all my adult life I have stayed with my own people, whom I understood and trusted, and who protected me. But it has been happening to Judge Morrison for many years, so many that he now has what is called a crocodile skin. I don't think anyone will quite dare to take these stories to him. If they do, they will regret it. If he hears rumors, he will ignore them. So if you are worrying about the Judge, don't. He can take care of himself. And if you are worrying about me, don't. People who know me will be as scornful of such talk as you are. People who don't know me have no basis for opinions about me, and any silly or ugly things they say reflect on them, not on me. The Judge and I have lived too long to value words very highly. All that matters is the truth which is or is not in them . . .

"So this leaves only you two to worry about. You are young and good, and the evil in the world can crush the young and good if they let it. It is not enough to be young and good. One must also be brave enough to face the fact of evil, and strong enough to stare it down. One must also grow wise enough to find the truth and recognize it and hang onto it. You feel, John, that somehow you should have been able to stay with that church and keep it open. But isn't it the truth that those who know God will not lose contact with Him by worshiping under another roof, that the effort you and others have made to keep that building open was not justifiable, that too many churches in one small town not only are divisive factors but so dissipate the energies and attention of churchgoers that they exhaust themselves acquiring and preserving the trappings of religion, rather than refreshing themselves at the fount of wisdom and resting and learning at the feet of God? . . . I don't say this is the truth. You know

better than I. But if it is, would your sacrifice in staying —
or going back — to be consumed have served God's purposes?
If not, what course would serve them better? That is what is
important. And that only you can decide — in prayer . . .
Now let's have our supper."

When they have eaten, Rosamond sends them for a walk.
She cleans the spoons she bought of Vera and packs the
china to be sent away for repair. Tranquillity has descended
upon her. She sings softly as she works.

It is dark when John and Eileen come back. They tell
Rosamond that, if she still wants them, John would like to
build over the studio into a home for the child that is coming, and to hold afternoon services at the church through
the summer, and to be a carpenter like the Elder.

Rosamond says, "Of course I want you."

She has not lighted the lamp. There are streams of moonlight across the kitchen floor, like paths which had their
beginning far away and which may or may not have an ending; if they do, no man has yet reached it.

It is mid-June and Sandy finds Rosamond in the studio one
evening. She is wrapping glass and china in newspapers and
packing it in barrels for removal to the barn. John has built
shelves in all three horse stalls and put in big windows behind
the stanchions to overlook the pasture and the sunsets.

She lifts her head at the sound of his step, surprised and
pleased.

She says, "Hello, stranger." She has not seen him alone for
weeks.

He says, in some embarrassment, "I'm sorry I don't get over
oftener. But I know you don't need me now John and Eileen
are here. And I've been working on the counter at Commons,
so I stay over all the week. Saturdays there's been the crowd to
work at the church. And Sundays I've been taking Sheila out

unless the folks wanted the car. They do more, this weather. If they did, I studied." He grins. "It's been something of a problem to fit the studying in, lately."

Rosamond nods.

"I believe you, Sandy. And don't apologize. It's true I don't *need* to see you often. John does our errands — any Eileen and I don't do ourselves. I only need to know you're out there, pulling your weight and getting ready for heavier responsibilities. But it's always a pleasure to see you. Isn't it almost Commencement time?"

He takes the bundles from her and stows them in the barrel. She notices how careful he is. His hands are like his father's. Broad, bony palms, and long, thin fingers.

"This next weekend. Finals are over. I think I did all right. Now I'm on the clean-up crew for campus and buildings. The only students still around, beside the seniors, are on the crew. Sheila's gone home, you know. She's going to be a camp counselor this summer."

"She told me last Saturday. That will be a very good experience for Sheila."

"Makes it look like a long summer, though. Our days off aren't going to coincide. I probably won't see her again until fall."

"It's a small part of a lifetime. Make it count. Use it to grow in. And get to be good letter writers."

"We'll get plenty of practice, that's sure . . . I've been brushing up on geography this week. Three of the seniors from our house are going to drive a jalopy West, working their way. I've been studying maps with them. Looks like quite a country."

"It is."

"They're lucky to have a summer free for that. Two of them have big fellowships for graduate study next fall, and the other is going into the Air Force in September . . . Other guys have been telling them they ought to take this chance to go abroad, but they couldn't work their way to a European trip. Besides, they say they have a corny idea Americans should see America first."

"I don't think it's corny. I think it's right. I've always thought it was a fortunate person who first knew his own dooryard, every rock and tree and blade of grass in it, then his own neighborhood, then his own town and state and section and nation. With that in his pockets, he has a basis for seeing the rest of the world, for making comparisons and judgments."

"All of us expect to get overseas, either east or west, before long, in the service."

"Yes." Rosamond is wrapping her bundles more slowly. Suddenly she says, "Sandy, couldn't you go with those boys?"

He is startled, incredulous.

He says, *"Me?"* She remembers Joe Kowalski. "That's a wild idea. I'm working at the Harbor Country Club, starting next Monday. Made over five hundred dollars there last summer, don't forget; and I've needed every penny of it this year."

"I haven't forgotten."

"And there's another year to go. The most expensive year yet. After which I hope —"

"I know what you hope. But Sandy —" She drops into her chair at the desk and sits looking at him as he leans toward her across the barrel, his hands on its edge as if about to roll it away, but his eyes fixed on hers. She laughs. "Stop looking at me as if I were a giant firecracker about to explode. I'm not going to explode. I'm just thinking."

"When you do that, I smell danger."

"If you knew how much of it I do, your olfactory sense might become less keen. Or more reliable . . . Now just wait a minute. Calmly. My father used to quote someone as saying, 'Keep ca'm. If you can't keep ca'm, keep as ca'm as you can' . . . All right; now listen. You needn't answer. In fact, I hope you won't, tonight."

She reminds him that he was one of the last generation of her pupils at the district school, and its most promising member. (She thinks, "Poor Sandy! All my professional and maternal dreams center in you. Fortunately you have always seemed to bear the burden with ease, and on occasion to toss it around quite impudently. But it is impossible for me to stop running after you in my mind, sometimes trying to get a little ahead of you, in the hope of warning you of a bridge that is out, or of saving you precious time, or of catching an opportunity by the tail and holding it until you get there.")

She says he knows his dooryard — and hers — his neighborhood, and his state; he has already spent five summers at the Harbor in various capacities and relationships to the natives and the summer visiters. Once the wise and sensible course for a young American was to apply himself closely to school and work, progressing directly to self-support and then applying himself to doing so well in his first position that he would be promoted and could then marry and establish a home and family. In those days travel, unless it was part of his work, was self-indulgence, recreation, a kind of decoration on life, and likely to be postponed by the conscientious until the successful middle years or even until retirement. Now tremendous numbers of Americans are rushing about the world, many of them on a go-today-pay-later plan, apparently seeking distraction and escape. She doubts that either attitude, either motivation, meets the needs of the present and the future.

There is no denying his is a critical period in history. Our country faces a great challenge. By some means, Sandy's generation must overcome a colossus. In the classroom he has studied history, economics, comparative religions, philosophy, psychology, cultural heritage, political science. Should he not now find out for himself how the North American continent looks and sounds, what the American way of life has produced? Because he is one of those who will, not only in his lifetime but before his prime of life, see it strengthened, improved, expanded, partly by his own efforts, or see it destroyed, either suddenly, catastrophically, or slowly, insidiously, but no less surely.

"You know I am no alarmist, Sandy, no pessimist. But it must be clear to us all that we cannot maintain and improve our democracy with less than an all-out effort, and to make an all-out effort we need to know, first of all, what we are sacrificing and struggling to preserve — and then the nature and extent of what threatens it. And *should* we fail — I don't believe we shall, but we must face the fact that we *could* — and should all or most of what you would see if you crossed the country this summer be struck from the face of the earth, you might be one of those Americans who would survive to tell of what once was, or whose records in written words and pictures would one day be taken from a basement box or from under a stone to become the inspiration of those who need proof of what can be accomplished by free men in a free world."

She says it seems to her that records of the past and of the present are becoming every day of more vital importance; records carried in men's minds, in objects men have contrived, in printed matter, and in portfolio; they are needed now for close study and constructive action, and may in the future be the only foundation by which civilization can gain a foothold and pull itself out of the mire of a dark age.

She thinks, she says, of the story of the United States as in the past threatened people have thought of their family silver, their jewels, their paintings. With no way of knowing what would happen to them as individuals, as human beings, they foresaw a time when someone, somewhere, might need and value these treasures; so they buried silver deep in garden beds, sealed jewels behind chimney bricks, and plastered over paintings on the walls before going out to meet the enemy or tying up the last bits of bread and meat in a cloth and fleeing into the wilderness, perhaps to die there, perhaps to wander the face of the earth as exiles for many years, or perhaps to return when the fires were out and the cannon stilled and find all as they had left it, with birds nesting in the orchard and flowers in bloom at the door. Our heritage and the achievements of our society in the course of three hundred years are our family silver, jewels, and art. We must recognize them, evaluate them, photograph them, list them, describe them, keep them secure in themselves if that is possible, but in any case carry the knowledge of them in our minds and hearts as long as we live and, as long as we live, seek and find and use the means of passing on that knowledge to those now too young to understand their significance or as yet unborn.

"Please just think about this, Sandy," says Rosamond urgently. "I shall not mention it again unless you do. I trust your judgment for yourself more than my own for you. But unless you are sure I am wrong, find out whether these boys would like another member in their scouting party, and how much money each expects to need as a backlog. If you decide that you want to go with them, let me make up financially whatever difference there is at the end of the summer between what you have saved and what you would have saved if you had worked at the Harbor. You know my family provided me with an income which meets my personal needs. My antiques business gives me the opportunity of preserving and distributing some of the treasures of our past, of making contacts with the world of today, and of contributing, through others, to the future I believe in . . . Oh — and fair warning! If you make this trip, I expect to profit greatly from it. I would insist that you make it with your eyes and ears and heart open and alert, that you carry and use a camera, and that you keep a journal faithfully . . . Now! Did you have any special reason for coming tonight?"

After a minute, Sandy says, "If I did, I have forgotten what it was. I'll go over to the House now, and get the information we need. See you tomorrow sometime."

Tomorrow he comes with the word that he needs a hundred

dollars for the kitty, that he is on his way to the Harbor to
say that he must be replaced on the golf course as he is going
west as far as the Mississippi, south to Louisiana, across
Texas and the Southwest to California, up the Pacific Coast
to Washington, back over the Rockies, and across the plains
and prairies to the Great Lakes, Niagara, and through the
Catskills home. He is leaving early the next morning.

Rosamond says this is better than going herself. She gives
him the hundred dollars in folding money from the desk
drawer and adds the price of a good camera. She smiles at the
care with which he places it in a billfold worn through at the
seam and held together with an elastic band.

He says, "Some day I'll pay back whatever this summer
costs, Rosamond."

She says, "To your family, Sandy. To the world. To the
future. Not to me. Except that I'll be waiting to see your pictures and to hear and read your report. Please forget where
the money came from. Forget before you tell anyone. *Anyone.*
Better still, consider that it came from the past, as it did; part
of your inheritance."

They go across the yard to the barn to tell John what
Sandy is going to do. Eileen is there with John, painting
shelves wagon-blue. John's face lights up with surprise and
delight. Eileen rests her paintbrush on a can and clasps her
hands. Sandy says good-by to them and there is a tremor of
excitement in his voice. Rosamond goes with him as far as
his car. They shake hands, then suddenly he takes her into
his arms and rubs his cheek hard against hers, there in the
June sunshine.

He says, "Rosamond, you're the best friend a guy ever had."

"No. Only one of your best friends. One of the oldest." She
feels tears start, and as she steps back, willing the tears to
stay hidden, she hears herself say, "I was over to buy a few
things of your mother day before yesterday. She told me
she has a new linoleum for her kitchen, but it hasn't been
laid yet."

"Dad and I took up the old one after I got back last night. We'll put down the new one tonight."

"That's fine. She'll enjoy it while you're gone."

"Take care of yourself, Rosamond."

"I will."

"I'm glad John and Eileen are here."

"They're very good to me."

"I know. And so they should be. I'm sorry to miss the church services —"

"We'll think of you. We'll pray for you. And we'll have services in September to welcome you home."

"I'll look forward to that."

"But don't do too much looking forward. Live every day to the hilt. Work hard. Play hard. Take pictures. And write it all down."

"As I've said before, you're a slave driver. But, withal, so benevolent."

"Our most is none too much. Our best is none too good."

"Seems to me I learned that in school."

"You must have had an excellent teacher."

"Oh, I did. She was a tyrant, but she was — solid gold."

"Salt of the earth?"

"All wool and a yard wide."

"Oh, get along with you to the Harbor, quick, before you remind me of the time I accused you of letting Roger Lee copy your sentences. And you asked with those thick eyebrows all tied into knots, 'Miss Lacey, don't you *want* Roger to learn to write?'"

"You handled it all right. You said of course you did, but that as head of the school you should see the other teachers' lesson plans. You said that before Roger handed in a copy of my work, either he or I should tell you exactly what it was."

"I can't imagine that about other teachers was anything you could understand."

"It wasn't. I understood about telling you when any copying was done, though. And you see I remember the rest even though I didn't understand it. You often said things to me I didn't understand. Sometimes you still do. But working at it is good exercise."

"I'll spend the summer thinking up phrases and observations with which to confound you. Good-by, Sandy. Make every mile and every minute count. And come home safe."

When he has gone she walks slowly over the lane and up the trail to the pond. She sits on a ledge and looks across the water, remembers the story she has heard of how when her great-grandmother was twelve years old this was the Pond Field, and one day when her little great-grandmother-to-be was alone there raking hay she saw a waterspout. When she came home she told her family that every drop of water had been lifted out of the pond into a monstrous cone with a top like a toadstool, and she had seen the terrified fish flapping in the mud until the water came back with a thunderous roar.

Rosamond thinks, "The summer will be long. The sunshine will be pale. There will be foggy nights. And the flavor of wild berries will be mild. I feel undone. But I have not let him know it. I'm sure he does not know it. It would be something he could never understand, no matter how hard he worked at it. There are limits to what a teacher's, a neighbor's, an old friend's attachment can explain and account for. But I have never fooled myself. If Sandy Weymouth were not on this earth, I should not want to be here."

When she goes home, John and Eileen ask no questions. Eileen has lunch ready. She has made a casserole and a fruit salad and Scotch oatcakes. The coffee is fresh and strong. In the afternoon they go to the barn to see the painted shelves, and then to the studio to finish packing the barrels. Rosamond touches the sleighback as she passes it. A continent is a small part of earth, earth an infinitesimal part of the universe, and our universe only one of a number so large we may have no name for it.

"These are proportions," she tells herself, "in which humanity must learn to think. They make the Atlantic and

Pacific oceans seem separated by hardly more than a braided rug. Yet even as we struggle for a realization and acceptance of illimitable infinity surrounding us, we must at the same time hold harder than ever to the knowledge that all which is to be depends on what has been and now is, that every earthling is a potential Atlas holding up or letting sag, not the sky which is independent of us, but his bit of the future of mankind . . . Courage. Courage and conviction. Courage and conviction and the determination to act forthrightly according to the best we know or can learn. They are the prime essentials for the building of individual character. And human character so strong that neither serious mistakes nor terrible misfortune can destroy it is what this nation and this world must develop as fast as it can in order to survive and to merit a high place at the council table of any community of inhabited planets."

7

BY the end of June at least a few roses bloomed in every yard, and at the Lacey place they were a mass of pink and red and white and yellow at every doorstep, up the sides and over the roof of the studio, in the garden, tangled in the field grass, and even in clumps behind the barn. Strawberries were ripe. Corn was calf-high. Squash and pumpkin vines were in flower, cucumbers and peapods were setting on. The sleigh-back now swung from an overhanging arm at the corner of the barn. Stalls and stanchions were full of small antiques, and fine pieces of early furniture, grouped on the wide, worn planks of the spare floor, could be seen from the lane through the open door which had so often admitted pairs of horses pulling high-piled haycarts.

John had plastered the walls of the studio and built a stair-way to the loft which would become a bedroom. He worked in the studio on Saturdays. The first five days of each week he worked with the leading contractor at the Harbor, and was saving his money to buy brick and hire a mason to build a chimney. When he and Eileen had a sink and a stove in place, they would move out there. Rosamond would lend them any other furniture they needed until they could buy their own.

Each Sunday afternoon John held a service at the church and his audience grew each week. Nearly everyone in the neighborhood, except those of the Catholic faith, was there the second Sunday, even Suse George and her parents and all her little brothers and sisters; the Georges liked to sing and had good voices, all of them. People came from the village, too, including the curious, those who felt more respectable for going to church but who liked to sleep late in the morning, and the very devout who were happy when they left their own morning service to know that there would be another, not far away, to which they might go in the afternoon. On the second Sunday Elise Burrage, having found out why Rosamond was wearing a hat in the barn shop, rode up with her and the Struthers and sat in the Lacey pew with Rosamond and Eileen: Ray, good-natured about waiting for her, lay in the hammock under the Lacey maples and listened to the broadcast of a baseball game.

Vera Weymouth had not only a new linoleum in her kitchen but a new flowered wool rug covering her parlor floor. She was one of the few who had not yet come to church. She now wanted a white sink and nylon net curtains for her parlor windows more than she wanted the new hat she felt she must have before she could go to church. Roger Lee was another who did not come. Roger had worked for a month on a road-tarring crew — long enough to make a down payment on a '53 Chevrolet. Now he had stopped work, having no time for it. He haunted town dumps and junk yards looking for parts for his car, and was painting it fire red with his initials large in gold on the door. Roger worked — and even haunted — sleepily, stopping often to curl up under a tree for a nap or disappearing for hours across the state line to where liquor was sold. Young Joe Barron had just been married to a round-faced, dark-eyed girl from Canada; her name was Geneviève; her small brown hands fluttered like mating birds as she talked; they were living with young Joe's parents, but Joe and his father were building on a two-room ell. There was a new baby at the Thibedeaus', and Emilie acted as if it were hers, but she did not nurse it, and people suspected Rita had brought it back with her after a long stay in Boston where she said she had been looking for work but found none. Emilie, Rita's mother, was past fifty, which is old to bear a child; but she mothered this one as tenderly as she had Rita and the eight others after her. Rita worked as a waitress at the Harbor now, and came home only on her day off. The Pulaskis were putting roofing and siding on their barn; you could hear the hammers all day Saturday and every weekday night until dark.

These were the longest days of the year. Each one began early with the stirring of birds in their nests as the first streak of light came over the mountain, and ended late with the disappearance of a band of pearl-gray along the western horizon and a whippoorwill making the introductory remark to a long conversation with himself. The starlit hours were brief, sweet, and poignant.

It was that moment of suspension when the stage is set behind a velvet curtain. Those members of the cast to be seen as the curtain rises are in position, sitting or standing according to the directions in the script. Those to come on later wait in the wings or in dressing rooms. The dress rehearsal, on the whole, went well. Is that a bad sign? Who will remember his lines, and who forget them? If one is not given his cue, can he recover and keep the continuity? Are the costumes secure? Is the prompter ready? If needed, will he speak loud enough but not too loud? Lights are dim, shadows long. It is not easy to distinguish one figure from another. An onlooker, unfamiliar with the play, cannot tell which are leading characters, and which minor characters or extras. Is it significant that this one stands tall and that one crouches, that these five sit together and that one leans alone against the wall? All the faces are quiet, expressionless. No one speaks to be heard, but there is a murmuring like that of the wind caught in willow trees, or of small waves on a lakeshore, or of soot which has flamed up in the chimney. Suddenly silence falls, so complete as to startle the ear. Then the orchestra bursts into the overture, the lights of the house go down, a spotlight plays on the dark curtain as it stirs and rises slowly, heavily, portentously; but what the portent is — whether ominous or triumphal or delightful — no one yet knows. . . .

Until now, the Harbor season had been reflected on this side of the mountain only in the young people whom it magnetized, who went there in June to be gone until after Labor Day, serving as golf caddies, waitresses, busboys, chambermaids, pin boys, baby sitters, dishwashers, and grease monkeys; and in the occasional sale of a load of early vegetables or berries offered at the service doors of hotels, restaurants, or summer homes. This year, by early July, Harbor visitors were following the black road inland to Lacey's Lane, traveling in long, high-powered cars bearing the license plates of states all over the Union and of Canadian provinces. Stopping at Pulaskis' to inquire the way, they saw the baskets of wild strawberries the children had just brought in, and bought them, asking when they could get more; that night Ed and the boys, having finished repairing their barn, began building a roadside stand. Young Joe Barron and his father took a week off from the Navy Yard to devote to the new ell, and Joe and Geneviève decided that when their big kitchen and small bedroom were furnished they would not occupy them until fall, but would hang a FOR RENT sign on the door which was still so close to being part of a living tree that pitch oozed from it and clung there in golden drops like tears. Eileen, watching Rosamond's customers come, and linger, and go reluctantly, thought they must be thirsty for a cold drink on hot days, or would enjoy a pot of tea on rainy ones. After consultation with Rosamond, she posted a notice in the barn.

LIGHT REFRESHMENTS WILL BE SERVED ON THE FRONT PORCH ON REQUEST. TEA AND COFFEE, HOT OR ICED; LEMONADE; RASPBERRY SHRUB; BUTTERMILK — 25¢. CINNAMON TOAST; SCOTCH OATCAKES AND JAM; CRACKERS AND CHEESE; CHOICE OF COOKIES — 25¢ PER SERVING. THIS IS THE AFTERNOON MENU. COFFEE WITH OR WITHOUT DOUGHNUTS ALWAYS READY MORNINGS.

Many who sat at one of the two tables covered with red and white checked cloths, who were served by Eileen in a soft blue dress and crisp white apron with her hair pinned in braids to the top of her head like a crown, who ate her delicious tidbits from old china and with coin silver, peered through the door and asked wistfully if it were possible that they could see the house. Eileen asked Rosamond if she might show the hall and the two front rooms.

"But how could you? You're so busy already —"

"If I couldn't, I wouldn't. But often I could. Of course you should charge admission."

"*You* should. You do all the cleaning and all the cooking and serving and washing up. I'm afraid it will be too much for you, Eileen."

"Oh, I love it. Otherwise, what would I be doing all day while you're busy in the shop? And they're such pleasant people, collectors —"

"Not all of them, I'm sorry to say."

"Well, all those who've come to the porch so far. They act as if they like everything here so much they can hardly bear to leave. They're so appreciative — so *grateful* for an excuse to stay a little longer . . . And I'm doing so well. At this rate, in two weeks, I'll have cleared enough to buy our sink. John's proud of me."

"Bless your heart. Do as you wish. But use judgment. And any admission charge is yours. I have nothing to do with it."

"I'll love telling them the stories you've told me. Do you think fifty cents apiece would be too much to ask?"

"If they don't want to come in fifty cents' worth, you shouldn't take the trouble."

"It won't be *trouble*. But it will take time. And extra cleaning. I'm going to try it! I'll write cards and prop them against the sugar bowls on the tables. Oh, Miss Lacey, it's so exciting! I'm so lucky! I never thought I could be such a help to John!"

"You're a great help to me, too. How in the world could I manage this summer without you? I'm almost forgetting how to cook. Besides, after you feed and rest my customers, they often come back to the barn and buy *again!*"

Rosamond's business had become so lively that her chief concern with it now was keeping her stock large and varied. Every Saturday she was out all day buying, mostly from other dealers because this was quicker. The shop was supposed to be closed Saturdays, but if regular customers came John or Eileen opened it and waited on them. When calls came from homes where there were antiques to sell, Rosamond made appointments for the early mornings. Often when she rolled open the barn door at nine o'clock she had already driven fifty miles or more, invested perhaps five and perhaps several hundred dollars, and had brought home the small items, arranged for the larger ones to be brought in that night by Dick Thibedeau and his pickup truck.

One Friday she had not returned at nine o'clock and it was Eileen who opened the shop. On her way home Rosamond had met Charles Weymouth driving toward town and, knowing that Vera would be alone, she drove past the end of the lane and on to the Weymouth place. Even on a hot July morning it kept its look of being hasped and buttoned and bolted, not for protection of anyone within, not against intruders, but as a fine mesh screen to keep out whatever might impregnate it with life, with emotion, with the joy and the terror to which the human heart is heir. The black Weymouth barn and the white story-and-a-half house were a stark, well-kept mausoleum, side by side on a hilltop, erected long ago and maintained in perpetual care, the driveway graveled and the grass of the yard close cut. But not a tree stood now anywhere on the hill, every piece of farm machinery was under cover, hidden, and not a shrub was to be seen except the one rosebush under the parlor window, the faded petals from the last bloom clinging to its leaves.

The view from Weymouth hill was magnificent. Rosamond sat in her car for a minute to look at it. Gentler hills and broad valleys, fields and woods, brooks and a river lay below her, a dozen shades of green against the blue and white sky; but lay, it seemed to Rosamond, sufficient to themselves as the rosebush had bloomed, not expecting to be noticed, appreciated, gathered in and used.

It had not always been like this. Charles was the youngest of five, the others from five to fifteen years older than he, and when he and Rosamond were children the Weymouths were always giving parties — skating, sleighing, snowshoeing parties, sugaring-off parties, quilting and husking bees, nutting parties — and every year there was an all-day Fourth of July picnic on Weymouth hill, with fireworks in the evening. The barn swing was so long that with doors open fore and aft you swung backward through one and forward through the other, and the seat was so wide two grownups or three children could sit on it together; Charles always sat in the middle for his arms were long and strong. Rosamond could remember seeing his parents, already in their fifties, flying in and out through those open doors. There had also been smaller swings and padded barrel hoops hung in the apple trees, and a striped hammock from a branch of a big elm, double swingchairs near the back door. Lizzie Weymouth had been an herb woman. She had an herb garden and mixed medicines which her neighbors went to her for, in time of sickness, in the hope — usually realized — of avoiding seeing a doctor. Lizzie's comfortable, sensible cheeriness had been as likely a cure as her herbs.

"And now see," Rosamond murmured, "on what evil days we are fallen. But they will pass. Life can't be kept forever from such beauty. It will come again. It won't be the same, but it will come."

She felt she was speaking to the landscape, that here only it had ears.

She went slowly up the neat walk and knocked at the door. When there was no answer, she knocked again.

Vera's voice came through the only open window. One of two in the west end, upstairs.

"Who is it?"

"It's Rosamond, Vera. Just thought I'd run up. You busy?"

"Busy, lord, no! I'm abed."

"Oh. Not sick, I hope?"

"Well, I sure ain't very well."

"I'm sorry. Anything I can do?"

"No. Nothing anybody can do, I guess. Come to buy some more stuff, did you?"

"To see if I could. But never mind. I'll come again another time. I met Charles on the road. Will he be bringing you some medicine?"

"Doubtful, 'T'aint often he brings anything but grain. Door ain't locked, is it?"

Rosamond turned the knob and pushed a little.

"No."

"Didn't spose 'twould be. He'd never think what might walk in here while he's gone. Least of his worries he'll find me murdered or other ways dead in bed when he gets back. Come in then, if you can get in. I'll be down if I can make it."

"Take your time. I'll just sit here on the step. It's lovely out this time of day."

"Be heating up in another hour, though. I mind the heat this summer worst I ever did. I get these dretful dizzy spells. Sometimes lately everything turns black, 's if I was blinded . . ."

To Rosamond, sitting there on the step looking off at the view from Weymouth hill, the words in Vera's querulous voice, her heavy breathing, her small groans and gusty sighs came down as from a tower room where torture is dreaded and at the same time longed for as proof of suffering and, when the limit of endurance has been reached, as release from the dread of it, the hopeless waiting, the dark, gloomy incarceration.

"Seems as though I can't lift my feet. Or don't dare to. Best I can do is shuffle around. Stairs scare me so I made him put up a railing, but that's risky too. Sometimes all of a sudden all the strength goes out of my arm. Know how I get downstairs now, if I do? I crawl down. Backwards . . . And getting up again is the worst of it . . ."

Yet listening had not prepared Rosamond for the change two weeks had made. When the door opened, Vera supported herself with both hands on its edge. Her face and hands and bare feet and ankles were shockingly bloated. Her eyes had become slits. Her skin was a dark color. Her hair hung in two braids reaching nearly to her waist. She had tried to cover her nightgown with a topcoat Rosamond had seen Sandy wear; she must have taken it from the hall closet before opening the door; but it was far too small. The yellowed material of her nightgown was tight around her huge body.

"I must be a sight," she said. "It's two days since I had enough ambition to comb my hair. But it don't make much difference how I look. Come in. I didn't know how he'd left the house but it's decent, I guess."

The kitchen was as neat as the outside of the house, and as barren. The enamel stove shone, and so did the new linoleum. There was a white cloth on the table and two chairs drawn up to it. Other chairs were set back to each window. All cupboard doors were closed.

"See my white sink," said Vera. "I stayed up till they got that in and I saw water run down through it. Then I dragged myself to bed."

The sink was spotless, and bone dry. The faucets gleamed.

"It's a beautiful sink," said Rosamond. "I don't believe there's a handsomer one in town."

Vera sank into a chair.

"Go look at my wool rug in the parlor," she said. "I can't go any further. But you go."

Across the hall the green shades were pulled down to the windowsills. Rosamond raised one halfway. The rug nearly covered the floor. Only a few inches of wide pine boards showed below the wainscot. It was a geometric pattern in brown and green. The few pieces of furniture were Victorian, a small sofa and chairs upholstered in green plush, and a marble-topped table with a gone-with-the-wind lamp on it. Enlarged photographs (of men with black beards and women without teeth) in heavy walnut frames decorated the walls. Rosamond drew the shade to match its fellows.

"What a fine rug," she said. "That's a cool, quiet room, Vera. Do you sit in there on hot days?"

"Never have. I thought I might after he got the rug down, but I didn't. Wasn't natural, some way. And lately I'm best off in bed. But I shan't rest till I get them nylon curtains I been talking about. See 'f there's anything you want out in the shedroom cupboard. Cupboard's on your right out there."

In the unfinished room where Vera's zinc washtubs were upside down on a bench, a copper washboiler was upside down on an ornate black cookstove, an ironing board hung on the wall, and lines were strung from the ceiling beams for the hanging of laundry in cold weather, Rosamond looked for the first time into a built-in pine cuboard with long deep shelves.

"I was thinking in the night," called Vera, "if only I could make out to get one piece of new furniture for that parlor. One big handsome shiny piece. That, with the wool rug and the nylon curtains, would make quite a room of it, wouldn't it? But I can't make up my mind what other piece of furniture anybody would want. What's in your parlor, Rosamond, besides the table and sofa and chairs?"

Staring into the crowded cupboard, Rosamond answered, "Oh — bookcases. And Aunt Ruth's melodeon."

"Don't seems as though I need them. Nobody here can play, and all Charlie's and Sandy's books are on the shelves they built in Sandy's room. I never was no hand to read."

"Want to know what I think I'd put in there, if I were you?"

"What?"

"Something like a studio couch. John and Eileen have one. It was the first piece of furniture they bought after they were married and the only one they've bought yet. They had it in the parsonage living room. They're handsome and comfortable too. If you had one, you could rest on it whenever you felt like it."

"Rest in the parlor? Well, I don't know. I never thought of that. Wonder how much they cost. I'll see 'f they're in my catalogues. Studio couches, you say they are?"

"Yes. Studio couches. They come in all colors. They have box springs."

When Rosamond came back from the shedroom she had a copper lustre pitcher in her hand.

"Want to sell this, Vera?"

Vera lifted her head from her hand and blinked.

"I've gone dizzy again. Can't see much. What is it?"

"A pitcher."

"Lord, we've got pitchers enough. How much'll you give for it?"

"Twenty dollars. It's a nice one."

"You don't say. Well, take it, take it. I've as good as got them nylon curtains, and some left over, ain't I?"

"You certainly have."

Rosamond puts bills into Vera's hand.

"Drat it," Vera said. "Wisht I could see these. Well, I'll set here till I can. Anything else you want?"

"Yes. Several things. But this is all I can spend this morning. I'll be back. I hate to leave you to get upstairs alone, but I'm late about opening the shop already. How soon do you expect Charles?"

"What time is it?"

"Quarter of ten."

"Oh, he's most usually back around ten or so. Before you go, see 'f you can find my catalogues in that cupboard at the end of the stove."

There were three. Rosamond placed a chair side to Vera's knees, and piled the catalogues on it. Then she picked up the top one and quickly riffled the yellow pages.

"Studio couches," she said. "Yes, Sears has them. Page three-forty-two. Here they are."

She arranged the other two side by side, and on top the Sears open to "Studio Couches."

"There now," said Vera. "That's good. When my head begins to clear, I can see the pictures some time before I can make out the words."

"You be thinking what color you'd like. They come in all colors. I'll run along now, but I'll be over again in a day or two."

"Getting quite neighborly, ain't you, since you went into business? Well, I hope you're making a good thing out of it. Might as well be you as somebody else. I'm glad to get what you pay, I know that."

To another slyly casting a suspicion Rosamond would have said, "I'll tell some other dealers about your things. See if they will pay more than I do." But not to Vera. Vera needed the feeling that her possessions were of great value. It would not do for her — or for Charles — to know that Rosamond had difficulty getting from customers the amounts she paid Vera, and sometimes could not.

"Well, you're making a great change in your house, so we're both pleased," was all she said. "Shall I close the door behind me? To keep the sun out?"

"Yes, you better."

But before Rosamond quite reached the door, Vera called, "Lucky it's daylight, or you might run down somebody on the road and be surprised, when you got out to look, to see who 'twas."

Rosamond stood still in the entry, holding the copper lustre pitcher.

Vera chuckled. It was a strange sound.

"Two-three nights ago I was layin' awake. Couldn't hardly get my breath. So I raised up on my elbow and got as close to the window as I could. Got my head right into it, resting against the frame. Around midnight, I guess. There was a bright moon, and who d' you spose went sauntering down the road?"

"Who?"

"Well, the girl was Suse George. Course that was nothing to bother putting in the book. If she ain't riding, she's traipsing afoot 'til somebody picks her up in a car. But the fella was Roger Lee. Ain't it something new, her taking up with him?"

"I don't know, Vera. I hadn't heard."

"Well, now you have. Right from the old horse's mouth. I saw 'em myself."

"Could you be sure who it was? From here to the road? In the night?"

"I told you it was bright moonlight. Knowing 'em sence they was the two worst-acting young ones in the neighborhood and having a boy near their age, don't you s'pose I've watched 'em like a hawk for twenty years? Always knew they'd never bring themselves or anybody else anything but trouble. Just never happened to dawn on me they'd get together, being birds of a different color . . . If folks find out about this, maybe even Lizy George will feel a mite ashamed of how she's let everything slide, even her own young ones."

"I'm afraid Ramona Lee would suffer a good deal more than Lizy. She's tried so hard with Roger, and so has his father. If they heard he was with a girl like Suse, it would be almost more than they could bear. I hope they never do hear it."

As Rosamond hurried down the walk, Vera's voice followed her.

"Say! You don't believe that new one at Thibedeaus' is Emilie's, do you? It's Rita's, ain't it?"

Rosamond pretended not to hear. She swung in behind the wheel, dropped the pitcher on the seat beside her, and went roaring down the hill. Around a curve of the main road, half-way to the end of her lane, she pulled off to the side and stopped under a big hickory.

She looked at her watch. It was ten minutes past ten.

"How fast time goes," she thought, "when you are trying to get something done. But how it must drag when there is nothing you can do but wait for a miracle."

The effort she made to get out of her car and stand beside it when she saw the Weymouth car coming toward her would have been visible on her face if there had been anyone to see it.

Charles, who had been staring straight ahead, drew to a stop with a squeal of brakes.

"Trouble with your ladybug?" he asked.

Rosamond shook her head.

"I have to talk to you, Charles. Would you park off the road for a minute?"

He did so without answering, and came back to the hickory tree. His walk had not changed since he came and went from the principal's office. He had always moved slowly. She looked at him steadily for the first time in many years, and was sorry to see apprehension in his eyes.

"Heard from Sandy?" he asked.

"Not for a week or so. He was working at a filling-station on U.S. 66."

"We had a card since then." Charles relaxed a little.

"They'd got to the California border. Sent us a picture of it. 'Welcome to California.' Quite a trip he's having."

"Yes. Charles, I've been over to see Vera. Don't you think she's very ill?"

He took off his hat and ran a hand absently over his hair. The lines deepened in his face.

"Seems as though she's not so well lately. She doesn't get up much. Says it's just one of her spells."

"Has she had a doctor?"

"No. She's been to doctors so much she's lost all faith in them. Says all they can think of is starving her to death. She takes things she reads about in the papers or hears about on the radio. She's taking some patent medicine for her blood now."

"She must have a doctor, Charles. Unless she is a strong Christian Scientist, and obviously she isn't."

"I don't know. She's determined not to. I can't persuade her to do anything she doesn't want to. Sandy might — but I can't."

"We can't risk waiting for Sandy. I think we'll have to do the best we can, our own way. Unless you forbid it, Charles, I'm going to telephone Dr. Mansard when I get home and ask him to come to see Vera. If he isn't at the hospital, he may come before office hours. That is, he may be there by noon."

"Of course I don't — forbid it. But what shall I tell Vera? Or should I tell her at all?"

"I think you should tell her that you saw me, and I told you I was going to do this. Say you told me she doesn't want a doctor, but remind her I am a determined woman and that I said my shoulders are broad and I will take the blame. Tell her I said it is perfectly plain to me that she has to get over these dizzy spells and onto her feet to fix up her house the way she wants to — and that unless she humors me on this and co-operates with Dr. Mansard or some other doctor, she'll have to sell her antiques to somebody else because I'm not going to keep on going up there and seeing her in this condition. Tell her I'm her friend, whether she believes it or not, and I'm worried about her."

"All right. I'll tell her. I hope she'll appreciate it. Probably she will."

"One other thing, Charles. You know how she loves to sell things. Today she sent me to the shedroom cupboard. It is packed from floor to ceiling with nice old dishes. Did you know it?"

"No. I haven't looked in there for I don't know how many years."

"I think most of them were your mother's. I remember quite a number of them. Especially the Chelsea tea set. I don't remember that pitcher on the seat there, which I bought just now. Had she talked with you about selling them?"

"No. But whatever is in the house is hers. Always has been. She knows that."

"You don't think Sandy expects or hopes to have his grand-mother's china?"

"I don't have any idea he's interested in china. Do you?"

"I suppose not. Well, then, I'll be glad to buy as much of it as Vera wants to sell. She keeps getting new ideas about fur-nishings for the house."

"Funny, too. She never talked about it until within the last year."

"I think it's a good sign. A new interest is another reason for wanting to live. Often people die for lack of enough reason to want to live."

Charles stared off at the horizon.

"Just living is a great experience," Rosamond said softly. "Even the hard things are a great experience. Even dreadful mistakes, and sorrow, and anxiety, and monotony, and dis-couragement. They are part of human life, and come only to human beings. We should all be more aware of that. Perhaps Vera is just beginning to be, and to want all the life she can have, regardless of the confusion and pain it is bringing and may bring. We must help her with that, Charles. I realized this morning that she is a — courageous woman."

He nodded slowly.

"Yes," he said. "Yes, it takes courage. No doubt about that . . . Well, I'll go along and talk to her."

He went to his car and she into hers.

Through his window he said, "I'm obliged to you. All you're doing for her."

Rosamond answered, "There is no obligation, Charles. Vera is my neighbor. We are helping each other. I am glad to have her things in my shop. And I am learning from her, as perhaps she is from me. Remember that until lately we have both been — quite isolated."

As she drove over the lane she had the sense of grateful relief, the anticipation of a haven just ahead, which always came to her when she was nearly home. It came up from the ribbon of moss and feathery grass between the wheeltracks, from the twin ribbons of hard-packed clay, from the running blackberry vines at the roadside; in from the sweet fern and junipers overgrowing the bank, down from the great shade trees set out by her grandfather in his boyhood, down even from the sky above the Lacey place which had always seemed part of the Lacey property though for a long time now planes had had a right of way across that broad expanse.

That there were three cars in her yard did not disturb her. It was to be expected. Eileen waved to her from the barn door.

Rosamond called, "Thanks for taking over. Sorry I'm late. Be there in a minute. I have to put in a telephone call."

Dr. Mansard was at the hospital, but his wife said he probably would go to Mrs. Weymouth after office hours and before supper. She asked the way, as she did not think he had ever been there. Rosamond gave her own name and explained that she was a neighbor, calling because the Weymouths did not

have a telephone. She asked if she might call again in the evening to ask how he had found Mrs. Weymouth.

"I am sure he will talk with you if he is in, Miss Lacey,"
said Mrs. Mansard, suddenly formal. "Please don't call during
office hours. Try us between nine and ten tonight."

Rosamond washed her face and hands, ran a brush through
her hair, and went to the barn, taking the copper lustre
pitcher and a filled carton from her car on the way.

Five women, a man, and a young girl, scattered throughout
the barn, looked up as if startled as she came through the big
door. They had been expecting her, but she was not what
they had expected. They did not know now what they had
expected. They stood as if playing a game wherein, having
taken a position, one must hold it, and stared at her. One of
the women had a teacup in one hand, a saucer in the other;
two others sat on a bench just inside the door, smoking; the
fourth carried her eyeglasses on a chain and was holding
them ready to use as a magnifying glass for reading a price tag;
the fifth had been about to run a finger around the rim of a
glass bowl and, motion arrested, stood as if pointing at it. The
man held a long-handled iron fork in both hands, resting its
weight at midpoint against his knees, as a farmer does a hay-
fork while he waits for the cart to approach the haystack he is
to load. The young girl — twelve years old, perhaps — was
kneeling beside a cradle filled with dolls, and to see Rosamond
had been obliged to twist her head far to the right and tilt it
as high as she could.

Rosamond was reminded of the years when rows of country
children sat straight in the seats to which they had just filed
quietly from the playground and replied to her "Good morning, girls and boys" with a chorused "Goo' morn', M'sleazey."

She released her customers with a brisk "Good morning.
Going to be all-fired hot, as my grandfather used to say. Nice
you came in the cool of the day."

Eileen whispered, "No sales. I'll go in now."

As Rosamond was listing what she had bought earlier, one of the women on the bench stepped outside to crush a cigarette in the sand and then joined the man in the stall where wood and metal items were displayed. Rosamond glanced at the one who remained on the bench and saw that she was a very young woman. Hardly older than Sheila; but, except in age, there was no similarity. This girl was exceptionally tall, probably close to six feet, with the generous bone structure of a big woman, but so thin that she appeared almost emaciated. She wore no make-up. Her hollow cheeks were pale, and there were shadows under her eyes. Her full lips were slightly parted and there was a small space between her front teeth. But she had two features of extraordinary beauty. Her eyes were very large, and their color was green with flecks of brown. The color was that most often seen in those who have red hair, but the eyes of the red-haired are usually not large. And this girl's hair was dark, almost blue-black; thick, coarse, springy, naturally curly, and reached nearly to her shoulders; in a shaft of sunlight from the window behind her, strands of gold, purple, and dark red appeared in the dusky mass as if it were spun of stained glass.

She was not smoking her cigarette, only letting it hang between her fingers, and it had gone out.

Rosamond said, "I take it you're not interested in antiques."

"Not in the least. Nor in museums. Nor in mountains. Nor in waves beating on a rock-bound coast." She spoke in a husky drawl, as if she thought it was a monotone, but there was music in it like the stained glass of her hair. "In very little, actually."

"You came with someone who is interested in antiques, then."

"Yes. But more because I was brought. I'm like that. Someone says 'Come on,' and I think, 'Why not?' As a matter of fact, we were sent."

"Sent?"

"My father sent us. We saw him off from Idlewild day before yesterday, and then came on to the Harbor. I'm Margaret Frye."

Frye. Frye . . . The Congressman's daughter, from Minnesota.

"Oh, yes. Your father was here for a day's fishing in the spring."

As if she had been waiting for the conversation to reach this point the chubby, anxious-faced little lady in the print shirtwaist dress came from among the teacups, leading by the hand the twelve-year-old who was already nearly as tall as she.

"I see Margaret has introduced herself, Miss Lacey," she said. "I am Dorothea Frye. And this is our younger daughter, Brooke. My husband appreciated your hospitality very much. It was his first visit to your beautiful state, and he has been most eager for us to see it, too, and to meet you. What a delightful place you have here, and what fascinating things in your shop! Brooke is absolutely entranced with the dolls; aren't you, Brooke?"

"Oh, they're adorable," responded Brooke instantly, all smiles, but with a slight lowering of her head and a looking up through her eyelashes which was like a curtsy. "I was trying to decide which are china and which are wax. I've read of children long ago who left wax dolls in the hot sun or near a fire until their features melted. How *could* they have been so careless with such lovely things?"

"As Brooke became too old for just playing with dolls, she started a little collection. Her father adds to it when he travels. I suppose she would like very much to buy one of yours."

"Oh, Mummy, dear! Could I? Could I *really?*"

The anxiety in Mrs. Frye's face was swept away for an instant. Clearly this sweet, bright, well-mannered Brooke was the joy of her life. Impulsively she hugged the child, looking at Rosamond with proud, emotion-filled eyes.

"I hope so, darling. I think so." Then she looked at her

older daughter, and the anxiety returned. "I *wanted* Brooke to love dolls as I did. For some reason, Margaret always disliked them."

"Hard lumps," said Margaret. "Cold. Creepy. Horrid travesties."

"My own favorite doll was a rag doll," said Rosamond. "She had a lovely black face and hair of raveled-out yarn. I called her Sister Abbie and she slept with me every night."

"Didn't she have to be *washed?*" asked Margaret.

"I doubt very much," said Rosamond, "that she was ever washed. If we ever thought of it, we assumed she had a built-in self-cleaner."

"My teddy bear, Tawny, had the stuffing washed right out of him before I'd had him a month."

"But he was given to you when you had scarlet fever, Margaret. He *had* to be washed. He shouldn't have come apart. Your father brought you another one the next day."

"So you've told me before. I don't remember. It doesn't matter. As soon as they let me into the garden, I played my flute over Tawny's remains and buried him. After that, I slept alone."

Mrs. Frye looked helplessly at Rosamond.

"It's hard to believe she remembers that. She wasn't three years old. We think she must have got it from her baby book. I wrote about it there."

"I remember it," said Margaret, lighting another cigarette. "But it's not important, you know."

Brooke, still in the circle of her mother's arm, asked low, "May I choose, Mummy? Do you think I may *choose?*"

"Well, first we must ask Miss Lacey the prices, sweetheart."

Rosamond went with them to the cradle. Mrs. Frye and Brooke happily decided together on an old German composition doll with bright blue porcelain eyes, flaxen wig in a black lace snood, flowered challis dress trimmed with black velvet, and high-heeled bronze boots. Brooke would not have her wrapped.

"Don't worry, Mummy. I'll be *so* careful! Isn't she — *enchanting?*"

Margaret rose and walked out through the yard. She wore a white cotton jersey and faded blue bermudas, and her midriff showed between. Her broad shoulders were slightly stooped, and her bare legs looked painfully long and thin. She was barefoot, carrying tennis shoes in her hand.

Rosamond remembered that poor Vera had been barefoot too. Probably because her shoes no longer fitted.

Mrs. Frye bought a set of eight Alhambra cups and saucers. Rosamond packed them.

"We've enjoyed this visit so much, Miss Lacey, and we shall enjoy our souvenirs of it, I know. I hope we may come again before we drive on up the coast."

"Do, if you can."

The woman who had been studying price tags had already gone. Rosamond had known at a glance that she was one who did much looking and little buying.

The one who examined everything for chips, cracks, or dents explained now that she was a scout for a Harbor antiques shop and carried a little book in which she noted down items in which Mr. Evans might be interested. If he was, she said, she would come back.

"Of course whatever Mr. Evans offers has to be absolutely proof. He has a most discriminating clientele. He prefers the very rare, the really unusual."

"Naturally."

"Perhaps if you come across a piece you feel is in that category, you would like to let me know. Here is my card."

"Thank you." Rosamond wrote "Rare" across the corner of the card and dropped it into a drawer. "As you know, the rare is rarely found and vanishes quickly. Come again. You may be just in time to snatch something Mr. Evans would like."

The man came out of the horse stall carrying the long fork and rested it against Rosamond's desk. He went back and returned with a copper measure and a burl mortar and pestle. His wife followed with a horse's bit of hand-wrought iron and a wooden ladle with a handle as thin and delicate as if it had been fashioned of coin silver.

"I think he is going slightly mad," she said indulgently. "But I'm so happy he has a hobby at last that I wouldn't dream of discouraging him."

"Not mad. Just old," he corrected her. "Old enough to realize that everything I used to see around my grandfather's farm is something I want to recover. I'm sure this is the fork Jake, the hired man, used for rolling logs into the huge fireplace. This is the measure that was in the grain chest. The mortar and pestle were in the shed chamber and sometimes we brought them down for grinding herbs. And I'm sure that bit hung in the harness closet."

He did not seem old to Rosamond. He might have been seventy or more, but he was slight, agile, muscular, and had the vigor all healthy older men had had in her childhood. He had their confidence, too — the confidence which comes to a man who has mastered his environment, whatever it may have been. And his boyish pleasure in his possessions was enormously refreshing.

His silver-haired, young-faced wife in her pink polka-dotted dress and short-sleeved, pink cashmere sweater bound in polka dots was regarding him with amused tenderness, the expression of a mother watching her child with a new toy and that of a girl waiting for the boy she loves to finish painting his boat or to hurl his javelin or to reel in his line and then come for a walk with her among the dunes.

Rosamond said, "I think they are, too. They and you have traveled a roundabout way, but now you're together again." She glanced at her watch and said, "Why, it's half-past twelve. I'm hungry, aren't you? Come in and have lunch with us. Eileen is sure to have something good."

The woman exclaimed, "Oh, no, we *really* —"

But her husband interrupted her.

"Hush, Buddie. That's an honest-and-true invitation, Miss Lacey? Because if it is, I wouldn't miss the opportunity for — a house and a barn all stocked with cattle."

Rosamond never understood how so many of her customers knew her name; the direction signs John had put up were only arrows with the word ANTIQUES on them. She had stopped noticing it, took it now for granted. She quirked an eyebrow and smiled at the good old phrase for the best of everything — "a house and a barn all stocked with cattle."

She said, "Well, I can't promise that what Eileen has fixed is quite *that* good. But it is a fact that I'd take it as a favor if you would share it with us. As it happens, I've had a rather hard and depressing morning and I'd like to forget it for a while. I'd like a complete change of pace. You two radiate self-earned security, you know — a rare and lovely light these days, kind to the eyes, warming to the heart, and illuminating to the inner resources of the beholder. Let's go up to the porch and tinkle one of Eileen's little bells and see if she comes in what she calls her uniform. If she does, and if the uniform is complete, she will wear a blue ribbon in her hair."

At lunch she learned that her guests were Dr. and Mrs. Albert Bradford of Indiana and close friends of the Sid Lamies.

"The Governor-elect!"

"We certainly hope so. And that he will go on to the Senate. He is a man of integrity and his judgment is of a very high order. In fact I have more confidence than ever in it now; don't you, Buddie? Because he told us that the first thing we must do after getting settled for a summer in Maine was to look you up. Of course he didn't say you would ask us to lunch. Did your intuition tell you we are Republicans?"

"Actually, I hadn't thought of party affiliation until now. And I have been known to feed Democrats. But I do deplore, more than ever this year, the way their leaders seem to me to seek to sidestep the great challenges to American courage and stamina and faith in God and ourselves. Their hero of modern

times proclaimed that 'we have nothing to fear but fear itself.' Republicans understood that. I see no sign that Democrats do."

"Perhaps because their hero-teacher passed quickly from that
great truth to instruction on how to avoid rather than how to
face up to and stand fast against any threat to personal or national security. We know that only the brave can enjoy freedom from fear. It is not a right or a privilege which can be
guaranteed by others. Each must earn it for himself."

Dr. Bradford had been born in Indiana of parents who had
gone there from Deerfield Valley farms in western Massachusetts. They and their children had made long summer visits to
New England as long as the grandparents lived. His wife was
an Indiana girl. They had met during his internship. She was
a nurse. They had worked together until the children came.
They had had six children, lost two in the influenza epidemic
of 1918 — he had been in the army at that time — and their
first-born of polio when he was sixteen; but by that time they
had another son and two daughters.

"Tragic experiences faced together bring two people very
close. You think for a while your hearts are broken, but if
anything breaks it is the mind. The heart is a very tough organ. I should know, because I am a specialist in heart disease.
We have been very happy and very fortunate for the last
thirty years. Our daughters have married well; one son-in-law
is an army surgeon and they're in Germany for three years;
the other is an engineer doing great things in Brazil. Our son
is coming up fast as a legal adviser to an aircraft company on
the West Coast. We have ten grandchildren. We don't see
the children often, but we know they are busy and happy,
helping to run the world. What more can we ask?"

"Especially now that Al has agreed to take summers off from
his practice, and we have rented a dear little Cape Cod farmhouse, with an option to buy, and it has a fine black barn
which he seems resolved to fill with everything *but* cattle!"

"Actually, I have never been overly enthusiastic about cattle since I was five years old, giving close attention to the milking of a beast named Hannah and she, with deliberate intent and malice aforethought, switched her tail into my eye. Though I suppose I should be grateful to her for sending me to the hospital for four weeks. Four weeks out of the five we had to spend in the Valley! Because it was then I decided to study medicine. If I hadn't studied medicine, it is too unlikely I should ever have met Buddie. So blessings on you, brindled old vixen Hannah."

"You are proof of the adage that blessings often come in disguise. People of our age know that to be true. But it is young people who most need to be convinced of this and other truths. And today they tend to scoff at adages, believing only what they see — or think they see — with eyes blurred by youthful emotion and astigmatic from looking in so much and out so little."

"Sid told us you are doing remarkable things for young people."

"Increasingly I am becoming aware that there is only one thing their older friends can hope to do for them. That is to convince them that they *must do for themselves,* as individuals. Must think, and come to conclusions, and speak, and act, and become together the strongest driving power for good that the world has ever known. Otherwise, they will see Armageddon, and they will not survive it."

"Al, she makes me feel like what used to be called a slacker. An escapist."

He nodded and reached for her hand, looking at Rosamond.

"No. I don't intend that. You mustn't feel so. The way you look, everything you say, your whole lives bear witness to these truths, and you have brought up children who are bearing the same witness, and doing their share of what must be done. That accomplishment is not lessened but continues even while you rest and taste its rewards. By traveling halfway across the country for a summer holiday you spread it over a vast territory and share it with us."

The doctor said, "We should like to think so. Nevertheless if in the course of the summer you think of any way we can be of service to you, remember that we are only thirty miles away. Here is our address."

He wrote it on a slip of paper and pushed it across the table.

Rosamond, noticing that the slip was a prescription blank, tucked it into her blouse pocket, and they all rose. A car had just driven in.

"You're a great comfort," she said. "Both of you. I knew you were going to be. Please come again. And often."

She was busy all the afternoon. When supper was ready there were still customers in the shop and Eileen, having eaten quickly, went across the yard to take Rosamond's place at the desk. They talked for a few minutes in undertones about Rosamond's best price to a dealer on items a dealer present had been assembling on a drop-leaf table in which perhaps he was also interested. As Rosamond went toward the house she saw the Weymouth car parked behind the others.

She found Charles standing in the doorway between the kitchen and the sitting room which served as a dining room in summer, and John urging him to sit down for at least a cup of coffee and a piece of cake.

"No. No, thanks," Charles was saying, turning a stained straw hat between his hands. "Can't stop. Have to go downtown. I suppose — Rosamond's busy at the barn?"

"No, here I am, Charles. Eileen has taken over for me out there. I don't think you two know each other. This is Charles Weymouth, Sandy's father, John. Charles, this is John Struthers, Rev. Struthers. You probably knew he and his wife are staying with me for a while, and he preaches at the church Sunday afternoons."

They shook hands.

"Sandy's talked a lot about you," Charles said. "People say you have fine meetings. I — my wife and I've been planning to come some Sunday. But she hasn't been well."

"I'm sorry to hear that, Mr. Weymouth."

"How is she tonight, Charles?"

"About the same, as far as I can see. But what I came about, I thought you'd want to know the doctor came. Just left a few minutes ago."

"What did he say?"

"Well — says her condition is very poor. Says he doesn't like the sound of her heart at all, and that her blood pressure is over two hundred. I think he said two hundred and thirty. He wants her to go right into the hospital tonight."

"Tonight!"

"But she won't. She told him right off the bat she wouldn't. Said so far she had stayed out of both hospitals and jails and aimed to keep on staying out. Said if anybody tried to take her to either place she would kick and scream every mile of the way. He acted quite put out. Told her he couldn't take the responsibility for a case as serious as hers if she wouldn't cooperate. She told him she didn't want anybody taking responsibility for her, that she hadn't sent for him, and wouldn't have let him come except as a favor to other folks."

"Was she in bed when he came?"

"No, she didn't get back upstairs after you were there. She sat all day on the sofa in the parlor, trying to look at catalogues. I took her dinner in to her . . . When the doctor left, I followed him into the yard and he told me over again what he'd told her and said I'd have to get her to consent to his sending an ambulance for her. Said it was a question of life and death. She might — go any time . . . But it's just the way I told you this morning. I can't get her to consent to anything she doesn't want to do. When I went back into the house she said before I could open my mouth, 'Don't you aggravate me

now. Whatever he said to you, I'm not going to a hospital tonight nor tomorrow nor ever. I'm just getting this house the
way I've been planning it, and what time I've got left I'm going to stay in it.' All she wanted, she said, was for me to go
to the village and get her some ice cream. Said she had a han-
kering for ice cream. I didn't feel as if I ought to leave her
alone, after the way he talked, but she said I would go quick
enough if I needed grain; which isn't so. So I started. But I
thought you'd want to know —"

"I certainly did. John, did Eileen really eat?"

"As much as she ever does."

"And I see you're on dessert. So I'll just put my supper on a
plate . . . As I thought, there's plenty left for two. Will you
put the rest of the chicken loaf into a kettle, John? Right in
the pan. Pan's hot, so watch it. I think it will set in there on
top of the vegetable casserole if you turn the casserole cover
over. Put this sheet of aluminum foil over it and drop in a
few rolls. That's for your and Vera's supper, Charles. You
don't have to go to the village for ice cream because there's
sherbet packed in the freezer down cellar. You know where
we always kept the freezer when there was ice cream in it.
Take it right along, freezer and all. Tell Vera I sent it, and
that sherbet is better for her than ice cream. And don't go
until I come back from upstairs."

John and Charles were standing by the car when she returned.

John said, "I was just telling Mr. Weymouth Eileen and I
would like to call on his wife."

Charles looked — imploringly, she thought — at Rosamond.

"Fine," said Rosamond at once. "Why don't you go over
tonight? Charles, tell Vera I don't want her to eat until she
is back in bed and rested from the stairs. Then give her this
dressing gown. Tell her it was Aunt Rachel's and came from
Paris. When John and Eileen get there, if she wants to see
them, ask her to put on her fancy costume and they'll come up

for a few minutes. Whether she wants to see them or not, say I've sent by them to buy the pair of blue vases I saw in the shedroom cupboard this morning if she will sell them for thirty-five dollars . . . Meantime, Charles, don't worry. We'll all be thinking what to do next. I'm sure Vera will cooperate with us, within what seems to her to be reason. I'm sure she wants to live — and will even more as we all show her how much we want her to."

Charles, who had been looking at the ground as he listened, nodding, now lifted his head with an effort.

"I'm certainly much obliged. Without — you folks I'd hardly know which way to turn."

"You aren't the first one to feel that way," John told him. "I've been in the same place myself. But we're never alone even though we feel so. God is always near, and sends messengers too."

Charles was in the car when he said, "I've been wondering — should I try to get word to Sandy? I hadn't thought of needing to, and I don't know how anybody would. By the time we hear where he is he has gone on. And it would be quite an expense to him to come back by train or plane."

"There are ways it could be done," Rosamond said. "But let's not do it yet. Let's take a chance and wait a few days to see what we can do for Vera. It's hard to know how she would feel about his being called home. Maybe a little later we can talk it over with her. You go along now and have your supper before it gets cold."

"And let you have yours," said Charles with a sudden, shy half-smile.

The customers had gone now. When Eileen closed the barn door and came into the house John stood uncertainly by the table, looking down at his half-eaten cake. Rosamond's plate had not yet been touched.

"Where is she?" Eileen asked.

"She went into the front of the house."

Eileen followed, and found her standing in the shadows before her father's portrait. Darkness came first to the rooms on the east.

"Aren't you going to eat your supper? Aren't you feeling well?"

"Yes. I'm all right. I'll be out in a minute."

"Oh, Miss Lacey . . . You're — you're *crying* . . . Oh, you're tired. You've been so busy today — and it was so hot . . . Are you worried about something?"

"No, I'm not especially tired. And I'm not worried . . . Maybe you thought people of my age never cry. Well, you see they do. Usually for the most unlikely reasons. Maybe some day I'll tell you just what made me cry tonight, but now it's my secret . . . Yes, I'll come have my supper. You have a glass of milk with me. You've done at least as much as I have today, and the day isn't over yet."

 *8*

THE next morning early, when Eileen was in the studio ad‑ miring what John had done there, running over in her mind what he had still to do, and wondering when he would have time to do it all, a dark-haired girl drove up to the door. She was alone.

Getting out of the car, she said, "Remember me? I was here yesterday. Miss Lacey home?"

"No. She isn't. Anything I can do for you? I don't know quite when she'll be back."

"Just wanted to ask if it's okay to leave the car here. Would it be in the way?"

"Oh, perfectly all right. Nobody comes out here in the day‑ time but me. I don't often."

"I got curious about what is at the end of this road. Thought I'd walk over."

"It's a lovely walk. My husband and I have taken it several times. It's called Lacey's Lane. I don't know what you will consider its end. It leads into a trail that goes to a pond. If you go that far you'll see a rowboat. Those who know the woods can take the boat across to pick up another trail and follow it to the Harbor road. But if you take any trail, be sure you stay in it. It would be easy for a stranger to get lost."

"Thanks."

She walked away from the car without a backward glance and on out of sight. She walked with a slight roll, as Eileen imagined sailors do on shipboard, and swung her hands before her and then behind her until they met, parted, and met again.

When Rosamond came back at noon there was no one in the shop, and she and Eileen sat down to lunch together.

After a while Rosamond asked, "Whose car is that out there?"

"A girl left it. A dark-haired girl who was here yesterday. She walked over the lane."

"Margaret Frye. From Minnesota. Her father was one of those politician-fishermen."

"Oh. Maybe she wanted to see where her father went fishing."

"I doubt that. I'm afraid nothing but Margaret Frye interests Margaret Frye."

"It seems as if she's been gone a long time. It wasn't more than half-past eight when she left."

"The trees may be talking to her. Or, more likely, she's talking to the trees . . . My gracious, here's a truck with all that furniture I bought at the auction Saturday. Wouldn't you know it would come today?"

In mid-afternoon Margaret Frye came into the barn, nodded at Rosamond who was talking with a customer, read Eileen's notice on the wall, and went to the front porch. She said that, stupidly, she had brought no money with her, but could she be trusted for coffee and doughnuts.

"Coffee and sandwiches," said Eileen. "You must be starved. I don't serve doughnuts in the afternoon. Especially to people who haven't had any lunch."

"As you will. I've heard it said that beggars can't be choosers." The corner of Margaret's mouth twisted wryly.

"I shall add a glass of milk," said Eileen firmly. "Milk is good for you."

"I should like that," Margaret said, almost graciously. She added, "Even though you do sound awfully like an overconscientious mother."

"Can a mother be overconscientious?"

"Yes. Yes, *ma'am*. Believe me."

"I didn't know. My mother died when I was four years old."

A few minutes later, bringing the sandwiches, drinks, and a tossed salad on a tray, Eileen said, "I'm going to be a mother myself next winter. I'll remember what you said, and try hard to be just conscientious enough."

"Just don't try too hard. Don't get desperate about it." Margaret took a swallow from her coffee cup, put it down, and said huskily, "Oh, don't bother your head with what I say. You're sweet. How does it feel to be sweet? Good? Or sickening? . . . I honestly don't mean to be rude. I really want to know."

"Then I'll try to answer you as well as I can. My husband is much better at answering questions than I am. He usually —"

"Is he *sweet?*"

"I think so. I also think you're getting on thin ice, so please watch it. You may think I'm sweet but I do have a temper. The kind that explodes without the slightest warning to me or anybody else . . . You asked me how it feels to be sweet. As far as I know, it doesn't. I don't believe people who are sweet feel sweet. It's one of the qualities that are what they are because they're always going out. They don't stay inside to be mulled over and analyzed and felt. If they ever did, they'd die an instant death. In my opinion, people who feel sweet aren't, but probably quite the opposite."

"Ha," said Margaret almost savagely. She raised her left hand and made a circle with her thumb and forefinger.

Eileen had no idea what this response meant, but was relieved to see the girl bite hungrily into a corned beef sandwich and that four ladies in smart cottons and spectator pumps were tripping up the walk.

Later, when they had finished their iced tea and asked to be taken inside, Margaret murmured as Eileen passed, "Trust me for the price of admission, too?"

"Might as well, since you've opened an account. But be prepared for me to hound you. My profits are buying a cookstove. One that's heated by oil."

"You'll get paid tomorrow. Every penny . . . Sweetie."

"Stop that. It could kill the goose that lays the golden eggs."

"Shall I call you Goosey?"

"How about Eileen? It's my name."

"Howdy, Eileen. I'm Peg. To my friends, if any."

"Hi, Peg. Come on in."

"I will. Last. After the cash customers."

She did not join the group nor listen to Eileen's commentary, but waited in the hall, watching the pendulum of the grandfather's clock, until they left one room, then waited in there until they left the other. When the tour was over and Eileen went to the kitchen with a tray of dishes, Margaret was standing in the back entry doorway.

"Confession," she said. "I opened a closed door."

"Lucky for you it wasn't Pandora's box."

"I also cheated. I snitched a cookie from the pan."

"I'll add it to the bill."

"That's what a girl gets for being honest."

"Small beside what she gets for being dishonest."

From the back porch, Margaret said through the open window, "On second thought, I've decided you're certainly not cloying. Good grief, you may even be dangerous."

"It's a chance you take, with strangers," retorted Eileen.

She was surprising herself. She had never talked this way to anyone before. She wondered what John would say if he had heard her.

She thought, "I must admit it's fun. I wonder how I happened to. It must be something in her that set me off."

Margaret went a little way into the field and lay on her back under a twisted apple tree until hers was again the only car in the Lacey yard and she knew Rosamond was alone in the barn.

Then she wandered in, fists driven deep into the pockets of a striped terry shirt she was wearing over khaki bermudas, and asked, "Do you ever take overnight guests?"

"No. Why do you ask?"

"It's so peaceful here I hate to go back to the Harbor. Is there any place in the neighborhood where they do rent rooms?"

"There is a small apartment for rent at the Barrons'. If it isn't already rented. A couple inquired about it here yesterday. Aren't you expected back at the Harbor?"

"Yes, but I thought I could call my mother. Unless she needs the car tonight I could get it back to her in the morning."

"Well, of course you may stay here tonight if you want to. But I warn you it is not so peaceful as you think. Our pots may be invisible to you, but they're boiling at a great rate, I can tell you, and some of them may be about to boil over, others about to go dry. This is the wrong night to look for peace here. If you stay you will get put to work. I'm getting a reputation as an organizer. I know a boy about your age who calls me a slave driver."

"It's a chance," said Margaret, quoting Eileen, "I'm willing to take."

"Fine. Come aboard, cabin boy, for a short but likely stormy passage. Help me bring in the settee, the plant rack, and anything else out there that needs protection from the weather. Then we'll go in and you can call your mother after which we'll eat. I read the other day that food is the best tranquillizer and I can use tranquillizing tonight. Here comes John. John is a minister. He is also a good carpenter. As far as I have been able to find out in three months of having him in the family he is also a saint. So it behooves the rest of us to be as saintly as possible where he is."

"Eileen's husband?"

"Yes. It's an experience just to see a couple as much in love as they are."

"Real love?"

"Complete and perfect."

"I thought that went out with the Victorians."

"Watch them at supper and you will see how wrong you were. It hasn't gone out, though perhaps pride in showing it has, in too many places. I suspect that from what I read."

While Margaret was on the telephone, Rosamond said that she would probably spend the night, and set another place.

"A strange girl," Eileen whispered.

"Very. But we won't let her know we think so. Let's go ahead as we would if she weren't here, but include her. I've told her we're up to our necks in troubled waters and mysterious machinations. She seemed intrigued."

After John and Margaret were introduced, the supper talk during the main course was light and casual. The day had been cooler than yesterday. John had been tiling a bathroom; brown tile with dark red trim. The pieces bought at auction had been delivered. Eileen had served nine customers.

As Rosamond cut a pie into sections, John asked, "Have you heard from Mrs. Weymouth?"

Rosamond laughed.

"I've heard a great deal from Mrs. Weymouth."

"She is still at home?"

"She is still at home."

"Do you think we should go over to see her tonight?"

"Not you, John. You missed last night from your work in the studio. We must stop calling it the studio, and begin to say your house. And not Eileen. She's been on the run all day. No, Margaret and I'll go over to see Vera."

Margaret raised startled eyebrows.

Rosamond explained about Vera's illness, Charles's report of what Dr. Mansard had said, and John's and Eileen's call on her as her minister and his wife. She added that last evening she had telephoned Dr. Mansard and he had confirmed Charles's report, saying that Vera was so ill she must have hospital care and that she would probably never leave the hospital unless perhaps to go to a nursing home. She told Margaret that he sounded rather cold, and that John and Eileen thought this might be because he and his family had attended the village church of which John had been the pastor and from which he had resigned when he came out here. So then she had telephoned a heart specialist, a Dr. Bradford whom she had just met as a customer in the shop that afternoon, and who was spending the summer in a neighboring town. He had promised to come to see Vera today. All this John and Eileen knew.

She went on to say that she had gone to the Weymouths' this morning to tell Vera that he was coming and to stay with Vera while he was there because it was clearly going to take doing to persuade Vera to see and be reasonably polite to a second doctor. It had been hard enough for Charles to get her to see the first, and she had been far from polite to him. For both Vera's and Dr. Bradford's sake, Rosamond had been determined that every effort be made to have Vera on good behavior. This Eileen knew. Rosamond had not announced her decision until after John had gone to work.

The morning had been well spent. This none of the three had known, and John's and Eileen's faces lighted up, at the same instant, as if they could not have heard better news.

"I felt almost cruel," said Rosamond, "but I told Vera the truth. I told her that we certainly hoped she wouldn't have to go to a hospital, and for that reason we had to have a second opinion, so I had called a specialist and told him how she felt about hospitals. He understood and was sympathetic. He was coming to see her, and if he possibly could, he would plan some way that she could safely stay at home. But she must prepare herself to accept whatever Dr. Bradford said, because unless she began getting better, state police would be flagging down Sandy (that's the boy who calls me a slave driver, Margaret) wherever he was on the West Coast and sending him home by plane and that would take all of everybody's money so heaven only knew when, if ever, she would get her nylon curtains and studio couch and all the other things she wants for her house . . . Well, I held my breath, but she didn't go into a rage. She grumbled for a while and then she said, 'Well, if he's a specialist from Indiana, help me into my sick-chair and get me some water to wash in. While I'm out of the bed, make it up clean. I s'pose he's used to everything elegant.' So we were all ready for him when he came at ten o'clock —"

"Did she wear your Aunt Rachel's Paris dressing gown?" Eileen asked.

"Oh, yes. And a nightgown of Aunt Rachel's trimmed with Irish lace. I took it to her this morning. I always wondered why some of the trunks Aunt Rachel brought home with her were never even unpacked. Now I know. She had in them the things she wore when she was having her children, and she didn't have any children after she came home. They must have been very full even for maternity wear. They're plenty large enough for Vera, and she is really pleased with them . . . And I *wish* you could have seen Dr. Bradford in that room with Vera. He was as easy as an old shoe. Like a brother stopping by from the next farm. Of course he tested and listened and pressed and prodded, but he did it as if that was just his way of being friendly, as if he did it to everybody. I half expected him to saunter over and take my blood pressure. And most of the time he was talking of the ways Indiana is like New England, and asking if she remembered this and that about farms forty years ago and if she had ever made hogshead cheese, right along with how often she has dizzy spells and whether she has much pain and how her appetite is and if she has a cough. He told jokes and Vera laughed. He said, 'This is more fun than a barrel of monkeys. I like women who laugh at my jokes.'

"And about half-past eleven he began repacking his bag, tossing things into it as if he never expected to need *them* any more, and said, 'I don't see why anybody wants you to go to a hospital, Mrs. Weymouth. No reason why we can't fix you up right here, if you'll be a good girl. You say your husband's out baling hay. I'm going out and tell him how to take care of you, and I'll be back tomorrow to see how you're getting along.' You never saw anyone more relieved than Vera was. She reached for his hand and held it tight, tears running down her face. He bent over her a little and said, 'You'll be a good girl. I know you will. You don't want that boy of yours to come rushing home before he's seen all the sights. Besides you need time to do what you want to to the house before he gets here, so you can surprise him. Though as far as I can see it's nice enough for anybody just as it is.' "

"If I'd been there," Eileen exclaimed, "I'd have kissed him."

"How old is he?" demanded John.

"Seventy or so. But still a very charming man, as Eileen knows."

"I expect Buddie kissed him when he got home," said Eileen dreamily.

"Who's *Buddie?*" asked Margaret, in faint derision.

"His wife."

"Young?"

"Seventy or so. And a very attractive woman. Well, he went out to see Charles, and Vera was still crying happily when I went down to get her lunch but when I came back with it, you know what she had done? She'd put talcum powder on her nose, and she had propped herself up with pillows and was looking at her catalogues! . . . By then Dr. Bradford had gone, so I went to find out what he had told Charles, before I came home. Apparently his diagnosis was much like Dr. Mansard's, only he thinks that since she is so determined not to go to a hospital it would be unwise to upset her by insisting; that it is safer to try doing for her at home at least for a week or two, and see whether there is any improvement. He said her blood pressure and heart action should be checked every day. Charles asked him if he should try to get Dr. Mansard to do that, and Dr. Bradford said no, that he had stopped in to see Dr. Mansard on his way up and would see him again on his way back; that Dr. Mansard preferred not to take the responsibility unless Vera was in the hospital as he is expecting several baby cases in the next two weeks, but that he, Dr. Bradford, would be glad to drive over every day for a while if Charles was willing. He told Charles there would be no bill for his services as he was on vacation and just keeping his hand in."

"Honey," said John, "you can kiss him if you want to."

"It's too late now," said Eileen. "That was only a passing thought. I've changed my mind."

She stooped, holding a stack of dessert plates, and rubbed her nose against John's cheek.

"So the next thing," said Rosamond, "is for Margaret and me to go over to stay with Vera while Charles goes to the village to get prescriptions filled and corn oil and all the things Dr. Bradford wants her to take and eat and drink. The stores are open tonight. And Dr. Bradford says she mustn't be left alone. We can get her ready for sleep while we're there. Then when Charles gets back he can go to bed in Sandy's room. Poor Charles has *his* hands full, right here in haying time. I *am* sorry to leave you with all the dishes again, Eileen."

"Maybe I could do the dishes," said Margaret doubtfully.

"Oh, no," Eileen said. "I'll have them done in no time and be out with John."

"No," said Rosamond. "You come with me, Margaret. Or maybe you'll drive us over if you have plenty of gasoline. Mine must be low. The warning light was flashing all the way back from the Weymouth place this noon."

The sun was close to setting as they rode up Weymouth hill. Margaret had not spoken all the way over, but as she turned off the ignition she stared at the buildings stark against the ruddy sky and said, "Bleak, isn't it? Like a Grant Wood painting without people."

"Still more like a copy of a Grant Wood painting without people, made by one who did not have the skill to include the pulse which beats even in Grant Wood structures and crude tools. Some people's lives are as bleak as that. It's tragic. We have the gift of human life only once. If we don't — can't — use it, a creeping dryness sets in, as in a plant slip which doesn't put out roots in the glass of water on the window sill."

They went into the kitchen. Charles, dressed to go to town, was just coming downstairs with Vera's tray.

Rosamond introduced them, told Margaret to wait there until called, told Charles they would be here until he returned and not to feel hurried on his errands, and went up to Vera. She did not call Margaret until Charles had been gone some little time.

"This is Mrs. Weymouth, Margaret. She knows who you are."

"Pleased to meet you, Margaret. Never expected to see a Congressman's daughter in my bedroom. Seems like Main Street runs right through here lately."

". . . Margaret, Mrs. Weymouth has to get quieted down for a good night's sleep. I've been telling her one of us will read to her from her county weekly which came today, while the other tidies up the kitchen and gets the parlor ready for her to move into tomorrow if Charles can find a nice hospital bed to set up there. Dr. Bradford wants her to be where she can get up and around a little, soon, and he certainly doesn't want her climbing stairs."

"The pig he slept in the parlor," said Vera. "No way *I* ever intended to use the parlor. Soon as I get my studio couch that hospital bed will go back where it came from, and you can lay to that."

"We'll lay to it with a will," promised Rosamond cheerfully. "Which will it be, Margaret?"

"I've never read aloud much," said Margaret cautiously, "but I might be better at it than at tidying. I have something of a reputation as an untidy person."

"There are worse faults. It's all a matter of habit. All right then. I'll go downstairs and you read. If Vera falls asleep, put out the lamp and come down softly. You know how to put out an oil lamp?"

"No."

Rosamond turned down the wick, blew out the flame, then wrapped her hankerchief around the hot chimney, took it off, turned up the wick, lighted it, and put the chimney back on. Margaret watched, fascinated.

"Putting it out is very easy, you see. Lighting it is a little harder. That's true of many things. Good night, Vera. I wish I could come over in the morning but I guess I'll have to let you have Dr. Bradford all to yourself. I'm a working woman. But some of us will be over later tomorrow."

As Rosamond worked in the kitchen she thought the two in the room overhead must be in conversation for she heard voices by turns, both husky, but one young and one old. After she went into the parlor she heard nothing more until Margaret came into the room. Her bare feet on the bare stairs had been silent as an Indian's.

"She asleep?"

Margaret nodded.

"Good. I've finished here." She carried the carpet sweeper and cleaning cloths back to the shedroom, Margaret following like a magnified shadow. "Now what else can we do until Charles comes?"

"Shouldn't you just sit? For a change?"

"All right. I will. I'll sit at the kitchen table if you'll bring me — there where I can see it under the lamp — what is in this cupboard. Start with the bottom shelf. Better use both hands for each piece. Something of considerable value may turn up. One never knows. It's like digging where Captain Kidd *may* have buried some treasure. Here's a pencil. I'll make a list. Let's see, what can I write on? Oh, I'll take a paper bag from this rack."

The contents of three shelves had been listed and replaced when Charles opened the screen door. They had not heard him drive into the carriage house. He set a full carton on the white drainboard of Vera's new sink, and dropped his hat on top of it.

"You're all lit up here, I see," he said. "From down the road house looks like a ferryboat. Made me think of old-time serenades." He looked pleased, even a little excited, and Rosamond wondered how long it had been since there was gaiety in this house; but he kept his voice low. He glanced up at the ceiling. "She asleep?"

"Yes. Margaret read her to sleep. We're going now, and you'd better go to bed. Vera told me to make up Sandy's bed for you. Tomorrow'll be another big day. Haying and nursing, nursing and haying."

"There's a hospital bed we can have. I inquired around and they told me to see Dr. Mansard. I didn't know how he'd be, but he was very cordial. Said he's looked up Dr. Bradford and he's one of the best men in the country on heart conditions and we're lucky he happens to be around. Seemed gratified he and Dr. Bradford agreed on Vera's trouble. He had his wife call up the people who've been using the hospital bed and they're through with it — it belongs to the Red Cross. Stopped in at Thibedeaus' and Dick said he'd truck it up here first thing tomorrow morning. Told him I'd make it right with him, whatever it's worth, and he said he wouldn't take anything for it, had to go to the village to get something for his tractor anyway."

"That's good news. Didn't take you long. You find out from Dr. Bradford in the morning just how Vera should get downstairs. I think the room is ready and some of us will be over tomorrow night to see what's to be done next. Vera's going to feel like a queen in there."

Rosamond and Margaret were on the step when Charles said low, through the screen, "I've been — I've been watching some red lily buds — freckled lilies, some call them — yesterday and today, down in the field. I noticed them when I was mowing and didn't cut them off. They're getting big. I thought when they bloom Vera might like a bunch of them to look at."

"In a big redware jug she has in the cupboard. They'll be beautiful, Charles."

Margaret backed and turned the car and set off down the unfamiliar road with the complete, apparently instinctive assurance of a human being who regards as part of himself the machine he operates.

Then she spoke for the first time in an hour.

She said, "Tell me why so many are going all out for Mrs. Weymouth."

"I might say, because she's dying."

"So is everybody. I mean, it's just a question of when. Many live only a fraction of the time she has already. And some of the very people who are spending themselves short may die before she does. You, or instance. Or Mr. Weymouth."

"True. So 'Because she's dying' is a small part of the answer."

"What is the rest of it? I'm only an onlooker, and I just came on the scene, and I'm no sentimentalist. Frankly, I think she is an ugly old woman and that she has lived long enough, maybe much too long. Mr. Weymouth is miles too good for her. Why should he risk killing himself to keep her out of a hospital just because she doesn't want to go there? Why should this Dr. Bradford waste even a week of his vacation on her, to say nothing of maybe all summer, and give her the advantage of all he knows, for free? Why do the Struthers spend evenings with her when they have so much to do for themselves, where it would count? And especially why are you taking on this burden? What is she to you? She hasn't a spark of gratitude in her. She doesn't care in the least about anything but herself and getting her own way.

"She kept interrupting me when I was trying to read to her. When I read some item about somebody named Thibedeau, she interrupted to tell me with unholy glee that there was somebody named Thibedeau in this neighborhood who claimed a new baby was hers when everybody knew it was her unmarried daughter's. Now somebody in that family, I gather, is going to load and haul and unload a hospital bed for her; no charge.

"Something else reminded her of how she'd seen a white girl walk by the house with a colored boy around midnight last week. What if she did? What business is it of hers? And why tell me? For that matter, why tell me her husband has to be scared into paying her any attention, and you had never stepped foot in her house as long as she had lived in it until you found out she had things you could make a dollar on?

"I didn't say a word to her. I just read from the paper until she started spewing poison. When she finished I'd read again until she started again. I couldn't even bear to look at her, lying there in your Aunt Rachel's maternity nightgown. I kept my eyes glued to the paper the whole time. Matter of fact, I don't think she went to sleep. I think she just ran out of ideas. I don't believe she ever sleeps. I think she just lies there night in and night out, creating enough venom to last her through the next day. Wouldn't she be better dead? To say nothing of everybody else?"

"No," said Rosamond quietly. "Not yet."

They were back in the Lacey yard now, with the leaves on the lowest branch of the maples brushing the top of the car. The motor was silent. There was no moon, and no light anywhere except from a few stars and a lamp turned low in the kitchen. Knowing they could not see each other's faces, Margaret and Rosamond were not looking toward each other, but toward the barn ink black against the slate-colored sky.

"There are many answers to the questions you have asked. I don't know all of them, but I can think of some. Everyone does have to die, and many die at an earlier age than Vera, leaving more unfinished business than she would if she went out tonight, and mourned more than she will be whenever she goes. Yet, as you say, quite a number of us are doing all we can to keep her alive, and you ask why. Perhaps each of us has a different reason, most of them having nothing to do with admiration or love of Vera. John and Eileen hope for time to bring her closer to God before she goes; they want that for everyone, but her critical need of Him is clear and immediate. Dick will bring the bed because he and her son Sandy are friends and Sandy is away and Dick loves his own mother, Emelie, with a deep devotion. Dr. Bradford is taking her case because he knows it is a favor to me; because Vera is a country woman and it was in the country, when he was a small boy, that he decided to be a doctor, and he has never had a country practice; because it is a challenge to all his skill to prove to young Dr. Mansard that she can live as long outside a hospital as she might in it. Dr. Mansard is cooperative now because Dr. Bradford has handled him very well, and Dr. Mansard is proud to be associated with a specialist of Dr. Bradford's reputation.

"Her husband's reasons are more complicated. They have been married for nearly forty years. They had been married twenty years when their only child was born. Living together that long has produced set habits. One of his habits is trying to please Vera; even though he has never been successful, he has tried doggedly. One of her habits is complaining that he never does anything for her unless driven. I would guess that the root of both these habits is that — whether or not she once loved him, he has never loved her. If that is true, he is weighed down with a sense of guilt, because he did marry her, she did bear his son, and she has had no life apart from him. Now that he knows she may die at any time he has his last chance to look for and find something she wants or needs or at least will accept from him — a prescription filled, a bed, a bunch of red lilies — anything which may convey to her how sorry he is it is not more, how eager he is to make up for the wrong she may feel he has done her; anything to add a little color, a little richness to what he knows has been a dull, hard, barren life. Vera has to be kept alive and at home as long as possible for Charles to do for. It is his one need now, and will be his one comfort after she goes . . .

"My own reasons are perhaps the most difficult of all to explain. The only simple one is that Sandy was my favorite pupil during my last years of teaching and since then he has grown to seem almost like my own son. I think I am almost as grateful to Vera for having him as Charles is. But of course she does not know that, and it would make no sense to her if she did. Anyway, the kind of gratitude *I* feel to her for that does not obligate me to do anything for her. She certainly did not have Sandy as a favor to me. But my affection for and interest in Sandy is such that I would go to considerable trouble to prevent the necessity of his being called home in the middle of what I feel sure is a great personal and educational experience for him. If he felt toward Vera as Dick Thibedeau does toward his mother, I would know that he might never forgive us for *not* calling him home right now; but I am sure he doesn't. I'm equally sure Vera has no wish for him to come, no feeling of need of him. If she had, I can't say what his father's conscience and mine might tell us to do. Fortunately for her — and for all of us at this time — Vera is no more attached to any human being than any human being is to her. Vera is attached only to herself.

"And this brings us to my personal reason for what I do and ask others to do for Vera. Beyond wanting to save Sandy's opportunity and to give Charles his (Charles and I were playmates and schoolmates), I am trying to satisfy my own intense curiosity. Since getting acquainted with Vera I have seen what it can do to a person to live for at least thirty-five years with no love in her heart and with a steadily increasing antagonism toward everyone she knows or hears about, with no religion, no ideals, no ambition, no standards, no dreams, no friends, no hope, no achievement, nothing to think about except how big she was getting, how sick she was getting, and how to make other people at least as miserable as herself. The horror of such an existence has an awful fascination of its own. A living example of what enters the human system if it becomes and remains empty of any warm emotion, any constructive impulse, any urge to make the world a better place. What happens to such a system when it senses the approach of the final entry, like air creeping into the veins, or water into the lungs? It must be as instinctive for the human spirit to seek light when total darkness begins to fall as for the body to struggle for breath, however feebly.

"And I have discovered that Vera is not feeble. She has an extraordinarily strong grip on what is and has always been her main concern: herself. I suppose in some such people there would be an overpowering fear of fatal illness and death; they would pity themselves to the point of heartbreak, and beg and whine and cling. What can a life which has had and contributed so little in this world expect of the next? But Vera's courage is tremendous; one can't help admiring that and wondering where it comes from. If she knows or suspects she is dying, she never gives the slightest indication of it. Others might have retained a spark of the love we were all born with and be moved now to bring it up from the cellar to a sunny window. I suppose that even those they had neglected and abused would suddenly seem precious to them and even on their deathbeds they would try to make up for the lost years in this world at the same time that they groped for the hand of God, comforted by being assured that it is always there. Not so Vera. Vera is hoarding her strength and using her courage just as she always has — with grim determination to get as much as she can of what she wants. Not what anyone else might think she would want or ought to have, but what Vera wants."

"What does she want?"

"Well, a few weeks ago all I could figure she wanted, besides to keep on fighting anyone who came near her, was to get hold of money and spend it, and that all she could think of worth spending it on was furnishings for the house. Day before yesterday I realized that what she wanted was to pile up around her as many possessions as she could, as fast as she could, and live and die with them heaped up around her, where she could gloat over them and think, 'Mine, mine, mine.' That's why she wouldn't go to a hospital. She wouldn't leave her things, which are giving her for the first time in many long years a reason to want to live, to apply all her courage and determination to the business of living as long as possible. What poverty, Margaret, to have only *things* to live for! And so few things at that! But it is all she has, and time for her to enjoy anything is running out, so I find myself almost childishly eager to see her get more things. I'll buy her dishes, I'll take her French nightgowns and dressing gowns, I'll write her mail orders — all so that Magpie Vera may see her rough nest lined before she has to leave it . . .

"Today I have discovered, as she has, that there is something intangible she can use. That is attention. She is beginning to think it is almost as good as a thing. Not quite, for I am sure she would not use her money to buy it. But very good as a fillip to her last days, provided it comes to provide her with what she needs to go on living where she wants to live, to make her feel that as long as her wheel turns she is its hub, and to supply an outlet for the unkind, even vicious thoughts which you call poison. Maybe she suspects that they would shorten her life if kept inside, and probably she is right.

"It is also becoming obvious to me that she finds it most gratifying to receive attention from people she recognizes as important, even famous. Such as a heart specialist from Indiana, and the daughter of a Congressman from Minnesota. She would do nothing to deserve or to inspire these attentions; that would make them valueless to her. They must come to her exactly as she is, unrepentant and unimproved, for no other reason than that she is Vera, as she probably has read that a crowned head must receive homage simply because it wears a crown . . . But I am still curious. Here, close to the end of an empty life, she has discovered that she wants things, that she wants to be where these things are, and that she enjoys the attention of other people. What else may be there, stirring in her subconscious? Is there anything which might justify even a little of what she has been and done, and hasn't been and done? If so, will it reach the surface? Will she live long enough for it to reach the surface? We can only wait and see. But somehow, with all the great books there are to read, I cannot put down this poor little paperback mystery with all its loose and ragged leaves. I feel impelled to hold it together and to read as much of it as I can.

"So there you have my reason. Come, we must go to bed. Eileen said she would air Aunt Pauline's room for you."

They went up the walk together, and into the kitchen.

"Hungry?"

"No."

Rosamond took up the lamp and carried it upstairs and along the hall, Margaret following.

"Of course you don't have a gown or pajamas? Can I lend you something? We are about the same size."

"I never wear anything in bed in summer."

"The pitcher's filled. Hairbrush on the bureau here. I don't believe I have an unused toothbrush."

"It doesn't matter, really. I often skip."

"You shouldn't, of course. Unless you have to. Or so they say. I'm not sure that it harms the teeth of anyone who eats properly. I'll leave this lamp with you. You know how to put it out now. I can find my way quite as well in the dark. Good night, Margaret. We'll call you as soon as John has gone in the morning. I never go down until he has left. I think he and Eileen like breakfast by themselves."

She went out, but she had just closed the door behind her when Margaret opened it.

"Miss Lacey —"

"Yes?"

"Somehow, you've aroused my curiosity, too. My mother and sister are going on up the coast day after tomorrow. They want to see Bar Harbor and Quebec and maybe tour the Gaspé. I don't. They'll be gone three weeks or more. Would you be willing for me to stay here?"

"There is a great deal to see along the New England coast and in Canada."

"I don't understand scenery."

"There are many people to meet."

"I don't want to meet people. I've met thousands and thousands of people. Maybe I do need — to *know* a few . . . But I can see you're all awfully busy. I wouldn't want to be in anybody's way."

Rosamond came back into the room.

"Frankly, Margaret, we don't have time for a guest. As you've seen tonight, not even an overnight guest. We do need help. If after this trial voyage as cabin boy you want to sign on for a longer one, that's fine with us. We can use you, and I warn you I mean use. John needs more time for work on his house, Eileen needs help with the house, Charles needs time for his haying and errands, I need someone to take over the shop when I can't be there. You would have to be a jack-of-all-trades, and fill in any spot that was empty — sell, serve, nurse, clean and wash dishes first in one house and then in the other. It would be no vacation."

"The last thing I wanted this summer was a vacation. I wanted a job. The trouble was I don't know how to do anything. Besides, my mother wouldn't come East without me, and, good grief, it was easier to come with her than to have her stay with me."

"There'll be nothing easy about the next three weeks here, Margaret. They're bound to be strenuous for all hands. And our way of life is all new to you. Why, you didn't even know how to put out an oil lamp!"

"But I learned."

"That's true. And I showed you only once."

"Maybe I could learn the other things. From you and Eileen. I want to try a new way of life; I'm downright sick of the old way, I can tell you. And maybe you'll think I shouldn't say this, but I *have* to get away from my mother and sister."

"I think you shouldn't tell them that. There is no reason why you shouldn't tell me. And if you haven't yet had any experience in working away from home, I'd say it is high time you did. So talk it over with your mother tomorrow and come back if you can."

"I'll be back before supper tomorrow night. As early as she will bring me."

She left before eight o'clock in the morning, was back at eleven, ran upstairs with a suitcase, ran back to the kitchen and presented herself to Eileen.

"Cabin boy reporting for duty, Madam Commodore. What are my orders?"

Eileen closed one eye and inspected her sternly.

"Go put on a skirt, cabin boy. Also some shoes. If you don't have a ribbon to tie back that mop of hair I'll give you one; also an apron. That's your uniform for the galley. When you're called to the captain's quarters, take off the apron and be sure your hands are dry. Now off with you and come back a girl. A boy in the kitchen makes me nervous."

In the barn Mrs. Frye was telling Rosamond that she would be eternally grateful to her for taking Margaret in, that the real purpose of this trip had been to try to persuade her to do this — that is, to take Margaret as a boarder for a few weeks, if she possibly could — because the Frye family had been much concerned for a long time about Margaret's adjustment, and her father felt that Miss Lacey could straighten her out if anyone could. Of course Margaret had no idea that this was in their minds; if she had, no doubt she would have refused even to get out of the car the day before yesterday. For some reason, she opposed every plan they made for her.

"I didn't dare look beyond getting her here to meet you, Miss Lacey. I didn't even know she was coming here when she took the car yesterday. When she telephoned last night, I was so pleased and excited I could hardly keep my voice steady. As soon as I could hang up the receiver, I burst into tears; didn't I, Brooke?"

"Yes, Mummy. I was scared. And you didn't have any Kleenex. I ran to get you some."

"I know you did, darling . . . Oh, it's *too* wonderful that Margaret made up her own mind she wanted to stay here. And even more wonderful that you feel you can have her. I expect a call from my husband at the hotel tonight, and this news will make him *very* happy. We'll repay you in any way we can, though we can never fully repay you —"

"You and your husband have and will have nothing to repay me for, Mrs. Frye. Margaret has come here to work, and we need her help. We welcome an extra pair of hands and feet and a quick young mind. We are already too busy to straighten anyone out. It has always been my belief that this is something which must be done for one's self. If you ever consider her straightened out — and I hope and believe you will some day — have no doubt that it is her own achievement, and give her full credit for it, but don't tell her so. She will not want to be reminded that she was ever otherwise. In the meantime, don't worry. Forget Margaret for a few weeks. It will be good for both of you. And you and Brooke have a happy holiday together. Soon she will begin to grow up, and that is not easy for children or for adults who love them. It is hard — harder for some than for others — and it takes time. But it is necessary, and ultimately rewarding."

"Miss Lacey, you are so comforting. I hope you won't regret your kindness to Margaret. Brooke and I are sure to enjoy three weeks alone together; aren't we, honey?"

"Oh, yes, Mummy."

"Would you like another doll? To keep Dorothea company in the back seat on our way to Canada? She named her Dorothea for me."

They bought a tall china doll with painted black hair parted in the center, with brown kid hands, dressed in iridescent brown taffeta and wearing gold beads. Brooke said she would name this one Louise, for her grandmother, and her mother said Grandmother would be delighted. Mrs. Frye bought cranberry glass, a rare rosebowl, a pair of whale-oil lamps, and asked if they could be shipped to her home in St. Paul.

"Certainly," said Rosamond. "I suppose there is no great hurry. I'll have Margaret pack them as soon as she has time." She thought Mrs. Frye restrained a shudder. Before turning to another customer she said, "If you'd like to go to the house to say good-by to Margaret, please do."

Mrs. Frye said they had said good-by to Margaret before coming in.

"Well, then, you two are off for the Gaspé. We'll look forward to seeing you again in about three weeks."

Al and Hazel Bradford came in a few minutes later, and asked if the woman and little girl they had met on the bridge hadn't been here when they were a couple of days before.

"Yes. You don't know who they are? Mrs. Robert Frye of Minnesota, and her younger daughter."

"Isn't he in Congress?"

"Yes."

"I've heard Sid Lamie speak of him. They're great friends."

"They were fishing here together in the spring. He is abroad now. Mrs. Frye and Brooke are just leaving for points north and the Gaspé Peninsula. An older daughter, Margaret, is working with Eileen and me until they come back. You will see more of her. She was over reading Vera to sleep last night. But I suggest you don't mention her family to her. I'm under the impression she wants to Get Away From It All."

"We know how that is," grinned the doctor. "We've been through it three times and out the other side."

"You have to let them go gracefully, or you never get them back," said Hazel.

"The only one we worried about was the last one. We began to wonder if she was ever going to want to go! But she bolted finally. Now sometimes she calls us from Rio, as if she were in the next room. 'How you, Mom?' she says. 'Dad, old boy, old boy?' Then in ten minutes she finds out everything we've done and tells us the most exciting of what she's done since the last letter, gets the oldest child on to say, 'Love you. G' night,' and ends up with a 'Take *good* care of yourselves, darlings. We'll talk again soon.' Oh, it's a great life if you don't weaken."

He thrust his hands into his pockets and ambled off in the direction of the horse stalls. When he had disappeared into one, the two women by the door could hear his low whistling.

" 'Daisy,' " smiled Hazel. " 'Daisy, Daisy, give me your answer, do' — he *always* whistles that when he's alone. Unless he's reading or eating. Never anything else. That just goes on and on."

"My father's was about the grandfather clock which stopped short, never to go again, when the old man died. Yet somehow it always sounded very cheerful. I asked him once, 'Do you ever think of the words when you whistle that?' and he said, 'Not usually. The music for "stopped — short — never to go again" is as gay as a polka. If I *do* think of the words, I think, Too bad they didn't get your Uncle Lute to take a look at that clock. He'd have fixed it' . . .

"I wonder if the children of today remember their fathers whistling, and if when today's young people are our age the music they all heard when they were young will turn them quickly from strangers to old friends. And I understand that slogans are anathema today, also maxims. Yet how else can one speak a truth to inspire or to be remembered, in so few words? And those of us who were brought up on sayings accepted by everyone and constantly repeated have the bond of a shared language. I don't know when before I've heard 'It's a great life if you don't weaken.' It was never in the copybooks, yet to our generation it is as familiar as if it had been. And it's *true*. If the same observation, in whatever terms, could have been passed down to succeeding generations, would so many weaken so easily?

"Well, we can be thankful for what we had. When Al says that and whistles 'Daisy,' I feel as if we must have all gone to school together, and I'm conscious of the kinship of New England with Ohio and Indiana . . . In fact, everything you two do and say makes me feel that we are old friends and neighbors. So much so that I don't even feel surprised to see you sitting there. It seems you have been here all the time, and I talk about a dozen other things in a random way before saying what a pleasure it is to have you, and trying to thank you for letting Al's vacation, and yours, be interrupted by our neighborhood emergency."

"Don't be concerned about that. I like it. He likes it. It's reassuring to be needed wherever we go. We're proud to be associated with Lacey, Incorporated, and to see part of what is going on here from the inside. What fun we'll have telling the Lamies about it in the fall! And this is a very intriguing case you have given Al. I've just been to Mrs. Weymouth's with him."

"I thought you probably had. Did you go in?"

"Oh, yes. When we got there, the hospital bed had just arrived. Mr. Weymouth and a young man he called Dick were carrying it in. I told them they'd better leave it on the lawn while I scrubbed it. While Al was upstairs, we got the bed set up and Mr. Weymouth brought me things to make it up with. By the time he came down I had shown the men how to make a stretcher with two poles and a tent-fly we found in the barn loft. So before we left I'd bathed Mrs. Weymouth and got her into her *other* Paris nightgown and her robe with the flowered satin yoke, and Dick and Mr. Weymouth had brought her downstairs — and there she was, almost literally, sitting on top of her world. Spang in the middle of the parlor, looking through the hall into the kitchen, with a good view from windows facing north and west, and her precious catalogues piled beside her."

"Well! *All* that done this morning? What did Vera say?"

"Oh, she said a great many things in the course of an hour. She's a real character."

"She is indeed. But what did she say first after she was all settled? She must be the most comfortable she has been for weeks, if not months."

"I think she is comfortable. What she said was, 'I *wish* that dratted mailman would bring my nylon curtains. I hope he don't give 'em to Suse George. They say she's out there, twisting around the mailbox, every day when he comes along.' "

She sounded so much like Vera that Rosamond laughed aloud. Hazel was laughing too. Their laughter seemed to strike small lights which went dancing through the barn.

The woman who had been at the far end came up to the desk with a sauce dish in her hand.

"I'll take this," she said. "I couldn't help hearing bits of your conversation. What is this anyway — an antique shop, a politicians' back room, a child guidance clinic, a philosophy club, or a hospital annex?"

"That's for the audience to decide."

"I'd call it a five-ring circus. A good show, but distracting. You might sell more antiques if you concentrated on it."

"Perhaps. And I like selling antiques, but it is chiefly one means to several ends. It may be the multiplicity of ends which you find distracting. One of them, you see, is meeting interesting people with interesting ideas. I'm glad you feel it was a good show. There is no admission charge, you know. Are you sure you want this sauce dish?"

"Yes. I was able to recognize my pattern. There is no price mark."

"You should be proud of your power of concentration. The price is fifty cents."

"Fifty?"

"Reasonable, isn't it? But everyone likes a bargain. You'll come back some day to see if I have another. If I do, the price may be a dollar. You see I have my own crafty business methods. You might be surprised to know how many customers come and come again for the show, and while they are here buy antiques as if they were bags of popcorn. Human beings are of great variety. *They* are the greatest show on earth."

The woman went away with her sauce dish.

"Do you really think she will come back?"

"No. Nor do I think she will ever again pay a dollar for a sauce dish. She'd rather spend all summer looking for another one for fifty cents. I've given her a purpose in life. Can't you see her walking, walking, driving, driving, hunting, hunting for another proof loop and dart sauce dish with round ornaments, priced fifty cents? . . . Call Al from the ironworks, the tinsmith's, the turner's, and the cooper's, and let's have lunch."

"I *told* him we shouldn't come again at this hour."

"There is no reason why you shouldn't, and every reason why you should. We have much to talk over."

Eileen served them on the porch, but, before they finished, a car drove in and she had to go to the shop. Margaret brought out the dessert, her face intent, almost grim, and a slight shaking of her hands making the silver chatter against the china as she took away the salad.

"This is Margaret, Dr. and Mrs. Bradford," said Rosamond. "She is undertaking to save our lives for the next few weeks. See how I can keep on sitting here while Eileen goes to the shop? Pure luxury."

As Margaret refilled his coffee cup, spilling a little, the doctor touched a loop of the bow at the back of her neck.

"Are bows coming back, Margaret?" he asked. "Then the world is taking a turn for the better." And he sang, " 'Scarlet ribbons — scarlet ribbons for her hair —' "

She glanced over her shoulder at him, flushing a little, frowning uncertainly, and he looked back at her unabashed, with open, hearty, male admiration.

When she had gone — perhaps out of hearing — he added, "And *what* hair!"

"Isn't it?" said Hazel instantly. "I've never seen anyone else with such gorgeous hair as that. It's — almost extravagantly beautiful. That royal color. I noticed it, of course, the other day when she sat on the bench beside me." She added, as if it were irrelevant, "Do you remember when, if a delicate girl had long, heavy hair, the doctor might urge the parents to have it cut, thinking it might be sapping her strength?"

"I remember."

"Then I suppose the boys stopped noticing the delicate creatures and that's why so many of them had the vapors, went into declines, and died of broken hearts. People pay too much attention to what doctors say."

"Interesting to hear that from a doctor."

"Oh, I'm a doctor only when I'm with a patient. And only part of the time then. Too many doctors think of nothing but keeping people alive. What's the use of being alive if you don't live? And how can you live in this world if you have to keep your mind on what may sap your strength, walking for exercise (dullest walking anybody ever did), staying out of crowds, gargling three times a day, brushing your teeth five times a day, taking your vitamins, not getting too cold, not getting too hot, counting your calories, avoiding smoke, fog, and engine exhausts, poking yourself to see if you have a lump anywhere, having your drinking water analyzed, getting complete checkups, going to hospitals for observation, having exploratory operations?

"Jumping fishhooks! People used to live while they lived and then die. Once. Now a lot of them spend practically their whole lives dying. I tell you it's long-drawn-out torture, and the medical profession is at the root of most of it. People come to my office and tell me the only time they feel well is when a doctor has just told them there is nothing the matter with them. This lasts until they get home. I tell them that if I were in their place I wouldn't go home. I'd start on a slow boat around the world or on a hike to the Canadian Rockies. Some project that would take at least three years."

"I couldn't agree with you more. But if the medical brotherhood knew of these opinions, would you lose your membership?"

"They know," said Hazel. "They should. He says it wherever he goes."

"So you see how much influence I have, Rosamond. No, you don't lose your membership except for malpractice. They're glad to have me around to keep hearts beating. I tell them they wouldn't need me so much if they weren't scaring everybody to death by taking care of them so hard. They say I'm a throwback, that I ought to have been a general practitioner in days when all a doctor needed was a horse and buggy, a bedside manner, and what he could put into a battered old valise. I tell them men and women lived like men and women then, not like embryos in laboratories. They say many of them died who would now be saved. I say, 'Saved for what? For a proud, rich free life or for years of fear and suffering and semi-invalidism and for you to experiment on?' They say wait until I get a fatal illness myself, and I'll feel differently. I tell them that when I get a fatal illness, I hope to the Lord I can keep out of their clutches long enough to die. Living has been my business so far, I've done it in my own way, and, according to my bookkeeping, I've made a success of it. When it comes to dying, I want a try at doing that in my own way, too, on the chance that I can make a success of it. After all, it's my only chance, because *I'm* going to die just once."

"Now I understand better his interest in Vera," Rosamond

told Hazel. "She, too, is bound to do it only once and on her own terms."

Hazel nodded. "So he enjoys doing what he can to help her to live, not just to keep her alive. There's quite a difference, as he says. He'll advise her but he won't order her or alarm her. We'll offer, but we won't insist. We told Mr. Weymouth we'll be up every morning for a week or so, and while I'm there I'll get her ready for the day. It's fun to try my hand at nursing again. You find you can do perfectly well with the simplest of equipment."

"Bless you both," said Rosamond rising. "Shall we go back to the barn and relieve Eileen to help Margaret? I feel a maxim coming on. Many hands make light work. I used to get on very well with just one pair of hands, but that was when life was not so complicated — very pleasant, but less interesting. Now we are — let me count — six pairs of hands, and not one pair too many."

That night John and Eileen went to see Vera, while Margaret and Rosamond did the supper dishes, cleaned silver, and set bread to rise, talking as they worked. When the others returned, bringing some milk-glass animal dishes Rosamond had sent for, Eileen said that Dr. Mansard had been just leaving the Weymouths' when they reached there. She said he had greeted them quite cordially, asked John how he felt, and said he understood the church people had criticized him for not being able to cure John's headaches so that he would not have had to resign.

"He said probably Judge Morrison had told you the churches were trying out union services at least for the summer. John said none of us had seen the Judge for quite a while, but we had heard of the union services from some of those who came up to our afternoon meetings. Dr. Mansard said, 'I hear you get out quite a crowd up here,' and John said there was a good congregation; and he added that the cure for his headaches seemed to be using his hands more. Dr. Mansard said that was very likely, that manual work was known to reduce tension. Then he said people up here certainly had a Christian spirit to do so much for Vera whom he called 'something of a Tartar' as well as 'a very sick woman,' and she was fortunate indeed to have Dr. Bradford's services; that he had promised Dr. Bradford he would stop in, if he could, the next time he was up this way, so he had, but he wouldn't again unless called; he could see everything was being done for Vera that could be outside a hospital."

Then Charles had come to the door and said Vera wanted Eileen to come in and write an order for a studio couch.

"I've been waiting all afternoon and night for somebody to write it out," Vera said acidly. "All I get is doctoring and nursing lately, seems like. I want this order wrote, and Charlie'd never get it right. Wrong number or something. Here it is — right here. I been holding the place."

Out in the yard Dr. Mansard was asking John, "You know a colored fellow lives around here somewhere? Roger Lee?"

"I've never seen Roger. He's the older of the Lee boys. The other works in Boston. His parents come to church. But I haven't happened to see Roger. Why do you ask?"

"Well, Mrs. Weymouth has just made quite a point of warning me about him. What she *said* was that he may be laying out a piece of work for me. When I asked her what kind, she said it might be one kind and it might be another. She also said that Elder Struthers comes over to pray for her, but there are others around here who need praying for more than she does."

"I'll tell Mrs. Weymouth that I pray for us all," John said quietly.

"Just as I told her," replied the doctor, "that I take my work as it is handed to me. And sleep when they let me." He yawned and stretched. "Could you pray that when I get home tonight there'll be nothing to prevent my going straight to bed and staying there until morning?"

John said he would pray for the health of all, and for the

needed rest of those who care for the ill, and that words might be found which would open the doors to all the cold, dark places where the light and warmth of the Heavenly Spirit had so far been kept out.

The doctor shrugged and chuckled, struck John on the shoulder, and went away.

John went in to Vera. Eileen had written the order and addressed the envelope. Now she was collecting laundry to take home in a bag she had brought, laying out clean towels and a fresh gown for morning.

"Shall I read to you, Mrs. Weymouth?" John asked.

"No. That girl Rosamond brought here last night read the paper through . . . Can't you sing something?"

"We'll both sing. What would you like to hear?"

"I don't care."

She lay with half-closed eyes for a long time, as if strangely content and relaxed.

They sang the old hymns, one after another, all the verses of each one. Rock of Ages, cleft for me . . . How firm a foundation, my trust in the Lord . . . Onward, Christian soldiers . . . Blest be the tie that binds . . . The Lily of the valley . . . The little brown church in the vale . . . The old rugged cross . . .

Charles came into the hall from the kitchen and sat on the stairs to listen.

At last Vera said, "That's enough now. I'm getting sticks in my eyes. Where's Charlie?"

"Here I am, Vera."

"Put that letter she wrote into your coat pocket before it gets mislaid. I want you should take it to the village in the morning while the Bradfords are here. You'll have to get a money order at the post office. The money's in the envelope. I won't trust it with that mailman."

~~~~~ *9*

THE summer drifted on into August. The little meetinghouse was nearly filled now every Sunday afternoon. John had
put up between the doors a small sign which read OPEN FOR
WORSHIP, and as the doors were never locked, and often open,
it was not unusual to find, when one stopped in on a weekday,
that one was not alone.

Vera's condition had improved immediately upon the ar-
rival of her studio couch, which was delivered the day Rosamond and Margaret hung the nylon curtains. Triumphantly
she ordered the hospital bed out of her parlor, and slept on
the couch at night, napped on it during the day, but went to
the kitchen table for her meals, and padded about the downstairs rooms in one of her two Paris dressing gowns and the
most glamorous pair of jeweled velvet slippers Margaret could
find in Port City. She had found she liked to have Margaret
shampoo her hair and tie it back as Margaret tied hers, with
ribbons ordered by mail. Wallpaper had now been ordered for
the kitchen, and a full dinner set, eight of everything, two
each of red, two of turquoise, two of gray, and two of yellow.
They were guaranteed practically unbreakable. It was no
longer necessary for someone to be always with her, and she

was glad to be alone and "have a chance to get my head together." Charles had more time for his hoeing and haying, which he needed. The Bradfords came to see Vera only twice a week, on Wednesday mornings and on Sunday afternoons while Charles went to church. John called there one evening each week. Eileen continued to do the laundry and to take or send food now and then. Rosamond stopped in frequently to buy. Margaret did a weekly cleaning. A crisis seemed to have passed for the Weymouths, or at least to be held in abeyance.

At Laceys' the studio had become a house. The chimney was going up. Eileen had made of Margaret a good waitress, a good cleaning woman, even a good cook. They worked together with few words, except for occasional good-natured sparring, as if they understood each other without speaking. On the other hand, while Rosamond was teaching Margaret how to pack china and glass for shipping, how to tend shop and record sales, while they went on house-to-house buying trips and spent bright Saturdays at country auctions, the two carried on a conversation, a discussion which sometimes became an argument, a constant stream of observation and comment which had no end, only interruptions and postponements.

It had begun when Margaret finished packing her mother's dishes and addressed the carton to St. Paul, drops of perspiration running down her nose and mingling with the blood of cuts on her hands from the heavy paper and the cord which looked and felt as if made of haircloth. After "Frye" and before "St." there were small clouds of pale pink. Triumphant at last, she threw herself on the grass beside the barn door and lay looking straight up at the sky with her arms crossed under her head. She had kicked off her shoes, as she did at every opportunity.

After a while she said, "I love a time when nobody is saying anything."

"I like silences too. But you have broken this one."

"Just thinking aloud . . . I hate words. I've heard so many

of them. Words, words, words. Why don't people *do* more, instead of talking so much?"

"Doing is one thing. Thinking is another. You can't think without words."

"Good grief, Miss Lacey!" Margaret sat up. "I do my best thinking — practically my only thinking — when I'm alone. Or feel alone. Always have. And I *don't* talk to myself."

"But you think in words. There's no other way. Anything which doesn't come to us in words is a feeling or an instinct or a vague impression or a hazy memory. We don't *have* to express our thoughts, and often it is better not to. But if we *can't,* either we are not thinking clearly or we have lost the ability to communicate much as if we had lost our voices and the use of our hands. And if human beings, on a large scale, ceased to communicate with each other, how long would it be before there were no schools, no churches, no printed matter, no business, no professions, no government, no friends, no families?"

"You mean words are essential to civilization."

"Can you deny it?"

"Well, the words, maybe, of one person in a thousand. If the rest kept still, we could hear the important words better, and find out they were important and learn to listen to them. Most people's words bug you, they're so absolutely empty and mean-ingless and silly, and they go on and *on* and ON."

"Don't blame the words. No word is empty, though the one who uses it may be. Every word has meaning. It is a challenge to find out whether the one who uses it knows what it means and means what it says. We have to develop the ability to separate what is meant from what is not meant, the full ear of corn from the false, the wheat from the chaff. In a democ-racy, no one can or should be silenced. The man of wisdom must grow tall, his voice must be strong with confidence; he must convince by the soundness of his logic, the sincerity of his purpose, the human warmth of his heart; he can become a leader only by the will of the people whom he has taught to trust him; and he can continue as a leader only by demonstrating over and over again that he knows how to put his words into action . . . I say a man. Of course exactly the same is true of women."

"But most people have nothing to contribute to anybody. Even themselves. Or less than nothing."

"Not one of us was born with nothing to contribute. Every single individual has the capacity to become a force for good; whether from a mountaintop or a niche in the mountainside is not important. Where each of us is, that is his platform, his battle station, his garden spot. Any niche, or any mountaintop, which is defiled, or is left unguarded, or fails to produce sturdy plants from good seed, becomes a breeding place for weeds and pestilence and is ripe for occupation by any and all enemies of human growth and human freedom . . . I think you will see, Margaret, if you look, that in our country everyone is contributing something to himself and to others. By communication we can get a better understanding of just what each of all those around us is contributing. Not all of it is good, by any means, but all of it *can* bring out good in others if the others see it for what it is and react positively. We learn from our own mistakes and from mistakes we see made. We also can learn from a bad example as well as from a good one."

"That's — encouraging."

This was how the long conversation began. It was still going on when Mrs. Frye and Brooke came back from the Gaspé. They stayed at the Harbor for three days but Margaret still was not ready to go home with them and Rosamond said she had now made herself almost indispensable; if she could stay another two weeks, while Mrs. Frye and Brooke were in the Catskills, and then fly to New York to meet her father and the rest of the family for the trip home, everyone on the lane would be delighted. In two more weeks it would be close to

Labor Day, and after Labor Day the tourist season drew to a close. So Mrs. Frye bought a doll's house full of miniature Victorian furniture for Brooke, and a service of Georgian silver for herself, asking that these be sent, then told Margaret that when she left she might choose from the shop whatever she liked best.

"Thanks a lot, Mom," Margaret said. "I like to travel light, you know. Most of what I take away from here will be *in* me . . . In my head, I mean — like how much profit an antique dealer likes to make on each piece that sells." She winked at Rosamond. "It would shock you. But you see, what sells has to pay for what doesn't sell . . . Also in my fingers — like how to use a paring knife and how to make lamp chimneys shine. And don't ask me how I'm going to use these valuable possessions at Carleton this fall. That remains to be seen . . . I have to run now and get a jellied salad ready to chill, for I took Eileen up to Vera's this afternoon and I have to leave in fifteen minutes to get her or she won't be here when John gets home and John doesn't like that. Good-by, Brooke-be-good. Good-by, Mom."

With tears in her eyes, Mrs. Frye said, "Good-by, sweetie," and opened her arms. Margaret did not flinch. She hugged her mother, gave Brooke's small braid a tug, told them to take care of themselves and she would see them in a couple of weeks, and ran into the house, her red ribbon bouncing, her peasant skirt flying, and with sandals on her brown feet.

"What have you done to her, Miss Lacey?" whispered Mrs. Frye.

"Put her to work, showed her how to do it, and taught her what we could of the little we know," answered Rosamond. "She is a very apt pupil. For instance, that skirt she is wearing. She washed the India print spread that was on her bed, got some spots of bleach on it, insisted on buying a new spread to replace it, and then cut around the bleached spots to make herself a skirt. Isn't it attractive?"

"She looks lovely," said her mother. "Simply lovely. Doesn't she look lovely, Brooke?"

"Yes . . . Am I as pretty as Margaret, Mummy?"

"I'm the luckiest mother in the world," said Mrs. Frye. "I have two beautiful daughters. One of them is dark and the other blond."

They went away. A few minutes later Margaret left to get Eileen. When they came back, Rosamond was standing in the shop door talking with a man. Margaret glanced at him, looked again harder, ran behind Rosamond's car to look at his number plates, and surprised Eileen by dashing into the house by way of the front porch.

"Blacktop all the way from town to the end of the lane, and gravel to the foot of the hill beyond your house?" the young man was saying. "The shop outgrown the studio and moved to the barn? A Gorgeous Creature just putting out a 'For Rent' sign down the road —"

"That's Geneviève Barron. She was a June bride."

"Naturally. The gorgeous ones are always June brides. Last June's. Vegetables and fruit stands lining the roadside? Telephone wires piercing the gable end of the Lacey house? A parade of people coming and going?"

"You exaggerate. As is your regrettable habit, I believe."

"Why do you say that? What do you know of my habits?"

"Someone brought me a newspaper column of yours."

"Not — really!"

"Yes. Really."

"Well, I'll be — hornswoggled is the scientific term I'm reaching for. How did that happen?"

"It would take too long to explain. My point is that you exaggerate."

"I want the explanation and I hope you will find time for it eventually. I'll come back every day until you do. Now that I know I was on the right road I'm going back and ask Geneviève, bride or not, to take her sign down and let me in.

And I didn't exaggerate either in the column or in trying to convey my honest impression that there have been startling changes around here since last summer. I can't say I'm sure I like them. Does Geneviève serve meals?"

"No, but we do. Your column was a gross exaggeration. It's a pity if you don't like the results of it, I must say. I have borne up under them very well. People coming here to get me to speak to the PTA and furious when I told them what I would say. People lying in wait to crucify me because they claim I closed their church to open one of my own. People not daring to sit down because some member of my family may be occupying the chair. People who think I can work miracles and people who think I'm not right in my head. People who love art glass and buy so much of it I'm in such frantic pursuit of it not a cupboard, attic, or cellar barrel is safe from me, though I don't like it a bit better than I ever did. And *you* complain of changes! There is only one fruit and vegetable stand, you met only one car on the way in, and I moved out of the studio only because the minister and his wife are moving in."

"Whew!" He struck his forehead. "I don't understand. I'm bewildered. Seems to me we are carrying on at least three conversations."

"You started all of them, so I supposed you were used to it. I am. Often as many as six are going on here at the same time. With a buyer about prices, with a looker about New England traditions, with the doctor about immortality, with the minister about high blood pressure, with Eileen about how many cans of tomatoes are enough cans of tomatoes, and with Margaret about the trend toward lynching, figuratively, anyone who expresses a minority opinion. Of course, if Sandy weren't working his way across the Great Lakes to Niagara Falls, and Sheila weren't at camp, several other topics would be tossed into the ring. Or one of the rings. A customer — sort of — asked me one day whether this was an antique shop or a five-ring circus, and said it was her opinion I would sell more antiques if I concentrated on it. She was wrong . . . You know, I really didn't expect to see you again, Jason, but I must say it is a pleasure. Come on in to supper."

"Maybe I do need nourishment. I certainly need something. But isn't someone likely to come along and rent Geneviève's house, or apartment, or room, or whatever it is she has, while my back is turned?"

"Yes. It was only vacated this morning, unexpectedly. It is a two-room apartment. But the Barrons have a telephone too. You can call from the house."

In the kitchen Margaret was saying to Eileen, "He's from out home. I know he is. He has a Minnesota license plate, and I've seen him somewhere. Or anyway his picture. And here they come! He's coming in! In *here*. Eileen, I'm going upstairs. Can you manage, until he goes?"

"Yes. But what's the matter with you, Peg? What do you *care?*"

"Oh, *don't* you see? If I've seen him out there, he's seen me. Even if he doesn't know my name, Miss Lacey may tell him, and anybody in Minnesota who hears the name Frye thinks of my father; and if he ever has seen me, he'll put the two together. And there I'll be, the Congressman's daughter again. It's been such a relief just being me, you don't *know!* Vera's the only one here who has ever mentioned my father, and she hasn't for weeks. I'm not ready yet. I won't be —"

She was gone, for Rosamond was opening the screen door into the back hall.

"One more for supper, Eileen," she said. "Jason Schuyler. Jason, this is Eileen Struthers, our minister's wife, and one of my two household angels this summer. Jason is here for the second time, Eileen. He was my first customer last year. Only he didn't buy anything, as I remember it. I'm expecting better things of him this time. He wants to telephone the Barrons to ask if he can rent their rooms."

"Oh, yes; well, he can go right in. John's there. Supper will be ready in just a minute."

As soon as Eileen had heard Rosamond introduce John and Jason, she called, "Miss Lacey, could you come here a minute, please?"

Rosamond came back, lifted the cover of a kettle, and sniffed.

"Carrots," she said. "Those nice baby ones. What are you mashing? Oh, green pumpkin! Where's Margaret?"

"Upstairs. That's what I called you out to tell you. She ran away. Is this young man from Minnesota?"

"Yes."

"She thinks she's seen him out there. She doesn't want to be recognized."

"I'd thought of that. Particularly because he is a newspaper-man. I'll finish up the supper, Eileen. You go find her and say I need her to wait on the table tonight. Say I'll introduce her as Margaret West, and tell our guest she came to us from the Harbor . . . You see, she can't keep on hiding because he expects to be in and out of here for the next two weeks. If he gets those rooms at the Barrons', he would be your customer for most of his meals."

"Oh, yi-yi," Eileen cried softly, rubbing her palms together.

When Rosamond carried the casserole into the sitting room, John was just putting up the telephone receiver.

"I called for Mr. Schuyler —"

"Jay," came from the depths of a wing chair.

"For Jay, because I know the Barrons. Joe says the rooms are still available, and if Jay wants to get into them tonight the couple who said they would decide tomorrow will be told the space is already taken."

"That's the way we do business around here. No nonsense. Quick or you lose it."

"*Gracias, danke, spasiba, merci — tous la même chose —* Mr. Struthers."

"John. I'm glad you know so many languages because I know only two. Not that I need to be thanked, but I do like to know what is being said to me."

"I thank you, John. Not only for your influence with the Barrons but for the effort of calling them. I'll be in their rooms tonight if I can get out of this chair and to the table where I count confidently on being revived. At the moment I'm bushed. I've not only driven six hundred miles today. At the end of it I was inundated by totally unexpected developments and a flood of highly intriguing but also highly unintelligible chatter. Since I sank down here, I've been trying to figure out what language it was in. That's what led me to run through my pathetically small repertoire. All I'm sure of at the moment is that I have much for which to be grateful, even though I speak as from under water, hear as from a great distance, and see as through a glass darkly."

"It is good," murmured Margaret, who had followed Eileen down the back stairs. "The man is out like a light. Go in and be seated, ladies. Your minion will attend you."

"Just what I've always wanted. A minion," said Eileen.

"Don't forget, when you talk," said Rosamond, "to use your best New England accent."

"Too bad I'm not serving rawr oystas to one who has been long on the rud. But why should I talk? Peg West will content herself with bobbing her head."

When Margaret made her first appearance, with a basket of hot biscuits, she paused by Rosamond's chair and mumbled, " 'Bout the drinks —"

"Oh, yes, Peg. I told you I have two household angels this summer, Jay. This one likes to be called Peg. Peg West. She came in from the Harbor. Our neighborhood young people have gone to the Harbor to work summers for many years. Peg is in the process of reversing the tide. And she wants to know what we'll have to drink. Milk? Coffee, hot or iced? And now or later?"

"Hiya, Peggy," Jay said. He raised his eyelids as if by main force.

John and Eileen would have milk now. Rosamond would have coffee later.

"*Jay?*"

"Yes? . . . Oh, yes. Coffee, please. Now and later." He still sounded sleepy, or dazed, but his eyes were wide open. As soon as Margaret was back in the kitchen, he made a gesture in that direction and said, "Another last June's bride, I presume."

"Who? Peg? Heavens, no. Just a school girl."

"A *school* girl?" He whistled very softly. "What a school girl! You don't mean that, Miss Lacey. You're using another language I don't know. If *she* came up from the Harbor, she's a mermaid. Or else — you sure her name is Peg?"

"Oh, of course she was named Margaret. But aren't most Margarets called Peg or Peggy?"

Jay's eyes were fixed quizzically on Rosamond.

"Still that strange language! I suspect you are, for your own reasons, trying to mislead me, Miss Lacey."

Eileen held her breath. She strove to keep her eyes on her plate. A wave of thankfulnss went over her that John, when puzzled, was quietly puzzled, calmly waiting for revelation, and could be depended on not to explode with "What's all this? I thought you said *West*. Margaret's name is —"

"And what reason do you think I would have for misleading you?" asked Rosamond, offering Jay the basket of biscuits.

Margaret came in with a tray and placed the glasses of milk, the coffee cups. She filled Jay's cup from a glass pot, and disappeared again. Eileen knew she would not have come if she had overheard the conversation.

"Perhaps," said Jay, resting his chin on his fist and looking after her, "you are a kind-hearted woman, and think that I am in no condition to know the truth."

"And the truth is?" asked Rosamond. She thought, "If he knows, he knows."

"That her name is Nereid, and my coffee has just been brought to me by a sea nymph."

"Oh, now, *really*," Rosamond exclaimed. "Eat your supper and wake up. I know you deal in absurd exaggeration. If you are going to add fantasy to your stock in trade, I shall have to say, on second thought, that we cannot feed you for two weeks. It fair takes away a practical country woman's appetite, like sitting at table with a somnambulist. Eat, or I shall send you off to the Barrons at once, supperless."

Jay rolled his eyes at Eileen .

"I don't *think* she could be so cruel," he said, "but I will take no chances."

He picked up his fork.

~~~~ *10*

D U R I N G the next week Vera had a stroke. Margaret was
there cleaning at the time. Jay had driven her over and was
in the field with Charles. Margaret rang the bell Charles had
hung by the door and the men came. The nearest telephone
was Rosamond's and Jay drove there as fast as he could. Rosamond called the Bradfords who said they would come at once,
and went back with Jay to the Weymouth place.

"I'll send Margaret right out and you can take her home."

"Poor kid, she must be in a state of shock herself. When
Charles and I got here she didn't have a trace of color in her
face."

"She'll be all right. The first time anyone sees death actually
at the door it is terrifying. But after that it is easier to face it
— for yourself or with others. And women bear the experience
better than men, as if something in their chemistry prepares
them for it in advance. It's Charles I'm worried about."

As she went in, she saw Charles sitting bent forward over the
couch where Vera lay. Margaret was in the kitchen ironing.

"I was upstairs," Margaret whispered. "I heard her fall. It
shook the house. I ran down and spoke to her and she tried to
say something but I couldn't understand her. I don't see how
Mr. Weymouth ever got her up on the couch; do you?"

"He is very strong. And you're a brave, sensible girl. Go on home now with Jay. There were five or six customers in the shop when I left and Eileen has a cake in the oven. You'd better let her get on with the supper and you take over the shop. Have Jay help you. He might as well make himself useful as well as ornamental —"

"I think he's been *very* helpful!"

"You do? Well, I'm glad to hear it, I'm sure. Ask John to come over as soon as he has eaten."

Rosamond smiled at Margaret, gave her a quick spank, took the iron from her, tested it with a wet fingertip, and set it back on the stove. Snapping the wooden handle into a hot iron, she rested it on a trivet and smoothed the sleeve of a blue work shirt across the board.

When the car had gone, she went into the parlor. Charles had not moved. He held Vera's hand in both his, and did not look up.

"How do you think she is, Charles?"

He shook his head. "I can't tell. And she can't tell me."

"Dr. Bradford will be here soon."

"I'll — be glad to see him."

"I didn't think she would want me to call Dr. Mansard."

"No."

"Anyway, I think Dr. Bradford will get here at least as soon as he could."

"Yes."

"If you should need me, I'll be in the kitchen ironing."

The Bradfords were there within the hour. Vera was already more alert and when she spoke they could understand a word or two.

The doctor said, "Give me a break, will you, Charlie? *I* want to hold hands with Vera." A little later he said, "Vera, you had a little bad luck, but you're going to weather it. This is what happened. Your circulation slowed down almost to a stop. But it's going again now. It numbed your right side, but one leg feels about like the other one now, doesn't it? You gave my hand quite a squeeze when I asked you to, and your tongue is limbering up. Now you won't be over this in a minute, but you may be pretty well over it in a week if you're a good girl and mind Buddie and me."

Vera opened her eyes and asked, "How . . . know I . . . sick?"

"Oh, the old grapevine. Margaret told somebody and somebody told Rosamond and Rosamond told me. Can't keep any secrets around here."

"Tel'phone?"

"Sure."

"Char —"

"What is it, Vee?"

"See tel'phone . . . nex' . . . Money — for it . . ."

"What does she say?"

"She wants a telephone put in," translated Hazel instantly. "Says she has the money for it. I call that a very sensible idea."

"I'll see about it first time I go downtown," Charles promised.

"That's right now," said the doctor. "We'll go together because I have to pick up a few things. Including — and you hold your horses, Vera! — that hospital bed. Got to have more beds around here for the next few days, and that one is the best one for you. Then Buddie can have the couch. You see, we came fixed to stay a spell. Buddie brought her pajamas — the ones with red, white, and blue stripes; you'll see them tonight; pretty nifty; she looks like Mrs. Uncle Sam in them — and I brought my nightshirt. Can I bunk with you, Charlie?"

Vera said, "S'eep Sand' room."

"You'll sleep in Sandy's room, Al," said Hazel. "Takes Vera to figure things out."

"Oh, fine. I hear there's a rock collection up there. Make me a boy again just for tonight. Now Buddie's going to look after you while we're gone, Vera, so we can take Rosamond home on our way. Pretty soon we'll be back with the bed, and ready for supper. Buddie brought what she had in the refrigerator. After we eat we'll get you settled in style and after a good night's rest you'll feel like yourself again. Then a few quiet days, and by the time Charlie gets your telephone in you'll be answering it when it rings . . . Rosamond, come on. Buddie can finish the ironing."

"It's all done," said Rosamond. "The shirts may be a trifle damp. I've hung them on chairbacks."

The others had just sat down to supper when she got home. Margaret was at the head of the table. She had put on a sleeveless white piqué dress, tied at the waist with orange silk rope, and had pinned her hair high in a soft, dark, radiant knot.

"See where the lackey is," said Jay. "I put her on the throne just to see how she would look. I think she looks fine, don't you? Cinderella at the ball. Queen for a day."

"We didn't expect you so soon," said Margaret hastily, about to rise.

"Sit still," said Rosamond, "and start serving." She added another plate to the pile and, with silver in her hand, slid into the chair Jay had drawn up for her beside him. "Vera is better. Al says she had only a mild stroke. The question now is whether it is the first of a series. The Bradfords are going to stay with her for a few days. It's fine the house has just been cleaned and the laundry done. Can you girls do some extra cooking to send over?"

They chorused that of course they could.

"What's a little more cooking to them?" asked Jay. "May I be delivery boy?"

"If you give us your word not to eat it before you deliver it. Are you going over tonight, John?"

"If you think Mrs. Weymouth would like to see me. It is always hard to tell."

"I know. But she might, tonight. And perhaps you would know how to ask her if she would like for Sandy to come home a little sooner. He expects to be here in a week anyway. I had a letter from him today and he is selling souvenirs at Niagara

Falls. He told me where he was and that he expected to stay about three days, so no doubt he is still there. I could call him tonight if she wants me to."

"I'll try to ask her about it."

But when he came back he said he had arranged with Mrs. Bradford to ask her while he talked with Charles and the doctor in the kitchen; Vera had seemed to be asleep while he was in her room but whenever Mrs. Bradford spoke to her she responded. Mrs. Bradford had come out to say that Vera definitely did not want Sandy to hurry home, that there was no need of it, and the house was full without him.

"What she *said* was, according to Mrs. Bradford, 'Place like a beehive now. Doctors in the kitchen, nurses in the parlor, a minister buzzing in every corner.' "

That was Friday night. The Bradfords were still with Vera on Sunday when Charles Weymouth drove into the Lacey yard after eleven o'clock in the morning and stopped his car but did not get out. Margaret, who was putting the shop in order while Jay tied up some cartons to be taken to the express office the next day, was the first to see him and ran out.

A minute later she was in Rosamond's room, where Rosamond was dressing for dinner and the church service.

"Mr. Weymouth is here. Something has happened. I don't know what. He looks strange. He asked for John and I told him John was in his house working on his sermon. He said he would go over to see him, and got out of the car and walked that way. He walks stiff. After he started walking he said without looking around, 'Ask Rosamond to come out there.' It must be Vera is — worse, mustn't it?"

"It may be. I'll go right out. As you go down, tell Eileen what you've told me."

"Oh, poor Mr. Weymouth."

"Yes. Poor Mr. Weymouth . . . Margaret, dear, if you are ever sure you love a man and he loves you, marry him. But never, never marry anyone if there is the slightest doubt in your mind that you love him and he loves you, so much that your love will carry you both through whatever happens after that . . . Of course this must have been said to you at least a thousand times, but I —"

"No," said Margaret gravely. "No, no one has ever said that to me even once, Miss Lacey. When I was listening."

She went quietly down to the kitchen, and then to the barn where Jay, seeing the change in her face, asked, "What's up?"

"We aren't sure yet, Jay. As soon as I know, I'll tell you."

"I hope it's nothing to stop us from going to church. Partly because I like that little service, and partly because I hoped you would ride down to the Harbor with me afterward. I'd like to meet your family."

"We have to wait until we know what's happened."

"So much is always happening here now, isn't it? It wasn't like that last summer . . . I wish you'd been here last summer. Looking back, it seems to me it was like an allegory, or a fairy tale."

"Or like I imagine a happy childhood? Something wonderful to have once and to remember, not something you can or should keep?"

"You imagine. Didn't you have a happy childhood, Peggy?"

"No. Did you?"

"No . . . I wonder why we didn't."

"Maybe because we did a lot of thinking. When you have a mind for thinking and you use it that way a lot before you have much personal experience to base your thinking on, and nobody helps you with your thinking because nobody supposes you are thinking — how can you help getting more and more confused? And I was so proud; were you? I wouldn't ask questions because I didn't want older people to find out I didn't know the answers. I thought I ought to know as much as they did. I wanted to know more and better than they did. Sometimes I looked in books, secretly, for the answers, but I looked in the wrong books and only found more questions or learned what I only half-understood and wished I had never heard of. When people of my own age told me things they knew, I pretended I had known them for a long time, and it was years before I found out that most of what they told me wasn't true . . . I suppose a good many adolescents are like that, and some of them never grow up. But we did. We're lucky."

"How old are you, Peggy?"

"Twenty."

"You've grown up faster than I did. I'm twenty-eight."

John and Charles had been standing, facing each other, when Rosamond went in.

John said, "Mr. Weymouth has brought us very shocking news, Miss Lacey."

"What is it, Charles?"

He cleared his throat, and still spoke gruffly.

"Suse George was drowned last night."

"Was — *drowned?*"

"In the river. Her body was found this morning caught on the MacIntosh Mills dam. That's a mile below the village. Folks who saw it called the sheriff and he recognized her. He and two of his boys drove up to tell the Georges and stopped by to get me to go over with them, knowing Sim and I had been neighbors all our lives."

"What a hard thing for you to do!"

"The worst of it was, at first, Sim and Lizy thought Suse was right there, abed and asleep. Lizy said she always went out Saturday nights and came in real late, never got up till dinner time Sunday. Lizy even thought she'd heard her come in, around two o'clock. They both went up to her room and pounded on her door and then went in. But she hadn't been back. We waited at the door, and Lizy never came out again. We could hear her sobbing in the kitchen. The young ones gathered from all directions and stood staring. Sim said

Suse would never go into water; she hated the water; she had never learned to swim; wouldn't even go paddling when they went to the beach, just sit on the sand. But she'd *been* in the water, Dr. Mansard figured, seven or eight hours when they found her about nine o'clock this morning; so she must have drowned around midnight or one o'clock. Sheriff asked Sim if he knew who she was with last night, but he didn't; said that as often as not she started out alone and met some friend at the end of their road. Sheriff asked him if he noticed how she seemed to feel at supper time last night, was she in good spirits. Then Sim broke down. Said he never saw her act happier; she had a new white dress with red poppies on it, and red shoes, and he noticed that before she left she picked a red poppy that was blooming by the old cellar hole and fixed it in her hair. Last thing the sheriff asked him was if it was true, as he'd heard, that Suse was going around lately with Roger Lee; and Sim said no, he'd never heard of it, that Suse liked to have a good time and that cost something and Roger wouldn't work and didn't even have a car that he could put on the road."

Here Charles looked miserably at Rosamond. Both knew one source of the rumor that Suse had been seen with Roger.

"Finally they took Sim off to make the identification. The children stood there, one of them holding the baby, and waved to him as he left as if he had been going to town meeting. I came over to see if some of you wanted to go over to speak to Lizy. Seems as if she ought to have somebody."

"Yes. Could you and Eileen go, John?"

"Certainly we can. There's no question in my mind but that we should, right away. Thank you for letting us know, Mr. Weymouth. I'll get Eileen." He stuffed his papers into a drawer. "Will you be coming with us, Miss Lacey?"

"Not now. I think I'll just tell Margaret and Jay what has happened — and then drive over to the Lees'."

"You let me know," said Charles, "if there's anything I can

do. For anybody." They were all crossing the yard. As he got into his car, he said, "Trouble . . . Trouble, trouble, trouble . . ."

"Our faith will help us to surmount it all," John reminded him gently. "Jesus said, 'I am the light of the world; he that followeth me shall not walk in darkness.' "

One car went down the lane, then the second, and then the third.

Jay kept the shop until time to close it for the afternoon. Margaret prepared dinner for five, but she and Jay ate alone. They rode up to the meetinghouse at church time, but a notice was posted there saying that there would be no service today. John had written it, and left the doors open for private worship.

Standing irresolutely beside the road before the meetinghouse, a woman asked, "Why in the world isn't there a service? We've driven sixty miles —"

A man who had just read the notice and was on his way back to his car told her, "A girl near here was drowned last night, lady. There's talk it may have been murder. Shouldn't wonder if her folks need their pastor today. If they do, that's where he'd be."

"Murder!" The woman shivered. "And I came here because people said it was such a calm and lovely place. Little white church surrounded by woods and fields. Minister who is a carpenter on week days. His cute wife in the front pew. An old parlor organ, and untrained voices singing loud. Doors and windows wide open. Like being on a heavenly balcony —"

The man shook his head slowly.

"I guess it's just a corner of our old earth," he said. "Wherever human beings live, there's a pretty good sampling of all kinds. Question is what's going to get control of it, the better in us or the worse. Same as the country. Same as the world. Same even as what's up there in the sky, maybe, and beyond the sky, between us and God."

Jay and Margaret sat for a few minutes, waiting for a sight

of someone they knew. But there was no one, though several of those who drove up, read the notice, lingered briefly, and went away they had seen the Sunday afternoon before, and she had seen at services earlier in the summer.

"Don't know but the Struthers jumped out of the frying pan into the fire, didn't they?" . . . "Poor girl, they say she came here every Sunday with her family. All gifted singers" . . . "You been here before?" "No; ran up after we heard the noon broadcast; didn't know till then there was such a place." "One way to get on the map." (Laughter) . . . "Did you hear the police are looking for a colored boy? Lives right around here, but seems he's gone, skipped out." "No! Well, that's what you get —" . . . "Nobody's safe anywhere nowadays" . . . "This building had been falling apart for years until a woman took it into her head to get it fixed up and open it. An antique dealer. Looks like she thought of it a little too late." "Maybe she thought it would draw trade." "Well, I don't know about trade but she'll have a crowd around for the next few days, anyway. A good deal longer if somebody goes to trial for this thing." . . . "Behind every case like this there's a family — or families — with no sense of responsibility. . . ."

"I can't stand this," said Margaret suddenly. "I think I've been listening in a trance. Of horror. I feel murderous impulses rising in *me!*"

Jay turned on the ignition.

"Where do you want to go?"

"Home. To see if anybody's there."

She meant Rosamond, Eileen, or John. None of them was. Two cars waited before the closed barn door, and Jay explained to their passengers that it would not be open that day. He was not sure whether it would be open the next day. It would be safer for them to telephone before driving over from the Harbor. He gave them the number.

Margaret was packing a basket of food, filling a thermos jug with coffee.

"Will you take this over to the George place, Jay? Probably

Eileen will come to the door. I don't suppose anyone there has had anything to eat since morning. Then will you go down to Lees' and ask Miss Lacey if there's anything she wants us to do? Tell her I'm roasting a chicken for supper."

"Yes, ma'am. Do you know you sound like her? You even stand like her."

"Do I? Call me the apprentice, filling in for the expert who's been training me. But I'm getting uneasy, being so long without orders."

"You're a fine girl. Your mistress will be proud of her apprentice. And so am I."

The chicken was in the oven and Margaret was shelling beans for succotash when Judge Morrison drove in. Never having seen him, she did not know him, and thought he was a customer. But after a glance at the closed doors of barn and studio, he came heavily up the walk toward the house. She set the pan of beans on the table and went to meet him.

He stood on the porch holding his hat in his big hands.

"How do you do. Is Miss Lacey at home?"

"No, she isn't, sir."

"When do you expect her back?"

"I really don't know. I hope she'll be here soon, but I don't know."

"I see. You don't know whether she might be at the George home? I've just returned from a few days out of town, and hear they have had a — tragedy."

"Yes, sir. But Miss Lacey's not there. Reverend and Mrs. Struthers went over to the Georges' before noon, and Miss Lacey went to the Lees'. I haven't seen any of them since."

"To the Lees'!"

"Yes, sir."

"I see. Well, if I may, I'll wait a little while."

"Of course. Come in."

"No. No, thank you. I'll sit in the car. If she doesn't come soon, I — may look for her at the Lees' . . . Beautiful day, isn't it, after the heavy rain?"

"It was this morning, sir. We've hardly noticed since."

"No, I suppose not. I understand that whatever happens in this community reaches into this house. It always has. That is why I drove out at once."

He walked heavily back to his car, putting on his hat as he went.

He had been there perhaps fifteen minutes when Rosamond drove in. She had sprung out and was beside him before he could open his door. He could not remember that she had ever before greeted him without a smile.

"William! I was never so glad to see anyone in my life! I was on my way to call you. I told them I was going to call you. I've wanted to call you for hours, but I didn't feel I could leave until Jay came to take my place. Oh, the blessing of a telephone! I've set my heart on seeing that before winter every house around here has a telephone. You're so *dreadfully* cut off without it!"

He was beside her now.

"You couldn't have reached me, Rosamond. I've been at meetings in Rockport for three days, and only reached town half an hour ago. Haven't even been home. They told me at the paper store about the George girl and I came directly here."

"Oh, bless you, William. Come in quickly. Margaret will give us some coffee, and I'll tell you — I have so *much* to tell you."

What she had to tell him was that when she had reached the Lee house the state police had already arrived there. They were just going up the steps to the porch where Ramona was sitting in the hammock peeling potatoes.

"Mrs. Lee? You have a son Roger?"

Ramona dropped her knife and clasped her hands.

"Yes, officer. What is it? What's happened to Roger?"

"We don't know as anything has, ma'am. We want to see him. He isn't here?"

Ramona breathed a little easier. She said no, he wasn't there.

He hadn't come home last night. Sometimes he didn't, but she always worried when she didn't know where he was, and when she saw who they were the first thing she thought of was that Roger might have been in an accident, for he had taken his car though it wasn't in the condition it ought to have been to be driven.

"Have you heard of any — accident, ma'am?"

This question surprised her.

She said, "Why, no, we haven't heard of any. But I know there are lots of them, especially where the traffic's heavy. We always tell Roger to keep out of heavy traffic, but you know how boys are —"

"When did you see him last?"

"I guess it was around ten o'clock last night when he left. The last time. Why?"

"You mean he left here in his car around ten o'clock last night, and you haven't seen him since?"

"Yes. It might have been half-past ten. It was dark. I couldn't see the clock . . . Why are you asking me all these questions about Roger?"

They sat down, one in front of the hammock and one at the end of it. They were very polite.

"Because we want to see him, Mrs. Lee. You say you don't know where he is, and we have to find him . . . You say he left the last time about half-past ten. Had he been away from home earlier in the evening?"

"Yes, but he came back."

"Had he been out in the car before?"

"No. He was walking somewhere, I guess."

"You don't know where?"

"No."

"Does he have friends around here he goes out with?"

"Not that I know of. Once in a while he goes over to the Thibedeaus'. They're real nice to him. But most of his friends are down around the Harbor, I guess. That's where he goes when he can get his car started."

"Did you see him when he came in around ten or half past?"

"No. I didn't see him, but I heard him. His father and I had gone to bed, and I guess his father was asleep. But I heard him. He came up to his room and I thought he was getting undressed, but he was changing his clothes. He went back downstairs, I thought to get something to eat, but he went right outdoors and started his car. I wanted to call down and ask him where he was going, but I knew I'd only wake my husband. Roger wouldn't hear me . . . You sure you don't know where Roger is, officer?"

"No, ma'am, we don't. But he may come home any time. If he doesn't, we'll find him. You say he was changing his clothes. How do you know that?"

Paul Lee had come up from the pasture and seen the cars in the yard. He stopped beside Rosamond's and asked her if she knew what was going on.

Rosamond said, "They want to see Roger, Paul. They drove in just ahead of me. Ramona doesn't know where Roger is, and they're asking her questions. You'd better go and help her."

He said, "You come, too."

So she went up on the porch with him just as Ramona was saying, "Because he left the clothes he took off in a heap on the floor."

"Could we see those clothes, Mrs. Lee?"

"Why do you want to see Roger's clothes?"

She began to cry and when Rosamond sat down in the hammock she turned and hid her face against Rosamond's shoulder.

One of the officers said to Paul, "You Mr. Lee? I'm sorry about this, but we'd better see those clothes."

"Are they up in his room, Monie?" Paul asked, touching her shoulder.

"No . . . in the basket . . . head of the shed stairs."

Paul brought the basket. There was a pair of chinos in it and a short-sleeved white sport shirt. Nothing else.

"They're very wrinkled," said one of the officers. "And they're quite damp. I wonder how that happened. Did you wash them last night, Mrs. Lee?"

"No," Ramona sobbed. "I wish I had. I don't *like* for people to see his clothes look like that."

"Then why are they so wrinkled and damp?"

"Because they were wet. That's why he changed them, of course."

"How do you think they got wet?"

Now Ramona was crying too hard to answer.

Paul said, "We talked about that at breakfast this morning. He must have fell into water. Probably slipped in the dark, pulling in a boat."

"He has a boat, does he?"

"Not a boat of his own, no. But there's an old boat on Lacey's Pond anybody can use. And sometimes he takes Thibedeaus', on the river."

"You mean anybody can take the Thibedeau boat? Or does he ask them if he can borrow it?"

"Not anybody. They keep it down back of their house, where the river runs through the meadow, and it's just tied to a tree. But they keep the oars in kind of a little camp they built for their children, and the camp is locked against strangers. They let Roger have a key to it, though, same as they did our other boy. So they could take the boat any time it was there. The boys around here go eeling at night sometimes."

"Mrs. Lee, try to tell us this one thing. What makes you think it was around ten o'clock, or half-past, when you heard Roger come in and go out last night?"

She sat up and tried to get control of herself.

"I know I hadn't been to sleep. I'd heard the clock downstairs strike ten. It hadn't struck anything else when I heard him come in. It strikes the half hours."

"Did you hear him, Mr. Lee?"

"No. I'd worked hard all day, and I sleep sound."

"Well, I guess that's all then. For now. We may be back later. We'll go see if we can find him."

Paul went to the car with them. Ramona watched the three, watched their faces as they exchanged a few words. When Paul came back, she got to her feet.

"Paul, what did they say out there?"

"Well, I asked them — if the boy was in any trouble that they knew of. They said they hoped not. Said of course they couldn't tell, any more than we can, till they find him. Said if he should come home to be sure he stays here until they come back. Because they're going to keep looking for him until they find him. They'll stop by here every now and again until they do."

"Oh, Paul, I wish he'd come. I wish I'd see him driving up that road the next minute. I wouldn't *care* how fast."

"I think he will. 'Most any time now. You try to stop worrying, Monie. Let's all go in and see if there's still some coffee in the pot."

But Ramona would not leave the porch. Rosamond went in and pulled the coffeepot forward on the polished stove-top, found cups and saucers on orderly shelves edged in paper lace, and spoonbread under a plastic cover in the cellar cupboard. She carried this to the porch on a tray.

Paul said, "Monie painted the flowers on that tray."

"It's pretty. Maybe I shouldn't have used it. It's pretty enough to hang on the wall."

"It's all right," Ramona said. "I put three coats of varnish on it."

She would not eat anything, but she drank a little coffee.

Then the state police came back.

"Has Roger come?"

"No."

"I was thinking again about the clothes he changed out of. Wasn't he wearing anything but a shirt and pants?"

"Hot weather, he don't wear underclothes."

"Socks? Shoes?"

"No socks. An old pair of sneakers."

"Where are they, ma'am?"

"In the shed. I didn't put them in the basket. They're all muddy."

"We'd like to see them, ma'am."

"His old muddy sneakers, full of holes, and splashed with paint?"

"Yes, ma'am."

Paul brought them, wrapped in newspaper. The officer was careful. He took the loosely wrapped package out on the grass to open it. He crouched there, turning the sneakers over, studying their worn rubber soles. The other officer stood beside him, looking down.

"We'll have to take these with us," the first officer said, rising. "Be sure Roger waits here for us, if he comes back while we're gone."

"*Why* do you want his sneakers?" cried Ramona.

The officer, getting into the car, said without quite looking toward the porch, "We found the Thibedeau boat overturned and caught on a stone a couple of miles down river. Haven't found the oars yet. The Thibedeaus didn't know it was gone until we told them. We have to find out who took it. The camp was unlocked. There are tracks in the muddy bank where the boat was tied."

They were gone again.

Ramona looked despairingly from Rosamond to Paul.

"Oh, dear Lord above! Roger must have been out in that boat. But how could he have upset it? And if he did, why didn't he right it, and pull it ashore even if he'd lost the oars?"

"That boat's pretty heavy, Monie, and Roger's never had much strength in his arms, I've noticed. Like enough he couldn't right it."

"And it was so dark. If he had his flashlight with him, that was gone too. If he didn't take it, it was in his car. And that must have been where he went in the car — down the road to where he left the boat. With light to find it, and maybe a tow-rope to pull it ashore by —"

Rosamond wondered silently, "Then why did he take time to go up to his room? Was his car key there? And why did he stop to change his clothes?"

"So why didn't he find the boat and get it ashore, Paul?"

"Maybe he did find it, right where the officers found it, and couldn't dislodge it, or thought it was safe there, and he went on hunting for the oars. Oh, if only he'd told me he was in a jam! If only he'd ever told me, hadn't always tried to keep things secret until they piled up and looked worse than they were."

"We've begged him not to do that. We've told him it made it look as if he was a bad boy. And Roger isn't a bad boy. We told him we'd always help him if he'd just come to us in time . . . But *where is he now*, Paul? He couldn't — couldn't have drowned, could he, trying to get the oars?"

"No, Monie, no. You know better. One thing Roger can do is swim. Nothing could happen to him in that river. Even if it could, they'd have found his car wherever he left it . . . No, Roger's off somewhere in that car, and, the way I see it now, he doesn't dare come back just because that boat is two miles down the river and the oars are lost . . . Poor, foolish boy. If he'd called me to help him, we might have got the boat and the oars back to the camp all right. If we couldn't, and he'd told the Thibedeaus first thing this morning, they'd have taken it all right. They know accidents happen. We'll get them another pair of oars."

"But how long would he stay away because of that?"

"He'll be pretty hungry by night. I don't believe he had any money with him. I'd say he'd start home as soon as it gets dark, anyway." Paul added a little grimly, "But now he's got the state police after him, they'll find him, and he'll probably be here sooner."

"That'll scare him almost to death. He's been terrified of police for years. And that only makes them more suspicious of him."

Ramona began to cry again.

Rosamond took the dishes back into the kitchen and washed them, thinking, thinking, but still aware that the iron sink had been rubbed to a gleam with kerosene, the pine boards of the floor were spotless, the glass in the windows shone, the dish towels smelled of sun and wind, the cretonne covers on couch and chair cushions were clean and crisp, and yet the whole room had a comfortable, much-lived-in feeling. There were newspapers and magazines on a stand, books on a set of hanging shelves, a big framed print of "The Blue Boy" on the wall, and the clock which struck the hours. And the half hours.

At last the Lees came in. Ramona swayed a little as she walked, and reached for chairbacks. Paul, just behind, watched her anxiously.

"Do you have any ammonia? Spirits of ammonia?" Rosamond asked.

"There may be. In the cellarway."

"I hope there is. It would make you feel better."

Paul found it. Rosamond poured a little into a glass of water and added sugar. As Ramona sipped it, she looked at the clock.

"It was awful good of you to come," she said. "I don't see how you happened to, just then. And now it's past church time. You're missing church."

"We're all missing church today," Rosamond answered. "We'll go next Sunday. Drink it all, Ramona."

Standing with the empty glass in her hand, she said, "You look so tired. Did you stay awake long after you heard Roger go last night?"

With a sigh, Ramona pressed her thumb and second finger against the outer corners of her eyes and slowly upward across her temples.

"I don't believe I slept a wink last night. After he left I tried to lay still. But after the clock struck eleven and then half-past it seemed as if I was twitching all over. Not that he isn't often out that late, because he is, but because he'd started so late. I couldn't understand it. So I got up and went into his room and lit the lamp, and there was that pile of wet clothes. So wet I took each piece to the window and wrung it out and the drops fell like rain on the syringa bushes. Then I took them down to the shed and shook them out and dropped them in the basket.

"When I came back to the kitchen I fixed myself a cup of hot milk, and while I was drinking it the clock struck twelve. I tried to read, and I paced the floor, and it was hot and I went out on the porch and lay in the hammock. The clock struck one three different times and then I may have half-dozed off, but when it struck two I heard it and jumped up and went out in the yard and listened to see if I could hear Roger coming. I couldn't hear anything but the belled heifers across the river, and the mosquitoes were thick, so I came back in and put out the light and went up to bed. But I heard the clock every time it struck the rest of the night. And I was up before sunrise. Did a big ironing before Paul came down to breakfast."

"I wish you'd lie down, Monie. Stretch out here on the couch."

She lay down, to please him, and then he went back to the porch. Rosamond thought they must wonder why she did not go home, but knowing what she knew and they did not know, she did not dare to leave them alone. She felt that if Roger should come she must be there to help them keep him, and then, when the police came, to warn him that he should refuse to answer questions except in the presence of a lawyer. If he did not come, but someone else came and told the Lees about Suse, she wanted to be with them when they heard it. So she took a magazine from the stand and pretended to read it while

Ramona lay with her eyes closed and Paul waited on the porch, the cretonne-cushioned wicker chair creaking faintly whenever he moved.

"Oh, if only they had a telephone here," thought Rosamond. "I'd call William and ask him to come and tell us what to do."

"You will do what you can for Roger, won't you, William? When they find him he must have somebody, and the Lees have very little money. I can't tell you how glad I was to see Jay coming, Margaret. I ran out and told him as much as I could of what I knew, very fast, and asked him to stay while I came home to call you, William. I reminded him of what to tell Roger about his right to counsel, and said I was glad he is a newspaperman because if there was more questioning while I was gone he would remember it . . . I'm afraid it is looking very bad for Roger. The evidence will pile up, and his reputation is against him."

"I'll do what I can, Rosamond. How much can be done will depend, of course, upon what actually happened last night and whether or not it can be proven conclusively. The boy's own story, when he is found, will be very significant."

"I hope you will hear it when he tells it. First, I wanted you to hear what Ramona and Paul have said today. I am convinced Ramona was telling the absolute truth. She knew of no reason not to, and she would anyway. If Roger did take the Thibedeaus' boat and overturn it — as almost certainly he did — it was no later than ten o'clock. And Suse was not drowned until two or three hours later."

"But where was Roger two or three hours later?"

"None of us know. Will you come to Lees' with me now, William? He may have come back."

"Yes. Yes, let's go down there."

As they were leaving, John and Eileen drove in. They said it had been a heartbreaking day at the Georges'. Lizy was close to collapse. A man from the district attorney's office had been there asking questions about poor Suse, her companions, her habits. After he left, Sim found a bottle and began to drink. Fortunately, Dr. Bradford had come over and given them both sedatives. John had taken the children up in the woods for what he called a Sunday School picnic while Eileen did what she could to put the downstairs rooms in some kind of order. There was almost nothing to eat in the house except what Margaret had sent. After they had eaten something themselves, they would go back with more food for the family and get the children to bed. Then John would bring Eileen home, but he would go back and spend the night there.

"How are the Lees?" asked Eileen. She had shadows under her eyes. "Have you seen Roger?"

"Margaret will tell you all I know," said Rosamond. "Jay is there now. William and I are on our way down."

"Wait just a minute," Eileen said. "I want to tell you this, Miss Lacey. After the Georges were asleep, Dr. Bradford told us that the man from the district attorney's office had also been over to see Vera."

"Vera!"

"He said he understood she had some information he needed. He had heard that she had seen Suse and Roger pass her house in the night. Mrs. Bradford was trying to keep him out, but Vera heard what he said at the door and called for him to come in. You see, she knew what had happened to Suse. Mr. Weymouth had told her. So the man came in. The Bradfords stood by the bed and they said Vera lay there, propped up with pillows to help her breathing, and roared, 'Who told you I said that?' The man said he was not at liberty to reveal. Vera said, 'Be something to know how you make up your mind what to reveal and what not to. Supposing I did say I saw them go by? What would that prove? It's a public road, ain't it? And how do I know what I see three feet away, to say nothing of three hundred yards in the dark? Part of the time I can't see a blamed thing. You work you up a case and drag me into court on a mattress and I'll swear that if I ever named two people that went by here in the dark within the last month or six weeks anybody that believed me was a fool. I might have thought I saw somebody go by, but I can't swear who it was, I can't swear it was men or women or a man and a woman, I can't swear there was more than one of them, I can't swear it wasn't a few scarecrows swapping cornfields. Now you'd better go along before I have another spell and there's two to bury in this place. Keep this up and nobody around here'll have time for anything but answering questions and going to funerals.' "

Rosamond said softly, exultantly, "Well, good for Vera! That's *true*. And she found it in her heart to say it after the fun she had spreading that malicious little story! . . . I think Charles must have been proud."

"Oh, he was. Dr. Bradford said the man left as if he'd been blown out, and Mr. Weymouth kissed Vera and said 'Bless you, Vee,' and a tear ran down Vera's cheek. But then she said, 'I *wisht* you'd bring me something decent to eat. Getting red of that ghoul took all my strength. I can't get my strength back on *slops*.' "

They laughed a little, the first laughter in many hours. Laughing, Margaret put her arm around Eileen and drew her toward the house. John followed with the empty picnic basket.

At Lees', Rosamond and the Judge found Paul and Jay talking quietly on the porch. Rosamond had told the Judge who Jay was and when she introduced them the older man said, "I knew your product, my boy, before I knew you. Are all your columns of the quality of one which was published last winter about how you didn't go fishing at Lacey's Pond?"

"Did you see that, sir?"

"It was he who brought it to me," said Rosamond. She left the men and went to the other end of the porch where Ramona lay in the hammock. The pan of potatoes half peeled, which she had put down when the state police car first drove in, was still on the floor under it. "Have you heard anything more, Ramona?"

"Yes. They've found him, Rosamond. One of the officers came to tell us they'd found him."

"Where?"

"On some woods road up back here. They said he was asleep in his car."

"Where is he now?"

"Over at the sheriff's office at the county courthouse, they said. I *don't* see why they took him so far. I asked the officer that, and he said they had to ask him some questions. Paul said, 'Why don't you tell us what this is all about? There's something you're keeping back from us. You don't go to such lengths about a pair of oars, do you? The boy didn't steal them or the boat, even if he took it. The Thibedeaus let him have the key. They'll tell you that.' The officer said they had told him that; he'd been to see the Thibedeaus. He looked kind of funny and then he — said there was the tracks of a girl's shoes beside Roger's sneaker tracks around where the boat was tied . . . Shoes with high heels . . . Said they had to ask Roger who the girl was he had with him, because nobody around seemed to know he had a girl . . . We didn't either. Far as we know, he never went out with any girl. Of course we can't swear he didn't, and if they found the tracks together — but what business of theirs is it if he did? What's that got to do with a pair of lost oars? Why did they have to take him all the way to the county courthouse? I don't suppose he's had a mouthful to eat for 'most twenty-four hours now."

Rosamond turned quickly to William, who was just behind her, and he nodded to indicate that he had heard it. Ramona, seeing him there, struggled to get up, but he put a big hand on her shoulder.

"Stay quiet, Mrs. Lee," he said. "Troubles young people get into — large and small — are very hard on parents, perhaps especially on good mothers. Take it as easily as you can."

"This is Judge Morrison, Ramona —"

"A — *judge!*"

William chuckled.

"Once a judge always a judge, they say, Mrs. Lee. I was the magistrate of our district court for many years, but for some time now private practice has filled my time. I am a lawyer, and a friend of Rosamond who is a friend of yours. If you and Mr. Lee wish me to, I will go up to the county seat now and find out how things are with your boy."

"Oh, would you, sir? Could I send him something to eat? Paul, did you hear what he said?"

"My wife and I'd be mighty glad if we could know, Judge. But it'll take you some time, won't it? Twenty miles up and back. We'd pay you, though, as soon as we can. Probably I ought to get the oars first, and find out if there was any damage to the boat —"

"I suggest you let that go for now. About the boat. Wait and see if your boy says he took it. And there'll be no charge for my going up to the county seat. I go there several times every week, like to say I could drive over the route with my eyes shut. I'd better not wait for you to put up a lunch, Mrs. Lee. If your boy hasn't eaten, I'll find food for him."

Ramona was on her feet now. The Judge bowed to her and shook hands with Paul. There was new hope in both their faces.

"I'll see you all later, then. I trust with good news. Are you coming, Rosamond?"

She made a sudden decision.

"Yes, I think I will. As far as the end of the lane. Ramona, I think you need some young life to keep you cheerful while you wait. There's a fine, bright, capable girl helping me this summer and when I get home I'm going to send her over to visit a while. Only she won't want you to make company of her. She'll help you get supper for Paul and Jay, and maybe get your mind cleared a little before Judge Morrison comes back."

Jay went along to the Judge's car, and said, "Lady, I sure would be glad to see that fine, bright, capable girl of yours coming — barefoot, I assume — round the mountain. But since all is quiet at the moment on this front, can't I take you home and bring her back? It would take me off duty no more than ten minutes, and add ten minutes to my personal life. Don't forget, in all the excitement, that old Jay Schuyler has a little less than one more week here."

"Of course," said Rosamond. "Excellent idea. Because I should have one car at home. I may need it. And you know perfectly well I wouldn't ask her to walk over, after such a day as she has had. This sets you free, William. Bless you."

"Collecting material for another column, I suppose," said William to Jay, a twinkle in his eyes. "Perhaps a whole series of columns this time. I think I shall subscribe to your paper. And if you should ever get around to fishing *in the Pond*, let me know. I know where the trout hold their conventions."

Rosamond thought, "Who but lawyers can separate their minds from their hearts so completely? I imagine many people doubt that William has emotions. But I know he does."

～～～ *11*

JOHN and Eileen had gone back to the Georges'. As Margaret left with Jay, she said, "Ships that pass . . ."

Rosamond was glad to be alone. She sat on the step to eat bread and milk, with Pansy beside her daintily lapping some of the same from a cereal dish. She went slowly to the well, and pumped, and drank from the long-handled tin dipper which hung there. She walked on into the old orchard, picked up a Red Astrachan from the grass and bit deep into it. The bread and milk, the water, the apple all tasted as they had when she was a child and then a young girl. In the years since, which had brought far more changes than the two hundred years before had brought, truth had not changed.

"And the truth was and is," thought Rosamond, "that we really need only two rules to live by, to live well, even nobly, and without fear of anyone or anything. The first rule is, ask God to stand beside you while you look earnestly into the book of your own mind and heart to find out what is right. The second rule is, do it . . . When we make mistakes, it is because we have not looked carefully enough to find what we needed to know, or because, having found out what it is, we fail to do it and try some other way which we think may be quicker, or easier, or safer; but it never is . . . I was taught this lesson with the taste of milk, bread, water, and apples. I have said it to myself many, many times, like a rosary. I am sixty years old, and still repeating it, for the reassurance, the confidence, the strength it always brings me . . . How do people live who never repeat it, never having learned it, and even never having heard it? Yet many do. More last year than the year before, I am afraid, and more this year than last. Because those who have learned it are embarrassed to repeat publicly a lesson so familiar in the history pages of mankind that they assume everyone must know it. They should realize that a lesson long enough untaught is torn from the text. If one generation has not learned it, who will teach it to their children? . . . Grandparents? Then much depends on today's grandparents, actual or potential. We must tell what no one else knows, or dares to tell. And we must act — quickly . . . It is already too late for Suse. She had heard it — at least from her teacher in her early days at school — but she was a slow learner; she did not hear it often enough or long enough; it slipped from the fringes of her mind . . . Is it too late for Roger, too?"

She went into the house and did the supper dishes. The hot water from the tank at the end of the stove, the thick bar of white soap, her own kitchen china and glass — though the one was cracked and the other chipped — felt good to her hands. Thankfulness for this began to extend to thankfulness for many other blessings and was like a soothing ointment spread over the aching grief and anxiety of the day. Her house, her fields, her lane. Her business which had opened so many doors to her and to others. The meetinghouse open and a service there next Sunday when all that could now be done for Suse would have been done and perhaps the Georges would come to be with their neighbors and to listen, even if they could not yet sing. John and Eileen, and the studio almost ready to become their home. Sandy no farther away than Niagara Falls, and perhaps nearer; he might come up the walk any time now.

Margaret able to make a friend of Jay; perhaps her first real friend near her own age. William, after all these years, still standing by, kind, reliable, selfless, wise. Vera gravely ill, but with a new willingness, determination, to keep the rules she had been taught at the same time Rosamond learned them. Though she had many times ignored them, today she had observed them; and for this she had been and would be tenderly cared for by neighbors who had hardly felt acquainted with her until two months ago, by the Bradfords who a little while before did not know that she existed, and by Charles, her husband, whom her illness had brought closer to her than he had been for many years, and whom today she had made proud.

Rosamond heard herself singing low and listened to hear what she sang. It was a song she had heard several times on Jay's portable radio as he and Margaret sat in the grass or under a tree with music playing softly as they talked.

> When the dog bites, when the bee stings,
> Then I just think of my favorite things . . .

When John brought Eileen home about nine o'clock, Rosamond was asleep on the sitting-rom sofa. When Jay brought Margaret back about ten, she was still asleep. Yet in her sleep she must have sensed that Eileen and Margaret were there, for when the third car drove into the yard, she sat up quickly, saying, "What? Girls, is that William?"

They came in from the kitchen, and Eileen answered, "Yes, it is. I'm so glad you had this good sleep —"

Margaret said, "He may be William to you, but he's the Judge to us. Oh, I never supposed I'd be holding my breath to hear what a judge would say."

"Can you bear to hear it, Miss Lacey?" asked Eileen. "I don't know as I could if — if it's what it may be."

"Yes, you could," Rosamond told her. "We have to know whatever he can tell us."

But the Judge did not come in. He waited in his car, and

Rosamond went out and joined him. There was no moon that night. The stars were obscured by clouds.

"Tell me what you feel I should know, William. I am more ignorant than I should be of legal practice and ethics, and so I hesitate to ask questions."

"You — don't read many detective stories then?" Though the words were light, the tone was heavy. He sounded tired, preoccupied.

"The only one I have ever read is *The Moonstone*. It's not helpful to me now."

She waited.

"Well, Rosamond . . . I can tell you that Roger has been treated very well, and that he is still being held. He was told as soon as he reached the courthouse that he need not tell his story or answer questions until he had legal counsel and his lawyer was present, but he said he did not want a lawyer, he wanted to tell them what they wanted to know and go home. All he said and all that was said to him was taped, and the earlier part, which took place before I arrived, was played back to me. No one there is trying to conceal anything from me, at this point. About half-past eight they stopped the questioning for the night, and Roger and I had an hour alone together. (Yes, I had brought sandwiches with me, and the sheriff's wife brought us coffee. But neither of us ate much.) Roger told me the same story he had told the sheriff and the district attorney."

Roger said he had not been home after leaving around half-past ten the night before because he could not find the Thibedeaus' boat which he had taken about nine o'clock because Suse George wanted him to. He had met Suse on the road in the evenings several times during the summer and she had told him that maybe when his car was fixed up for a good long ride, like to Boston or the White Mountains, she would go with him. He liked Suse, and he had never had a date, and he wanted to take her; that was why he had been hunting so hard for parts for the car. Still, she always seemed to be laughing at him whenever he met her, the way she used to at school; he didn't feel very sure she would ever go for a long ride with him. So when she told him one night the middle of last week that she wanted him to take her out in the boat Saturday night and teach her how to row, he thought he was in luck and he said he sure would. She told him to meet her in front of the Thibedeau camp at nine o'clock and he did. First he rowed down the river a little way, then back, and then they changed over and she rowed down, which was easy with the current; and he rowed back, and so on until she wouldn't give him the oars but just kept going and laughing at him.

Finally he told her it would be a far piece to row back against the current in the dark and they would have to change over, and she laughed, and he was getting scared, so he got up and tried to take the oars away from her, and she got mad, and said, "Do you think I come here to boatride up and down with you, you silly kid? I'm going somewhere. In case you'd like to know there's a *man* waiting for me just below here and *he's* got a car. When we get there, you can have your old boat and welcome, because *we're* going to Boston and then we're going to New York, and I'm never coming back to *this* hole in the ground."

This made Roger feel bad, and it made him mad, and besides he only half believed her. She might keep on rowing downriver for miles and then just sit and laugh if he couldn't get the boat back to Thibedeaus' camp. So he kept on trying to take the oars away from her, but she was strong, stronger than he was, and pretty soon over he went into the water. The water was deep there and he went away down. When he came up, he couldn't see anything, but he could hear her laughing and saying, "Swim, sucker, swim," from so far away that he didn't think he could catch up with her. So he swam to the bank and ran through a field to the road. On the way home he passed Thibedeaus' house but it was all dark there and he was afraid to wake them up and tell them he had let Suse use their

oars and now she had gone off with the boat. He thought he
would tell them in the morning.

By the time he got home he thought he could never sleep for
lying there thinking of what he could say to the Thibedeaus
in the morning, so he decided to change out of his wet clothes
and take a chance on his car and go down to the Harbor where
Rita Thibedeau was working, and tell her. It would be easier
to tell Rita than to tell her folks. She might help him figure
out how to find the boat and get it back so nobody would ever
know he had taken the boat at all that night. Rita was a smart
girl, and sometimes at school when Suse laughed at him Rita
used to say, "Cut it out, Suse. Leave Rodge alone. Rodge is
okay."

He got to the hotel where Rita worked, about eleven o'clock.
He went into the lobby and asked a man who was sitting there
if he knew Rita, and the man said no. Roger said she worked
there, and the man said he guessed the help stayed at the
building out back. Roger went around back and Rita was sitting on the steps but when he went up and spoke to her she
said she couldn't talk to him at that time of night; it might
wake people up. He asked her to get in the car and said they
could go where they wouldn't bother anybody. She said no, she
couldn't do that either, and he'd better go home, and she
started to go in and he felt desperate so he said he *had* to talk
to her and he was going to stay right there until she let him.

She went on in, and he sat in his car for hours, mostly because he didn't know what else to do. Finally she came back
to the door. She whispered, "Roger, are you still there?" He
got out of the car and went toward her, and she whispered,
"For heaven's sake, go home, Rodge. It's almost two o'clock."
He said, "Let me talk to you, Rita. About some trouble." She
whispered, "I've got troubles enough of my own. Go on now,
and don't come here again. Go on, or I'll call the police." That
scared him, and he drove away. He went toward home, and
once in a while a car came up behind him, and he always

thought it was the police until it passed. So finally he drove off on a woods road he knew, and stopped there, and fell asleep, he was so tired.

When he woke up it was broad daylight, and for the first time the thought came to him that when Suse got to the place where she was going to meet this man they might not have bothered to pull the boat high enough on the bank so that it could not be swept along away down to the mouth of the river and out to sea. Taking the blame for the total loss of the boat seemed to Roger more than he could face. He decided to wait there in the woods until dark, then drive as far as the little gasoline he had would take him, then walk and walk and walk. He was so scared and hungry he felt dizzy. He supposed he would have to steal food before he could walk very far. He was afraid to steal because once he had taken a case of Coke from a truck and been caught by the driver and made to bring it back and tell his name, and the driver told him he was going to give his name to the police so that if he ever stole anything again he would go to jail and stay there until he was an old man. Thinking about that, Roger had to get out of the car and be sick. After a while he got back in again and fell asleep again. When he woke up, an officer was shaking him and asking, "Are you Roger Lee?" He didn't answer at first. He was bewildered with sleep and hunger, and shaking with fright, and he thought he was going to be sick again. But the officer kept on asking him until he said yes, he was Roger Lee. Then they took him to the courthouse. On the way they didn't say anything to him, but they stopped at a place and one of the officers brought him a paper cup of tea and a couple of rolls to settle his stomach. Then he began to worry about his car, for fear somebody would find it and take it away, but the officer said they had locked it, and had the keys, and it would be all right. Roger felt a little better after that.

"This was Roger's story on the recording I heard," said the Judge, "as well as when he told it to me later. It took him a long time to think it out and tell it. Between the taping and the hour we were alone together, there were several hours of questioning during which he was frequently confused but in the main his story was not changed by the questions. Finally, the district attorney asked him suddenly, 'Roger, you know that Susan George is dead, don't you?' The boy stared at him blankly. 'Her body was found this morning on the MacIntosh Mills dam. You struggled with her, didn't you, when you made advances to her and she laughed at you? And that struggle tipped the boat over, didn't it? . . . Maybe you didn't know she wasn't a good swimmer like you. Or maybe you tried to rescue her, but the current was too strong? So you started to run for help, because you didn't really mean the girl any harm, but you were scared and you knew pretty well it was too late, so you went home and changed your clothes and ran away. It was around midnight or later when you got home. That's the truth, isn't it? . . . You'd better tell us just how it was, Roger. If you didn't mean to kill her, it wasn't murder. But if you keep on lying to us, don't be surprised if we think the worst. How'll we know you didn't hold her down? . . . Come on now, Roger. It's late and we're all tired. You and she tipped over the boat and went into the river together, didn't you, around midnight last night? Just tell us the truth about that, and you can have some supper and go to bed.'

"But when Roger could say anything he said he was the only one who went into the water, and it couldn't have been ten o'clock then because he ran all the way home and changed and was at the Harbor at eleven o'clock. He added that he knew Suse couldn't swim and had never been in a boat before, and he was trying to take care of her but she was stronger than he was. Then he rather went to pieces and the district attorney sighed and said the rest could wait until morning . . . The rest, no doubt, will include the use of a polygraph."

"What is a polygraph?"

"A lie detector."

"William, do you think he is lying? And that Ramona is lying about the time he came home wet?"

"You know Ramona, and you say she would not lie, so I believe she is telling the truth. Though if this comes to trial, his mother's testimony might not carry much weight with a jury. Anyhow, even if he did come home wet around ten o'clock, it has been established that the girl lived two or three hours after that. Who knows that Roger was not with her between eleven and twelve or one?"

"Why, William, you've just told me that he says he was out back of the hotel where Rita Thibedeau works, trying to talk to her. Why don't they ask Rita?"

"Oh," said the Judge wearily, "I'm sorry to have to tell you, Rosamond, that as soon as Roger told his story the first time, a member of the district attorney's staff left the county seat at once for the Harbor. While Roger was being questioned, Rita was found at work, waiting on dinner guests. She was called out and asked when she last saw Roger Lee. She said it must be months, probably a year or two; she couldn't remember when she had seen him. The investigator asked, 'Wasn't he here to see you around eleven o'clock last night and stayed until one or so?' She said certainly not, and what was this anyway, a sneak attack? She said she had worked two weeks straight without a break, went to bed with a sick headache as soon as she came off duty at nine-thirty last night and did not get up until noon today when she had to go back on duty, and if he didn't believe her she would call her two roommates and they would tell him the same thing."

After a minute Rosamond put her hand on his arm.

"Thank you, William. You must be dead tired. Go home now and get your sleep. Unless you forbid it, I'm going to the Harbor to see Rita."

"Tonight?"

"Yes. The sooner the better."

"Why?"

"To ask her to tell me about last night. I feel that Roger's story is true, though I have known him to lie about other things. If it is true, I don't understand why Rita would deny it."

"She didn't deny it knowingly. The investigator didn't tell her what Roger had said, or that he was being held on suspicion of a crime. Perhaps she had not even heard of the drowning. The body was found, of course, too late for it to be reported in today's papers. It probably has been on the radio but by Rita's account she has had no time to listen to broadcasts. And I doubt very much if there has been a leak yet that Roger is being held and questioned on suspicion of being involved in the girl's death."

"But Rita has said she did not see him last night. Roger says she did. I want to know the truth. And I am convinced that whatever Rita tells me will be true. She was my pupil for several years, sometimes a difficult pupil, but to the best of my belief she never lied to me."

"I know of no reason why you should not ask her. Only that you, too, should be getting some rest."

"I have just had a long nap."

"If you are resolved to go, I shall drive you. It is too late for you to be on the road alone."

"I don't deny that I should like to have you."

She went into the house for a coat, and told the girls to go to bed, that she would be away for a while but was taking her key.

As the Judge turned the car into the main road, he said, "The passing years have not affected your determination, Rosamond. I always admired it, even when I suffered from it . . . If this case is to come to trial and I am to be the attorney for the defense, perhaps I should appoint you as my assistant."

"Without portfolio," said Rosamond. After a minute, she added, "Actually what you call my determination — what I would call my resolution, my confidence that what I believe to be right is right — has increased with the years. It used not to be so unshakable as it may have appeared. Sometimes then I could be persuaded against my own judgment. I was stubborn, which is not the same thing as being resolute."

"I am surprised to hear that."

They rode on silently until Rosamond told him the name of the hotel where Rita worked, and he drove in behind it. In what had once been a livery stable and now was a dormitory only a few lights were on.

"I'll go to the one on the first floor," said Rosamond, "and ask which is Rita's room."

"You don't mind if I come with you?"

"No."

The door of the lighted room was closed, but there was a bright streak under it and between the shrunken panels. Rosamond knocked. A severe-looking elderly woman in a flowered housecoat and with her hair in pin curls peered out.

"Does Rita Thibedeau live here?"

"Yes. I suppose she's asleep. Who wants her?" She looked from Rosamond to the Judge and asked doubtfully, "You her folks?"

"We are her friends and neighbors. I used to be her schoolteacher. I'm sorry to disturb her — and you — at this late hour. But it is very important that I see her right away. So if you will just direct me to her room —"

"Oh, you'd have a time finding it. I'll go tell her you're here. What name'll I say?"

"Miss Lacey. Rosamond Lacey. It's too bad to keep you up."

"Me? I'm awake most of every night. Girls say I'm worse than a mother. Can't sleep until they're all in and generally one of them, anyway, is out till one or two o'clock. I get my sleep while they're on the job up front. Lucky I can —"

She was still talking as she disappeared down the dark upper corridor.

Rosamond murmured, "Was she up late last night, too? . . . Will you wait for us outside, William?"

Rita came running downstairs. She had thrown a raincoat over her pajamas.

"Miss Lacey! What is it? What is it? Has something happened at home? Is it Dad who came with you? The baby — is the baby sick?"

The woman was following her closely, curiously.

"No, no, dear. Everything is all right at your house as far as I know. But I have a personal reason for wanting to talk to you. Personal and confidential. Will you come out to the car for a few minutes?"

They went to the car together and Rosamond opened the door to the back seat. They got in together. William was already behind the wheel, and Rita looked wonderingly at his shoulders and the back of his head.

"A friend of mine," Rosamond explained. "I didn't want to drive down alone . . . Rita, tell me. Was Roger Lee here about this time last night?"

Rita opened her mouth to answer and then closed it. When she opened it again, she asked angrily, "Why is everybody trying to make trouble for me about Roger Lee lately? Roger Lee's nothing to me but a kid who was still going to school when I got through. I never had a date with him in my life, so why does anybody think I did? I haven't been out with anybody all summer long. Roger Lee, nor anybody else. Not once."

"Rita! Listen to me! I'm not asking you if you had a date with Roger, only if he was here in this driveway last night."

"What difference does it make whether he was or not? There was a guy here this morning asking the same question, a stranger —"

"I know there was, Rita. And you told him you hadn't seen Roger for months, maybe a year or two; you couldn't remember when you had ever seen him. I'm not a stranger, Rita. We've known each other all your life. All I am asking you is if it is true that, as far as you know, he was not here last night?"

"No. He *was* here. He asked me to go out with him, but I didn't. He's nothing but a crazy, mixed-up kid. I told him to go, and finally he went. That's all there was to it. I tell you, I don't date *anybody*. So what's all this fuss about? Why is everybody at me? I should think when a girl —"

"Rita, I'm not doubting you. I knew you would tell me the truth. So Roger was here. About what time did he come, and how long was he here?"

"Well, he was here a long time. But I wasn't with him. He drove up right after the Town Hall clock struck eleven. I happened to be sitting out on the steps because it was hot in the room and my head ached. I didn't know who he was until he got almost up to me and spoke. He asked me to come to ride, and I said no and started to go in, and he said he would wait there until I did, and I said 'Don't be a fool, Rodge,' and went upstairs. But I was scared for fear somebody had given him drinks and he might make a racket and I'd be blamed for it. That old woman watches us girls like a hawk. She ain't had any reason to complain of me to the management yet and you can be sure I don't want her to. I'm getting big tips on this job and believe me I need them for the rest of the summer. I woke up my roommates and told them I was scared and we all lay on the bed by the window and watched him. He just stayed there for two solid hours. I thought my head would spilt. Then I made the girls sit on the stairs while I tiptoed down and told him if he didn't leave I'd call the police. Then he went . . . There, that's all there is to it, Miss Lacey. Now what *I* want to know is, who's telling around that I go out with him?"

"Rita, dear, I've never heard anyone say that you did, or ever have. All you have been asked is whether you saw him last night. We wanted to know where he was."

"Why? What's he done now?"

"Nothing wrong, apparently. But he is under suspicion. You know how painful that can be . . . Roger is sleeping in the county jail tonight. Perhaps you can save him from sleeping there tomorrow night. I don't know of anyone else who can."

"Jail!"

"For questioning. You haven't heard anything about the case?"

"No. What case?"

"Much of it is still a matter of conjecture. Roger is suspected of having done something in our town last night which he could not have done if he was here at the time it happened. But only you know and can swear — if you will — that he was here."

"Gee-e-e . . . Poor old Rodge . . . And I told that guy he wasn't! . . . Who was the guy, anyway, do you know?"

"Only that he was an investigator, trying to get the facts."

"You mean I have to tell that guy I lied to him this morning?"

"If he asks you. Because it's true, isn't it? For an honest person — and you are, Rita, naturally, I know that — one lie told is likely to lead to the telling of many truths, and a good deal of effort to prove what is true. If you're willing, we'll tell the investigators that you want to take back what you said this morning and tell them the truth. One or more of them will probably come to see you. When you have told them the truth, they may try to check your new story with your room-mates, with the woman who is in charge of the house, with anyone else who might be able to give them any information on it. They may ask you to take a lie detector test, as Roger also may be asked to, tomorrow morning."

"And that's the only way to get Roger out of jail where he's been put for something he didn't do?"

"The only way I see, Miss Thibedeau," said the Judge, turning for the first time.

"This is Mr. Morrison, Rita," said Rosamond. "A lawyer who wants to get Roger cleared, so that no charges will be made against him."

"Then I'll do it," said Rita, gloomily. "It'll be tough, but I'll do it. Have to ask for time off while I go to get a friend out of jail, and everybody gossiping about how he sat out here for two hours in the middle of the night. Bet the management will tell me to turn in my uniform and never mind coming back. But who am I to think I can keep out of trouble, no matter how hard I try? No use, it comes and climbs on my back as if I was a magnet for it. I'm beginning to think I might as well be killed for a sheep as a lamb. I'm in for it, whatever I do or don't do. Same as Rodge, looks like. Brothers under the skin, you might say. Born to trouble."

"As the lark flies upward, Rita. To me that always meant that it is not easy for men and women to overcome weakness and fear, to grow strong, wise, confident — but it is not supposed to be easy. To the extent that we achieve it, it is our triumph, we are rewarded by the grace of God, and we soar."

"You always talked that way in school, Miss Lacey . . . I don't know . . . Seems as if I just can't get off the ground."

Rita bent forward, pressed her forehead against her knees, and sobbed quietly.

Rosamond got out of the car, reached for Rita's hand, and said, "Come. You and I are going up the beach."

They stumbled together through deep sand, and huddled together, wrapped in their coats, on stone which stormy waters had left barren and cold. They could hear the waves breaking at a little distance and lapping close to their feet, but it was too dark to see them. They saw each other only as black shapes.

"Rita, you have answered well the only question I had to have an answer to. You are going to do whatever you can do, in strict honesty, to help Roger. I wish I could help you in whatever battle it is you are fighting. That is why I'm going to ask you some personal questions. Of course you needn't answer them if you don't want to. Roger told you last night that he wanted to see you because he was in trouble, didn't he?"

"Yes. I guess so. I didn't pay much attention. I didn't want to get mixed up in it, whatever it was . . . What trouble was he in, anyway; do you know?"

"He had borrowed your father's boat and gone out in it around nine o'clock. He took somebody with him. This other person pushed him out of the boat and went on downriver in the boat. It was as dark then as it is here now. Roger was scared. He didn't know how to get the boat back. He knew he couldn't do it alone. He didn't dare tell anybody — either your folks or his — for fear he would be blamed, wouldn't be believed. You were the only person he could think of who might understand and help him. Your father and his were a good deal nearer than you were. Either one of them would have gone with him in search of the boat, and that would have made a great difference. If he had done that, it would have spared him and all of us much of this day's suffering. But he thought your father or his would blame him for losing the boat. So he got into his car and came all this way from his responsibility to talk to you."

"And I wouldn't listen to him. It figures."

"You are going to more than make up for that. Roger has made many mistakes in his few years of life so far, and missed many opportunities. But the fact that he sought someone last night — you — to whom he could tell the truth and who might be able to help him find the way to make things right turns out to be of prime importance to him now. It was not the wisest or the bravest action he could have taken, but it was far better than running away entirely, going off to hide by himself. He did run away and hide later. He was running away a little when he came to you. But he did not run far enough soon enough to be lost; and therein lies his hope for the future . . . Would you like to tell me why you wouldn't talk with him last night? I know you have a kind heart. You must have had a good reason."

"I thought I did. It was late. Roger's been in trouble before. I've been fighting like a wildcat to get what they call a good reputation. I wanted to keep this job and get a recommendation at the end of the season. I need a good job. I'm trying — to help my folks . . . But what's the use? It's tumbling around my ears like a house of cards. Don't think I don't know they're telling around home that — the baby's mine instead of Mom's."

"None of us can afford to worry about what is told about us that isn't true. Life is too short. Is the baby your mother's child?"

"No . . . He's mine . . . I don't think you'll tell anybody I said so, but if you do, so help me God, I'll hate you as long as I live."

"God won't help you to hate, Rita. And you are absolutely right that I shall never tell anyone what you have told me . . . I just want you to know that I feel very proud of you tonight, Rita. You have told me the truth. You have agreed to take such risk as there may be to you in telling the truth about Roger, as you know it, to others, and in proving it. I don't believe you run much if any risk, but even if you do you are ready to take it . . .

"You have made mistakes in the past, and you have suffered for them as we all do from our mistakes, great or small, but you haven't run out on them. You didn't take your baby's life. You didn't give him to strangers. You brought him home and are working to support him, to be all his mother ought to be. You have been and are so brave and strong, and are doing so much that is right that it grieves me for you to feel bitter and afraid . . . I wonder where this bitterness and fear comes from. It seems to me they would both disappear if you proudly and humbly claimed your little boy as your own, and began working openly and joyfully instead of secretly, fearfully, and angrily for his welfare and his mother's and his grandmother's . . . But all decisions concerning him must be your own for a long time. You are his mother. I have never been a mother, only a teacher. My former pupils are the nearest to own children that I can ever have. That is why every one of them is precious to me, and why I feel such personal pride in you to-night, as well as such a great longing for you to be happy . . . We must go back. We shall all be up early in the morning."

They went back past the dark hotel toward where the car

waited. A figure rose from the steps of the rebuilt stable and beckoned.

"It's the old woman that lives in the shoe," muttered Rita.

"Hi. I've been waiting to speak to you folks. You all live in North Pelham, don't you?"

"Yes. We do."

"Since you went out, I turned on my radio. Just happened to, to take up the time. There was a special newscast. They said some girl in that town was drowned last night. I suppose you knew her, did you? That's maybe what you came to tell Rita."

"We hadn't told Rita. But we did know this girl."

"*Drowned!* . . . Who was it, Miss Lacey?"

"Suse George. Around midnight to one o'clock last night."

"Oh — oh, poor Suse —"

"They said on the newscast there's some thought it may have been murder, or manslaughter anyway. They say the sheriff and the D.A. have picked up some young feller and are questioning him."

"I heard that, too, but I think he'll be released soon. He wasn't with her at the time. He was right here in this yard, trying to get Rita to come out and talk to him. She is going to testify to that. He and Rita and Suse were all schoolmates."

"Oh, was *that* who that was? I saw him drive in. He asked Rita to go to ride with him but she wouldn't. She told him to go, but he hung around a long time, till she told him again to go. He kept getting out and walking around his car, smoking cigarettes. Thin, small feller. Dark-complected."

Rita said suddenly, "Would *you* testify to that, Mrs. Wilson, if you were asked to?"

"Sure I would. Why not? When's the trial going to be?"

"We hope there won't be a trial," Rosamond said. "We hope the boy will be released tomorrow. It has been a hard day for his parents and his friends."

"Gee-e-e," said Rita. "Gee — thanks — Mrs. Wilson. It's sure — lucky you keep an eye out —"

She sobbed and ran up the stairs. Mrs. Wilson looked after her curiously.

"Broke Rita up, didn't it? She didn't show any interest in this feller last night. Too young for her anyway, isn't he?"

"He was a little boy in school when she was a big girl. She was always kind to him."

"Oh, Rita's goodhearted. She's smart too. And steady. One of the best girls in the house."

"She was a good pupil in school. A quick learner," said Rosamond. "Good night, Mrs. Wilson. I hope you can go to sleep now."

The next afternoon Judge Morrison drove Roger back to where his car waited on the woods road. It had waited as a child waits for its vanished parent, a bride for her flyer missing in action, a dog for his master (that old, old man who has been carried away on a stretcher), knowing he will come back soon, surely soon, or anyway by and by; or so it seemed to Roger to whom his car was child, bride, and dog, all three, all he had to call his own, his one favorite thing of which he had been thinking and for which he had been longing all the twenty-four hours they had been separated, while "the bee stung."

Roger slid out of the big car before it had quite stopped and stood staring with his hands in his pockets.

"Whee," he said softly. He withdrew a hand slowly and moved it toward the hood as if trying to make friends with a wild bird. There was no flutter of wings. His hand touched the hood, rested on it, moved in a long, tender caress up to the windshield, down to the door handle. "Whee," he said again. This was his thanksgiving. Then he began to get excited. His hand shook as he put the key in the lock. He flung the door wide, sprang in, and turned on the engine. He sat listening to its sweet music, a grin curved his mouth and ran up to his eyes, his hairline. He lowered a window and shouted exultantly, "She still runs, Judge. Runs fine. Runs fine as silk."

"So she does, Roger." The Judge came over and peered in at the gauge. "All she needs to get you home is a little gas. She shows empty. There's a can full in my trunk. You fill her up."

The father brings milk, the master bones, and the flyer and his bride dine by candlelight. Roger tipped the oil can high, draining the last drop.

"That's a gallon, ain't it, Judge? I ain't got no money on me, but first I get I'll pay you for this. Sure glad to get it. She was bad thirsty." With difficulty he brought his mind to bear on another matter. "I owe you for trouble you been to to get me outa this scrape, too. You write it down, and I'll pay you soon's I can. I'm going to get me a job. I'll go looking for one to-morrer morning."

"That's fine, Roger. On your way you stop in at my office and I'll have the bill ready. In the meantime, I want to make you a proposition. How would you like to drive to Boston tomorrow — maybe take your folks along — and spend a week or so with your brother and his wife? If you would, I can let you have a loan. Enough to put your car in condition for the trip and to get you there and back and have something to spend while you're gone. Your brother might find you a good job up there. If you come back, you can pay off the loan and my fee by working for me. I need somebody to look after my grounds and my office. Later on maybe you can get something better."

"Yuck, yuck," said Roger. "That sure sounds awful good, Judge. I'd sure like to do that." After a minute, he added, "I don't see why you're doing this stuff for me."

"Well, I'll tell you, Roger. I think you've had a pretty hard time and so have your folks. You all ought to have a change and get a new line of thought. Besides that, I want to see you make your parents and Miss Lacey proud of you. You can do that by finding a job as soon as you can, and sticking to it until you get a better one, and paying your own bills, and not getting into any more scrapes. That's not too much for them to ask, is it?"

"No. Judge. 'Tain't. That's a fact."

"No, because you're a man now. A man has duties to his family and his friends and himself, and it's high time you settled down and started discharging them . . . So I'll go my way now and you go yours. Your folks are probably pretty eager to see you. They know you're coming because I telephoned Miss Lacey before we left the courthouse and she said she would send them word. I expect your mother is cooking up a feast. I'll see you at my office around nine o'clock tomorrow morning then?"

"Yes, Judge. You sure will."

The Judge reached through the window and they shook hands.

"Good luck, Roger, from here on in."

Late that afternoon Rosamond for the first time was free to go to see the Georges. By then everyone in the neighborhood, even the Georges, had heard by the mysterious route news travels even where there are few radios and telephones that Roger Lee had been taken by the police for questioning about Suse's death because they had gone out together in a boat but that he had been released because, at the time she was known to have drowned, he had been at the Harbor with Rita Thibedeau.

Sim's sister had come from downstate to help with preparations for the funeral, and when Rosamond went into the always crowded little house the kitchen was more crowded than ever, with washing and ironing, and the best room with cutting and sewing.

"Well, you got here, Rosamond," said Lizy in a weak, tired voice, from above the ironing board. "The Reverend and his wife said you would as soon as Lees could spare you. Seems as if they ain't hardly enough of anybody to go round here lately, don't it? There ain't a spot where you can set down, I guess, nor one I can clean off. We've got so awful much to do before tomorrer. They say Roger's been let out. I 'spose his folks is thankful, and I'm glad for 'em. Different with us. Awful different. Ourn — ourn can't never come home agin. Little did I think Saturday night when she come a-running down the stairs in her red shoes, nor Sim when he see her put a poppy in her hair. I don't blame Roger for nothing. He hadn't ought to took her out in a boat when she'd never been, but she needn't a gone with him if she hadn't wanted to. Must have just took it into her head.

"Only thing, I don't see what made him leave her alone out there and go running off to see Rita Thibedeau. I 'spose he got mad about something. She just never ought to a got into that boat. Sim'll be sorry he wa'n't here when you come. He's took the boys to town to git 'em some shoes and pants. We was going to have to git 'em some before school started anyway. I only hope Schaeffers'll trust him a week or two till we get a few dollars together. Lucky we don't have to buy more clo'es than we do. Mame, that's Sim's sister, she brought shirts for the big boys. Vera Weymouth sent Charlie over with a nice black dress for me; must have been her best one, it's real nice; a mite big but better that than too small; Mame's took it in some and shortened it. I'm not as tall as Vera. I guess she's pretty bad off, ain't she?

"Oh, I don't see why life has to be so hard. Anybody goes through agony bringing young ones into the world, and works their fingers to the bone to bring 'em up . . . It might seem heartless to some folks, but we've took poor Suse's dark dresses and skirts to fix up for the big girls to wear tomorrow. They can wear her shoes, too, even if they don't just fit. Suse would want it that way. She had a lot of clo'es — some way she could always get a hold of something new to wear — and she don't need 'em now. We ain't going to take the little ones to the funeral. The Reverend says his wife'll stay with 'em while we're gone. She's real handy with the baby. Kind of looks as if she might be going to have one of her own. Poor kid, I pity her.

"It's a long hard row to hoe. Folks have been awful good to us. Neighbors and some I never saw before have come and brought us food. I ain't had to cook a thing since I got breakfast here Sunday morning, and the cupboard's full of meat and cakes and pies. Somebody sent a whole crate of oranges. I don't know who. Charlie brought 'em when he brought Vera's dress, but he said he didn't buy 'em. The young ones was tickled. Don't get oranges here very often, I can tell you. You got to go, Rosamond? Well, it was awful good of you to come. I wisht I hadn't had to keep at the ironing, but we've got an awful lot to do. You coming to the funeral tomorrer? Sim and I went down there this morning to see her. She looks nice, real nice. You'd think she was asleep."

"Yes," Rosamond answered. "Of course I'll be there, Lizy . . . I always think of Suse as a little girl with yellow hair, drawing big letters on the blackboard."

"She never liked to go to school, but she used to say you treated her nice. Not like teachers she had afterwards."

"I loved her," said Rosamond. "She was one of my children, and I loved them all."

On her way home she stopped at the Weymouths'. Charles and Dr. Bradford were sitting in old rocking chairs beside the shed. They drew pipes from their mouths and waved them.

"Hello, stranger. We hear you've turned lawyer overnight and won your first case. To tell the truth, I'm a little disappointed. Buddie and I kind of thought we might win you over to the medical profession."

"Seems to me it was high time she started doing *something*," Charles said. "Not just go on crocheting and playing solitaire the rest of her life."

"Very funny," said Rosamond. "I don't know which one of you is funnier. Now I *like* to find two people comfortably rocking and pipe-smoking their way into the sunset!"

"The reason we have these chairs to rock in," said Dr. Bradford, "is that Vera ordered them out of the house an hour ago, when her handsome new lounge chairs were delivered."

"She's got them in her room," said Charles. The parlor had become Vera's room. "She was hoping somebody would stop in today to see them."

"I'm on my way."

But when she looked into Vera's room, Vera lay with her eyes closed and did not open them. Hazel waved silently from the kitchen where she was getting supper.

"Everything is so clean here," Rosamond whispered. "Everything smells so good . . . I've just come from Georges'."

"Poor souls. Isn't it dreadful?"

"But I don't think they quite realize, somehow."

"And that's a blessing. It's fine the Lee boy has been cleared. Vera has been simply thrilled ever since she heard it. She seems to think she cleared him, singlehanded."

"How is she, Hazel?"

"She isn't gaining at all. She's drowsy a good deal of the time. But sometimes she is surprisingly alert. When do you think Sandy will get here?"

"Before the end of this week, I'm sure."

"That's what his father thinks."

"We must make plans right away so that you and Al can go home. We hadn't meant to let you stay here so long. It will be Labor Day soon. The summer is almost over."

"We'll stay until Sandy comes. You must all go to the service tomorrow. Charles is to be one of the bearers. It's an experience for us to be here like this, you know. It's many years since Al and I have worked so closely together on a case. Vera and I get along fine, and Al and Charles have become great friends. It's as if they had been boys together, the way they sit and reminisce. And I'm flattered because Charles praises my cooking. He says it tastes —"

"Who's whispering out there?" called Vera.

Rosamond hurried in.

"I was speaking to Hazel, Vee. We thought you were asleep."

"Rosamond?" She knew it was, though she had not opened her eyes. "They say Roger Lee's got home."

"Yes. He came back this afternoon."

"His folks was glad to see him, wa'n't they?"

"I suppose they're the most thankful tonight they have ever been in their lives."

"Ramona know they tried to get me as witness against him?"

"Not yet, Vee, but she will."

"No matter whether she does or not. I give that investigator what-for. Told him a thing or two. Told him if he wanted to drag me into court I'd make him wish he hadn't. I'd lose his case for him, I promised him. It's one thing for a sick old woman to chatter for the sake of hearing herself talk, I told him, and another thing to get her to swear to it. I may be down but I ain't out. I've still got my wits about me."

"You have, Vee. You certainly have. You know what is true and what isn't. And there's nothing so powerful as truth."

"Sandy'll grin when he hears about it. He's always had kind of a soft spot for Roger. When I used to sputter about him going anywhere with Roger, he'd say, 'Rodge can't hurt me, Ma, and I wun't do him any harm. Rodge may turn out all right.'"

"Sandy'll be glad Roger has been cleared. And he'll be proud as a peacock of you."

"Remember that grin of Sandy's?"

"Yes, Vee. I do . . . You'll be seeing it in a day or two now."

"Kind of cute, hain't it? I lay here thinking about it. He'll have a lot to tell over when he gets back."

"And you'll have a lot to tell him."

"I wouldn't let them call him just because I got sick. That would have been foolish. When anybody's set out for any-where, they ought to go . . . Besides that, I wanted to have the house fixed up some before he got here. Looks good, don't it?"

"Lovely."

"You see my new chairs, come today?"

"Indeed I do. One of them. It's handsome. I'm in the other. It's like floating on a cloud."

"I'll have to try them out tomorrow . . . I've got together everything I had my mind set on. Them chairs was the last of it . . . Suse George run off and got drownded. Roger Lee might have gone to jail for it, hadn't been for me . . . But my boy's all right. He went to college . . . And he got him a nice girl . . . Say, he's in California now; you know that?"

"He is, Vee?"

"Yes, sir. Worked his way clean out to the Golden Gate. I never see but two states in my life, and not much of them. But he has . . . He'll be home tomorrow. And when he walks in here I got a surprise ready for him. New kitchen linoleum . . . and a white sink . . . Telephone a-coming . . . Wool rug in the parlor . . . Curtains . . . Studio couch . . . Two big easy chairs . . . I don't . . . thinks likely . . . anybody anywhere's . . . got a better home than . . . my boy . . ."

12

$IT'S$ so still, isn't it?" said Margaret the next afternoon.
"Even when a breeze stirs, it is so faint that I can feel it only
with the palms of my hands and on the back of my neck."

"But you hear it among the leaves," said Jay. "Like a
Quaker grandmother coming down the church aisle behind
you."

"I wonder why Quaker grandmothers rustled more than
other grandmothers."

"I don't suppose they did, really. But their rustling was
noticed more because of the silence around it."

"That's like here, too. We are both speaking low. But it
sounds loud . . . I love this spot."

They had driven to the foot of the mountain and climbed
the trail to the top. The road was narrow, between bushes
which scraped both sides of a car; deep sand ruts and smooth
bare ledges by turns. The trail was so little used that no
stranger, even if he had risked driving over the road, would
have noticed where it began or been able to follow it once his
feet had been set upon it. Jay had come here the first time with
Joe Barron. This was the third time he had brought Margaret.
The first time she came they had found a boulder with a flat

top and pushed and pulled each other until they could sit on it and look off over the poplars and white birches to where Lacey's Pond lay like a crumpled, sky-blue kerchief. This had become their boulder.

"Why, Peggy? Tell me why."

"When I was little I wanted a crystal ball. More than anything. I used to ask for one for Christmas or when people were going away and asked what I would like for them to bring back to me. Until I had been laughed at too much. 'We think our Margaret's secret ambition is to be a fortuneteller' . . . 'Darling, Santa Claus makes just about everything but crystal balls' . . . 'Couldn't the child think of something easy, like spinning straw into gold?' I suppose they thought I wanted to see into the future. I didn't. That wasn't the kind of crystal ball I wanted at all. I wanted one that would show me what people I knew were doing when I wasn't there, what they said when I wasn't there, and most of all what they were thinking that they didn't say. I just wanted to understand . . ."

"So you love this spot because —"

"Obviously because it gives me my crystal ball. Of course not just as I had imagined it. A crystal ball has a magic all its own. But I can see a pond and I know it's Lacey's Pond. I see an old-fashioned little girl in a sunbonnet raking hay beside it; suddenly all the water rises up toward the sky and I see fish flapping and gasping in the mud, and then plop! Back comes all the water again."

"Did its weight kill the gasping fish?"

"I can't tell. They are still under it . . . I see the Lacey place. The shop is closed. The screen doors are hooked. It is deserted, but only for a little while. There will be at least five for supper there . . . Most of the houses are deserted just now, because down in the town a tall, homely young man is saying words over a girl who was drowned . . . I see small children in the yard of the George place. Eileen is telling them a story, holding a baby on her knees. It is a girl baby, too young ever to remember a sister who died at the age of twenty-four; died in darkness and cold, struggling to find light and warmth . . . I see Vera Weymouth asleep; and the Bradfords sitting together in the rocking chairs beside the shed; her quick little hands are idle, for once, in her lap, and one of his covers them. They are not talking. There is nothing they need to say or to hear . . . Only at the Lees' are house doors locked and barn doors bolted. Because they have gone to Boston. But Paul's cattle are in the pasture and Ramona's hens burrowing in the sand under the sunflowers, and tonight Pete Thibedeau will come to milk the cows and give them grain, fill pans with water and scatter corn and pick up eggs . . ."

"You must wear contact lenses that magnify, to see such detail. Such as which doors are hooked and which bolted. I can't do that."

"What do you see?"

"Down there? A settlement in the foreground with others like it in the distance. Last summer, when I first saw it, I thought it was absolutely unique; or rather I didn't see it as a settlement at all, but as one incredible woman dressed in the magnificant robes of a wondrous past and secure within the moat which surrounded her castle. I went away and wrote about her, not expecting anyone to believe what I said, only half-believing it myself by then. But other people *did* believe it, or some part of it, and I see now that the reason they could believe it was that they had lived in one or more of the settlements which surround this one in spreading circles reaching out and out until they take in all the territory so far inhabited by mankind. So had I, but the difference between us was that they knew it, or at least suspected it, and I didn't . . .

"So the moat was drained and the bridges lowered, the past receded, the future approached, and this incredible woman is revealed as not incredible at all . . . She says that what I wrote was a gross exaggeration, and she is right. What she does not know is that she herself is something of a living exaggeration. She says she is ordinary and that I wrote of her as if she were fantastic. She is not fantastic, and neither is she ordinary.

She is extraordinary simply in that she has more than most people of several commodities the world needs more of — health, enthusiasm, intelligence, pride, forthrightness, conviction, steadiness, the will and the ability to find these qualities in others, to whatever degree they exist, to dredge them up even if they are flapping and gasping in the mud, clean them off, give them a polish, and put them to work."

"In short, she stops at nothing which contributes — or might — to making her world the kind of place she wants to live in."

"Exactly. And that's what's extraordinary. Her concept of what the world should be, her belief that it could be so, will one day be so, and even now sometimes is; her unquenchable spirit which admits no self-doubt, no fear of ridicule, of the results of taking responsibility, or of ultimate defeat; no suppression either of her own opinions or those of others; no wasted — and wasting — sympathy. She is a woman of both thought and action and inspires other people to thought and action . . . Which leads me to say that I have been doing a good deal of the former lately and shall now proceed to the latter. Peggy, this is a fine spot, I agree, but we are now going down off this mountain, get into my car, and go to see your family."

"I don't think they're at home. In fact, I'm sure they're not."

"How do you know? Have you talked with them by telephone lately?"

"No. But I know their — habits."

"Their habits may have changed. You haven't been to see them lately, have you?"

"No."

"Why do you keep stalling on our driving down? Do you think they wouldn't like me?"

"They would almost certainly like you, Jay. Doesn't everybody?"

"No . . . Do you?"

"That should go without saying."

"Not with me it doesn't. Say it."

"Yes. I like you."

"You don't like your parents?"

"I've never felt — close to them."

"I'd gathered that. But is that their fault or yours? And is it any reason for not going to see them once in a while, when you have a chance? For acting as if they didn't exist? I feel as if I know you so well, Peggy, even though you've told me so little about yourself and nobody else has told me anything — but the one thing I can't understand is your not having any contact with your family or even mentioning them. I know everyone your age wants to be on his own, independent of older generations, free of unwanted advice and all that, but you carry it to extremes."

"You'd better not lecture me, Jay Schuyler."

"Lecture you! Holy Moses, Peg West — if that's your name, and sometimes I have a crazy idea it isn't — we've spent ten days together. If I ever act as if I'm really thinking about anything but you, that's just what it is — an act. As it happens, I've never been in love in my life until now, so maybe this isn't love, but it's *something* brand new to me. Sometimes I want to do more than lecture you. But you're hiding something. What is it? Is it just one thing or a lot of things? I have just two more full days before I'm slated to head back to Minnesota. I can't leave without knowing where to write to you, for instance. Where are you going to be this winter? Home? Where's home? Away at school? What school? Sometimes I wake up in the night thinking, 'Good God, how do I know she's not secretly married?' "

"Oh, poor Jay. I'm not married. That I swear."

"Say it again."

"I'm not married."

"In love with anybody?"

"I'm not — quite sure."

"As long as you're not quite sure, tell me this: how much longer are you staying at Miss Lacey's?"

"I'd planned to leave Saturday."

"The day after I do . . . *Where are you going?*"

"To New York."

"New York! That's not a long flight from Chicago, if I . . . what in blazes are you going to New York for?"

"To meet my parents and sister."

"They're in *New York?*"

"They will be by Friday night. It's — a trip. We'll only be there a few days."

"Well, no wonder you — Peggy, I just had a great idea! I'll drive you to New York! You can leave one day early, can't you? Wouldn't that be fun?"

"Yes. Yes, I'd like that, Jay."

"We'd be there by dinner time, and I could meet your family then, couldn't I? After all, who knows when I'm going to be able to label this feeling I'm feeling, and come dashing back across the country and pound masterfully on their door? That will be rough enough on them, if it happens, even if I'm not a total stranger. However you feel about them, I want to meet them. And they have a right to meet me."

"I know. And that's what we'll do, Jay. I'll ride down with you, and on the way I'll tell you all about my family. Then we'll meet them together. I'll telephone the hotel tonight and leave a message to say I'm coming Friday with a friend who will have dinner with us. They'll like you, and you'll like them, and I'll like everybody — which is a brand-new feeling *I'm* feeling lately and one which has to be adjusted to before I can weigh it in ounces and pounds . . . I have an uncle I've never seen. He went to live in Australia when he was a young man and used to write me letters which he signed, 'With tons of love,' and sometimes 'Tons and tons of love.' I couldn't imagine a ton of anything. Besides, I had forgotten what he looked like, and liked his letters mostly for the stamps. He married, of course, and had children of his own, and I suppose they are basking or whatever it is one does in a ton or more of love. He hasn't written to me for at least ten years . . . You've said you exaggerate, too, Jay. Let's never exaggerate what we feel for each other. Let's never pretend. Let's take our time, and see what comes, and be absolutely honest. I haven't *liked* keeping secrets from you about my family. But I did, for a while, because I wanted you to know me before anyone else was involved . . . No more secrets, Jay. Ever."

"No more secrets."

"Now let's not talk any more. This is our place, but we won't be coming to it again for a long time. Let's just *be* here, and watch my crystal ball."

"You watch your crystal ball. I'll watch you."

The sun was just rising Friday morning as Margaret and Jay left for New York, and Rosamond, on the porch steps, saw the sky above the mountain turning from dusty pink to a metallic brilliance. This would, she thought, be a strange day. She would be spending it entirely alone and with little to do. She and Eileen had cleaned the house the two days before, with help at times from Jay and Margaret; and they had baked. All was in readiness for the opening of the shop today for the Labor Day weekend. But she would not open it.

"What shall I do?" she asked herself. "I must do something. This is one day when I must not think . . . Well, there are the breakfast dishes —"

An hour or so later she loaded her car with big metal cans of water, a broom, a mop, a bucket, brushes, cleaning cloths, and drove to the meetinghouse. The sight of it standing quietly against the harshly brilliant sky, its plain lines, its dignity, its gentleness were soothing to her. It was as alone as she, and unthinking as she wished to be.

She pushed open a door and went to sit for a few minutes in the Lacey pew. The clock on the wall had stopped. All the windows were closed. There was the smell of old books, old carpet, old wood blended into the fragrance of a simple faith.

She bent forward, resting her elbow on her knee, and her forehead on the back of her hand.

Love beareth all things, believeth all things, hopeth all things, endureth all things . . .

Rosamond rose and opened both doors and all the windows. She swept and dusted, cleaned the lamps, washed the woodwork. Hour after hour went by and she never paused in her work nor raised her eyes from it. She was unaware of weariness or hunger. If cars passed along the road she did not hear them.

She did not know that anyone was in the room until a familiar voice exclaimed, "Well, so here you are!"

Then she looked up and saw him in the doorway. The tall young man, hardly more than a boy; his crisp hair curling damply in the heat; his blue eyes twinkling out at her from a face as brown as leather; his shirt missing a button; his long, bare, brown arms. She saw him and could not speak. If a word had come it would have been the wrong one.

"Well! Do you think you're looking at a ghost?" he asked. "Weren't you expecting me?"

"No, I — well, how *could* I expect you to find me here? And who gave me any warning? Besides, you're two inches taller and six shades darker —"

"That's more like it. Giving me heck the first thing. Now I know I'm home."

Sandy came toward her with his broad, bright grin. He took her into his arms, soapy cloth and all, and hugged her.

"Hey, am I glad to see you, whether you're glad to see me or not! Thought once I'd be here a couple of days ago, but I got delayed. More on that later. I've got so much to tell you it may take most of the weekend, and it can't take more than that because Monday's Labor Day, and more on *that* later. Come on out and meet the guys. They're in a hurry because they've still got what Bill calls a fur piece to go, but I told them I couldn't ride by the end of Lacey's Lane without turning in after three months of pioneering out West. Then — nobody home but Pansy! When I saw your car out front here,

I let out a war whoop. I said, 'Thar she is, boys. Sure as shootin.' Come on out. See the car that has crossed the continent even if we did have to carry it part of the way."

She saw that their car looked top-heavy under a rack filled with suitcases, cartons, and blankets. She saw boys springing out of it from both sides, and felt the grip of their hard young hands; all brown like Sandy, two tall like Sandy, one short and stocky. She heard names and loud laughter, said travel evidently had agreed with them.

"Well, we'd better get going, Wey. Have to get rid of him, Miss Lacey, and then drive three hundred miles on beyond. Lucky there's a superhighway going north."

"I'll be over tonight, Rosamond. Have I got stories to tell! And news for you! For John and Eileen, too. Especially John. Wait until you hear it . . . Shove over, chum. I'll bring the old crate to the end of the line. My line, that is."

Sandy was sliding under the wheel when Rosamond said, "Just a minute, Sandy. Will you come back into the church? There is something I should tell you. Before you go home."

He followed her in. The grin was suddenly gone from his face, and the twinkle from his eyes.

"What is it, Rosamond? You sound as if —"

"Yes, Sandy. If it — had to happen, I wish it hadn't happened when it did. Your mother died last night."

"Mom?"

"She had been ill most of the summer, but she didn't want you to know. She said that when a person sets out to go somewhere, he should go. She has been very brave. No one could have been braver. And she might have lived weeks longer, but she didn't. They would have been hard weeks."

"How's Dad?"

"He's all right. John went over to see him as soon as the word came, and stayed the rest of the night. When he came home to breakfast, before going to work, he said your father was all right."

"He's home? Alone?"

"As far as I know, he is there. But he isn't alone. Eileen has been there all day. And he has other friends with him. He — and your mother — have had no lack of friends this summer. But it will be a great comfort to him to see you, Sandy. So go along now."

She still had her cleaning cloth in her hand. She stood, waiting, until the sound of the car died away. Then she knelt and began to scrub the floor around the pulpit, though she had scrubbed it thoroughly an hour before.

She was alone again, and the sun only halfway down the sky.

~~~~ *13*

T H E night was warm for late September.

Rosamond was sitting on the porch when William came. He eased himself gratefully into the chair beside hers, folded his hands around the hat on his knees, and sighed.

"The air is good out here," he said. "Different from anywhere else, somehow. I've always noticed that."

"No place is just like any other place," said Rosamond. She thought of the Chinese communes, shivered, and added, "Nor ever will be in a free world."

"No. But the difference in the air here is marked. There is something which doesn't yield even to seasons. It blends with mayflowers, apple blossoms, lilacs; roses, berries, drying sweet grass, goldenrod, stacked corn, frost on the pumpkin; snow and ice. But it's always here, and it's not only the fragrance, the flavor. It's a quality, and affects sight and sound as well; makes both more distinct."

"I feel so, too. I wonder if it really does. When I become aware of it, I ask myself if it can be explained by my reliving the way it impressed me when I was very young; when all my senses had the keenness of childhood and I saw and heard and smelled whatever was around me with delicious, intense, almost electrifying distinctness."

"That doesn't explain it for me. I was past thirty years old the first time I came here."

"So you were, William."

"So if there has to be an explanation for me it is that this is where you are."

"Oh, William, dear — I hope you don't still —"

"Yes, I do still, Rosamond. But not in any way which should put a regretful note in your voice. I am happy to have been able to do exactly what you asked me to do, forty years ago. I found and have lived a satisfactory life apart from you. But you did not ask me to share it with another woman. If you had, I should have refused, difficult as it would have been for me to refuse you anything. And as it still is. Ever since I met you, I have wanted your happiness more than anything else. Which is not to say that what I wanted for myself did not once appear to me to conflict with what I wanted for you, or that when it did I didn't suffer from the battle. But what I wanted most won, and since then I have been content to the degree that you have seemed happy whenever I saw or heard from you. I can tell you now that your continuing to come to me for any legal advice you needed, as your father had done, was most gratifying to me. And now it has led to what I had never dared hope for — our association this summer in various activities of interest to us both, and my feeling no hesitation about driving out, as tonight, to sit and talk with you for a while as a lifelong friend whom I greatly admire."

"And I am at least as grateful for such an association as you are . . . I surely never thought of going to anyone else with Lacey legal matters. You have always had the complete confidence of our family, in every way. And it was a great comfort to me to see you now and then during my father's illness and after his death . . . Though I will admit it was a bit unsettling always to see that 'purple' cow holding down the papers in the basket on your desk."

Now why had she mentioned that? She knew too well. It had escaped her because of a sense of guilt as spontaneous as the irritation of forty years before which had led to his having the Delft cow and which had led so soon after to her ending the relationship between them.

During her first year of teaching after her graduation from college, the new young lawyer in town had been a member of the school committee. Though they had long conversations after school whenever he visited it that year, he was scrupulously careful to show her no attention publicly until the summer vacation. Then he began inviting her to ride in one of the first automobiles in the town, to band concerts in the square, to picnics in Pelham Park, to Chautauqua programs; and she had accepted his invitations for many reasons which did not include any serious intention of joining her life with his or even of continuing to go out with him after the summer was over. But her parents read significance into her acceptance; so did her neighbors; so did William. Suddenly she found everyone happily assuming that Miss Lacey and Attorney Morrison would soon announce their engagement.

Her own intentions then became ambivalent. She asked herself why not; ten years older was not too much older; he was a fine-looking, able man with the build of a fullback — a position he had played on the Dartmouth team in his undergraduate years before going to Harvard Law School; his future was assured, he had no bad habits, he was the soul of consideration; her family loved and admired him. She told herself she could not and would not, because, though she also admired him, *she* did not love him. She asked herself if she could not learn to love him and she answered no. Her no called for a reason. It seemed too absurd for a girl to be unable to love such an estimable, eligible, and personable young man unless she was in love with someone else. Unwilling, either consciously or unconsciously, to give herself the real reason, she sought almost desperately for a flaw in his personality. The one she found was the lack of a sense of humor; at least, of a sense of humor which she could appreciate. Sitting beside

him for hours when he was deadly serious, already a little
pompous, was as much as she could bear. Hearing him begin
one of his familiar, heavy attempts at being humorous became
altogether unbearable the winter night when he picked up the
Delft cow from the what-not for perhaps the twentieth time,
and for perhaps the twentieth time recited:

> "I never saw a purple cow,
> I never hope to see one;
> But I can tell you, anyhow,
> I'd rather see than be one."

That was the night she cried out — it seemed to her she
screamed — "It's not purple! It's blue! And don't you know
that afterwards Gelett Burgess wrote:

> 'Ah, yes, I wrote the Purple Cow —
> I'm sorry, now, I wrote it!
> But I can tell you, anyhow,
> I'll kill you if you quote it.' "

Instantly the cruelty of what she had said and what she was
doing smote her like a physical blow, and the result was a
flood of shame and tenderness.

She put her hand over the ornament William was holding,
smiled at him, and said, "But you like the silly thing, don't
you? I do, too. Aunt Rachel brought it to me from Germany
when I was three years old. I want you to have it, William.
As a keepsake. I hope it will be a talisman, and bring you all
the good fortune you so richly deserve. Come, I'll put it in
your overcoat pocket. Good night, William."

In the sleepless hours which followed, she had seen clearly
for the first time the way she must follow; and when next she
sat down with William it was to tell him that she could not
go out with him again, that she could never love him, and that

he must not let her decision darken his life or she could never forgive herself for any encouragement she might have given him to think that her decision would be otherwise.

Now, after forty years, the Delft cow was again between them, arousing latent feelings of guilt and regret in her but a quite different memory for him. He sat treasuring his for a minute, looking up under his eyebrows through the maple leaves at the sky where a sickle moon swung. Then he turned to her, smiling, and said:

"I never thought it might be unsettling to you, Rosamond. It has always been there, ever since you gave it to me. That evening was one I like to be reminded of, and shall never cease recalling with pleasure. You had always been so self-contained. But that night you were in a gay mood. You teased me. You seemed very young. Then you became a little angry with me because I called the cow purple. You had never done that before. I was — enchanted by it. Finally, suddenly you were sorry you had been angry, and though you were too proud to say so in words, your face and your voice said it, and, like a child, you offered me as a gift something you had treasured since you were three years old. I tried to decline it, but you wouldn't listen. You put it into my overcoat pocket yourself . . . That night I went back to town with enough happiness to last a lifetime, even though afterward, for a while, I did not know it. I have long wanted to thank you, Rosamond, for being of the stuff of which fairy tales are made and letting me know you long enough so that I came to love you. Otherwise, I doubt that I should ever have known what love is."

Now it was her turn to look at the sky until the blurred rim of the moon had become sharp.

"If you feel you have anything for which to thank me," she said, low, "I am glad. And grateful. You are such a fine man, William, and have always been, I wish that nothing you valued need have been denied you."

"I've had a great deal," he answered comfortably. "I have not for a long time felt denied. It is enough for me that we are friends." Then he chuckled. "You spoke just now of that 'purple' cow. I assure you I have never called it purple since you told me in such certain terms that it is blue."

She laughed with him.

It had all happened so long ago.

"The light in the studio makes me feel that your father must be over there cleaning his brushes and stretching canvas for tomorrow's painting."

"I know. But it's Eileen and John. They moved over day before yesterday. It's really a charming little house, and they're so proud of it."

"Does it seem strange to you to be alone again?"

"No. I don't feel alone. I never have. Of course I see almost as much of Eileen as I ever did. I'm very fond of her. And of John, too. I'm glad they won't be leaving before the baby comes around the first of the year."

"Leaving? Are they thinking of leaving?"

"People who came up from the Harbor to the services were very much impressed by John's sermons, and perhaps even more by his prayers which are extraordinarily moving and memorable. Several of them have sent members of their church boards to hear him this month. He has been asked by two churches in Connecticut and one in New York to come as a candidate this fall."

"I have never happened to hear him preach."

"You really should, William."

"I will. Next Sunday. Lately I have been hearing from others that he is a splendid speaker. Interesting that I never heard that when he had the Methodist church."

"I doubt if he was then. He was too disturbed. Really crushed by trying to carry more responsibilities than he had the strength for, by struggling to do what he could not do well and what he personally could not feel was essential and thereby exhausting and disappointing himself so that he failed in what he wanted to do most . . . But he is well now, and his call to full-time ministry is very strong. I feel that if they are asked to serve in a parish where he would have an assistant primarily to work with social and fund-raising groups, they will go there. John is by nature a spiritual leader."

"Then I wish we could offer him that opportunity in North Pelham. It would be possible if our pulpit were vacant or about to be, and if the Methodists would unite with us. But they are still having supplies and our minister, though a poor speaker, is much loved in the parish."

"In any case, I believe John and Eileen should begin again, when they do, in a place where they are unknown. They would be handicapped in the village by their earlier experience there, and by misunderstandings . . . He has said that, wherever he goes, it will be for no more than ten months of the year, and they will spend every July and August in their home here, holding our services as he has been doing. He has learned he needs the country, and time to work with his hands. And we need him . . . How is Roger doing, William?"

"Very well. Like any boy, he needs training and watching. I try to provide both, along with criticism and praise wherever it seems indicated. He has agreed to let me hold his bankbook, which he takes and returns to me every payday. So far he has saved over twenty dollars besides paying a dollar a week on the fifty he owes me. Most fortuitously, he and I found a pair of oars overhead in my garage and I sold them to him for fifty cents, so he is square with Mr. Thibedeau."

"You are a good friend to him, William."

"He seems to regard me so, I'm glad to say. Sometimes I wonder if I should try to guard against his becoming too devoted to me."

"Why?"

"Perhaps he could do more rewarding work than cleaning my office and taking care of my grounds and car. He polishes my car every single day . . . I have been thinking of suggesting that he take some evening courses at the high school in Port City. How good a pupil was he?"

"The last term I taught he was eight years old. He had been

coming to school for three years and had not yet learned to read. He could count quite well, and even add and subtract small figures. He was extremely shy. I think Roger has been discouraged most of his life by the fact that Larry, his brother, two years younger, is extremely bright. Larry graduated from high school at the age of fifteen, went to stay with relatives in Boston and did very well in a school of accountancy. He is now a certified public accountant. Paul and Ramona are very proud of Larry. They have mostly worried over Roger, and that hasn't helped . . . I think Roger needs to be devoted to someone, to get a feeling of accomplishment, and to taste success. I was very pleased when you asked him to stay at your house through the week. When he comes home for the week-ends he is treated like a prodigal son and he needs that. He comes to church with Paul and Ramona . . . I wish you would keep him for a year, if he wants to stay. Then perhaps he could take aptitude tests. If he has any special ability, it is probably in mechanics. He certainly loves cars as if they were living things, and I can imagine the delight it is to him to polish yours."

"What a difference a young person makes in a house!"

"Especially in houses like yours and mine where no young person has lived for a long time. And you began with a really young one. When Eileen and John first came to stay with me, I saw them as practically children. But then Margaret Frye came, and within twenty-four hours I knew that the Struthers were adults. How touchingly young the really young seem to people like us who haven't been with them through all their days and nights since babyhood! Especially if we feel respon-sible for them, as I know you do for Roger and as I did for Margaret. I was somewhat prepared by Sandy Weymouth who has been running in and out here with his friends since the last year I was his teacher. But they never seemed to be asking me to teach them anything, to train them as you express it. When I felt called upon to teach them, it was my own idea and I had to corral them, take and hold them by the ear, so to speak, while I did it. To me Margaret was in her way as Roger is to you in his. She felt a great need of me; of Eileen and John, too, but as a child needs an older sister and brother. Of me she was silently asking the key with which to open the door of her life. I knew that and she knew I knew it. I was her last resort, as you are Roger's. Because keys produced too late rarely fit the lock."

"What do you hear from Margaret?"

"Very little, directly. I didn't expect to. Really hoped I wouldn't. She wrote us one letter immediately after flying home from New York with her family. (Someone was driving their car through for them.) She thanked us for a wonderful summer, said she and Jay had had fun on the ride to New York and she was waiting for his telephone call as soon as he reached home; she must go shopping for fall clothes but wouldn't leave the house until Jay had called; would write us again after returning to Carleton. She concluded with, 'Here I am, a Senior! THEN what????' I've had a fine, warm, appreciative letter from her father, and two from her mother, all exuberant; they are delighted with Margaret, and delighted with Jay. I only hope they restrain themselves from expressing this delight too freely. But now Margaret is back in college and on her own, as she should be. I know this from Jay who writes me two or three times a week — long, rambling, amusing, enthusiastic letters stuffed into big envelopes along with clipped columns, editorials and news stories about Mr. Frye, and ticket stubs and other souvenirs of his dates with Margaret. He took her back to Carleton when she went, and goes down to see her weekends."

"How do you feel now about what that young man did to your life by writing one of his columns about you?"

"Well, as I have convinced him, he didn't write about me but about his own feeling, at the time, that today's civilization was an alder thicket in which he was lost, and about a lady genie whom his need conjured up to give him a sense of direction . . . Nevertheless, he chose to give this unearthly creature my name, the column happened to be read by such diverse citizens as a Mrs. Crawford who wanted to fill a blank space on her PTA program and a Mr. Frye who was more or less aware that his daughter needed what Jason Schuyler claimed to have found."

"And then the avalanche."

"Not exactly. It was not that sudden. And because of my obvious limitations it has never and can never become that big. But gradually, since that column was published, I have been given many opportunities I should never have had otherwise and which I did not know I wanted, but for which I am very grateful."

"For which many other people also have reason to be grateful."

"As we should all be grateful for our opportunities, and prove our gratitude by seizing them. In my school we used to choose, by vote, every September, a motto to be drawn at the top of each blackboard. The most popular, judging by the fact that it was chosen many times, was 'Seize the Opportunity.' Because an unforeseen opportunity came to me and was seized, others came to you, and to Sandy Weymouth, to the Struthers, to the Fryes, to Jay himself; to the Barrons, the Lees, the Thibedeaus, even to Vera Weymouth — and all were seized. It has made a very lively summer, and I hope the end is not yet."

"I'm sure it isn't. You mentioned Sandy Weymouth. He has returned to the University, I suppose?"

"Yes. Oh, you haven't heard the news about Sandy? After spending the summer working his way to the West Coast and back he went to see the girl he had been going with for several months. She was helping to close the girls' camp where she had been a counselor. He was there when Vera died, as a matter of fact. We hadn't let him know that Vera was ill; that was her wish. Sandy and Sheila, by correspondence, had agreed to be married this year, if Sheila could get a campus secretarial position to help finance them until Sandy has his degree, after which they hoped she could get hers. When he saw her at the camp, she told him she had the position. When Sandy reached home he was bringing the news that they were engaged and would be married at Christmas. As things were, I did not hear of it until the evening after Vera's funeral. Sheila had come for the service, and after they returned to the house, they told his father of their plans. Then Charles insisted that Sheila stay overnight with me. But she got supper there for the three of them, and they had a long talk, in the course of which Charles told them that Sandy's mother, in her will, had left Sandy the thousand dollars which her father had left to her, and the contents of the house; and he pointed out that the Weymouth place would be Sandy's when he was through with it. He asked if this wouldn't make it possible for them to be married at once and for Sheila to return to her studies and graduate with Sandy, if they lived at home there this year to reduce expenses and to 'look after' him.

"Naturally they found this not only possible but eminently desirable. It was all settled when Sandy brought Sheila over here that night, as prearranged by Vera's telephone which was installed the very day she died. They were married at Sheila's home on September tenth. Charles went up there with Sandy. I went with Al and Hazel Bradford. We four were the only guests beside Sheila's family. Charles came back with us and went on for a few days' visit to the Bradfords. Sandy and Sheila came home late that evening and found the house cleaned, aired, lighted, flowers in every room, and a feast spread. Eileen, Ramona Lee, Rita Thibedeau, and Geneviève Barron had done that. The next day, the very first day of their honeymoon, Sandy took Sheila to call at every house in the neighborhood. We were all so pleased it was like a royal procession. We did everything but stand on the roadside and toss flowers as they passed."

"Too bad Jay wasn't here to make a column of it."

"So he said, when I wrote him about it. Also said he was green with envy and asked, in case he ever persuaded Margaret to marry him, and if they were careful to do it during June, say, or more likely September, when John and Eileen don't expect to be here, what the chances were that they could have the studio for their honeymoon. I replied that when he could fairly claim he had a bride-to-be, he could take up the matter of reservations with the Struthers if he still wished to."

"More opportunities seized, or about to be . . . What I would like to know, Rosamond, is which of all the new opportunities which have come to you this year you have seized and used with the greatest satisfaction to you, personally?"

"Of those which have so far come . . . It is hard to select . . . I have enjoyed them all."

She paused to reflect. He waited patiently, his chair creaking faintly with his breathing.

"I might say it was finding by experience that I am Lizzie. At least that I surely am not Laura. But —"

"Wait a minute. Enlighten me. *Who* is Lizzie?"

She laughed.

"There is a poem by Christina Rossetti, called 'The Goblin Market.' About two sisters, Lizzie and Laura, who lived alone together, happily isolated, until one day Laura was tempted to visit the goblin market and tasted its fruit which drew her back to eat of it again, over and over. At last Lizzie ventured out to learn what was hypnotizing Laura. She learned a great deal that day about the evils of that market place, but she was not hypnotized by it, and with the knowledge she brought home she was able to save Laura. Her pleading, 'Oh, Laura, come: come with me home . . . Let us get home before the night grows dark,' had fallen on deaf ears because she did not know what she was calling Laura from, what it was she feared for Laura, for herself, for their way of life. But when Lizzie had gone forth, and learned, and knew, 'Laura awoke as from a dream,' and came home."

"So what is it Lizzie fears for Laura, for herself, for her way of life?"

"The Lizzies of this world don't really fear, I think, a known enemy. They set to fighting it, and they fight with relish . . .

So I will say that the new opportunity which brings me, personally, the greatest satisfaction is that of engaging, in my own way, in the battle against forces hostile to a truly democratic system; of saying as often as I can and as loudly as I can what I believe to be true. I used to assume that all of us had that opportunity and used it whenever we wished to, as the people I grew up with did. Now I discover that a shocking number of individuals don't dare to express their own honest opinions on anything unless or until they have made certain that these are the opinions of the majority. As individuals or as members of minority groups, they fear loss of their means of livelihood, the vicious personal attacks of their opponents, the crushing power of the press even when it prints half-truths or complete falsehoods, the icy stares of those they had thought of as friends but who now reveal they cannot feel friendship for anyone who disagrees with them or dare not show friendship for anyone not on the approved list of those on the winning side.

"This is not the democratic way, but a dark, malignant threat to it. I am most grateful to be so placed that at least a few can hear me say I am against the suppression of individual opinion wherever it occurs, and it occurs in both high and low places. If we live too long without knowing what our neighbor honestly believes and without expressing what we, within ourselves, honestly believe, democracy will be lost to mob rule and then to dictatorship as surely as we sit here tonight in this place where two hundred and fifty years ago, and even fifty years ago, not a person who breathed this same air we are breathing would for an instant have supposed it possible."

"I agree with you. But what would you say has brought us to this pass?"

"A blind, deplorable, growing lack of emphasis on integrity. Integrity is based on the confidence of the individual that he knows or can find out what is *right* (perhaps not popular, not necessarily of advantage to himself, almost certainly not easy, and not just a means to a possibly good end) but *right* in itself;

and then doing it. Only a person who has integrity is safe from the worst others can do to him, or can be trusted with anything of value. Only by promoting integrity in our citizens can we recreate a national atmosphere where honesty is recognized and respected as it should be, where true religions and true education can flourish, where we get our just deserts in the courts, where a man's vote contributes to what he believes in, where the people do not wait to be told by leaders and leaders do not wait to be told by the people, where we shall be clearly on God's side and therefore invincible."

"It seems to many in my profession that for some time there has been an alarming trend toward placing compassion above everything else."

"At best a limited compassion, felt and expressed only for the weak, the handicapped, the misguided, those suffering from their own mistakes. At worst, a pseudo-compassion, not felt at all but expressed because the expression of it covers a multitude of sins and brings the speaker what he covets. Only those who have integrity can be and are constructively compassionate, having a strong sense of justice for all."

"Justice is a word rarely heard nowadays. When it is used, it does not imply impartial justice. She used to be painted and sculpted as a magnificent creature. Now she would be shown, I think, with a cruel face."

"But justice is not cruel. The circumstances which lead a man to judgment may have been. Justice per se is neither kind nor unkind. Whatever is, is not justice."

"That is your answer. And mine. But many are seeking answers these days. It is not easy for those of our generation, who remember earlier excellencies, to believe that any answers generally accepted will be those with which we could agree."

"Not easy. But no more difficult than for people like us to accept passively the possibility, even the probability, that they will not be. We are old war horses, and must fight on with spirit, perhaps through our descendants, until the final, conclusive shot is fired. It may yet come from a modern weapon modeled, at least in a most important particular, upon our old muskets."

After a minute William asked, "Does it grieve you at all, Rosamond, that you have no lineal descendants? It does me. That you have none, I mean."

"No, no. We who are childless can have a much larger progeny than those who are blood-parents if we try in the right way, and often can correct mistakes parents are heir to. We have our special opportunities and responsibilities. No, really, William, the world could not do at all without those who have few family ties and so can give almost their full attention to a larger community. For me, a larger community means a greater number of individuals. I have nothing to give to groups. I've always known that. That's why my teaching ended when the district school was closed. I knew very well that I should be of little use shut up in one room with forty-two children aged eight, either mentally or chronologically, or with thirty-nine children aged twelve."

"You were the finest teacher I ever saw in action, and I have seen many."

"Thank you, William. I won't say you may have been prejudiced at the time. I'll just say thank you, and put the words away in the box with the school notes and little homemade valentines and other souvenirs I treasure of those teaching years . . . I wish I had seen you in action, and many other lawyers in action, so that it would mean something for me to say you are the finest lawyer I have ever known. But if I had, I'm sure I could say it."

"So I'll say thank you just as if you had. And put that among *my* souvenirs."

"Along with your purple cow?"

"It's not purple! It's blue!"

They laughed softly. It was growing late. The lamp at the Struthers' had been turned out.

When William left she walked to his car with him, and they shook hands.

"Good night, Rosamond."

"Good night, my good friend."

For a minute she was in the flood of his great headlights. She raised her hand and smiled, though she could not see him. The car backed and turned smoothly, quietly, and went slowly down the hill toward the old mill bridge.

She thought, "I suppose he is reluctant to leave me. Here alone. In the dark. I think he is a little sad, both for himself and for me. It seems to him that we are old, because so many years have passed since we were young."

But she did not feel old. When the night was still again, she walked from one maple tree to another, pausing by each one to touch it with her hand and to press her cheek against it as she had so many times when she was a child. Having caressed them all, she stood in the clearing with her feet apart and her hands clasped behind her, feeling the night wind on her face, flashing a knowing, almost a mischievous smile at Venus.

To Rosamond it seemed that no one could be old for whom there had lately been so many beginnings, and for whom a dream long despaired of might soon break out of its cocoon, unfold brilliant wings, and fly.

Surely before Earth had made another journey around the sun, it would be Charles who would come and sit beside her of an evening, for they too were old friends, again in communication after many silent years, and, with Sandy and Sheila, they would have been together many times in his house and hers.

But the first time he came alone to talk with her, whenever that might be, she would not say to him, "Charles, I hope you don't still —." She would not wait for him to say whether he did or not.

She would at once freely and frankly make her confession. She would tell him that when she came home after her graduation from college she had been at first puzzled, then hurt, then deeply resentful that he did not come to see her, that whenever she encountered him he only nodded, or spoke a gruff word, and hurried on. She had had too much false pride, too little faith in herself and in him ever to stop him before he passed and to say, "Charles, give me an explanation. After the happy summers we have had, the letters we have written, why do you ignore me now that I have come home to stay? If you were not speaking the truth when you said you loved me, or if you have changed your mind, you have a right to say so. You also have a duty. You have no right to leave me without an explanation, as if it had never been said."

She would tell him that, to her shame, she had accepted William's attentions only in the vain hope that Charles would be driven by this association to seek her out again; and that for this trickery she had been justly punished. The night she informed her parents that she had told William she could never love him and so would not go out with him again, her mother asked, "Why, Rosamond, why? Why can't you love so fine a man who loves you with all his heart?"

She would tell Charles, "I have never been able to forget the look on my mother's face as she asked that question."

Her answer had been forced by the pain within her and by the pain she had caused William and was now causing her parents. "Because I can love nobody — in that way — but Charles Weymouth. I have tried, but I can't. And now I know I never shall. For if I could love any man but him it would be William."

She would tell Charles, "Nor shall I ever forget the look my parents then exchanged. It was so stark, so almost horrified that I was frightened and cried, 'What is it? What have I said to make you look like that?' "

Her father asked her to come and sit on the sofa between them. He put his arm around her. She could feel her mother trembling. He told Rosamond that they had had no idea of the depth of her feeling for Charles; that just before her graduation, when they knew she had decided to return home and to apply for the school, they had talked over with some concern the possibility that she might continue to be seen constantly with Charles out of a habit established in childhood and so both would miss opportunities for associations which might lead to marriage, which obviously — it seemed to them — this one never would. They discussed warning Rosamond, but felt that it would have no effect; that she was too loyal and too kind to refuse Charles's invitations, to hurt his feelings. It seemed to them that the only way to protect them both was for Rosamond's father to have a talk with Charles, to point out to him that his friendship for Rosamond would be best demonstrated by not carrying over a boy-and-girl companionship now that they were adults.

"My dear child," her mother said, "you must believe it never occurred to us that you loved Charles. We don't see how you could — after your four years at Wellesley while he was here working on his father's farm."

("Neither of them had been to college, Charles. They didn't know that education does not affect the heart.")

Her father said, "But now that you have told us, my darling, I shall make everything right at once. If this is truly the way you feel, I will see Charles as soon as possible and tell him that — that in advising him I was tramping where angels fear to tread — that I apologize for interfering between you —"

("But I still had that foolish pride, Charles, that little faith in myself and in you. My reaction was to burn with fury. In my struggle not to blame them, I drove myself to place the blame on you. I told myself that you should not have listened to my father, you should have come to me. This even though *I* had not gone to *you*, still would not go to you, nor let anyone else. . . . I sprang up from between them. I stood in the middle of the front parlor. I remember that my arms were folded. And I said, 'No, Father. If either of you says one word of this to Charles, I will never marry him, even if he asks me a thousand times!' . . . So another year went by, and I never saw you, except when we met and passed with a nod or a short greeting. And then you married Vera . . . Remembering all this, I suppose we are by no means the only people of our generation to whom something like this happened, both because of what our parents were, and because of what we were. It couldn't happen now, could it? Parents and children still make mistakes, but rarely the same mistakes which used to be made. And that, as far as it goes, is a reassuring note in a troubled world.")

She went quietly back to sit on the porch alone with the night.

Surely before Earth had made another journey around the sun . . .

Teach us patience, God, with ourselves and with one another. The boy will try the bicycle again tomorrow, and ride away; the girl will take up the needle again tomorrow, and sew a smooth seam.